POLONAISE

'A marvellous, absorbing book. You'll be the richer for having read it'
New York Times Book Review

'A great pleasure to read' *Financial Times*

'An experience: it gradually draws you into its complex web, persuades you to indentify with its leading characters and leaves you much wiser about a country and its people ... a considerable achievement'
MARTIN GOFF, *Daily Telegraph*

'In the best sense, a historical novel'
Newsweek

'If Dostoyevsky were reincarnated as an Englishman, he might write novels like Piers Paul Read' *Time*

Piers Paul Read is the author of twelve novels and three works of non-fiction, including the international bestseller *Alive*. Past novels have won the Hawthornden Prize and the Geoffrey Faber, Somerset Maugham and James Tait Black Awards. Piers Paul Read is married with four children and lives in London.

Polonaise

PIERS PAUL READ

PHŒNIX

A PHOENIX PAPERBACK

First published in Great Britain by
The Alison Press/Martin Secker & Warburg in 1976
This paperback edition published in 1997
by Phoenix, a division of Orion Books Ltd,
Orion House, 5 Upper St Martin's Lane,
London WC2H 9EA

Copyright © 1976 by Piers Paul Read

A CIP catalogue record for this book
is available from the British Library.

ISBN: 1 85799 634 8

Printed and bound in Great Britain
by The Guernsey Press Co. Ltd,
Guernsey, Channel Islands

Part One

One

A succession of national disasters led to the downfall of Count Kornowski. The droughts of 1924 and 1925 halved the crop from his estates at Jezow; a fall in the world price of timber and sugar meant lower prices for what he could sell; and finally, in the middle of 1925, came the German tariff war against Poland which cut him off from his best customers. A man who was shrewd and careful might have survived these blows of fate; but the Count had an aristocratic disdain for the details of business. He sustained his extravagant way of life by borrowing money on the security of his estate. And in 1925 he gave a party lasting from Christmas Eve until Epiphany which he paid for with the money set aside for his daughter's dowry.

His wife, the Countess Kornowska, was not well. The lines of suffering were now added to those of sorrow and disappointment on her oval face. Her days were spent sadly with her daughter Krystyna, musing on her open features and slender figure, remembering how she too in her time has been earmarked by the local landowners for their eldest sons, and how she had chosen for herself a witty, gallant young cavalry officer – Count Stanislas Kornowski. Like every woman she had married with dreams and ideals: yet within a few years the Count was taking his gallantry to other women, and the wit for which he had once been so famous had degenerated into that pose and affectation which for centuries had been the disease of the Polish aristocracy.

Both of the children – Krystyna and Stefan – were born in their parents' country house at Jezow which was ten miles from Staszow in the Maulopolska. It was a long, low house of yellow stucco set in its own estates of woods, pasture and cultivated land. Until 1926 they lived in Warsaw in the winter: but by then the Count was so short of money and so deeply in

3

debt that they gave up their flat in the capital and lived at Jezow all the year round. Only Stefan went to Warsaw during the term to continue his studies at the Catholic lycée of St Stanislas Kostka. There he lodged with a maiden aunt (his mother's sister) who lived in Sluzewska Street.

Krystyna, who was two years older than her brother, remained with her parents at Jezow. Her only education came from the former governess of a neighbouring family who had retired to Kielce, but she was quite content that this should be so. She loved the country and was treated by peasants like a little princess. She was also glad to be able to take care of her mother, whose disease was now diagnosed as emphysema.

During the autumn the condition of the Countess grew worse. She lay on her bed, set into a niche in the wall, gasping for breath. She wore a white nightdress and a black silk bed jacket edged with black lace. Over the bed hung a huge crucifix. On the table beside her bed stood photographs in black frames of her husband and children with small flowers pressed under the glass. Her hands stretched out over the sheets, and groped every now and then for the smaller, plumper hand of her fourteen-year-old daughter.

The walls of the Countess's bedroom were covered with lithographs of the Virgin, various saints and church altarpieces. It was to one of these in particular – a depiction of the Virgin of Czestochowa – that Krystyna directed her gaze, praying desperately for her mother's life. When Stefan returned from school, he too knelt with his sister and prayed for his mother: but neither their prayers nor the doctor's prescriptions could save her. She died on Christmas Eve.

Two

By the summer of 1929, when Stefan was fifteen and Krystyna seventeen, the Count's mismanagement of his own affairs had reached a point where he was threatened with bankruptcy.

He was a small man with close-cropped hair, an aquiline nose and bow legs, whose only pleasures were to shoot birds on his own estate and play cards with his friends. As a Pole and an aristocrat, he did not deign to consider whether or not he could afford to lose so consistently to his neighbours, or to entertain them on such a lavish scale. And when, from time to time, he went to Cracow to borrow money from the bank on the security of Jezow, he received the money as if it was his feudal due.

He was remote from his children and did not confide in them. The death of the Countess had not changed the routine of life at Jezow. It had made Stefan and Krystyna more attached to their home, and to the soft, fat peasant women who cared for the family: but since their father was so often distracted by his pastimes, they were left very much on their own – especially Krystyna, who did not go away to school. She would spend her afternoon wandering around the rose garden with its unpruned plants trailing onto the brick pathways, talking to the gardener about the rotting frames of the chocolate-coloured french windows; or to the mason about the holes in the yellow stucco which still remained from the Great War. She was busy too in the kitchens, ordering the food to suit her father's digestion or making sure that the sheets were aired before they were stored in the painted chests on the landing.

The first intimation she had of her father's financial difficulties came when certain shopkeepers in Staszow told her that they could no longer give credit. She also noticed that a plump, unhealthy man called Stets came with increasing frequency to see her father at Jezow; and that after these visits her father would shout at the peasants and beat the banisters in the house with his riding-crop. This made her curious – even fearful – but she knew that it would humiliate her father if she interfered with his affairs, so she said nothing and waited.

One afternoon in August Krystyna rode across to play tennis with Toni Zulawska, whose father's estate bordered on Jezow. The two girls were friends but also rivals. The rise in the fortunes of the Zulawski family was an awkward contrast to the fall of the Kornowskis: for while the Kornowskis had many quarterings in their coats-of-arms – and had been married in the past to Radziwills, Zamoyskis and Sapiehas – the Zulawskis had Silesian coalmines and large sums of money invested abroad. These inequalities might have balanced one another were it not that Krystyna was slim and pretty while Toni was plump and plain – something which mattered more to those girls at that age than their families' finances and connections.

At tennis they were evenly matched. Krystyna was the better player but was diffident, while Toni put more effort into the game and cared very much if she lost. That day in August she did lose and immediately afterwards, as they changed their clothes, she told Krystyna that she had overheard a conversation between her father and his bailiff about Jezow.

'What did they say?' asked Krystyna.

'Did you know that your father was in debt?'

Krystyna blushed. 'Yes, perhaps, but I'm sure it's only for a time.'

'Pappi said that your father came over last week to borrow a thousand zlotys,' said Toni sweetly, 'and that he wouldn't lend it to him because he knew he'd never get it back.'

'I'm sure that's not true,' said Krystyna quietly.

'He said that he'll have to sell Jezow to pay the bank, and that if he didn't the bank would take it anyway.'

'Take Jezow?'

'That's what he said. The house and the estate. And then, he said, we might buy it from the bank . . .'

'But it's ours. We live there.'

'I'm sure Pappi would let you go on living there if you paid him the rent.'

Krystyna now went red in the face. For a moment Toni cringed as if she was about to be struck or spat at; but then Krystyna turned, ran to the stables, snatched her horse from a groom and rode back to Jezow without staying for tea. The tears in her eyes made her vision vague but the trees and fields were so familiar that she did not need to see where she was going. The horse, too, knew its way.

The Count had spent the afternoon wandering around his house. He was dressed in riding-breeches and carried his crop. His head was bent as he moved and his eyes were on the scrubbed tiles of the passages or the polished wood of the floors. Every now and then he would stop and stare at the portraits of his

6

father, grandfather and great-grandfather which hung in the hall. He would make faces at them – especially a kind of grimace which was a mannerism of the male members of his family. Then he would grunt, lash out at the banisters with his crop and continue his rounds.

Krystyna found him in the dining-room, standing quite still with his arms crossed, brooding over the large bowl which was placed in the middle of the table. In the corner, by the window, a woman was on her hands and knees polishing the floor, but the Count did not seem to notice her presence. Nor did Krystyna pay any attention to her. She went straight up to her father and said: 'Papa, Toni says that you borrow money from her father and don't pay it back.'

The Count did not move but continued to gaze at the bowl. 'She says that you will have to sell Jezow to pay your debts.'

The Count now made a grimace – not at her but at the bowl.

Krystyna's voice had trembled as she spoke to her father. Now it rose in tone and her face went red. 'Tell me, Papa, tell me if that's true.'

The Count now swung round, gave a croak and struck his daughter across the face with his whip.

Krystyna's hand went up to her face. She stood still for a moment, looking with astonishment and pain at her father's contorted expression. Then she turned and left the room.

She ran out of the house and across the rose-garden to the summerhouse where her brother Stefan sat puzzling over the loftiest riddles of our existence – its purpose, value, significance, etc. – which was how he passed the time of day.

Stefan was taller than his father but had similar features and, like the Count, was inclined to make faces – especially the disdainful Kornowski grimace. His face twitched with this expression as he saw his sister enter the summerhouse.

'Did you know that Father borrowed money from Mr Zulawski?' she asked Stefan, her voice breathless and excited.

Stefan did not move from his wicker chair; indeed his eyes moved to the table where he sometimes lay on his back to shut out distractions. 'From Mr Zulawski? Did he?' he said.

'Toni told me. And she says that he owes so much money to the bank that we'll have to sell Jezow.'

'Yes.'

'Did you know?'

'Yes.'

'Who told you?'

'I . . . read a letter.'

'So it's true?'

'Yes.'

'But where will we live?'

Stefan shrugged his shoulders. Krystyna leant her slim body against the table and looked out at the garden. Stefan glanced at her long legs and then followed her gaze at nothing in particular.

'But it's impossible,' said Krystyna.

Stefan shrugged his shoulders again.

'When did you find out?' she asked.

'A week ago.'

'Can they make us sell the house?'

'It's a mortgage. They . . . foreclose.'

Krystyna glanced at her younger brother, impressed at his use of technical terms which she did not understand.

'But not if we pay, surely?'

'No. Not if we pay.'

'Then we must pay.'

'How?'

'Uncle Max . . .'

'He has no money. None of them have any money. That's why they came here in June. To save money.'

Krystyna could not dispute what he said. Ever since she was a child she had known that they were the rich Kornowskis. 'But how . . . I mean, what will happen?'

'Mr Stets is coming tomorrow.'

'For what?'

'The money. Or the house.'

'I hate that man.' Krystyna clenched her teeth as she thought of the unsavoury regional representative of the bank.

'You may hate him,' said Stefan, 'but our fate is in his hands.'

'How can you say that?' said Krystyna. 'Our fate is in the hands of God.'

'If he exists.'

8

Krystyna went slightly pale. 'What do you mean?'

'I don't believe there is a God,' said Stefan.

She clenched her fists. 'How can you say that? It's a most terrible thing to say.'

'God is all very well as a myth for the peasants,' said Stefan. 'But if one is at all educated, and if one applies some sort of method . . .'

'But you *must* believe in God.'

'Pray to him, by all means,' said Stefan with an adolescent shrug of his shoulders: then, with an ironic smile he added: '"Ask and you shall receive."'

'I will,' said Krystyna. 'To God and to the Virgin. *She* won't let him come and take our house.'

Again Stefan shrugged his shoulders. 'Pray then,' he said. 'Pray that Stets does not come tomorrow . . .'

'I will pray,' she said.

'Just as you prayed for Mama.'

She blushed. 'You'll see,' she said. 'He won't come.' She turned and Stefan saw the red line which ran across her cheek. 'What happened there?' he asked.

'Papa did it,' she said.

'You should keep out of his way.'

'I had to ask him.'

'He's upset.'

'He's a fool,' said Krystyna, wiping the two tears that had appeared in her eyes, and going to the entrance to the summer-house.

The brother and sister parted – Stefan returning to his Cartesian speculation, Krystyna to her room. There she knelt before her crucifix and prayed to God and the Virgin that Mr Stets would not come, and while she prayed she wondered what she would do if he did.

The next day was dark and damp and Mr Stets, when he arrived from Cracow, looked ill and irritable. His appearance, even on a fine day, was not healthy. He was a man of indeterminate middle age, with a huge belly, a sagging face and grey skin which grew yellowish around the eyes and mouth. He was partly bald and what hair he had was greasy. He was not tall and waddled like a toad.

9

Krystyna had been watching, and she came out of the front door to meet him. Stets's expression, which until then had been irritable, changed to a leer and he took Krystyna's hand and kissed it with the same soft, hot impress of his lips. Krystyna did not draw her hand away quite as quickly as she usually did, but invited Mr Stets into the house, took his coat and then led him into the drawing-room. 'Do sit down, Mr Stets,' she said to him. 'My father will be down in a minute. They've gone to look for him.'

Stets lowered his wide body into an armchair. 'No hurry, Miss Krystyna, no hurry. I can assure you, your company is most pleasant . . .'

Krystyna sidled up to the sofa and leaned against its arm. 'I asked them to bring you some mineral water,' she said. 'Isn't that what you like?'

'Oh yes, certainly it is,' said Stets. 'How considerate. An ulcer, you see. I have an ulcer that plays me up if I don't give it some water.'

A peasant woman entered with a bottle of water on a tray. Stets examined the label, shrugged his shoulders, muttered about the brand but accepted a glass when it was poured out for him.

Krystyna started to pick at her brown dress as if there were specks of dust she should remove from the bodice. She smelt the scent she had dabbed under her ears and felt ill at ease in her own body and conscious that the dress was not the sort of thing she would normally wear on a weekday. She said nothing for a while. Stets seemed not to notice nor even expect her to stay in the room – his mind was on the mineral water – until Krystyna looked up and spoke to him quite abruptly. 'Mr Stets,' she said. 'I wonder if you would be good enough to tell me the address of the bank you represent . . . that is, the address of its headquarters or its chief branch. I don't know what you call that sort of thing.'

'Head office,' said Stets.

'Its head office, then. And the name of its president.'

'The Chairman of the Board.'

'Yes. Good. The Chairman of the Board.'

Stets wobbled in his seat. 'They are all on the letters from the bank that your father must have . . .' he said.

'My father does not like me to interfere in his affairs,' said Krystyna, 'and . . . and he keeps his desk locked.'

'In that case,' said Stets, glancing at her as if she was more of a child than he had imagined, 'I am not sure that it is for me to go against your father's wishes.'

Krystyna sat down on the sofa. She had no idea of what she could say to Stets, but was determined not to tell her father he was there until she had found out more for herself. For a moment she hid her face in her hands, trying to think of something to say. Then she heard a creak in the floorboards and, fearing that Stets might be about to leave the room, she looked up. Instead of Stets, however, she saw behind him the figure of her father, the Count, dressed in the full uniform of an Austro-Hungarian Hussar. His sabre was drawn and raised in both hands above Stets's head. The eyes of the old man met those of his daughter for just a moment; then they flickered and all expression died. The arms reached higher still and began their descent over the head of Mr Stets.

In the space of that second Krystyna leapt forward to stop her father or save Stets, but as it happened the bank official from Cracow, quite unaware of who or what was behind him, had leant forward himself with the leer once again on his face saying: 'Come now, Countess Kornowska . . .'

As he did so, he heard the cry of Count Kornowski and a rush of air behind him. He turned to see the sabre buried deep into the back of the armchair, its point only inches from his back.

Realizing what had happened, Stets went white and got to his feet. He ran towards the door which opened out onto the veranda, but when he turned to see if he was being pursued he saw that the Count was kneeling, immobile, at the back of the armchair, his hands still gripping his sabre. Krystyna, who had been standing clenching and unclenching her hands around a small, scented handkerchief, now ran to her father and called at the same time for the servants. Two women came running and with Krystyna they pulled the Count back from the chair and laid him on the floor.

It was hard to say whether he was conscious or unconscious. His eyes were open but they were glazed as they had been the moment before he had struck the blow at Stets's head. Saliva dribbled from his mouth and his lower lip was quivering. Otherwise he was still and silent.

Stets, seeing that he was in no danger from the Count, strode back across the room. 'This is preposterous, quite preposterous,' he said. He looked for a moment at the Count on the floor; then, with an expression of great self-importance, he waddled into the hall shouting at no one in particular: 'Where are the police? We must have the police. I have been subjected to an assault. Yes, distinctly an assault. An assault on my life.'

At that he turned white once again. A sudden understanding came to him that the straw and sawdust which had leaked out of the armchair onto the drawing-room floor should have been his brains. He felt weak and sat down on a bench and repeated, much more weakly: 'An assault, an assault on my life.'

He sat shivering as the inert body of the Count was carried past him and away by the two women. Krystyna, who followed, stopped beside Mr Stets.

'I am sorry,' she said. 'You see, he isn't well.'

'Ha,' said Stets, rising from the bench. 'Not well? No, he's not well. He's mad as a hatter. Where's the police?'

'In Kielce,' said Krystyna. 'You'll have to send to Kielce if you want the police.'

'Of course I want the police. He tried to kill me. He would have killed me if . . . if I hadn't moved forward, just then . . .'

Again the thought of how near he had come to a split skull made Stets feel weak, and he sat back on the bench.

'You must have a glass of vodka,' said Krystyna, watching his trembling hands and wobbling, grey cheeks. 'It's the best thing for a shock.'

Then suddenly Krystyna started to cry. The phrase 'it's the best thing for a shock' had been her father's – a joke of his in front of the fire after his children had hidden and surprised him.

The effect of her tears on Stets was to remind him that she was a young girl – in some ways hardly more than a child. He stood and placed a stubby arm around her delicate, heaving shoulders.

'We should both have a glass of vodka,' he said. 'We have both had a shock.'

Krystyna went with him into the dining-room where two

trays had been prepared, one with hors-d'oeuvres, another with various decanters filled with different sorts of vodka. Some were pure spirit and colourless, others tinted brown or green by the addition of herbs, and one contained long strands of grass which had been added to give a particular flavour. It was from this bottle that Stets poured himself and Krystyna first one and then another glass of vodka.

The alcohol enabled Krystyna to recover herself and stop sobbing. Stets too seemed to forget his ulcer and the episode with the Count and the sabre: his face settled into a fat smile.

After a final sniff and a sigh, Krystyna invited Stets to sit down on one of the heavy, dining-room chairs. This he did, placing his glass on the table. Krystyna then went to the door which led towards the servants' quarters to make sure that the door was properly closed; then she crossed the room to the door which led into the hall and shut it. Finally she sat down at the dining-room table opposite Stets and looked at him with a serious, slightly sour expression on her face.

'Mr Stets,' she said. 'As you can see, my father is not himself. He is not quite normal . . .'

Stets shrugged his shoulders.

'And it must be clear to you that he cannot really be held responsible for his actions.'

'Even so . . .'

'I quite agree. We shall have to do something about him – that . . . incident, I know. And if you want to inform the police, clearly you have the right.'

'Of course . . .'

'No, you have the right. And I am quite sure that the court – that is, if there was a trial – would put my father into the hands of a doctor which is, after all, just what I shall do.'

'Is there no one else? I mean, you're very young, Countess.'

'I am old enough, thank you,' said Krystyna.

'Of course.'

'And I hope you will agree, now, that I have the right to interfere in my father's affairs.'

'Well of course, up to a point . . . but you're not of an age, legally . . .'

'Legally, no, of course not,' said Krystyna, brushing aside the concept of legality as if it was unimportant. 'I dare say my

13

Uncle Max will act as our guardian – but that is not the point because he hasn't any money.'

'So . . . no, well, I understand that there were no other members of the family . . .'

'So the responsibility is mine,' said Krystyna.

'Yours?'

'Because this house is my home, and the home of my brother Stefan and we have no wish to leave it.'

'I see. Yes. The mortgage. But I am afraid . . .'

'That is why I asked you earlier for the name of your . . . that is, the Chairman of the Board, and the address of your head office; because I am sure that if I went to Warsaw and explained to the Chairman exactly what our circumstances were . . .'

Stets laughed. Krystyna blushed.

'Why are you laughing?' she asked Stets in a low, cold voice.

'My dear Countess, oh dear, I am sorry. I'm not laughing at you. It's just the idea . . . that, you see. Well, it's a very big bank. One of the biggest in Poland, and the Chairman of the Board . . . well, he doesn't know about such small details and anyway, he wouldn't have the power . . . I mean to say, he represents the shareholders . . .'

'Then I could talk to the shareholders . . .' said Krystyna – but in a less certain tone of voice.

Again Stets burst out laughing. 'The shareholders, oh no, you see there are tens of thousands of shareholders.'

Krystyna became impatient. 'Well who can I see? There must be someone.'

'See about what?'

'About the mortgage.'

'Ah.' Stets's expression suddenly changed. He scratched his cheek.

'As I understand it,' said Krystyna, her voice trembling slightly as if more tears were pushing up from under the surface, 'this house is in a mortgage . . .'

'Mortgaged. Yes.'

'Yes, mortgaged. Which means, I don't understand why, that it somehow doesn't belong to us any more.'

'It was security against a loan to your father which he promised to repay by the end of last year.'

'And he hasn't repaid it?'

'Not a zloty. Nor has he paid the interest.'

'It has been a bad time for agriculture,' said Krystyna solemnly.

'It has been a bad time for us all,' said Stets. 'Even for banks. And worse times may be coming.'

'Even so,' said Krystyna – a tone of pleading coming into her voice – 'there must be someone who could, well, I mean . . . for such a big and important bank, this house and estate can't mean so much.'

Stets stroked his plump, grey cheek. 'There are occasions,' he said, 'when bad debts are written off, or repayment postponed.'

'Written off, yes,' said Krystyna, catching at the word because it fitted her image of a ledger where figures could be crossed out or rubbed out or 'written off', as Stets put it. 'Who . . . who could decide when a loan could be written off?'

'Well,' said Stets, his eyes falling from nowhere in particular and coming to rest on the neck and shoulders of Krystyna. 'It could be a matter of recommendation from their regional representative.'

'Their regional representative. I see.'

Krystyna looked up at Stets and she saw his eyes on her body, which produced in her a sudden and unpleasant sensation of which the outward sign was a slight shudder. Then she gripped and twisted the skirt of her brown dress, and cringed as she remembered how she had dressed so carefully and had studied her appearance in the mirror. Nevertheless she looked into Stets's eyes and asked: 'And who is the regional representative?'

Stets looked up. 'I am,' he said; and his eyes met hers with a smug leer.

'I see,' she said, looking aside out of the window. She crossed her legs and thought for a moment. Stets said nothing.

'And would you,' began Krystyna, her voice shaking. 'Would you . . . or rather, if you made a recommendation . . . to write off the debt . . . would they accept it?'

'Almost certainly.'

'I see,' she said again.

Stets said nothing. He too turned and looked out of the window.

'And would you?' Krystyna asked.

'What?'

'Make the recommendation?'

Stets shrugged his shoulders. 'For a man who has just tried to kill me?'

'No, I do see . . .' said Krystyna. 'But . . .'

'What?'

She hesitated and then said in a quiet, low voice: 'There isn't just him.'

'No, of course not,' said Stets briskly. 'But then what are you to me?'

'No, I know. We don't really know you.' Krystyna trembled as she spoke and there was a further silence.

'Of course, if there were bonds,' said Stets, smiling at his delicacy, 'bonds of one sort or another . . .'

'What then?'

'Then it would be different.'

'You would make the recommendation . . .?'

'Of course.'

Krystyna stood. She walked to the window, stared out over the rose garden to the pine forests beyond, and then turned to face her guest. 'Mr Stets,' she said in a breathless voice, 'Mr Stets, I am prepared to marry you.'

For the third time Stets laughed. He laughed and laughed and poured himself another glass of vodka while still shaking with laughter so that he spilt the vodka over the tray. Krystyna stood quite still, her face red and her jaw set. She said nothing.

'Oh Countess,' said Stets, laughing between each phrase, 'I assure you, I . . . I am most flattered . . . it's too kind, I do realize . . . but really, I can spare you the trouble . . . I mean, that is . . . I am already married.'

'I see,' said Krystyna. 'I'm sorry. I didn't know.'

'Of course if I wasn't . . .' said Stets.

'What bonds did you mean, then?' asked Krystyna, still standing by the window.

'Oh, there are other bonds, I assure you. Between a man and a woman. If there was anywhere . . . private where we could go . . .'

'Why?'

'Then I could show you.'

'Do you mean . . . away from the servants?'

'Yes, away from the servants.'

Krystyna bit her lip. 'I don't know,' she said. 'Not in the house.'

'Outside, then. A summerhouse, perhaps, with a chaise-longue . . .'

'Not the summerhouse.'

'Or a barn?'

'There's the hayshed, yes. We could go there.'

Stefan lay like a corpse on the summerhouse table. His body was motionless but his eyes were open and fixed on the tarred beams above him. From time to time they would follow the progress of a spider as it ran to weave a cocoon around a gnat caught in its web. But then a frown would appear on Stefan's forehead and he would look away from the spider and resume his gaze at nothing in particular.

Stefan was thinking. He was thinking, or trying to think, about the fundamental questions of life and death; and the summerhouse, in spite of the spider, seemed the best place in which to do it. Here he was protected from the distractions of the outside world – his father, his sister, the peasants – above all the young peasants . . .

The reason why Stefan, just at that moment, was 'taking stock of his philosophical situation' was his recent decision that God did not exist; for since he had been brought up to believe the opposite, this decision was of some significance. He felt he had now to reconsider all his past assumptions, and build a new system of values based on reason or, as he termed it to himself, on 'sublime common sense'.

Until his mother's death, he had accepted and practised the Catholic faith which in Poland was as pervasive as the air itself. He had taken Communion and confessed his sins along with everyone else – and he had prayed, especially to the Virgin of Czestochowa for his mother's life and health.

His prayers had not been answered, and for a time he had accepted the 'mysterious ways' of the Lord: but the memory of those days and nights spent on his knees at his mother's bed – with the sound of his own and Krystyna's 'Hail Marys' mixing with her agonized breathing – was so painful to him that afterwards he could not pray. If he tried, he would feel again the misery and panic of those terrible days, and to avoid it he would think of anything rather than Christ or the Virgin of Czestochowa. And into this space in his mind came doubts. As he knelt at Mass, watching the priest mutter in Latin, he began to wonder if the Catholic faith was not as much a myth as the religion of the Greeks and Pharaohs?

'After all,' he said to himself, 'I am a Catholic only because I am a Pole. If I had been born in China, I would be a Buddhist; and if I had been born in the jungles of Africa, I would be a pagan, praying to a totem-pole instead of the Virgin of Czestochowa.'

When he returned to school in Warsaw – to St Stanislas Kostka – he asked the priests who taught him certain questions which they found it difficult to answer. 'If Faith is a gift of God, why is God more generous to Poles than he is to Arabs?' 'How does it accord with the infinite Justice of God that a man born in Berlin has so much less chance of salvation than a man born in Warsaw?'

The questions were never adequately answered. Most of the explanations were like that given by the parish priest at Jezow to explain the death of the Countess – the ways of the Lord are beyond human understanding – and when Stefan persisted, he was beaten for insolence. As a result he kept his doubts to himself, but now they were triumphant. He did not believe a word of the Papist myth, and never again would he be taken for a 'cosmic fool'.

And yet, if he was not a Catholic, what was he? If the aim of his life was not to love and serve God, then what should its purpose be? If all inherited beliefs, myths and prejudices were rubbed from his mind, what was left? And what could be constructed with reason?

These were the questions which preoccupied him on that morning in summer while his sister was treating with the regional representative of a Warsaw bank. He was trying to construct a system of values and had started by attempting to define his own person. He saw no other way to begin.

His first experiment was to discover in what sense he would cease to exist if he ceased to think. 'I think therefore I am: I am because I think. If I did not think, I would not be.' Hence his position on the table and his annoyance at the distraction of the spider.

It was not easy to stop thinking. He found that either he had to think about not thinking, or his mind would wander – onto the spider, or over the wall to those boys and girls from the village . . . And when Stefan stopped to wonder whether he existed, he would be forced to admit that he had existed for a number of minutes because he had been thinking of Jan, Jerzy, Maria, Wanda – that is, the boys and girls from the village whom he had played with as a child but played with no longer. This, above all, was the thought which distracted him – the thought that he had lost the knack of talking with the peasants of his own age, above all of talking to Wanda, who was now so plump and pretty, who laughed at him and looked at him and nudged him with her eyes, sweating . . .

The thought of her sweat – above all the thought of her sweat in the crevices between her legs and breasts as she returned from the fields with her brothers – elicited from Stefan a physical reaction which took him to a certain stage in his philosophical speculation. 'My head exists because it is a magic lantern with images of Jan, Jerzy returning from the fields, and Wanda running, sweating beside them; and my penis exists because it reacts to the image of her legs shaking and sweating, and her breasts swaying and sweating . . . I am, therefore, a head and a penis – and in an hour or so, when I begin to get hungry, a stomach too. A head, a penis and a stomach.'

Stefan did not sweat. He might have done so if he had gone to the fields with the young peasants as once he had done: but now his body was thin and white from studying at St Stanislas Kostka – while theirs were thick and brown. He therefore preferred to watch them from a distance and talk to them only when they happened to pass with such remarks as: 'Well, Jerzy, the good weather's holding out.'

'Yes, sir, Master Stefan. We'll have a fine harvest.'

'Don't you work too hard, Wanda . . .'

'Whyever not, Master Stefan, sir? I'm as strong as my brothers . . .' Strong words with a strong glance and sweat and eyes so animal that Stefan looked away and, with some other inconsequential remark, walked on, a gun under his arm.

Stefan was no fool. He knew that the magic lantern in his head was the inspiration of his loins, and if he wanted to carry things further – to take Wanda's thick, sweating, brown body

into his languid embrace, and have his penis do what it would –
it was only to clear his mind of distraction for further philosophical speculation. Or so he argued to himself. Unfortunately
the thought of taking things further in this way only inflamed
the whole question, so that once or twice he had leapt off the
table with the momentary intention of running after Wanda
and . . . and what? What could he do? What could he suggest to
her? He knew that he must catch her on her own, and whisper
in her ear – he even knew, or felt confident, that she would
listen and accept and meet him in the hayshed on the other side
of the garden. Only one thing was missing. The facility. The
knack. The knack of finding her alone, of whispering in her
ear . . .

Stefan's preoccupation with Wanda was not fresh. It had
tormented him throughout the summer and had grown to such
strength that anything which stood in its way had been swept
aside. Indeed Wanda, or the thought of her, had entered into
his theological speculations, enticing him away from Christ, his
apostles and the whole tradition of Catholic Poland. It was
Wanda who had driven him from agnosticism to atheism; for
there had been a time when Stefan was prepared to concede
that God might exist even if Stefan Kornowski did not believe
in him. But the sweating Wanda refused to cohabit with even
such a wispy deity as this in the confines of his philosophical
system; and when it came to the day of the visit of Mr
Stets, Stefan had reached this point in his creed. 'I have
tried to cease to exist by ceasing to think but have failed. I
retain, however, a strict definition of what I am by accepting as
real only those thoughts which I cannot dismiss by a simple
effort of will. I exist, therefore, partly because of the spider,
but more precisely because thoughts of Wanda and her sweating
limbs come into my head and animate my penis; and also
because, around lunch time, my stomach grumbles and that
too, therefore, exists until such a time as it is filled and I can
forget about it. There are also my bowels and bladder. I am,
then, a head, a penis, a stomach, a bladder and bowels; but all
of these can for a time be put out of existence except the head
and penis – because they are blocked by the image of Wanda.
This sticks in my mind and defines my identity. If I could have
her, that too might cease to exist – for a time, at any rate – but

I cannot have her because I have lost the knack of whispering in her ear. And why have I lost the knack which Jan and Jerzy almost certainly possess? (And, who knows, perhaps they have her in a haystack?) Because I am not a sweating, brown-bodied peasant, but a Warsaw-educated thinker and a Count with quarterings on my coat-of-arms: and while quarterings and a facility for conversations with peasant girls may not be incompatible, philosophy and this facility almost certainly are; because those who do not think, like Jan and Jerzy, can have Wanda on the haystack and believe in God both at the same time; whereas I cannot – not because I disbelieve in the forgiveness of sins, but because of what Wanda and logic have made of me. I think therefore I am. I think about Wanda and about having Wanda. I am therefore a sweaty limbs-loving entity which is incompatible with a God-loving entity because the notion of God repudiates sweaty limbs and sweaty limbs laugh at the notion of God.'

This was the point that Stefan had reached in the middle of the morning of the day of Stets's visit to Jezow. The fact that Stets was there – or any memory of his conversation with Krystyna the day before – did not distract Stefan from his speculation. His slow but sure progress towards an acceptable philosophical system was still far from encompassing such notions as mortgages, bankruptcies and banks. His father existed as the dim butt of certain subjective emotions. So too did Krystyna until – out of the corner of his eyes – Stefan saw her walking up the garden towards the hayshed with a plump, balding man beside her.

What they were doing would not in itself have been enough to arouse his curiosity. He knew that Stets was due, and might have thought it natural that he should want to inspect the property that he was about to appropriate for his employers. There were details, however, which contradicted this casual interpretation of what he saw. They had gone up the path which led only to the hayshed, yet had not crossed the lawn in front of the summerhouse – the most natural course from the house to the hayshed – but had skirted the lawn, walking on the longer grass behind a row of apple trees. Nor could he mistake the stealth in a glance that Krystyna had directed towards the summerhouse before she disappeared between the shrubs.

Stefan suppressed his curiosity, looked up at the ceiling again and watched the spider sit still in the corner of its web. Involuntarily, however, his mind returned to what he had seen – not so much to his sister or to the man waddling beside her, but to the path they had taken and the solid, secluded wooden building that lay at its end. He had often been there in his mind – dallying with Wanda in its dark, warm corners, his whispers and her laughter muffled by the dried-out bales of hay: and as he thought about it now, and the two who had walked towards it, an enormous curiosity came into his mind. In the space of four or five minutes it had hatched like a cuckoo's egg and thrown all the other birds out of the nest – even the image of Wanda's sweating legs – until Stefan was forced to admit that at that moment he *was* his curiosity, and that like hunger, it was something that could be satisfied by sitting up, getting off the table and sneaking across the garden to the hayshed.

In a moment he had done what this new personality demanded of him. He stood up, left the summerhouse and crossed the garden towards the hayshed. Having reached it, he was momentarily frustrated because the door was shut and there were no windows in the walls but only slats in the wooden roof. At the side, however, there was an opening through which the hay was thrown when the stacks inside had reached a certain height; and since this was open, with a cart beneath it, Stefan was able to climb up into the barn near to the top of the mountain of hay.

For a moment he lay where he had landed. He could see nothing until his eyes became used to the dark, and even then he could only see hay. With great caution he crawled forward, over the summit, and started to proceed down the other side until he heard, almost in his ear, the heavy breathing of a man. The sound was so close that Stefan did not dare lift his head but he listened to the breathing, to the sound of movement in the hay and to a slight whimpering in a higher pitched voice. Then came a grunt, then a cry (in a higher pitched voice), then a grunt, then another grunt, a curse, a grunt – all quickly together – and finally a long-drawn-out curse which ended in a sort of sigh.

Still Stefan did not dare lift his head. There was more rustling and movement a few feet from where he lay and he only looked up when he heard the man's voice some way below him saying: 'How I hate young girls. Why aren't you a woman? I'm not a hammer and chisel, am I? No, I'm a man, that's all. Not a *battering ram.*'

No one replied. Stefan looked down towards the floor of the hay shed at a moving grey shape which he suddenly recognized as a white pair of buttocks belonging to Mr Stets who, dressed only in a shirt, was looking for his trousers.

'Is that all?' said a girl's voice (Krystyna's) quite close to Stefan's ear. He quickly hid his head again.

'Of course that's all,' said Stets from below.

Stefan heard a movement in the straw and when he looked up, cautiously, a moment later, he saw his sister's naked body climbing down towards the floor. He buried his face again not because he thought he might be seen but to shut out the sight and the thought. He remained still in that position – his mind as blank as his vision. He heard Krystyna say: 'I'll go and see to lunch. It must be almost ready.' The door to the barn opened, letting in more light; then it closed again. When, eventually, Stefan looked up, there was no one else there.

Lunch was eaten in the dining-room without the presence of the Count. Stefan was late since he was not to be found in the summerhouse. No one spoke. Stefan kept his eyes on his food. Krystyna's hands shook as she held her knife and fork, and she gave orders to the servants in a slightly frenzied tone of voice. Mr Stets made no attempt at conversation. He gobbled down his food with a frown on his face. He asked for wine as well as mineral water in a bad-tempered tone of voice; and as soon as he had finished his food he rose to go.

Krystyna sent the servants to call for his buggy; and then went herself to fetch his coat. She walked with Mr Stets to see him off and held up her hand, which he kissed more casually than usual. Then she came back into the house to see to her father. As she did so she passed Stefan in the hall. She stopped him, took his hand and looked into his eyes. 'I've arranged it, Stefan,' she said. 'We won't have to sell Jezow.'

Stefan nodded and smiled but avoided her glance and said nothing; and a moment later he had removed his hand from hers and was on his way back to the summerhouse.

Three

Two days later Stefan went back to Warsaw, to the flat of his aunt Cecylia where he always stayed during the term. It was on the first floor of a building in Sluzewska Street, and consisted of two bedrooms, a dining-room, a drawing-room, a kitchen and a bathroom. The drawing-room and dining-room were enormous – large enough to entertain twenty people at a time. The bedrooms were small: one was for Aunt Cecylia, the other for Stefan. The old servant, Mamuska, slept in a cubbyhole in the kitchen.

At the beginning of November Stefan returned from school to find the hallway of the flat filled with trunks and packing-cases. He climbed over them to get into his bedroom, dropped his satchel onto the bed, and then went into the drawing-room to find Aunt Cecylia serving tea to his father and sister.

'They've come to stay, dear,' she murmured.

The Count said nothing but smiled and nodded. He did not seem to recognize his son; nor did Krystyna greet her brother or meet his eyes.

'Whose is that luggage?' asked Stefan.

'Ours,' said Krystyna.

'They've come for a long stay, haven't you, Krysia?' said Cecylia.

Krystyna did not reply.

'I don't know where you're going to sleep,' said Stefan.

'Krysia can share my room,' said Cecylia – a thin, distinguished lady who had never married – 'and perhaps your father could share your room . . . for the time being?'

The Count started to hum. Cecylia looked anxiously in his direction, then leant towards Krystyna. 'Is he . . . is he?' she murmured.

'He doesn't understand,' said Krystyna sharply. 'They think he may have had a brain storm . . .'

'But isn't there anything that can be done, darling?'

'No, nothing. They said we could send him to a clinic, if we had the money . . . which we haven't.'

Aunt Cecilia nodded, raised her eyes (as if to Heaven), and then turned away so as to present her profile to her nephew and niece.

'But why have you brought so much luggage?' asked Stefan.

'Some of it's yours,' said Krystyna.

'Mine? I have all I need in my bedroom.'

'What about your riding-breeches and tennis clothes?'

'Why should I need those here?' asked Stefan.

'Darling . . .' murmured Cecylia.

'Someone might ask you to stay,' said Krystyna.

'Then I can have them sent from Jezow.'

For the first time Krystyna looked at her brother. 'No,' she said. 'Not now.'

'Why not?'

'It doesn't belong to us any more. It belongs to the bank. All of it. The house. The fields. The furniture. Everything, except what's in those damned suitcases . . .' She stopped, and her fierce eyes became wet with tears. She sobbed and rushed to her aunt, who embraced and comforted her.

The Count's brother Max was soon at the flat in Sluzewska Street, often with a cousin, Alfred, who was a painter. They would establish themselves in Cecylia's drawing-room, drink tea, eat cake and discuss the disaster that had come upon the proud family of Kornowski.

Each had his own line. Max saw the whole thing as a political plot. 'Inflation,' he said. 'It's all part of the same phenomenon. Why, five years ago a man could live on his income – pay for his club, a cab, the theatre, that sort of thing. Now I'm damned if I can pay my own rent. And it's all because of Bolshevik agitation, pushing up wages, prices, then wages again. The Freemasons are in it too, and the Germans. It was their tariff war of '25 that started it all. They're in it with the Bolsheviks – out to destroy Poland . . .'

Alfred, the painter, was sure that they had been swindled.

'Those Zulawskis, you say, are going to buy the place? I wouldn't trust them. Hand in glove with the bank, I wouldn't doubt. Taking advantage of poor Stanislas . . . Good God, one can see that the man isn't well, there, I mean . . .' – he tapped his head – 'and they go and take advantage of him . . .'

'I saw lawyers in Cracow,' said Krystyna. 'There was nothing we could do.'

'Jews, I should imagine,' said Max.

'The papers were all signed by Papa,' said Krystyna, 'long before he was ill.'

'All bankers are Jews,' said Max.

'It's the same with the art galleries,' said Alfred. 'They'll get you to sign papers when you need them . . .'

'Only my mother's property is left for us,' said Krystyna.

'The Bolsheviks are Jews,' said Max.

'Some jewelry,' said Krystyna, 'and a small income. That's all.'

'You'll find that somewhere along the line they've swindled you,' said Alfred.

'And somewhere there's a Bolshevik,' said Max.

It was clear that there was not room in Aunt Cecylia's flat for the Kornowski family to remain there for ever: it was also clear that the small income that came in from government bonds left to the children by the Countess would not be enough to pay the rent of a similar flat in a similar part of the city.

It was Krystyna who now started to search for somewhere to live in the cheaper areas of Warsaw. Her first expedition was by tram to Mirow; she returned in the evening quite pale and shocked by what she had seen.

'What was it like?' asked Stefan. 'Was there room for the three of us?'

'It was big enough,' said Krystyna.

'And cheap?'

'Yes, but . . .' She hesitated, and then shuddered.

'Shall we go and live there, then?'

'No.' She shook her head, and looked up at her brother. 'Stefan, you don't know . . . you couldn't imagine how some people live – in damp rooms with no daylight, and only a bucket on the stairs for a lavatory which is used by all the other people: and a tap, one tap, where you fetch water for cooking and washing . . . We couldn't live there, we couldn't. I'd rather die.'

'Then what shall we do?' asked Stefan.

'I don't know,' said Krystyna. 'You can always stay here with Aunt Cecylia.'

'No. I shall stay with you and Papa. In fact there's no reason why I shouldn't leave school and get a job of some sort . . .'

'No. If anyone is to get a job, it's me. In the meantime we've got a little money and Mama's jewelry. We can always sell that.'

In the days that followed, Krystyna made further expeditions into the suburbs and returned each evening exhausted and shaken by what she had seen. By the beginning of December she still had not found a flat to live in. She had also run short of money and had sold one of her mother's rings.

Then the concierge at Sluzewska Street stopped her one morning and told her that the family who lived on the fourth floor of the building were going to live in Poznan. 'Of course it wouldn't really be suitable for you, Countess, under the roof, but I knew you were looking for something and I thought you'd like to know.'

The following week, when the flat was vacant, Krystyna went with her aunt and Mamuska to inspect this flat, which had originally been rooms for the servants. They peered around the small rooms, which smelt of the people who had lived there before, and had pale patches on the walls where their furniture had stood.

'This is more the sort of thing . . .' said Krystyna.

'It would be convenient,' said Cecylia.

'But the fourth floor,' said Mamuska. 'His Excellency living on the fourth floor!'

'It can't be helped,' said Krystyna severely. 'It's much better than anything else I've seen . . . and it's near Stefan's school.'

'Of course, of course,' said Cecylia. 'We mustn't forget that.'

'We'll take it,' said Krystyna, going back towards the door.

'Is it expensive, dear?' muttered Cecylia.

'It's not as cheap as some of the others,' said Krystyna. 'But it'll be all right because I'm going to get a job.'

'Oh no, dear, you mustn't work. You should study.'

Krystyna said nothing but left the flat and went down the stairs ahead of her aunt and Mamuska. She let herself into the flat on the first floor and went to the bedroom which she shared with her aunt. There she took from her suitcase a box containing the finest piece of her mother's jewelry – a diamond and ruby necklace – and put the box into her handbag. Then she went into the drawing-room, to make sure that her father was all right, before setting off once again into the streets of Warsaw.

There was a jeweller's shop near the Europejski Hotel called Blomstein's. It was here that she had sold the ring, and it was here that she took the necklace.

It was easier, this second time, to tell the girl behind the counter that she had not come to buy but to sell. The girl gave her the same contemptuous glance which had humiliated Krystyna on the first occasion, and then led her behind the counter, and through a door with panels of frosted glass, into the office of Mr Blomstein.

He was a man of about fifty – small and stooping, with a large head, a reticent manner and calculating eyes. He looked up from his desk as Krystyna came in – and after a moment recognized her.

'You have something more you would like to sell?'

'Yes, Mr Blomstein.'

'It's a bad time,' said Blomstein.

'I know,' said Krystyna, 'but I have no choice.'

Mr Blomstein sighed – a sigh of satisfaction disguised as a sigh of sorrow. 'Let me look, then,' he said. 'Sit down, sit down.'

Krystyna sat on the chair facing his desk. As she took the box containing the necklace out of her bag, she heard the girl leave the office and saw Mr Blomstein fix his jeweller's glass into the socket of his eye. He took the case from her hands with suppressed impatience, opened it, and placed the necklace on the cloth in front of him. Then he focused the lamp, leant over the necklace, and studied the stones.

'I wondered also, Mr Blomstein,' said Krystyna, 'if you could give me a job.'

He looked up sharply. 'A job? Here?'

'Yes,' said Krystyna. 'In the shop.'

28

Blomstein bent over the necklace and looked at the stones. 'Very well,' he said. 'A month's trial at one hundred zlotys a month: after that, one hundred and fifty if you stay on. And for this . . .' – he looked up and pointed to the necklace – 'one thousand zlotys.'

'Very well,' said Krystyna.

'Do you still want to sell it,' asked Blomstein, 'now that you have a job?'

'Yes,' said Krystyna. 'I have to furnish a flat.'

When she got back to Sluzewska Street, Stefan had returned from school and both her Uncle Max and her cousin Alfred were eating cake and drinking tea and discussing the political situation. The Count was leaning forward as if listening to the conversation, but every now and then he would grasp at the air as if catching a mosquito.

'I hear that we're taking the flat upstairs,' said Stefan.

'Is it true?' asked Uncle Max.

'Yes,' said Krystyna. 'On the fourth floor.'

'The fourth floor?' said Max, with a doubtful look. 'Well, I suppose beggars can't be choosers.'

'I shall give you some of my pictures to hang on the walls,' said Alfred. 'Well, I shall lend them, anyway.'

'Why not make a gift of them?' said Max, taking another slice of cake. 'You know that no one will ever buy them . . .'

'Nonsense,' said Alfred. 'If it wasn't for the galleries . . .'

'Can we afford it?' Stefan asked his sister.

'I can help a little . . .' Aunt Cecylia said in a timid whisper, her face in profile.

'You won't need to,' said Krystyna. 'I've taken a job.'

There was a silence.

'A job?' asked Alfred. 'What sort of job?'

'In a shop. Selling jewelry.'

Another silence.

'Impossible,' said Max at last.

'Darling . . .' Cecylia began.

'Will you like it?' asked Stefan.

'Not much,' said Krystyna, 'but it pays quite well.'

'But . . . but . . . which shop?' asked Max.

'A jewelry shop. Blomstein's.'

'Blomstein's?' Uncle Max said, spluttering as he spoke. 'But that is impossible.'

'Quite impossible,' Alfred repeated.

'Impossible,' said Max again. 'A Kornowski working behind the counter . . . impossible. Quite impossible. It would besmirch the honour of our family for generations . . . generations . . .'

'Impossible,' said Alfred yet again.

'You're young, Krysia,' said Max. 'You don't understand these things, but I can tell you, as your uncle – your guardian, really, in these . . . er . . . distressing circumstances . . .' – he gestured towards his brother – 'I can tell you that it is *out of the question* that you, a Countess Kornowska, should go and work in a jeweller's shop . . . behind the counter . . . for a Jew . . . a mangy Jew.'

Krystyna sat quite still. 'Perhaps you could pay our rent?' she asked quietly.

'You know I can't, my dear,' said Max, less confident than he had been a moment before. 'All our family fortune was in the land and . . .'

'And that has gone,' said Krystyna. 'So unless you can find me a better job, I shall start at Blomstein's on Monday.'

The Kornowski family now settled down to a life which was regular and quiet. Krystyna rose at half past six in the morning to make breakfast for Stefan and her father. She left the house at half past seven with Stefan. At the corner they parted; Stefan walked towards St Stanislas Kostka and Krystyna waited for a tram. The Count remained in the flat. He spent most of the morning there with a book in his hands – usually a volume of sporting prints which Krystyna had found in a second-hand bookshop. At mid-day he would go down to his sister-in-law's apartment and have lunch with her. It was a system which worked well because Aunt Cecylia was lonely and liked to talk; she did not mind that Count Stanislas did not concentrate on what she said. After lunch she would go with him for a walk in the Ujadowski Park and then leave him in her flat to play chess with the servant – the old woman called Mamuska. Stefan would return at about four; Krystyna at about six. They would all eat together in the evening unless their Aunt Cecylia had guests, in which case the Kornowskis would go up to their own flat with a dish of something prepared by Mamuska.

In ways this was a satisfactory life and certainly, from their expressions, none of the three Kornowskis would have been judged unhappy. Stefan, after all, lived the sort of life he had always lived in term-time – the same routine and the same friends. The Count might have been unhappy if he had not been protected by his insanity: as it was he took his walk and played chess with apparent enjoyment.

It was Krystyna who concealed her feelings. Only once or twice did she cry – when, for example, clumsy illiterate letters arrived from the peasant women at Jezow; or on Christmas Eve as they drank punch around the Christmas tree in the flat of her Uncle Max. Otherwise her manner was brisk, even cheerful, and there was no one to look into her eyes when she sat alone and remark upon their expression of bitterness and sorrow. Only Stefan, on occasions, would notice this mood of hers; and it was only to him that she would complain as they carried bags filled with cabbage, potatoes and milk up the four flights of stairs to their flat.

She loathed Warsaw. Every step she took in the dirty streets, every splash of mud from a passing car, tightened the spring of her hatred for the city. Even their flat, which was light and had a view, seemed to her like a shoe-box. She was exhausted and humiliated by the continuous cooking and cleaning (though she did it well and without complaint) just as she was humiliated by serving at a shop counter.

What sustained her at Blomstein's was her contempt for the customers; but she had such control over herself that not one of the dashing young men – or the fumbling older ones – could have guessed at the furious feelings of the girl who served them. Their attention, in any case, was distracted from her mood by her face and figure, which had become prettier still as she had grown from seventeen to eighteen and eighteen to nineteen. She knew why the old men hovered over her; she knew too why Blomstein himself was kind to her. Day after day she felt his sensual eyes watching her as she moved but he never made any gesture or any remark to which she could take exception.

She was frequently asked (in an intimate whisper) for an assignation by the customers. Sometimes she had only to glance at them for the confused and embarrassed man to change the subject and pretend he had not made the proposition. It was not only with strangers that she declined to go out at night. Krystyna never went out with men – even though her cousins and friends of her cousins invited her. She would go to parties or to the cinema in a group, but if ever one of the boys wanted to see her alone she would make the excuse that she had to stay at home and look after her father.

The only exception to this was Jan Zulawski, the plump son of their former neighbours whose sister Toni had been her friend. Krystyna had heard nothing from them since she had come to Warsaw: she had assumed that they were ashamed because their father had indeed bought Jezow from the bank. Then, one evening in the spring, Toni telephoned to say that she and Jan were in Warsaw and would like to go out with Krystyna. Toni's voice on the telephone had a funny tone to it, and she giggled once or twice for no apparent reason; but Krystyna agreed to meet them at the Café Ips at eight the next evening.

As soon as she had put down the telephone Krystyna went into her room to examine one or two of her better dresses. Those she had to wear in the shop were in quite good condition, but her only evening dress was emphatically in the style of the year before.

Next day in her lunch hour Krystyna bought a new dress. She did not enjoy spending this money on herself, and the dress was not particularly pretty – a compromise between what was elegant and what she could afford; she knew too that Toni would immediately recognize it as something cheap from a department store. All the same it was at least in fashion and so she walked into the Café Ips that evening with rather more confidence than she might otherwise have done.

It took only a minute to find Jan Zulawski, sitting solidly at a table drinking beer. Toni was not beside him, and for a moment Krystyna felt relieved to be spared the patronizing glance that she had imagined would be on her friend's face when she first saw her. She greeted Jan quite affably and sat down beside him.

He grinned and said: 'It's good to see you.'

'Where's Toni?'

A shadow of guile and confusion passed over his face but the grin remained. 'Oh, I'm afraid she had a most awful headache and couldn't come. She's most terribly sorry. She gets them, you know. She said she'd ring you tomorrow.'

Krystyna nodded and said nothing. She thought of leaving at once, but could not think of a pretext and so accepted the offer of a drink. Jan talked. She replied but there was not much spirit in the conversation. The dull, plump boy had become a dull, plump youth who made coarse jokes and laughed at them himself. As a child Krystyna had teased him – indeed he had been like a tame pig which Krystyna had led by the ring through its nose – but now, in Warsaw, she could not muster the same mood. Nor did she believe the story of Toni's headache.

They went from the Café Ips to a small restaurant in the Old Town with walls of padded pink silk hung with framed pictures from *La Vie Parisienne* of twelve or fourteen years before – girls lifting their petticoats and kicking up legs clad in old-fashioned underclothes.

It was dim at the table and Krystyna shrank back from the price of the food on the menu; but Jan seemed unaffected by the expense. He ordered champagne and pressed her to choose the costliest dishes.

Krystyna ate everything she was given but she drank little, whereas Jan left much of his food but drank a lot – one, then another bottle of champagne. The more he drank, the less he seemed to mind the subdued mood of his companion, or the small part she took in the conversation. He continued to tell her dubious anecdotes and then laugh at them himself. Once he leant across the table and asked Krystyna whether she had *changed* in Warsaw. She hesitated and was about to answer when he answered for her. 'Of course you have, of course. In a big city. Away from prying eyes. I know. And you work for a Jew, don't you, in a jeweller's shop?'

Krystyna said nothing. Jan laughed and went on with another story about some peasant girls and a stallion.

When they left the restaurant, Krystyna asked to go home. It had depressed her particularly to see so much money go into the silken hands of the restaurateur – and to watch the bundles of notes that Jan pressed into the hands of the waiters.

'I must go home,' she said. 'As you know, I work and so have to get up early in the morning.'

'Of course,' said Jan, leading her towards a taxi which stood at the kerb. He opened the door, helped her in and then gave the driver some mumbled instructions.

'Do you know where I live?' Krystyna asked him.

'Sluzewska Street, isn't it?'

'Yes.'

She sat back in her seat and immediately Jan was upon her, slobbering at her mouth as he tried to kiss her, clutching at her body and muttering endearments.

'Get off, Jan,' she gasped, pushing at him and seeing at the same time the grin of the driver who had turned around to glance at them as they stopped at a red light.

'Come on, old girl,' said Jan, as if she was a horse afraid of water.

'Was this what you planned?' said Krystyna, drawing back from him into the corner of the seat. 'Did Toni plan it too?'

'I won't tell Toni, old girl. You can trust me,' said Jan. 'I won't tell anyone.'

'Leave me alone,' cried Krystyna, almost weeping because she saw that her dress had been torn at the shoulder.

'Here we are,' said Jan, sitting up in the taxi and opening the door onto the pavement.

'Where? This isn't Sluzewska Street.'

'We'll go there later.'

'Go there later?'

'We'll have a drink here first.'

He pointed towards the door of a hotel – a small, dingy hotel – at which they had stopped.

Krystyna clutched the arm of her seat. 'Are you mad, Jan? What . . . what on earth do you think I am?'

'Come on, old girl. You know I've always liked you.' He took her by the arm and tried to pull her out.

'Come on, lady,' said the driver. 'I've got to be getting on.'

But Krystyna clung to the handle of the taxi door and Jan, after tugging at her for half a minute more, suddenly changed his expression from the grin that had been on his face all evening to a petulant frown. 'Come on, for God's sake,' he said. 'Papa gives me money now, so I can pay you just as much as that old Jew of yours.'

Krystyna stopped struggling for a moment and Jan stopped pulling her hand. 'What do you mean?' she said.

'We know all about Stets,' he said.

'What about Stets?'

'That your father tried to kill him . . .' Jan hesitated.

'What else?'

'And what you did so that he wouldn't go to the police.'

As if ashamed of what he had said, Jan let go her hand. As soon as he did so Krystyna opened the door of the taxi and got out onto the street.

'Come on . . .' said Jan.

Krystyna started to walk, then to run, down the street.

Jan started to follow her, but he had not paid the taxi. As he took his wallet from his pocket he shouted after her: 'I don't see why you won't do for me what you did for him . . .'

Krystyna ran faster. She rounded a corner and turned to see if Jan was following her. He was not to be seen, so she slowed her pace to regain her breath.

It took her half an hour to walk home through the wet streets. When she entered the flat she heard no sound from her father or brother. As she washed and changed into her night-dress she could not stop herself from crying and Stefan, who was awake, heard her tears.

Four

The most satisfactory aspect of the Kornowskis' first years in Warsaw was Stefan's education. The priests and boys at St Stanislas Kostka found him strange, but he worked well and amused them all by his eccentricity. It was known that his father was 'loopy', which gave an edge to his behaviour and was one reason why the Jesuits were so tolerant of his atheism. They assumed that it was only a stage in his precocious in-tellectual development; and as long as he continued to join in school prayers and go to Mass, they were content to leave him alone. Stefan in his turn was willing to conform to the practices of a religion in which he no longer believed because (or so he told his friends) he despised 'unnecessary sincerity'.

Stefan became so unlike any of the others that there was something of a Kornowski cult in his last years at the lycée. His provocative cynicism both enraged and amused his friends. For example he scoffed at their adolescent patriotism and talked of the 'inalienable inferiority of the Poles'. He ridiculed their ambitions yet worked quite hard himself and after taking his school leaving certificate in 1931 he applied for a place in the faculty of law at Warsaw University.

This choice of discipline came as a surprise to his family and friends. He had been expected to study literature, but he defended his choice of the law on the grounds that there was no Polish literature to speak of 'except Mickiewicz, and one cannot spend five years studying Mickiewicz'. He was full of such aphorisms in the company of others, which kept them amused, but there was a private side to his character which was different. He was conscientious towards his father and sister; he would do some of the shopping, braving the ridicule which might have been attached to it; and he always found time to take the Count for walks in the Park.

He was also more earnest in his own mind than he was with his friends. On the whole his fellow-students were interested in drinking, dancing, flirting, politics, and not, like Stefan, in 'the meaning of life' or 'the death of God'. For his thoughts still turned to these same, fundamental questions, as they had done in the summerhouse at Jezow, and he spent much of his time in cafés or at home turning them over in his mind.

He now accepted his existence to this extent: he had failed to cease to exist by ceasing to think, and was not yet prepared to try the further experiment of ceasing to exist by throwing himself out of his bedroom window. He had also established that his existence was not pure and free, but limited by many internal and external factors, some of which were susceptible to change, some of which were not.

He had a name – Stefan Kornowski – which could with some difficulty be changed – say to that of Raymond de Tarterre: but that change of name would not make him into a Frenchman.

Not even a change of nationality could do that. He might become a citizen of France, but he would always be a Pole. However dissatisfied he might be with that condition, there was nothing he could do about it.

Nor was there much to be done about his body. He had a flat, white stomach and a chest which would fit the same description. Certainly, if he was to spend the summer toiling in the fields, the chest and stomach might take on more form and change their colour to brown; but Stefan had also come to recognize and accept his physical condition: nature had not made him a tosser of hay.

He had also come to recognize and accept certain bonds of feeling which held him to others. He disliked the bonds, and they were not strong, but it was futile to deny that he was fond of his father, his sister, his aunt Cecylia and Mamuska the maid. There were also cousins and friends whom he met in the cafés or occasionally brought home; and so by the age of eighteen or nineteen, he appeared to be much like any other young man of the same background, strutting around like a country gentleman, affecting the opinions of the species and treating the absence of a country estate as an unimportant detail.

There was a difference, however, between Stefan and his friends. While they were mostly what they seemed to be, he was not. He was consciously playing the role of the sort of person he ought to be. Within himself he was quite different – that is, he was nothing, a potentiality, a blank page. As easily as he had put on the clothes of a dispossessed squire, he could take them off again and adopt the habit of a priest or the tunic of a soldier. It was as if a fear of commitment had inhibited the development of his personality. Pose, affectation and cynicism were the shield, armour and spear which protected and disguised a vulnerable body.

There was, however, a germ which penetrated the armour. Hormones flowed in his blood to his brain, infecting it with their narrow obsession. He could not stop thinking about women. He sat in his room, day after day, with desire like lead in his loins. 'Half the population of Warsaw are women,' he would say to himself. 'Why can't one of them be here, naked, on my bed?'

But who would oblige? The silly, tittering girls – the sisters of his friends – were too Catholic to do more than kiss him. There were always the whores, but Stefan had no money and he was afraid that they might be diseased. Friends of his had saved up their money and had survived; but the idea of going alone into the seamy streets and accosting some unknown woman deterred Stefan from following their example. He felt irritated and frustrated that such a trivial business was not easier and nearer at hand. 'Half the population of Warsaw are women,' he would repeat to himself. Why not one for him?

In this frame of mind he drew up a list of the women he met in the course of a week and the reasons why he either could or could not sleep with them; and immediately after the list came the first fragment of his fiction – a sketchily-written fantasy quite clearly dictated by a somewhat perverse desire.

Aunt Cecylia: would not oblige. Furthermore, it might kill her (shock, scandal).

Krystyna: would not oblige. Furthermore, would render me liable to prosecution under the Penal Code.

Jolanta: too pious, and might laugh at me.

Cousin Maria: might oblige, but no opportunity since she is always with her child.

Irena: might oblige, but mortal risk if her husband found out. Too dangerous.

Mamuska: too old. Has veins in her legs.

The old servant . . . she climbs the stairs every day with . . . A student, S. lives alone, studying . . . his mother, an invalid, is out for a walk. It starts to get dark. The door opens. The cook from the flat below enters with a pot of goulash. S. watches her as she stoops to put the pot on the stove. He plunges – he reaches under her skirts, and shoves his hands deep into the mass of wool, flesh and bulbous veins. Mamuska: a noise like a hiccup. She turns. She is hypnotized by the cruel eyes of the student. He removes one hand, inserts another, rummages around to find an orifice. Hooks it with his finger and leads the old peasant to his room. She lies on his bed. He covers her face with her skirts. The stink. He climbs on her, buries his face in her bosom, hugs her, fucks her. Later she scuttles downstairs to prepare dinner. She never alludes to it. Nor does S. But he remembers the scent, and the touch of her bulbous veins . . .

A month passed before Stefan wrote anything else in the notebook which was intended for his legal studies, but within that month the idea seems to have come to him that he might write more deliberately; for the next piece of writing was more self-conscious – a stylized fable which he never completed, but gave a title – 'The Princess of Volhynia'.

The dragon-like winds of dawn swept over the damp plains of Volhynia. The honey-coloured hay lay in the mounds on the ground – damp with the dew, yet warm in their kernels from the rampant sun of the eve. Trees bowed and waved in the cold morning light . . . etc.

Between silken sheets, high in a turret, the languorous limbs of the Princess of Volhynia stretched as she awoke. Her toes, more precious than the pearls of a queen, wriggled as the veil of sleep was lifted from her recumbent form . . . etc.

'Come, boy,' she said to the jester, 'you can surely do more than make me laugh.'
The jester looked into her fathomless eyes and saw the laughing invitation in their sparkle. And when he took her into his arms, the twinkle changed into a languorous look of desire.
'Come, now,' she said to the (puny-bodied) jester, 'you *can* do more than make me laugh.'
'Make you do what?' he asked.
'If your cock is as big as your comb,' said the Princess, 'just see what you'll make me do.'
'A most indecorous way for a Princess to speak.'
'Get on with it.'
'Your word is my command.'
When both were naked, the Princess poked his stomach.
'It's so flat and white,' she said.
'God made it so.'
'God is dead, or so you told me.'
'Then nature made it so.'

39

'Which made me pink and soft,' said the Princess, smoothing her own stomach.

'Just so,' said the jester.

Her hand crossed to his body. 'I like *that*,' she said.

'We always like what we haven't got.'

'Then give it to me.'

'Your word is my command.'

'Come on, then.'

'Shall I cut it off?'

'Don't tease your Princess.'

'How and where would your highness like it?'

'Here, here, can't you see? There's a place just made for it.'

'Your obedient servant will see what he can do.'

Some of his critics – his literary 'enemies' – were later to say that Stefan Kornowski was not a writer at all; that he was incapable of completing anything but the shortest of short stories or plays; that he belonged to no tradition; that his writing was either too didactic, too cerebral or too pornographic to be considered as literature. His admirers would answer that the absence of endings to Kornowski's longer works was a psychological, not a literary, question; that there was no Polish tradition to which he could belong; and that all art is inspired by passion of one sort or the other.

Whatever the truth of the matter may be, these two fragments were his first excursions into literature.

In the early summer of 1932, Stefan was seen less in the company of his old friends from St Stanislas Kostka and more with a fellow-student who was to all appearances quite his opposite – a tall, impassive young man, a year or two older than he was, who dressed in a deliberately proletarian manner and gave off an air of earnestness which was in marked contrast to Stefan's flippancy and affectation.

One Saturday in June, Stefan went so far as to ask his aunt if he could invite his friend to lunch with the family the next day. His aunt, of course, agreed, and it was thus that Bruno Kaczmarek was first introduced into the Kornowski family.

When he arrived, Krystyna was putting knives and forks onto the dining-room table and to show her fury at this unwanted guest she did not look at him but walked through the hall to the kitchen as if she was a servant. Stefan, who recognized her mood, made no attempt to introduce his friend until Cecilia drifted into the room, smiled weakly, and allowed the lips of the visitor to kiss her hand. After this Bruno was presented quite formally to the Count, and to Uncle Max, who had come as he often did for lunch on a Sunday.

The guest himself had an undecided expression on his face. He might have been embarrassed to find himself suddenly in such intimate surroundings with total strangers – his hand resting on the frayed, stained arm of the beige sofa, his eyes flitting from the eyes of the others to an eighteenth-century bureau which was too large for the room. Above all there were the smells which came to his nostrils – smells of Cecylia's and Krystyna's scent, the pork and cabbage from the kitchen, lingering steam and smoke from the bathroom and the aroma of stale cigar smoke which rose from Uncle Max – these were quite private and awkward to assimilate. Yet Bruno was not embarrassed, and he was only uncertain because he knew less than the others why he was there.

They drank vodka, ate herrings and gherkins and talked in a stilted way about nothing in particular, waiting for Krystyna or Mamuska to bring lunch to the table. Stefan, who was the link between the family and the visitor, said less than anyone else but watched with lizard eyes each twitch and mumble. Every now and then he would make the Kornowski grimace as if that in itself was a contribution to the conversation.

Eventually they sat at table. Krystyna still would not look at Bruno – not even at her uncle, who had started on an anecdote which she had heard before. At the other end of the table Cecylia – with her head turned away to present the profile of which she was so proud – began asking the guest about the university. 'You study law, do you?' she asked Bruno.

'Yes I do. I'm in the same year as Stefan.'

'Did you meet . . . at a lecture?'

Bruno looked across at his friend. 'Where did we meet?'

'I asked to borrow your notes.'

'That's right.'

'You see, Aunt Cecylia,' said Stefan, 'there are times when . . .

in a lecture . . . my mind wanders. But Bruno's mind never wanders. And he takes comprehensive notes in a neat hand . . .'

'He is trying to make me sound more pedantic than I am,' said Bruno.

'You will make a better lawyer than Stefan,' said Cecylia, 'if his mind wanders . . .'

'And his client will go to prison . . .' said Bruno.

'If I practise . . .' said Stefan.

'I don't know what else you'll do,' said Max from the other end of the table . . .

'But will *you* practise?' Cecylia asked Bruno.

'I think so, yes, in one way or another.'

'Bruno has a sense of mission,' said Stefan.

'Mission? Really?' said Cecylia. 'How interesting.'

'He wants to help the poor.'

'Really?'

There was a short pause: then Krystyna suddenly looked at Bruno and said: 'Aren't you older than Stefan?'

'Yes,' said Bruno. 'Three or four years older.'

'Why didn't you go earlier to university?'

'I had to work.'

'Why?'

'For the usual reason. I had no money.'

'Couldn't your father get you some?'

Bruno laughed artificially. 'He's a schoolteacher in Silesia.'

'I'm sure schoolteachers are frightfully rich,' said Krystyna: then she shook her hair over her face to hide the blush which came from speaking without thinking first.

'If they're as rich as you think,' said Bruno, 'then perhaps Stefan should learn to teach.'

'I'd rather be a teacher than a lawyer,' said Stefan.

'But *you're* not going to be a teacher, are you?' Krystyna said to Bruno – a sneer re-established on her face.

'No,' said Bruno.

'You've got better things in mind.'

'I'm not good with children.'

'So what are you going to do?'

'I mean to go into politics . . .'

'To fight for the nation?' said Uncle Max.

'To fight for the people,' said Bruno – whereupon there was a

42

grunt from Max, a snort from Krystyna and a sigh from Cecylia, with Stefan's eyes flitting from face to face until he saw that his aunt was about to change the subject. Then he said: 'Bruno is a man of the Left.'

'How typical,' said Krystyna, glancing at her brother, 'and I suppose you think it's funny to mess about in that sort of thing. How typical. Student Communists . . .'

Since Krystyna so rarely spoke to him so directly, Stefan was a little taken aback by what she said, but his aunt looked mournfully at Krystyna and said: 'Really, darling . . .' The Count smiled at them all, and Max, usually prepared to weigh in on a political discussion, merely muttered to himself about Bolsheviks and Jews, and then filled his mouth with pork and cabbage.

It was Bruno who replied to Krystyna – and again he showed no embarrassment. 'I was a Communist before I was a student,' he said. 'I am a student because I am a Communist.'

'Why don't you study in Moscow?' said Krystyna.

'Because I'm a Pole.'

'There are plenty of Poles in Moscow. Why, you might even end up head of the GPU like Dzerzhinsky, and kill as many innocent people.'

Bruno said nothing. Krystyna stood to clear the plates. 'Or do they want to keep you here for their next march on Warsaw?' Without waiting for an answer, she flounced out of the room towards the kitchen.

'I wish she'd sit at table,' Cecylia said to Stefan. 'Mamuska could clear away the plates.'

Stefan paid no attention to his aunt but stretched across the table for a piece of bread. He showed no sign that he was either embarrassed or upset by his sister's treatment of his friend. He had watched what had gone on with no expression on his face. There was a silence. Cecylia, who had thought that Bruno had such a nice face, was confused by his Communism and could think of nothing to say. Suddenly Stefan leant across the table and said, in a loud voice; 'What do you think, Father?'

The Count looked up, agitated.

'Bruno is a Bolshevik,' said Stefan, again in a loud voice as if his father was deaf, which he was not.

The Count now looked frightened – not of Bruno but of his son.

43

'Don't, dear,' said Cecylia. 'He doesn't understand.'

Stefan continued watching his father until Krystyna returned with clean plates, followed by Mamuska with a compote. Once again Krystyna adopted a servile role. She put a plate before Bruno as if she had never been introduced to him.

In the weeks which followed this lunch, no mention was ever made of Bruno either by the Count, by Uncle Max or by the two women until one evening, about two months later, Krystyna suddenly turned to her brother and asked what had happened to Bruno.

'Nothing,' Stefan replied.

'Is he still at the university?'

'Yes.'

'And do you see him?'

'On and off.'

'You never bring him here.'

'You didn't seem to like him.'

'I didn't say that I didn't like him.'

'You weren't particularly polite.'

Krystyna blushed. 'Oh, I'm sure he can take a tease, can't he?'

Stefan shrugged his shoulders. 'He's a serious person.'

'I'm not completely frivolous.'

'No . . .' Stefan hesitated.

'What?'

'What do you want me to do?'

'Nothing. I was just wondering why you kept him away.'

'I'll ask him again, if you like.'

'Tell him he should study me as a specimen of the masses who toil in jewellers' shops.'

Stefan mentioned his sister to Bruno when he saw him next.

'She didn't sound as if she could ever be interested in what we are trying to do,' said Bruno.

'You never know.'

'She was so antagonistic when I came to your flat that time.'

'I think she was nervous. She hadn't met a Communist before.'

Bruno thought for a moment, rubbing his thumb on the spine

44

of a textbook which he held in his hand. 'Look,' he said. 'Let's take her to Praga. If she saw the conditions that workers live in . . . real workers . . . that would do a lot more than any arguments of mine to bring her round.'

'Are they bad?'

'Appalling. Your aunt's flat is like a palace compared to theirs.'

'Good,' said Stefan.

'And it might interest you,' said Bruno.

'It might,' said Stefan doubtfully.

'We talk a lot about history, about the progressive mission of the Party and the Proletariat, but we should never lose sight of the concrete injustices which the historical process will put right. Damp walls, rats, hunger . . .' And Bruno went on with one of his soliloquies, which Stefan rather admired because they were cogent, sincere and almost convincing.

At ten on a Sunday morning Stefan and Krystyna met Bruno in Pilsudski Square and they took a tram across the river to Praga. It was a sharp, cold morning and their breath could be seen in the air. Krystyna sat next to her brother; Bruno sat opposite. Each had his own thoughts. Bruno watched the passers-by, and mused on the masses. Stefan pondered on the care his sister had taken over her appearance – her newly-washed hair falling over the fur collar which she had sewn onto her coat the night before. And Krystyna studied Bruno – his strong, even features and tall, slim figure which would have gone better with the uniform of an Uhlan than with the ordinary, unfashionable clothes that he was wearing now.

The city changed. They passed out of the old town where the houses had the elegant style of their period, crossed over the wide, placid Vistula and entered an area where factories and large blocks of flats had been built only for their utility. When they descended from the red tram at the end of the line, they were engulfed by this drabness. It was evident in every detail of the life around them. The windows of the shops had sparse shelves with bare cuts of meat or dusty apples laid out like medicines. The people who scuttled along were wrapped in coats which were old, worn and colourless. Some shuffled in feet protected from the cold by sacking.

Bruno knew his way. He led them from the tram terminal down a street of ordinary width, passed the great gates of a factory whose product might have been anything because, like any factory, it showed only its blocks of brick buildings, grey pipes and smoking chimneys.

Beyond the factory they turned right into a smaller street, and then into a large tenement building. The façade of the building had some form of decoration around the windows – a cursory touch of the baroque. Behind it, however, there were courts which were dark and bare – the fourth to which they went being the drabbest of all. The stairs at the bottom were made of concrete and lit by a dim electric bulb on the half-landing. At the bottom, two or three children aged around twelve stared at the three intruders.

Krystyna, regretting her attempt at elegance, cringed under the fur collar of her coat; but Bruno strode up the stairs as if he had more right there than the children, and Stefan followed behind him. On the fourth floor they stopped, and Bruno knocked on a door. It was opened on a chain by a man, then closed, then opened completely to admit them. Bruno shook hands with the man, addressing him as 'comrade' and then introduced him to Stefan and Krystyna. 'They are friends,' he said.

The man was heavy and unhealthy in appearance. He shook their hands with a measured warmth. 'Comrade Kaczmarek told me that you were interested in our living conditions,' he said, leading them from the cramped vestibule into a small living-room, and indicating a sofa where they should sit down. Stefan did so; Krystyna smiled at her host, just at the moment when his eye fell on her fur collar. She blushed deeply and sat down, wondering whether the dirt of the sofa would come off onto her coat.

A woman now appeared from another room. Around her shoulders there was draped a peasant's shawl, though there was little of the peasant in her physiognomy. The man, Jozef, introduced her as his wife and explained that their children were playing in the courtyard. 'There's no school for them,' he said, 'and we don't have time to teach them.'

Stefan, meanwhile, was looking around the room – at the damp patches on the walls and the dingy furniture.

'Not much of a place to live in, is it?' said Jozef, following the direction of his eyes.

'Well . . .' Stefan began.

'And I can tell you, ours is better than most. There's an old lady on the ground floor – well, the sun never reaches her flat and she's too old to go out and find it. She had might as well live in a dungeon . . .'

'Or a grave,' said the wife.

'Does no one do anything for her?' asked Krystyna.

'From time to time,' said Jozef. 'But the worst thing about living in conditions like these is that it takes away your will to make things better – for others, or for yourself.' He looked around the room. 'I dare say that there are things we could do to this place which would hide the damp; or brighten it up a bit. But it just doesn't seem worth it. A bright cushion just reminds you how drab the rest is.'

There was a silence.

'But we can provide some vodka, can't we?' he said to his wife with a deliberate, comradely chuckle.

The woman got up without a word and went into the next room.

'There's only one thing which sustains us,' said Jozef, looking alternately into the faces of Stefan and Krystyna. 'That is the certainty that in the future it will be different.'

'It *must* be,' said Krystyna.

'It will be,' said Jozef, 'it will be if we can organize the workers in the factories and the inhabitants of these tenements, and make them realize that conditions need not be what they are; that if the proletariat would seize power for themselves, the millions of zlotys which at present go in profits to the cartels would be redirected into schools, hospitals and homes for the people . . .'

'Have you made any headway?' asked Stefan.

'Some,' said Jozef. 'We have Party cells in most of the factories, and one or two in the tenements. But there are obstacles . . .'

'Not just here,' said Bruno.

'What obstacles?' asked Stefan.

'First, the religious sentiments of the people. And then there is still some mistrust of our patriotism – if you see what I mean.

Some people still think that we want to give Pomerania to the Germans, and unite the rest of Poland to the Soviet Union.'

'But that isn't the Party line,' said Bruno.

'No,' said Jozef, 'but it was before the Second Congress – and a lot of workers remember that.'

'So they support Pilsudski?'

Jozef shrugged his shoulders. 'Tacitly, anyway.'

His wife returned with some ersatz coffee and handed a cup to each of the visitors. She also offered them some cake, which looked stale, but was accepted by both Stefan and Krystyna for fear of seeming snobbish.

The two comrades, Bruno and Jozef, now began a quiet conversation about Pilsudski and the 'May error' of the Party whereby Communists had actually helped the dictator take power. Stefan and Krystyna, both unfamiliar with the terminology of Marxist polemics, let their minds wander onto other things. Stefan kept glancing at the large, red nose of Jozef's wife who sat listening to her husband and Bruno. His eyes never looked at her directly, but every now and then he would stretch or sigh, and under this camouflage give a look at its length and colour. He began to imagine the nose in different conditions and situations – quivering when she was angry, vibrating while she snored, twitching when she sniffed. He wondered too whether the other parts of her body were as ungainly as this nose – and he theorized (to himself) as to whether the nose was a product of its environment, or whether the conditions were somehow the fault of the nose.

As he thought about the nose he felt an impulse – which grew stronger – to interrupt the earnest conversation of the other two men with the remark: 'One thing's for sure – the revolution won't change that nose . . .'; and as their conversation continued, the impulse grew stronger and stronger. Stefan did what he could to think of something else – he turned his attention to his coffee cup, his finger nails, to St Stanislas Kostka – but none of this helped to dampen the impulse, and in the end, to prevent himself saying anything so dreadful, he jumped to his feet but involuntarily shouted as he did so: 'One thing's for sure . . .' and then only prevented himself from saying more by coughing so violently that he retched.

Krystyna, meanwhile, had been thinking calmly that while

the living conditions of the working class were undeniably appalling, and should be changed – by a revolution if necessary – they were in no way improved by her presence. Nor was she likely to benefit from any prolongation of this inspection – indeed she was liable to suffer as they suffered – to feel the damp and cold enter her bones, and to dirty her fur-trimmed coat on the filthy furniture. So when Stefan jumped up with his cry of 'One thing's for sure . . .' she too leapt to her feet – and while he choked, she moved towards the door. Bruno and his comrade were then also on their feet, slapping Stefan on the back; the commotion was such that no one thought of asking Stefan what one thing was for sure.

They took their leave – Jozef giving their hands an even, fraternal clasp, while his wife remained as sullen as when they had first come in.

Stefan and Krystyna were relieved to escape from the dingy, worker's flat but they felt indignant and outraged that anyone should be expected to live in such conditions. Krystyna, in imagining for a moment herself in a flat of that kind, was clasped by the memory of the days when she had trudged around Mirow and Miranow looking for somewhere to live. Bruno, walking beside her, took that shudder as a gesture of revulsion at the injustice of capitalism and he nodded righteously.

Emancipated from the nose, Stefan quickly forgot the remark he had been impelled to make, and rambled off on a vague assertion of the opposite – that history was on the side of progress, that progress would mean prosperity which in its turn would mean better housing and more frequent trams between Warsaw and its outer suburbs. These discussions continued on the tram (when it came) and in a café on the Novy Swiat where they went to get something to eat – and it was here that Bruno gradually introduced his more profound analysis of the social malaise which led to the paradox of affluent rich and suffering poor in the same city. 'Capitalism,' he said, 'is a necessary state in the development of man's productive capacities. But in the process of its development it distorts his nature. On the one hand it creates the bourgeois who is possessed and enslaved by profit; on the other it produces the destitute worker who is paid as little as it is possible to pay a man just to keep him alive.'

'But why is it all inevitable?' asked Krystyna. 'Why can't the two classes reach a compromise of some sort – pay the men more and cut down the profits . . .'

'Because profits are necessary for the creation of capital, and without capital there is no development of productive capacity . . .'

'So the businessman is only doing what history expects him to do?' said Stefan.

'Yes,' said Bruno, 'until you reach a point where a society is ready for revolution.'

'When capitalism is fully developed?'

'Usually, yes, but there can be situations such as that in Russia in 1917 when the proletariat takes power before the full development of capitalism, and itself directs that development during a socialist phase . . . And this is the stage we are at in Poland. Capitalism has served its purpose. The only use served by the system now is in preserving the privileges of those who find themselves in the bourgeoisie. What do they care if their capital "comes dripping from head to foot, from every pore, with blood and dirt"? They never go near the factories and see the dirty source of their money. They just take it in clean bank-notes and spend it on their own indulgence.'

Krystyna looked uncertain. 'Uncle Max would say that workers like Jozef live in such squalor because they're too lazy or incompetent to do better for themselves!'

'Jozef is paid less than five zlotys a day,' said Bruno.

'It's very little, I know,' said Krystyna, 'but there were peasants at Jezow who were as poor as he was, yet their houses were always clean and tidy.'

Bruno nodded. 'It's true that Jozef and his wife . . . and many workers . . . do let things go. Their spirits are broken by the monotony of their work. Marx called it alienation. Labour starts as a creative process through which a man expresses himself; but profit demands the division of labour and the worker finds that as an individual he no longer makes anything. He has become an adjunct to a machine. It is that – the spiritual dehumanization of man – just as much as his material degradation which is our inspiration and justification in the Party. Our revolution will not be just to take wealth and power from one set of people and give it to another; it will liberate the spirit of man which has been crushed by the inexorable development of his productive forces.'

'But if this development of socialism is inevitable,' asked Stefan, 'if it is historically predetermined, then why should you or I or anyone else do anything but sit back and wait for it to happen?'

'Because,' said Bruno, 'every objective development has a subjective factor which is essential for the realization of that development. People think that Marxism is cold and mechanical, but Marx himself wrote that: "History is nothing but the activity of man pursuing his aims." On the other hand, though men make their history, they do not make it just as they please; they do not make it under circumstances chosen by themselves, but under circumstances directly encountered, given and transmitted from the past. It is the interaction of these objective circumstances with the subjective will of men that makes for progress; and it was the genius of Comrade Lenin that he had both the will and the analytical intelligence to achieve the October Revolution.'

They talked late into the afternoon, always sitting in the same café, ordering every now and then a new cup of coffee; and Stefan occasionally smoking a cigarette. Their voices were low, their heads close together, for fear of attracting attention by the nature of their conversation, which gave an added intimacy. Of the three it was the eldest, Bruno, who spoke most – keeping an even tone which became infused with a particular sincerity and warmth whenever he strayed from the technicalities of Communism to its higher ideals.

His voice was pleasant, and once he had described a concept, such as the theory of surplus value, which the other two found difficult to understand, he would smile and ask Krystyna if she would like some chocolate cake to help it down. He had the manner of an older brother, and both Stefan and Krystyna listened to him as if that was what he was: but it became clear, as the afternoon went on, that an extra factor was entering into the equation – a subjective factor, as it were, in an objective development. Like a jealous sibling Stefan noticed that Bruno had started to pay more attention to Krystyna than to him – to address his remarks to her, to answer her questions and to direct at her those delightful, ironic smiles.

He noticed too that Krystyna was listening to Bruno with a concentration that could hardly be justified by her interest in historical materialism or the class struggle. Her eyes looked into his eyes – or wandered down to his lips. If he looked at her she would look away and blush, but as soon as he was off again she would return to a study of his features, and even lean forward, her chin on her hand, her elbow on the table, as if straining to hear what he said.

By five o'clock, when it was already dark, Stefan stood up and said that it was time to go. Neither Bruno nor Krystyna moved: indeed Krystyna merely turned to him and said: 'If you're hungry, there's some food in the kitchen . . .'

'I may not be going home . . .' said Stefan.

Krystyna frowned, briefly. 'No, well, never mind. Mamuska will see that Papa's all right.' Whereupon she turned away from her brother and returned her attention to Bruno.

On Saturdays Krystyna was in charge of Blomstein's jewelry shop. Because it was the Jewish Sabbath, Mr Blomstein himself did not come in, and there had been a time when it was closed like most other Jewish enterprises: but Blomstein was reluctant to lose business and did not like to think that his cosmopolitan customers should find the shop closed like any grocery in the Jewish quarter.

These feelings coincided with his growing confidence in Krystyna. Since he had employed her she had shown herself to be so competent and trustworthy that now, every Friday night, he would give her a set of keys – one for the shop, one for the safe and one for the top drawer of his desk. In this drawer he kept a black notebook in which was written the number of every article of jewelry in the shop, and beside the number two prices – a minimum and a maximum. If, in the course of a day, a customer asked for a ring or a bracelet, Krystyna would consult the list, ask for the highest price, but know that she could go lower without incurring the displeasure of her employer.

He had taught her more than just the reading of figures in a book. Many of the bankers and pawnbrokers who bought diamonds and pearls at Blomstein's because they kept their value and could be smuggled abroad would rather haggle with

Blomstein himself than with Krystyna. She was not deceived by their slavering talk of the beauty of the stone or the delicacy of the setting – nor by the brown badges they wore in their lapels to show that they had contributed to the National Loan. She met their pleading, wheedling eyes with a hard, blank expression. To Krystyna they usually paid the asking price.

On this particular Saturday (the Saturday after her visit to Praga) at eleven in the morning, an aristocratic young army officer – a species she particularly disliked – came into the shop and asked after a necklace in the window. Krystyna went out of the shop with the officer so that he could point it out to her, and immediately she recognized the diamond and ruby necklace which had belonged to her mother.

She went back into the shop, removed it from the window, and laid it out in front of the officer. He fingered it, and asked its price. Krystyna told him to wait while she inquired. She then took the necklace into Mr Blomstein's office, opened the drawer, took out the notebook and matched the number of the label to the number on the list, and saw that the low price was eight thousand zlotys and the high price ten. Blomstein, she remembered, had bought it from her for one thousand zlotys.

She returned to the counter and told the young officer that the necklace was ten thousand zlotys. He bit his lower lip and fingered the necklace. 'What a pity it isn't eight,' he said, smiling up at Krystyna.

'Impossible, captain,' she replied, with an unusually sharp tone to her voice. 'The price is ten thousand zlotys.'

The officer looked down at the necklace. For a few moments more his plump, well-manicured fingers fondled the stones. Then he shrugged his shoulders and said: 'Very well, ten thousand zlotys.'

Krystyna picked up the necklace and placed it in its box.

'Never economize on love,' said the officer, winking at her, and taking a wad of notes from his wallet.

Krystyna did not reply. She wrapped up the box and handed it to the officer. He counted out the ten thousand zlotys, glanced at her hand, clicked his heels and left the shop. As she watched him go – with her mother's necklace in his hand – Krystyna suddenly sat down on a chair: something she would not have done if Mr Blomstein had been there.

She returned home as usual by way of the grocer's shop, and bought food for their evening meal. She carried it up the four flights of steps to their flat and then sat for a while in the living-room. No one else was there – all she could hear was the faint noise of traffic in the street below.

Then she went to the kitchen and started to cut up the meat and wash the vegetables. Eventually Stefan returned with the Count – they had been downstairs with Cecylia – and they all settled down for an evening like any other evening. Stefan came into the kitchen to see if he could help his sister, and he noticed at once that her mood was fierce.

'Put the knives and forks on the table,' she said sharply.

He started to take them out of the drawer.

'You may be right,' said Krystyna suddenly alluding to an earlier conversation she had had with Stefan, 'that the peasants were poor, and we took rent from them which they couldn't afford . . .'

'I didn't say . . .'

'But that doesn't mean that we can't be on their side now.'

'Of course not.'

'Perhaps losing Jezow was not a disaster, as we used to think, but a kind of liberation which enables us now to see things as they really are.'

'Perhaps,' said Stefan.

'It helps me, anyway,' she said. 'Just think what I would have been like if we had stayed there. I'd have married some preposterous landowner, just as Mama did, and I'd have led an absurd, unreal life . . .'

'Perhaps,' said Stefan again.

'I wouldn't expect you to agree,' she said with sarcasm. ' "The spirit that forever denies", like Mephistopheles.'

Stefan blushed. 'That forever searches,' he said, 'like Faust.'

'But you'll never find anything,' said Krystyna, still peeling carrots at the sink. 'Whereas I . . . I think I have found some sort of truth . . .'

'Where?'

'In what Bruno told us.'

'But he's a Communist.'

'I know. But one shouldn't be afraid of that, should one, if one thinks that it might be true?'

'But you're a Catholic . . . you go to Mass.'

'I know,' she said, 'but that's habit.'

'Don't you believe in God?'

She shrugged her shoulders. 'Not really, no. Not since that afternoon . . .'

'Don't you confess?'

She blushed. 'No.' She hesitated, then said: 'I once told a priest about something that . . . happened. I didn't feel that it was a sin, but I told him all the same. He said that I would go to Hell unless I repented. So I said I was sorry but I didn't mean it. How can you feel sorry for something that at the time you had to do?'

Stefan smiled. 'You should have asked the priest.'

'What use would that have been? They're so smug in their cassocks. They can't really understand.' She put the carrots into a pan, and the pan on the stove. 'Your friend, on the other hand,' she said, avoiding Stefan's eyes, 'he seems to understand.'

'Yes,' said Stefan.

'And he seems ready to do something . . . to act.'

'Yes,' said Stefan.

'Is it rubbish, what he says?'

'No,' said Stefan. 'I'm half convinced myself. He seems so sure that a revolution will cure the human condition that one is tempted to give it a try.'

'Do you understand what I mean, then, about being liberated from our background?'

'Oh yes,' said Stefan. 'I've felt that for some time.'

Eight days later Bruno Kaczmarek paid his second visit to Sluzewska Street – invited there by Krystyna for lunch on a Sunday. Cecylia was in Cracow, so they ate upstairs – just Bruno, Stefan, Krystyna and the Count.

The three talked without stopping. Marx, History, the Revolution, bounced back and forth across the table like pingpong balls; but the tone of their talk was different from what it had been before. There was no argument now, but a joint journey of exploration and discovery into the philosophy of Revolution until, by the end of the meal, they had reached Rosa Luxemburg, and through her came onto the equality of women.

'At one time,' said Bruno, 'she was as prominent in the Party as any of the others. And if, now, her ideas are rejected, it is not because she was a woman, but because she was wrong.'

'Where was she wrong?' asked Stefan.

'She was excessively internationalist in outlook,' said Bruno. 'She wanted to merge the Polish Party with the Bolshevik Party; she wanted Poland to be one of the Soviet Republics . . . an attitude which was quite common up to the Fifth Congress.'

'There are no women in the Russian Politburo, are there?' said Krystyna.

'No,' said Bruno.

'And from what I've heard,' she said, 'Soviet women are given equal opportunities to be doctors and engineers, but they're still expected to cook and clean when they come home in the evening.'

'A real Communist would share that kind of work,' said Bruno.

'Then Poland will never be Communist,' said Stefan.

'Women are badly exploited,' said Bruno. 'In many homes the husband is the exploiter . . .'

'Not here,' said Stefan, smiling and getting to his feet. 'We share the burdens. I take Papa for a walk in the park . . .'

'While I wash the dishes,' said Krystyna.

'To prove that I mean what I say,' said Bruno, 'I shall stay and dry them.'

When Stefan and the Count had left the flat, Krystyna went to the kitchen sink and Bruno began piling up the plates, scraping the scraps of food from one plate to another. 'Where did you get these plates?' he asked Krystyna. 'They're old, aren't they?'

'We've always had them,' said Krystyna.

'And what is the coat-of-arms?' asked Bruno, scraping off the grease from the pattern of the plate.

'Ours,' said Krystyna.

'They must have seen better days,' he said, handing the pile to Krystyna who sank them into the hot water.

'Oh certainly,' she said.

'And you?'

'I used to think so.'

Bruno picked up the dish towel and, somewhat self-consciously, started to dry the dishes. 'Stefan told me that you lived on a large estate . . .'

She smiled. 'Once upon a time.'

'Not so long ago.'

'No. Three years ago. Papa went bankrupt and then . . . mad.'

'It must have been hard.'

'Hard, yes. But it saved us from the life of a landowner. We won't have the exploitation of peasants on our conscience. We are free to be on the right side.'

'Do you mean that?'

'Yes,' she said. 'It was difficult at first . . .' She turned, looked at him, and laughed. 'Like you, drying the dishes. You look quite absurd.'

'I'm not used to it . . .'

'But then one does get used to it,' she said more seriously, 'and one lives knowing that one is doing what is right. That is important, isn't it?'

'Yes,' he said. 'That is the most important thing of all.'

'It was easier for Stefan and me anyway,' she said, 'because we are young. It would have been hard for Papa, but he is protected by his madness . . . He has withdrawn from the world and anyway, it was his own fault.'

She finished washing the dishes, wiped her hands on the apron she was wearing, untied its strings and hung it up on a hook on the door. 'Leave the rest,' she said to Bruno. 'It was very kind of you to have helped at all – even if it was for ideological reasons.'

'They weren't just ideological,' said Bruno, putting the towel down on the table.

Krystyna smiled and walked out into the hall. She sighed. 'Now,' she began. She turned. Bruno was close behind her and they found themselves face to face. 'Shall we go for a walk?' she asked.

'A walk, yes, why not?' he said; but instead of moving towards the door he took hold of her hand and drew her towards him.

For a moment Krystyna's face had that look of passive concentration which comes to a girl when she is about to be kissed: but then she seemed to be seized by panic. She did not pull away from Bruno but looked away – her eyes staring wildly at familiar objects and furniture through the door in the living-room. Bruno was not put off. He folded his arms around her and drew her body into a tight hug. As a result his lips met her ear; and seeing it there he kissed it once, then again – softly, gently, quietly.

For Krystyna the noise of this kiss was amplified by her ear; and the choice of the ear itself exaggerated her agitation. It was more ordinary than her lips but somehow more intimate. She had never imagined that a man might kiss her ear. As a result she began to tremble, then to shake, then to cry.

Another man might have taken against a girl who behaved in this way, but Bruno noticed that though she cried and trembled and struggled, she did not draw away; indeed she clung to him, digging her fingers into the material of his jacket. He therefore held her tightly with one hand, and with the other moved her head around until his lips found their proper quarry and the two mouths were joined.

The shaking did not stop; nor did the tears. But once Krystyna felt his lips, his teeth, his tongue, his saliva, she crushed her mouth against his in the same way as she clung to his shoulder. She felt his hand move her head back so that his lips felt softer and hers were not crushed against her teeth. Both mouths began to move with pleasure or affection or whatever it is that goes into a kiss; and as they did, her trembling and shaking, which had started as an expression of panic and neurosis, grew into a rhythmic movement of both bodies, rising to a crescendo which left her whimpering and supine in his arms.

They went into the living-room and sat on the sofa. Neither quite knew what had happened. Krystyna looked into Bruno's eyes with joy and he looked into hers with an amused affection. Of course nature had not set its seal on him in quite the same way as it had on Krystyna. The kiss had served her body as well as her soul, and she was now content just to look into his eyes and hold his hand: and Bruno was too polite, too sensitive and too disciplined to impose his needs on her when hers had so evidently been satisfied.

He also was in a slightly awkward position, for though he knew from the kiss that she liked him, that her heart belonged to him, that even the shabby sofa on which they sat together had somehow entered his personal world, he did not know what attitude she would take to more intimate acts of a physical nature. Too gross an interpretation of her delicate sentiments might smother them. She was not a Party intellectual, but the Catholic daughter of a dispossessed nobleman whose plates still bore his coat-of-arms. Krystyna looked into his eyes and smiled. 'Let's go out,' she said. 'I don't want to stay indoors all afternoon.'

'Shall we go and find Stefan?'

'No. Let's go out on our own.'

They put on their coats, went down the four flights of steps and out into the street. The air was dry and familiar. They walked hand in hand, going in no particular direction. They did not speak but every now and then they would glance into each other's eyes. At a street corner they stopped. They looked at each other once again, and this time did not look away.

'I'd like to kiss you again,' said Bruno.

'Yes,' she replied, her expression unchanged. 'Where can we go?'

'Come back to my room,' he said.

'Yes.'

And so she returned with him to his lodgings, where he made love to her in such delirium that he had no memory of it afterwards.

Five

Krystyna Kornowska and Bruno Kaczmarek were married in Warsaw. Aunt Cecylia and Bruno's mother, the schoolteacher's wife, who had come from Silesia for the wedding, cried as they watched the young couple take the solemn vows; while Stefan turned down the corners of his mouth, which was as good as a smile of satisfaction.

Rarely can there have been such an auspicious beginning to a married life, for the two were not only physically besotted, but had become ideologically entwined. Krystyna now identified all those by whom she had suffered with the Bourgeoisie and associated herself entirely with the suffering Proletariat. A month before her wedding she had joined the illegal Communist Party of Poland; and her new convictions, together with the risk of arrest and imprisonment, were quite as exhilarating as the air on the high Tatras where they went for their honeymoon.

Then Bruno returned to his studies and Krystyna to Blomstein's, but their life was quite different from what it had been before. They were drunk on history. People were poor, trade was depressed and Hitler was now Chancellor of Germany, but this only heightened their excitement and they went secretly and separately to the meetings of the same Party cell, or took their turn at the clandestine Party press printing illegal leaflets.

For Krystyna Communism was the perfect vessel for her various conflicting emotions. It met her need to love and do good, yet hate and revenge herself at the same time. It even hallowed her new-found sexuality and saved it from degenerating into enfeebling self-indulgence. She was now cheerful when she got up in the morning; she would sing at the sink when she peeled the potatoes, or argue energetically about the Comintern's policy on the Popular Front. She was still as conscientious as she had been before – Uncle Max came to lunch on a Sunday, she still made tea for Aunt Cecylia, and took her father for walks in the park – but her concentration was entirely removed from these character actors, so far removed from the main drama of her life.

This change in her personality did not go unnoticed by her brother. He saw what her new ideals had done for her and, though wise enough to realize that some of her happiness was in Bruno rather than the Party, he still envied her the particular intoxication which came from her historical self-righteousness. He envied it, and after a time he determined to share it, but it was a hard path for him to follow. No tangible, human love led him on: and in accepting any set of ideals he had always to struggle with his own cynical reflexes and sardonic personality.

When talking with Krystyna and Bruno, he found himself neither convinced nor unconvinced by their arguments. The slow construction of a system of values by which he might lead his life had taken him little further than the foundations he had laid in the summerhouse at Jezow. It was tempting, therefore, to vault up into the fortress of Marxist speculation – to leave the isolation of a disinherited aristocrat, a landowner without land – and join a universal cousinship more exclusive still.

For Krystyna, faith had been more important than understanding: but Stefan felt that he must know just what it was a Communist must believe. He laid aside his law books and started to read Marx, Engels, Plekhanov, Lenin, Luxemburg . . . He became infected with their passion, their vehemence, their outrage and their certainty. The people who passed him in the streets ceased to be people, but formed ranks as Bourgeois, Peasant, Proletarian. The piggy smile on the face of a rich man became the snarl of the exploiter; and the simple expression of the worker became lines of sincerity, honesty and heroism.

Nowhere did his new convictions find better expression than in his writing. The clogged little texts of disguised desire were replaced by flowing stories of the Class Struggle. Here, at last, was inspiration; here was an inexhaustible source of grand, heroic themes. A writer must have drama, and Communism, with its clear-cut rights and wrongs, gave Stefan the meat for his fiction.

Three months after his sister's marriage, Stefan followed her into the same cell of the Communist Party of Poland.

The first piece he wrote in this Communist phase was called *Arbeit Macht Frei* (Work makes you Free) – an allusion to the motto above the entrance to the concentration camp which had just been built by the Nazis in Dachau. It was a straightforward story written in a simple style about the alienating effect of labour in a mattress factory. Jan, the hero, is a young worker, newly married to a peasant girl, Maria. She loves him but taunts him for the servility of his profession. 'You work for a pittance, making soft-spring beds for the gentlefolk of Warsaw; while we lie on a straw palliasse, worse off than the beasts of my father's barn.'

Jan has been unemployed. He knows that at least they have food to eat and a roof over their heads; thus, when his wages are reduced to 'conquer inflation', he accepts the cut and refuses to join a strike called by some political activists among his fellow-workers. When Maria hears of this, her frustration at their wretched life is transformed into a contempt for her husband. She spits in his face and goes out herself to join the pickets.

That night she does not return home, but goes to the room of a young striker. The next day she stands once again with the pickets, her lover at her side. A fight breaks out between them and the workers who wish to return. Jan finds himself face to face with his wife, a hammer in his hands. He sees in her eyes that she has betrayed him. She taunts him; he strikes her and she falls down dead. The story ends as Jan is led away in handcuffs by the police, and the workers return to the factory, their strike defeated.

In writing this story, Stefan had suppressed all the eroticism and frivolity which were so evident in his earlier pieces. There was no trace of any indulgence in his depiction of the adulterous encounter between Maria and the militant worker. ('He closed the door, and they shut out the world in the languid embrace of two bodies that were tired yet strong.') In its place there were conscientious descriptions of sweat, grime, steel and smoke; and ironic allusions to the scented silk handkerchiefs of the capitalists – to the whining of their pampered womenfolk about tepid tea or soggy éclairs. Indeed the story was written and constructed with such deliberateness that it could be said to have lacked spontaneity or a sense of humour. Stefan might have said this himself, but he was quite content that it should be what it was, that he had done what he had set out to do – write a story which was artistically and politically sound. He made up his mind to submit it to the review *Skamander*.

Before doing this he wanted to show it to his comrades in the Party cell. He did not have to do so but in his enthusiasm for his new friends, he wished them to be the first to appreciate this blow he was about to strike for the toiling masses.

The meeting was held in the apartment of Michael M. (they never used their family names, though they knew quite well what they were), who was a lecturer in mathematics at the university. Present there besides Michael M. were Rachel Z. (student), Krystyna K. (shop assistant), Bruno K. (student), Andrzej G. (janitor), Janusz B. (stoker), Jan D. (student) – and of course Stefan K. (student and writer). In the background the wife of Michael M. wandered irritably, reminding them as they came in that a child was sleeping in the next room.

Stefan was nervous. He sat in an armchair where Bruno had told him to sit, clutching his manuscript which he had rolled up like a baton. It had been agreed the week before that this meeting of the cell should discuss his story, and the expressions on the faces of the different members showed anticipation of a different sort. Rachel Z., a dark, pretty girl, looked at Stefan with eagerness; Andrzej G. and Janusz B. – the janitor and the stoker of the university furnace – both older than Stefan, looked at him with some suspicion. Krystyna sat back from the group, as if her presence might inhibit her brother, while Bruno sat opposite Stefan with as much encouragement in his expression as he could muster.

The mathematician, Michael M., a plump, balding man, began their discussion. 'As you know, comrades,' he said, clasping and unclasping his long fingers, 'we decided to give over this evening to a study of our Marxist aesthetics – in relation to literature, and particularly in relation to a story written by Comrade Stefan who as you know is a writer . . .'

He stopped, looked at Stefan, then drew himself up as he normally did when he started a lecture.

'Now it would be an error, comrades, for us to become so obsessed by the political and economic criteria which govern our activities that we forgot the value of aesthetics – especially of literature . . . As Marx so aptly put it, Charles Dickens did more for the English working classes than all the social reformers of the nineteenth century put together . . . And even here in Warsaw, you may remember, five or six years ago, the essay by Julius Brun in *Skamander* – and the controversy over Zeromski which followed. Well this sort of thing – one novel, one essay – can do much to create a revolutionary consciousness in our people, reaching into the minds of those who would never otherwise be open to our ideas . . .'

Michael M. hesitated, and Bruno – knowing how much this particular comrade liked the sound of his own voice – interrupted to suggest that Stefan should read his story first; and that the discussion of its value – as art or propaganda – should follow.

'Of course,' said Michael, 'of course we must hear the story.

63

I only wanted to say, well, that we must not look upon it as light entertainment. We must listen and criticize most seriously. It is as much part of our Party work as anything else . . .'

'I quite agree,' said Bruno, 'and I only suggest that we press on because I myself am keen to hear the story . . . politically and artistically keen . . .' He smiled at Stefan.

'I hope you won't all be disappointed,' said Stefan.

'Go on,' said Bruno. 'Read it.'

Stefan began his story, *Arbeit Macht Frei*. At first he read it too quickly, but then he grew less nervous and slowed the pace to express the sound of his words and the rhythms of his sentences.

Jan trod the dank, dark steps from tenement to factory, from factory to tenement, as he had now for thirteen years, as he would for thirty more, as his son would tread them, and his son's son. He was chained by need to routine – he was destined to fit linen over springs for the buttocks and backs of men and women in a different world of parasols and scented handkerchiefs . . .

The cigarette smoke grew thicker. The wife of Michael M. shuffled around the room as silently as she could, giving tea to the audience and a glass to Stefan. He sipped it and continued; and in three quarters of an hour he had finished his story.

He looked up into Bruno's smile of approval. At the back of the room, too, he thought he could see an expression of satisfaction on the face of his sister. At the same time Rachel, the Jewish girl, clapped her hands and said: 'That was awfully good,' before anyone else could speak: but the others – Michael, Andrzej, Janusz and Jan, the other student – cleared their throats and looked away from Stefan towards the plate of petits fours which the mathematician's wife had left out of their reach on her husband's desk.

'Well,' said Bruno, looking around the small group which made up this cell of the Communist Party of Poland. 'I can certainly say that I enjoyed listening to Comrade Stefan's story . . .'

'Yes, yes,' said Michael M. 'I certainly agree that technically – artistically, that is . . .'

'It had a German title,' said Janusz B., the stoker of the university furnace – somewhat abruptly, almost aggressively. 'I didn't understand it and I don't see why a Polish story should have a German title.'

'Yes, well,' said Michael M., glancing at Stefan, 'I took the title to be ironic – a reference to the fascist detention camp . . .' Stefan nodded.

'It has, you see,' said Michael to Janusz, 'a message – a kind of motto over the gate which says "work makes you free". Ironic, of course, because no one who goes into the camp is likely to get out of it – especially not our German comrades. And I take it that the author's intention was to compare the factory in which his hero worked – the mattress factory – with the camp. Is that fair?'

'Yes,' said Stefan.

'Then I don't see why you didn't have the title in Polish,' said Janusz, 'because a lot of comrades who come from the east wouldn't catch the meaning, if you understand me.'

'No, that's true,' said Michael, 'that's certainly true. But I suppose that if the title was not in German, then the allusion – the symbolic parallel, as it were – would be lost.'

'Symbolic parallel . . . no, well, I don't really know,' muttered Janusz.

'Literary criticism is rather a hobby of mine,' whispered Michael to Bruno before sipping his tea at close quarters to his comrade's ear.

'My criticism of this work,' said Jan, a sharp-faced student of economics, 'goes beyond the title. First – there is no positive hero; and second, it undermines the reader's belief in fundamental proletarian solidarity. The cause of these mistakes seems to me to lie in Comrade Stefan's complete ignorance of working-class conditions. He has not, I presume, set foot in a mattress factory; yet he writes – blithely, one might say – about factory workers . . .'

'Ah yes, of course, that could be a weakness,' said Michael.

'Nor have you set foot in a factory, Jan,' said Bruno, 'so you're in no position to judge.'

'I don't aspire to write about factories . . .' said Jan.

They all looked at Andrzej and Janusz. Andrzej, the janitor, sucked at the pipe he was smoking and said: 'It could have

65

happened. My wife complains, right enough, but it only makes things worse and I tell her so.'

'I was unconvinced,' said Jan with a look of condescension at Andrzej, 'but then all art is bluff, and so if it works for Comrade Andrzej, then I dare say it will work for a great many others. But this makes it all the more dangerous because there is no positive hero. From beginning to end our sympathy is for Jan – the suffering lumpenproletarian. The only worker with a socialist consciousness portrayed in any detail is the Communist who seduces his comrade's wife . . .'

'She goes to him,' said Rachel.

'All right. Perhaps he just takes advantage of her.'

'But do you say that it couldn't happen?' asked Bruno.

'I'm sure it could,' said Jan.

'It could,' said Andrzej. 'My cousin's wife . . .'

'But what is the effect on the reader,' asked Jan, 'above all of the Polish reader, imbued with Catholic prejudices against adultery? The political symbolism of the story – the factory as prison, Jan as alienated man, shackled to his work, raising the hammer not against his oppressor but against his wife – all this, which is good in itself, acceptable, straightforward propaganda – is overshadowed by the drama of his wife's infidelity. That, in the mind of the reader, drives him to his crime. And what is its significance? Nothing. Yet who is the partner in sin? Our Communist.'

There was a silence. Michael sipped his tea. Bruno looked at his knees: Krystyna withdrew into the shadow at the back of the room.

'Perhaps,' said Andrzej, 'perhaps she should sleep with the foreman.'

'Why not?' said Janusz. 'That's it. The foreman. And have him rape her. That would set people off in the right direction.'

Stefan gripped the arm of his chair. His eyes blinked as if tears were rising under their lids. 'Perhaps, yes,' he said, 'but I had meant . . . you see, the certainty, the calm of the Communist, is what attracts her . . . and then, they must come face to face at the picket line . . .'

'It *must* be the Communist,' said Rachel, 'and he doesn't *seduce* her. He is kind, protective – he takes her in. He makes love to console her . . .' She looked fervently at Stefan. 'I think it was beautiful, that passage. I think the story is beautiful. He is like Wozzeck. The whole system destroys him. It's quite clear in my mind that the effect of the story is what we want it to be.'

'I don't agree,' said Jan.

There was another silence. 'Perhaps we could compromise somehow,' said Michael, looking uneasily at Stefan. 'Of course we don't want to interfere with your artistic judgement, but if the story is to be published, and if it is criticized, then our whole cell will have to bear some responsibility . . .'

Stefan said nothing.

'I don't think you can compromise,' said Bruno. 'I think Stefan's sincerity . . . his ideals . . . the very fact that he belongs to the Party, means that we should trust him.'

'Yes,' said Michael in a quicker and quieter voice, directed particularly at Bruno, 'but all the same, this business of a positive hero – I mean there is a point there. And *Skamander* is widely read, so that Comrade Lenski . . . I mean, he might not notice, but if he did, it could become an issue and get muddled up with . . . well, you know. A slur on a Polish Communist, you see, might be taken as a Trotskyite error and, well, who wants to get involved in all that?'

Bruno nodded. 'How would it be,' he said to Stefan, but blushing as he spoke, 'if the wife went to the Communist striker who took her in, out of pity, but did not actually . . . well, that they spent the night together like brother and sister, and the next day the husband *assumed* that . . . well, it might even add something?'

'Excellent,' said Michael. 'Excellent. It keeps everything but saves us the snag. Jan, what do you think?'

Jan shrugged his shoulders. 'Certainly, that would improve it.'

'Fine. A noble thing,' said Michael. 'He is attracted to her but from a feeling of solidarity with his fellow-worker, he does not touch her. A kiss on the cheek, perhaps . . .'

'And he sleeps on the floor?' said Janusz. 'How about that? He gives her his bed and sleeps on the floor?'

'That's settled, then,' said Michael with a sigh of relief. 'She goes to the Communist worker, she spends the night with him, but nothing happens. And there . . .' – he pointed to the manuscript which Stefan still held in his hand – 'there you have something which will strike a real blow for our cause.'

It was an established precaution that when the meeting of a cell came to an end, each member should go his separate way – so that Bruno, Stefan and Krystyna, for example, would all take different routes back to Sluzewska Street. On this particular evening Stefan was among the first to walk down the stairs and out into the street. And instead of taking a tram, Stefan walked so that the odd tears of chagrin which were blinked onto his cheeks were camouflaged by the spots of rain. His feet splashed in the puddles because his mind was not concentrating on where he trod, but grappled with confused emotions – rage and humiliation countered by loyalty and idealism. His face, as he walked, twitched and twisted – contorting into the Kornowski grimace, then relaxing into an expression of disdain.

His anger came from frustration; the frustration from conflict. On the one hand he had asked for criticism from his comrades: his art was in the service of the Party and it was right that the Party should judge its utility. On the other hand the actual individuals who had criticized the story were so clearly unqualified to do so. If everything had to be understood by a fool like Janusz, then he had better write children's books: and Jan, who was clever, seemed to hate him. They had all criticized details – only the girl had praised the general effect of the work. Most of all, Stefan felt insulted by the attitude of Michael M. and Bruno, the leaders of the cell, who had thought up the compromise.

He stopped at a café and ordered a glass of beer. He knew that Bruno and Krystyna, who would have taken separate trams, would now be home – eating, perhaps, or reading but worrying about him and trying not to show it, for why should they have cause for concern?

He smiled to himself as he pictured their anxiety; but while his mind was on this image, his actual eye fell upon a young officer who sat opposite him with a girl. The officer sat back on the bench, his hands pushed down into the pockets of his tunic, his legs crossed – one polished boot resting upon the other. His frame was languidly inclined towards the demi-mondaine, and his eyes had an expression of sardonic lechery.

The girl leant forward on the table. She wore a dress of grey silk whose simplicity betrayed its expense. It was fitted to her body so well that where it protruded – her shoulders or her bosom – the surface was soft and smooth, while in the shadows of form it hung like fluted stone. Her hair too had been set in precise and perfect waves; and her lips and eyes were shaded so subtly that her complexion seemed most perfectly pink and natural and her eyes large and clear.

Stefan had started to watch them before becoming conscious that he was doing so, and it was only gradually that the inner fulmination against his critics in the cell gave way before his fascinated observation of the couple. They were, in a way, a tableau of decadence and charm. The young man was obviously aristocratic and rich; there was a bottle of French champagne in a bucket beside the table – and the public sensuality of the girl, her nakedness under the silk, seemed to demonstrate that she was a semi-professional. Stefan could not hear what they said, but the officer's expression was as good as a public caress, and the girl's charming, pretty smile and arched eyebrows were a lewd response. Moreover she moved her stockinged legs together under the table: Stefan could see that better than her partner. They moved together, then slightly apart, then together again, as if his words were touching them. The grey silk of her dress formed folds, then stretched, then creased again. Her heels lifted, then sank onto the floor.

At the table next to them an old lady fed biscuits soaked in tea to her poodle. No sooner had the little dog caught his eye than Stefan imagined that he was the dog, snapping the biscuits in the air or licking them up from the marble floor – and with the dog he slipped the leash and went under the next table to watch the moving legs of the girl. He looked up and under her skirts, his little eyes staring into the dark cavern between her legs, his moustached snout sniffing the smells of scent and sweat. Still giggling, and still listening to the casual patter of the officer, the girl lowers her hand to stroke the dog which jumps up towards her knee but catches his head under her skirt and loses itself in the silken slip, snuffling, licking . . .

Stefan's fantasy was brought to a halt by the officer, who was no longer talking to the girl but stood before him. Stefan drew back and lifted his hand as if to protect his face from a blow – forgetting for a moment that the officer had no way of reading his mind – but the Uhlan only beamed and said: 'Kornowski, isn't it?'

'Yes,' said Stefan.

'Don't you remember me? Onufry. I was in your class at St Stanislas's.'

'Of course,' said Stefan, seeing suddenly beneath the uniform a former classmate from the lycée.

'I thought it was you,' Onufry said. 'My . . . er . . . friend . . .' – he gestured towards the girl – 'she thought it might be your dog.'

'No,' said Stefan. 'It belongs to that lady . . .'

'Yes, of course. But I wondered . . . well, how are you getting on?'

'Fine.'

'Are you, what, studying?' Onufry asked, but did not wait for an answer. 'Anyway, come and join us,' he said, taking Stefan by the forearm.

Hesitantly Stefan rose from his seat and crossed to their table. Onufry ordered another bottle of champagne and introduced the girl as Valeria. 'Not celebrating anything except my leave,' he said. 'And now there's a reunion.' He turned to Valeria. 'This was the cleverest boy in our class,' he said, pointing to Stefan.

Stefan made a modest gesture with his hand.

'No, no,' Onufry went on, 'much the cleverest. Always thought so. And now you're studying, are you?'

'Law.'

'Law. You'll end up an ambassador or something like that.'

'I doubt it.'

'I'm sure of it. Me? Good for riding horses, that's all. So I joined the army.'

The girl, who was exceptionally pretty, smiled at Stefan who blushed and looked away. But even with his eyes aside, he could smell the expensive aroma that rose from her elegant figure; and when he thought that she might no longer be looking at him, he glanced at her, hoping for some blemish but loving her at once because she was so beautiful, so well-dressed and quite clearly amenable to the impure advances which went with champagne.

Not for one moment did Stefan wish to take the place of his friend Onufry. In his company or out of it he could never have thought of a single word to say to the girl – but in a world of women who seemed to conspire to deny men what they wanted, he was happy to see that there did exist this pretty young courtesan.

The officer too was charming. He had a tall figure, which bent elegantly when he moved forward to speak in a flattering, intimate tone of voice. He pressed Stefan to stay and dine with them, but Stefan, feeling that he was not only in the way, but had no money, made his excuses and left them. At the door of the café he turned for a last glimpse of the stylish couple; the officer had returned to his languid position, his legs crossed, his hands in the pockets of his greatcoat. He saw Stefan and waved; the girl smiled. Stefan went out into the night and trod more carefully to avoid the puddles.

The next day Stefan changed his story. In the mood he was in that morning, it irritated him to do it but he no longer felt humiliated or outraged. After all, the story had been deliberately didactic and he was a Communist, subject to Party discipline. In rewriting, however, he found that the piece had more life of its own than he had at first imagined. It was not difficult to have the militant striker and the worker's wife sleep apart – but then the problem arose as to why she should have returned with him in the first place, and why he allowed her to do so. If their feelings for one another were, from start to finish, those of brother and sister, then why spend the night in such discomfort? Perhaps her husband had threatened her, but if he had, that would lose the tragic effect of the end: no one pities a murderer who premeditates his *crime passionnel*.

Stefan compromised. The wife in the new version was attracted to the picket, and hoped to surrender to him sexually as she had done ideologically; and the picket was attracted to the wife – pity mingling with lust as he took her to his room. But there his feelings of respect for his fellow-worker proved stronger than his desire. The evening was spent in political discussion, and both slept the sleep of the just.

When he had finished re-writing *Arbeit Macht Frei*, Stefan showed it to Bruno, who read it and approved the changes.

'Can I leave the title in German?' Stefan asked.

'Yes . . . yes, of course,' said Bruno. 'The point would be lost if you put it in Polish.'

'You don't think that the Communist . . . the picket comes across as something of a prude, do you?'

'No,' said Bruno. 'No, he's . . . he's strong . . . principled. One admires him.'

'As long as you believe in him,' said Stefan.

'I do,' said Bruno, 'I do.'

Arbeit Macht Frei was accepted by *Skamander* and published in the spring. It produced little reaction in any quarter. The only criticism of the story appeared two months later in *Kurier Poranny*, written by a certain Jerzy Chomiski. In general he praised its style and structure – but there was one passage of adverse criticism which came at the end of the review.

The story takes place in a factory – an ambience with which this critic must confess that he is not familiar – though not less familiar, perhaps, than the author himself (do workers have cufflinks?). But let his imagination reign supreme and wander where it will, true only to the law that the reader must *believe*. And here, for the most part, he does believe until, towards the end, we come to a scene of such absurdity that tears give way to laughter and sympathy to derision. A woman, who is proud, violent in her passions, contemptuous of the weak, offers herself in the dark confines of his lodgings to a young stalwart of the picket-line. This hero, in his turn, longs for her but proletarian virtue triumphs! He resists. He sleeps on the floor like a seminarian while she lies chastely in his bed! So when in the end she is slain by her desperate husband, she is the victim not of life but of a misunderstanding. A tragic effect is lost. And it is hard to see why. The story promises to be harsh and true – to teach us something about the brutalizing effect of labour. Instead we learn something about the manhood of the Polish socialist – that he is either impotent or a prig. The wife too is ridiculous – women spurned are always ridiculous – and the murderer himself, the victim for whom we should weep, becomes in our minds a simple fool. '*Arbeit Macht Albern*' would have been a better title for the story . . . but Stefan Kornowski is young and interesting, and we may hope that he will learn from his mistakes.

Six

Stefan and Krystyna had joined the CPP at a time when it was in a state of some confusion. The government of Pilsudski – the régime of colonels – which the Party had helped into power and which was more firmly established than ever before, had now cast off all democratic garments to reveal a naked dictatorship. At the same time the Party in Warsaw had been weakened and demoralized by the expulsion of almost a third of its membership at the Sixth Party Congress. These 'agents of social-fascism' were the supporters of Trotsky. They had criticized Lenski, the secretary-general, and the Comintern line at that time, which forbade any form of cooperation with other socialist parties, or with other working-class movements such as the trades unions.

Bruno had some sympathy for the Trotskyites: he too had been exasperated first by the Party's tacit support for Pilsudski's coup (the May error), and then by its change to indiscriminate antagonism towards all other political move-ments. If he restrained himself from joining their ranks, it was because they were mostly urban Jews whereas he was by origin a rural Pole. And then there came the time when he felt they had gone too far – when the leaders of the Trotskyites in Warsaw openly advocated a Popular Front in opposition to the Comintern line, and then refused either to recant or apologize. As a delegate at the Sixth Party Congress, he had voted for their expulsion; and he had taken a firm line in the cell, sup-ported by Michael, Andrzej and Janusz, suppressing the Trotskyite leanings of Jan and Rachel.

Then, in 1933, Hitler had come to power and the Polish Communists lost their havens in Germany. The staff of the *New Review* had to flee from Gleiwitz to Danzig, and then from Danzig to Czechoslovakia. Lenski was himself arrested by the

Gestapo, and was only released through the intervention of the German General Staff.

One result of this Nazi triumph in Germany was a change in the Party line to the policy of a National Front of all socialist and democratic forces for the defence of peace and freedom against the menace of fascism.

Bruno, along with other members of the CPP, foresaw this change of policy – it was clear from Stalin's speech at the Seventeenth Congress of the Soviet Party in January 1934 – and took it upon himself to explain to the cell why the enemies of yesterday should become the allies of today. 'Hitler's consolidation of power,' he said, 'and the annihilation of the Party in Germany, changes the whole premise of our Party activity. The danger now is war – a war in which Hitler, supported by France, Britain and the United States, would march across Poland and attack the Soviet Union.'

'But our colonels have signed a non-aggression pact with Hitler,' said Michael M.

'Then they might join with him. Certainly the Quai d'Orsay would like nothing better than German and Polish soldiers fighting side by side against the Red Army.'

'But if it was wrong a year ago,' said Jan, with a look of mild disdain on his sharp face, 'to cooperate with the Bund and the PPS, then why is it right today?'

'Because of the German situation,' said Bruno. 'Then we had the German Communist Party behind us. We could risk revolution. Now we have only the German army, and our first thought must be for the defence of the Soviet Union.'

'Not the defence of Poland?' asked Jan – disdain turning to irony in his expression.

'What we must defend,' said Bruno, 'is the revolution – and Russia is the only place where it is established. Therefore we must defend Russia.'

'You know what they say about us,' said Rachel. 'That with us one never knows where the Polish Communist ends and the Soviet agent begins.'

Bruno blushed. 'Let them say it.'

'Yes, let them say it,' said Andrzej, the janitor. 'They've been saying it since 1917. And the Bolsheviks they said were German agents, but it didn't stop them and it won't stop us.'

74

'Perhaps not,' said Jan – irony now changed to scepticism – 'but it is hard to defend these volte-faces. At one moment we want revolution everywhere – the expropriation of the ex-propriators, the liberation of the toiling masses – and anyone who wants less is a fascist. Democracy is a sham and social democracy is a malign deception of the working class. Anyone who disagreed with this view was a fascist spy and was expelled from the Party. Then suddenly overnight Comrade Stalin and Comrade Dimitrov change their minds. Social democrats become our allies and democracy a sacred cause. The revolution is post-poned. We must close ranks for the defence of Russia because Russia is socialist and Poland is not . . .' Jan shrugged his shoulders. 'Quite frankly, I find it hard to take . . .'

'It's only hard to take,' said Janusz, 'if you don't want to take it.'

'Then perhaps *you* would explain,' said Jan – irony, scepticism and disdain all mingled now in his expression and tone of voice.

'I see it like this,' said Janusz. 'Conditions change. They may change in ways we don't know about. But they know – the Comintern. Our people send in reports from all over Europe . . . all over the world. So they know what's happening in Berlin, in London, in Paris. So if they say "change course", we change it because they know best.'

Jan shrugged his shoulders.

'All the same,' said Michael M., 'it is an advantage to under-stand *why* they say it. The Party must be informed.'

'We are informed,' said Bruno. 'We do know why . . .'

The discussion continued, and as usual two or three did the talking while the others listened – or seemed to listen. Stefan, as it happened, found it hard to concentrate on these inter-minable political discussions: phrases like 'social-fascists' or 'popular front' wafted in and out of his head like telegraph poles on a railway journey. Instead his mind would wander – perhaps to the girl who had sat in the café with his old school-friend Onufry, or back to the meadows around Jezow where the peasants had tittered while he had sniffed the hay.

Every now and then he would see Krystyna's eyes upon him; then he would try and concentrate once again: '. . . the letter of the Central Committee, which they have sent to the Bund, the PPS and the other parties of the Left, proposes a united front against the capitalist offensive and fascism – a front rendered necessary by the complicated international situation, the danger of new imperialist wars . . .' Stefan's eyes wandered around the room – once again they were in the living-room of Michael M. – but there was no object to hold them. He tried for a moment to read the titles of the books on the bookshelf, but they were too far away. Then he focused a little nearer, on a neck – the neck of Rachel Z., who sat on a chair in front of him.

Her black hair was pinned up in a bun: some wisps fell down around her ears and onto the back of her neck, and it was on this nape that Stefan concentrated his gaze. Certainly, he had seen it before (when they met in Michael's flat, they usually sat in the same places) but it was only now that he became aware of its beauty. Her neck was thin, long and it curved in a lean and graceful way towards her shoulders, where the line was interrupted by her dress. The colour of the skin was light brown: the wisps of hair were black; and the lobe of her right ear was pink. It was late on a Sunday afternoon. The light was fading. The combination of all these things – the light, the colour, and the shape – gradually put Stefan into a state of ecstasy; and while he was oblivious to the discussion that continued around him, he was quite conscious of his own thoughts and feelings. 'Here before my eyes is the highest attainment of mankind,' he thought. 'Rachel's neck. The wisp of hair, the lobe of her ear, all in the darkening light.' For half an hour or so he continued to contemplate the nape of her neck. Then he suddenly noticed that the others were talking and moving – that the meeting had come to an end. Rachel herself stood up; her hands came down onto the arms of her chair to help her body lift her torso with the neck on top out of the line of Stefan's eyes. He stood too; Rachel turned and there he saw her face, and saw that in its way it was worthy of the neck.

The face suddenly smiled. Stefan was taken aback, confused; he smiled awkwardly in return and then looked away.

Since Stefan's reading of his story there had been no meeting of the cell dedicated to literature – nor, since its publication, had Stefan submitted any more of his work to the literary reviews of Warsaw. But this did not mean that he had stopped writing; indeed he wrote more than ever, and his 'lecture notes' were usually outlines for his own fiction.

He wanted to write a novel, but before embarking on something so large, he intended to master the art of the didactic story. He was frustrated, however, by the unreliability of his characters, the unreliability of his own imagination. Carefully constructed 'positive heroes' would suddenly run amuck, doing absurd and obscene things which shocked their creator even as he was creating them. In a short piece called 'The Man Who Knew Lenin', the wizened hero lies dying, and tells those around him how he is content to die because he has lived on the side of history – fighting for the Bolsheviks and, in the course of the civil war, making the acquaintance of Lenin.

'Vladimir Ilyich was a man one would never forget. He was quiet and small, but whenever he came among us – be there ten men or ten thousand – his presence was felt, yes, among ten men or ten thousand, they always knew he was there. His mind, well, that always went straight to the point: he could analyse a situation like nobody else, and make the right decisions, yes, he always made the right decisions . . .'

There is a pause. The old man's breathing grows harder. His face assumes a more beatific expression.

'Tell us more,' a young grandson whispered. 'Tell us more about Lenin.'

'Vladimir Ilyich, ah, he was kindness itself. I remember that peasants from all over Russia would send him food, special food, mind you – caviare, sturgeon – and this at a time when people were starving. But Vladimir Ilyich never ate it himself. No, he always gave it away – to the people around him, or to the poorest soldiers, or the guards in the Kremlin like me. I tell you, there was something about him . . . you felt you could touch history, seeing him standing there. Why even his breath was sweet and the linen he used was never soiled, no, he didn't do things we ordinary people do . . . His farts were like a spring breeze; his dung was fragrant like moistened rose-petals. His piss, I tell you, it had the sparkle of champagne . . .'

77

It was at this point that Stefan stopped his story – baffled, confused, his spirit torn between tears and laughter.

Another story he planned to write had as its hero a young worker, Tadeusz, who emptied dustbins for the municipality of Warsaw. Through his work he saw the sufferings of the poor, who picked at the bins like cats, searching for scraps of food and clothing. He saw too the extravagance of the rich, who threw out what many would be glad to possess. The climax of the story was to be Tadeusz's discovery of a pair of brand-new leather boots in the dustbin of the Countess Y. At this point he is only halfway to class-consciousness: he still retains some respect for rank, and feels that they were thrown away by mistake. He knocks at the door to the tradesmen's entrance to return the boots: the servants ask him to wait and then show him into the drawing-room, where the young Countess sits languidly on a chaise-longue. She looks at him with contempt, throws the boots at him and tells him to take them away. 'Take them away,' she says. 'I don't want them. I don't like the colour.'

'But surely they would be good for someone,' he says.

'Why should I care about that?' says the Countess. 'The dustbins . . . the poor . . . it's all the same to me.'

The conversation continues; Tadeusz realizes how profound is the Countess's contempt for the poor. He leaves, resolved to change the social order which permits extravagance to coexist with distress.

This, then, was the plan for the story and it started well enough. The scenes in the poorer areas of Warsaw were well described (from Stefan's visit to the slum in the suburb). Tadeusz is approached by a worker's wife and asked if he has bones of a carcass which she can use for soup, etc. It was not until he neared the end that the narrative began to go awry.

On the first floor he was led into a small drawing-room with white walls edged in pink. The room was filled with flowers and elegant furniture, and for a while Tadeusz did not see the young woman who sat at the far end; but when he did he saw at once that she was staring at him – and holding the boots.

'Come,' she said, beckoning him as her servant had done.

He walked towards her across the room, noticing that the

elegance of her clothes and the delicacy of her figure and features were somewhat contradicted by the slovenly way in which she sat back on her chair with her legs crossed.

When he reached her he stopped. 'Madame . . .' he began.

'Countess,' she replied. 'I am the Countess Y. and my mother and father are out – walking, riding, shopping, paying calls . . . I don't know.'

Tadeusz was embarrassed to be standing there in this elegant room in front of an aristocratic young lady, dressed as he was in his filthy, working clothes.

'Countess,' he stuttered, 'I only thought . . . the boots . . .'

'I'm hungry,' she said. 'Will you ring the bell?'

She pointed towards an embroidered bell rope hanging from the wall, and Tadeusz crossed the room, tugged it and returned to stand in front of her.

'So . . . the boots,' she said. 'What do you think of them?'

'I only thought,' said Tadeusz, 'that they were so fine and so new that perhaps they were thrown away by mistake.'

'By mistake?' The girl smiled – she smiled under her brow, under her lashes.

'Yes, because they were new.'

'They are new. Brand-new. They were delivered yesterday.'

'Perhaps they don't fit?' said Tadeusz timidly.

The Countess cocked her head, glanced at her feet (in velvet slippers), then held the boots up to the light. 'But they were hand-made,' she said, 'from a plaster-cast of my foot.' She kicked off a slipper and pointed. 'This foot.'

'In that case, of course . . .'

'But that doesn't mean a thing. Cobblers these days . . . they're all Communists, so you never know.' She looked at Tadeusz and smiled. 'Shall we try it on?'

Tadeusz was confused by this suggestion, which was accompanied by a smile – almost a leer: but his position was saved by the appearance of the servant who had first shown him into the house.

The Countess looked at the servant and said: 'Were you told to look after me?'

'I was,' said the servant.

'Then bring me some food, I'm hungry.' She turned to Tadeusz. 'Would you like some food?'

79

'No, no, I must go.'

'You can't go,' she said – putting out one hand as if to hold him back, while waving away the servant with the other. 'You can't go until we've settled the question of the boots.'

'I'm sure, Countess, that it isn't necessary for me . . .'

'Of course it is.'

She thrust one of the boots into Tadeusz's hands and he took it without thinking and, without thinking, knelt like a salesman in a shoe-shop. The girl uncrossed her legs, and without moving her torso she stuck one of them out towards Tadeusz so that the toe reached beneath his nose. Her two hands took hold of her skirts, and with the leering smile once again on her face, she slowly pulled them up, trailing their hem along her shins, until it stopped just below her knees.

Tadeusz took hold of her slipper and removed it. The stockings were mauve and slightly too large for the slender legs. They had creased around the heel and the toes, and were dark where moist with sweat. The faintest of aromas reached his nose – not an unpleasant smell but noticeable all the same.

'Try it,' she whispered.

Tadeusz took the boot and held it open for her foot. She placed it in the boot and pushed, but it would not go on.

'Perhaps it is too small,' he said.

'How can it be too small?' she asked. 'Unless the plaster-casts shrank at the cobblers, or my foot has swollen since the plaster-cast was made. Perhaps . . .'

Just then the door opened and the servant entered carrying a tray. He crossed the room, laid the tray on a small French table next to the Countess, and left the room without speaking, or even glancing at his seated mistress or the kneeling garbage collector.

'Thank God,' said the girl. For the first time since Tadeusz had come into the room, she moved her body. She sat up and stretched out towards the tray and seized a wing of cold chicken with her fingers. 'I hate conventions, don't you?' she said, just before closing her jaw on the chicken's wing. Then, with her mouth full, she added: 'Help yourself,' and waved in a general way towards the tray.

Tadeusz looked at what there was on the tray – rolls,

butter, jam, cheese, a bottle of beer, a glass – and he shook his head.

'Come on, then,' said the Countess, pointing to her foot. 'Try again.'

Tadeusz took up the boot. He shoved up against her heel, but this time the Countess (busy with a chicken wing) did not push down with her foot. As a result her leg was pushed up and the hem of her skirt slipped further up her leg, beyond the knee, revealing (to Tadeusz) a further length of purple stocking.

'I really think it's too small,' he said.

The girl laid her hands (holding the chicken) on her lap. 'Then the cobbler is a swindler,' she said. 'They were made from a plaster-cast . . .'

'But didn't you try them on before?'

'Did I? I don't know. To be frank with you, I can't remember this pair of boots, so I don't know why I threw them away.'

'Perhaps they aren't yours?'

'Whose are they then?''

'Perhaps . . . your mother's?'

The girl laughed. 'She has a club foot.'

Tadeusz blushed. 'But if they don't fit you . . .'

'They must fit me.' She threw the chicken bone onto the floor and concentrated once again on the boot, on her foot . . . 'I know,' she said, 'it's my stockings. They're too thick. The plaster-cast was made without stockings . . .' She plunged her hands under her skirts and fumbled with the tops of her stockings.

Tadeusz was so taken aback (he still knelt in front of her) that he gawped and then looked away.

'Are you embarrassed by a woman's legs?' he heard her ask. 'Who would have thought it? You'd think you'd see everything in dustbins – afterbirth, underclothes, even chopped-off limbs . . . No? Well, you can turn around now. I've taken them off.'

A more noticeable odour. He turned and there, just as she said, were the two purple stockings discarded on the floor, and two naked legs dangling above them. The skirts of her dress had been rearranged to cover her knees.

'Now,' she said with a sigh, 'let's try again.'

Tadeusz by this time had reached a state of mind where everything was improbable. With little thought he did as he was told; he picked up the boot for her right foot and tried to fit it on. This time the Countess played her part. She pushed and pushed down, the delicate muscles flexing in the calf of her leg, little hairs starting out of her dappled white skin. And while the boot almost went on to her foot, it would not quite pass the obstruction of her heel. Tadeusz continued to try, all the same, because there was something undeniably pleasant about this proximity to such a perfect leg, covered with soft, pink skin and giving off a scent . . . a scent of soap. He looked up at her face. It was pink from the struggle, but she smiled at him and pushed harder still. It was no use. The boot would not go on.

'This is absurd,' she said. 'Either the boot has shrunk, or my foot has swollen, and I won't believe that. I won't.' She sat back in her chair and looked sulkily towards the tray; her lips stuck out in a pout.

'Perhaps,' said Tadeusz, 'perhaps it doesn't matter . . . if you don't want them anyway.'

'Of course it matters,' said the Countess. 'I always do something if I want to, and I want to put on that boot.'

Suddenly she sat up again. 'I know,' she said. She reached towards the tray and plunged the three middle fingers of her left hand into the butter which lay on the dish. Then she spread it over her foot and the calf of her leg. 'That should do it,' she said.

Tadeusz fingered the boot, uneasily, but remained kneeling at her feet as obediently as the wing of cold chicken lying beside him, until the right leg of the Countess was greased from her toes to her knee. Then she looked triumphantly at Tadeusz and held out her hands for the boot. He proffered it, she took hold of it, and with a quick tug she pulled it on to her foot.

'There,' she said. 'Who said it wasn't mine? It fits, it fits like a glove. But what a fool that cobbler is.' She looked at Tadeusz. 'Now what does he expect me to do? To go out with naked legs, all covered with butter?'

'I don't know . . . no, clearly, he made them too tight.'

'Too tight, yes, much too tight. So they're no use . . .' With another tug she pulled the boot off her foot again and dropped it onto the floor next to the chicken leg. 'That's why I threw them away. They're no use at all. No use.'

'Of course,' said Tadeusz, standing with the left-hand boot in his hand, and turning to pick up the other.

'Wait, though,' said the girl. She pointed to her butter-covered leg. 'What am I to do about this?'

'About the butter?'

'Yes.'

'Well, I suppose you could wash it off.'

She looked at him with her leering smile. 'But I'd like you to lick it off,' she said.

'But, Countess . . .'

'Come on, come on, man.' She talked to him as she would to a lapdog – coaxing and imperious. 'And to make it nicer – look . . .' She stretched once again towards the tray. 'I'll mix it with some jam.' She put the same three fingers into the pot of jam, and started to smear it on her toes, her foot, her ankle, her shin, her knee as if it was beauty cream – trailing her sticky fingers back and forth along the inside of her thigh. 'Come on,' she said. 'Come on.'

Tadeusz came towards her. He dropped the boot, knelt, looked for a moment into her smiling eyes, then lowered his lips to her sticky foot and started to lick between the toes. She murmured softly as he did so – she murmured, and her murmuring grew louder as his lips closed around her heels and licked the fine hairs that grew on the skin covering her calf. 'Good boy,' she whispered, 'good, good boy, there'll be a prize for you, a prize, I promise.'

He licked. He licked on. His tongue ached; his mouth was covered with grease and slobber and strawberries from the jam. He covered her knee. His hands gripped the side of her chair: he touched her only with his lips and tongue, and occasionally with the back of his head which bumped against the inside of her other leg.

Above her knee the skin became softer, softer than any surface he had touched before. His head was dizzy from the musty, airless atmosphere under her skirts, which she held over his head with clutching hands. She was writhing, too, which made it harder, and his nose was filled with kaleidoscopic smells of soap and jam and genitalia. 'The prize,' she gasped, 'the prize I promised, you are near the prize . . .' and indeed he was near – he could sense and smell and almost see; his mouth reached up, he was – when suddenly she lifted her skirts, opened her legs and thrust a chicken leg into his mouth, then clasped her legs around his neck, opened them again, and kicked him away onto the floor.

Tadeusz lay still, staring up at the plaster mouldings on the ceiling, and – nearer at hand – the bone of the drumstick which entered his field of vision beyond the end of his nose. He heard only his own heavy breathing and then, as that subsided, the scratching of a pen from the far end of the room. He turned his head and saw an elderly man sitting at a desk, writing with an old-fashioned pen. The girl sat still. She had straightened her skirt and was sipping beer. Tadeusz heard a bell. The light was fading, but he saw as the door opened the same servant who had shown him in: he came now to show him out.

Here the story came to an end. Finding himself with his hero in the street (in the sense that he too had been with him under the skirt), Stefan was brought up short by the fresh air, and obliged to consider just how his heroic collector of garbage could go on to rage against injustice with his lips still sticky from the thighs of a Countess; or how the whole sequence of events which he had just described could be said to create in the reader a heightened sense of class-consciousness or a greater revolutionary enthusiasm.

And yet, at the same time, Stefan could not suppress a pinch of self-satisfaction at what he had just written. He liked particularly the finale – the girl readjusted, sitting demurely on her chair; the old man (her father?) writing at his desk; the garbage collector lying on the Aubusson carpet in his overalls with a cold chicken leg stuck in his mouth.

It was clear that as it stood the story would be quite unacceptable to the cell. For a time Stefan tried to save it with symbolism – the girl as the bourgeoise, the servant the proletarian and Tadeusz representing Trotsky – but in the end he gave this up. The story was inescapably decadent, indulgent and meaningless.

Seven

Stefan and Bruno both graduated from the university of
Warsaw in June, 1934, and to celebrate their success they
decided to go with Krystyna for a week's holiday in the country.
Aunt Cecylia agreed to look after the Count, and Blomstein
gave Krystyna seven days off work. They had several discussions about where they should go – to the Baltic in the north
or the Tatras in the south – but decided in the end on the
Suwalki forests, which were near the Polish frontier with East
Prussia. Someone had told them about a small hotel which was
far from anywhere, and they determined to go to it and 'get
right away from Warsaw'.

They took a sleeper at ten at night, and the next morning
changed onto a smaller train which dawdled from one small
station to another. At mid-day they reached their destination,
and were met by a pony and trap sent by the hotel. The driver –
an old man – advised them to eat something before they set off,
which they did; and were later glad of the advice. They afterwards sat in the trap with their luggage under their feet for
three hours as the pony trotted through the green gloom of the
forest.

Enormous firs rose on either side of the road, and stood in
uneven ranks stretching back into darkness. The ground was
covered with a deep layer of discarded needles, creating an
exceptional silence which seemed to bewitch them and force
them to be silent. The only sounds were those of the pony's
hooves on the gravel, and of the steel-rimmed wheels splashing
in puddles or slipping in and out of ruts in the road. Occasionally
they heard a twig snap or leaves rustle quite near to them, as
some bird or animal – a wolf or a lynx or a capercailzie – took
fright and scuttled deeper into the forest.

Eventually they came to a clearing. The trees stopped

suddenly, there were fields with wooden fences, then a small village and, a quarter of a mile beyond it, a nineteenth-century hunting lodge which was now a hotel. Its exterior was somewhat pompous – the Germanic taste of the nobleman who had built it – but inside the furnishings were simple. They were given two rooms next to each other which looked out over a small lake towards the forest beyond. Children were playing in the water, and their cries and laughter were the only sounds from the late afternoon. In their room Bruno and Krystyna lay down on their bed to rest – Krystyna with her hands cupped behind her head. In his room Stefan shut the window because there were gnats in the air, and then sat at the table to write down in his notebook certain ideas which had come to him during the journey.

In the days which followed they did just what they liked. Bruno always rose early and went for a walk before breakfast. Stefan was usually up in time to join him at his breakfast. Krystyna had hers brought to her room at ten. Then the three, the two, or each one on his own, would go for a walk in the woods, swim in the lake or read in his room until it was time to eat the heavy, wholesome food which the hotel served for lunch. In the afternoon they would do what they had not done in the morning; and in the evening eat again and go early to bed.

After only three days the effect of this relaxed life became quite evident in Krystyna. She became cheerful and cheeky, teasing Stefan as she had done as a child, and flirting with Bruno as if he were a handsome stranger. Every now and then he would try and talk about the future – about what he was to do when he returned to Warsaw – but then Krystyna would frown like a petulant child and ask him not to spoil her holiday. Stefan too had to decide what he was going to do, but he also preferred to postpone the discussion.

'Why?' asked Krystyna on the fourth night as they sat eating their dinner and Bruno had once again mentioned the post he had been offered by the Party. 'Why talk about it now?' she asked. 'There'll be time enough in Warsaw.'

'I have to decide . . .' he muttered.

'But not now,' she said. 'There's no Party here – just bugs and

86

beasts and big black capercailzies which taste delicious . . .'
She filled her mouth to prove her point. Bruno frowned for a
moment, then shook his head.

'You see I'm happy,' said Krystyna. 'It's my holiday and I
don't want to think about dull and gloomy things.'

'Why is it dull and gloomy to talk about the future?' asked
Bruno.

Krystyna blushed. 'I'm only ever happy in the present,' she
said. 'The past has unpleasant memories, and the future has
fears.'

'You shouldn't think that. The future might be magnificent . . .'
Bruno drew in his breath, as if about to start on a speech,
but he thought better of it and turned to Stefan. 'Are you
pessimistic too?' he asked.

Stefan avoided his eyes. 'I don't know,' he said. 'Politically,
do you mean, or personally?'

'For me, they're much the same.'

'Then how can you be optimistic, with Hitler in power and
the KPD in concentration camps?'

'That's no reason to be pessimistic,' said Bruno, his voice
becoming insistent and conspiratorial. 'Revolution thrives under
persecution. The greater the assault by the bourgeoisie on the
working class, the greater the counter-attack when it comes.
Think of Russia in 1905. Never did things seem worse; yet
twelve years later, the Revolution had triumphed . . .'

'You're right, of course,' said Stefan.

'All the same, I'm afraid,' said Krystyna.

'But why?' asked Bruno.

'Because whoever wins in Europe – the Right or the Left, the
Nazis or the Party – poor Poland will get cracked like a nut and
eaten up. It's always happened and it always will.'

And Bruno did not remonstrate because he saw that there
were tears in her eyes.

On their last day in the Suwalki forests they thought they would
go on a long expedition into the woods, leaving early in the
morning and returning only when it was dark. The hotel provided them with a packed lunch, knapsacks, a map and a
compass, and soon after eight they set off. They went around the
edge of the lake and then followed foresters' tracks towards the

north-west – marking their route quite carefully on the map because there were certain military areas near the frontier which were forbidden.

The woods here were quite different from those around Jezow, which saved Stefan and Krystyna from the melancholy they usually felt in the country. The ground was wet – in parts a swamp – and covered by small blue flowers, a little like orchids. There were also a million insects which flashed their bright colours when caught by the sun; and these, together with the flowers, made the forest seem exotic and magical. Every now and then they would catch sight of a long-legged bird with an owl-like face, hopping onto the marsh, or ruffling the black and white feathers of its plumage.

At mid-day they stopped. They sat on a bank of moss, drank from the bottles of beer they had in their knapsacks and ate rolls stuffed with sausage and cheese.

'I'd like to live here,' said Krystyna. 'I'd like to build a hut in the middle of these woods and live on mushrooms and rabbits . . .'

'You wouldn't like it in winter,' said Bruno.

'Perhaps not,' said Krystyna, 'but I hate Warsaw all the year round.'

'You'd be bored in the country,' said Stefan.

'I'm bored in Warsaw,' said Krystyna sharply; and then added, 'Well, I'm bored at Blomstein's, which is where I spend most of my time.'

The two young men looked down at their feet. 'Can we talk about it now?' asked Bruno.

'About what?' asked Krystyna.

'About what we're going to do.'

'All right,' she said. 'But I wasn't serious. Blomstein's is boring, but it's not a hard job and it's well paid.'

'I know,' said Bruno. 'And I could also get a job now which would pay well . . . well enough for you to stop working. But the Party want me to work on the *Popular Daily* . . .'

'Then you must,' said Krystyna.

'It's badly paid. Only ten or twelve zlotys a week.'

'You can't expect more than that.'

'It would be important work,' said Bruno.

'You must do it,' said Krystyna. 'It shows that they think a lot of you. And I don't mind going on at Blomstein's. After all, it's because of Papa, really, and you mustn't give up your work for him.'

Bruno turned to Stefan. 'What do you think?' he asked.

'I don't think Krysia would be happy if you didn't do what you thought was right.'

'Exactly,' said Krystyna, with a light laugh. 'You'd be insupportable if you didn't work for a cause.'

'And what about me?' asked Stefan. 'What should I do?'

'Law,' said Bruno. 'You must go on with the law.'

'I don't particularly want to,' said Stefan.

'You must,' said Krystyna. 'Aunt Cecylia says that she'll help you as much as she can.'

'I know, but that won't pay for Papa.'

'I'll pay for him: but you must go to the courts. You could quite soon earn a good living . . .'

'I'd rather not,' said Stefan.

'Why not?'

'I'm always on the side of the murderers . . .'

'Then defend them,' said Bruno. 'You can do much more for the victims of society if you're a qualified advocate . . .'

They sat for a moment in silence. 'I'd rather write,' said Stefan suddenly. 'I'd rather go to Paris and write.'

Krystyna scowled. 'We'd all like to go to Paris,' she said, 'but we can't. There's Papa and there's the Party, and both mean that we have to stay in Warsaw.'

'I could take Papa to France,' said Stefan.

'Don't be ridiculous,' said Krystyna. 'Where would you live, and what would you live on?'

'I could find some sort of work . . .'

'Don't be a fool,' she said. 'I haven't worked in a shop for five years to see you throw away your education as a rootless bohemian in Paris . . .'

She stood up and started walking away into the woods.

'Let her go,' said Bruno. 'Here in the forest she feels free.'

They started to pick up the papers and bottles which were all that remained of their lunch, and put them back into the knapsacks. Then they too stood and followed Krystyna. Their worn shoes sank softly into the pine needles; their nostrils were filled with the smell of dead and living bracken, of toadstools and wild garlic. The sun shone into the dark woods like search-lights, dazzling them for moments, then leaving them blind in the green obscurity.

Ahead there was a clearing from which the light shone with such brilliance that Krystyna's shape a hundred yards ahead became difficult to see: for a time she became a wobbling line, and finally, as they came near to the clearing, she disappeared altogether into a cauldron of light. Then they too came out of the forest. They blinked, saw the grass at their feet, and then Krystyna standing stock-still, staring in front of her.

Fifty feet away there was a barbed-wire fence, and behind it stood a German border guard. He stood facing them, a machine-gun slung over his shoulder, his hands on his hips. His expression was impassive, stern: his boots were black and polished, his helmet hard and grey. The three Poles who had come out of the forest were mesmerized: they stood staring at him as if he were a snake. He too stared at them, and then quite suddenly he spat. He spat at the ground but at once looked back at the Poles as if to emphasize that his contempt was not for the earth but for them. Part of his spittle had touched his boot. With a languid movement of his leg, he wiped the boot on the grass. Then he turned and walked down the wide swathe of land that had been cut and cleared through the forest on both sides of the wire.

'Dirty Germans,' said Bruno, looking down at his map.

Neither Stefan nor Krystyna said anything.

'I didn't realize that we'd come so far,' said Bruno. He turned. 'Come on,' he said. 'We'd better go back the same way.'

Eight

They returned to Warsaw, where life was now harder than before. In ways it was the same – and monotonous because it was the same – but Bruno's work as a Party journalist was dangerous and took more of his time. The *Popular Daily* was suppressed by the police, but reappeared soon afterwards as *Face of the Day*; and when that was suppressed, as *Labour News*. Each time it was suppressed, there was a chance that Bruno would be discovered and arrested; and when he did not return until nine or ten at night, Krystyna did not know whether it was his work or the police which kept him.

Stefan also spent less time at the flat. After a day in the courts, transcribing the proceedings, he would look for some amusement in the cafés; and even when he came back to Sluzewska Street he would just take something to eat out of the kitchen, and then shut himself up in his room to work on a story.

Thus the only company for Krystyna when she returned from Blomstein's was her imbecile father, her simpering Aunt Cecylia and the servant Mamuska. On some occasions she would go out herself with some anonymous comrades to distribute leaflets – and of course there were the meetings of the cell, usually on Sunday afternoons – but she did not enjoy her work for the Party if it was not with Bruno, and for reasons of security this was not allowed. On most days of the week they would not see each other until ten or eleven at night, when Bruno would come to the flat – tired and hungry, expecting something to eat, irritated if it was cold or overcooked, preoccupied still with the work of the day, yet unable to discuss it with his wife for those same 'reasons of security'.

Their sexual life had suffered. The time had passed when a glance or touch would excite them: now Bruno would roll over onto his wife and make love like a machine. Krystyna endured it but did not enjoy it, and as a result she became disgruntled, depressed and finally exasperated. There came a night when she could take it no more – when she pushed his body off hers, said: 'Why don't you leave me alone?' and burst into tears.

Bruno cursed softly (at the situation), then sighed, then turned towards her and took her sobbing body into his arms. 'What is it?' he asked, kissing her cheeks and licking away her tears.

'I don't know,' she said.

Bruno sighed again. 'I'm sorry,' he said.

'I wouldn't mind . . . I wouldn't mind if you were there. I could put up with Blomstein's if I could look forward to seeing you when I got home . . . but now there's nothing. Just a dull evening with Papa and Mamuska, or handing out leaflets . . .'

'I know,' said Bruno. 'I'm sorry.'

'Couldn't you tell them that sometimes . . .'

'I will,' he said. 'But it's difficult . . . it's a bad time. Two of our people left last month, and they haven't been replaced.'

'There must be others . . .'

'No one they can trust.' Bruno hesitated – as if wondering whether to say what he had in his mind – then went on: 'Sochacki's been arrested in Moscow. They say he's been working for Military Intelligence.'

'Sochacki? A spy?'

'Yes. A provocateur and deviationist . . .'

'Impossible.'

'There's an article in *Communist International* saying that the whole Party here is infiltrated with spies, so no one trusts anyone else. I was even asked about Jan.'

'But he's gone.'

'Precisely. To work for the Comintern. They arrested him in Moscow last week.'

'But why?'

'They think he was in touch with Trotsky.'

'What did they ask you?'

'If I knew, or if I suspected . . .'

'And what did you say?'

Bruno looked up at the ceiling. 'I said I didn't know. I said he could be. He was always . . . internationalist. But then Jews always are, but if we expel them all we'll have lost half the Party.'

'Do they suspect you?'

He shook his head. 'No. I'm not a Jew.' He sighed and then smiled. 'I wish they didn't trust me so much. I'd have less to do.'

They lay side by side in silence.

'I'm sorry,' said Krystyna, timidly taking hold of his hand.

'It's my fault,' he said.

'No,' she said. 'I was thinking of myself and forgetting your work.'

They embraced; they made love; they lay side by side once again.

'He was conceited, wasn't he?' said Bruno.

'Jan? Yes he was.'

'But I can't believe that he was a spy. A spy would go along much more . . .'

'What will happen to him?'

Bruno was silent. Krystyna looked towards him but it was too dark to see his face.

'What will happen to him?' she asked again.

'I don't know,' said Bruno. He turned over, and they both went to sleep.

In the autumn, the Count caught cold. For a day or two he stayed in, sniffing and sitting by the stove. The three younger members of the family – who were anyway irritated by his empty, useless presence – avoided him to avoid his cold which, on the third day, was worse. The Count now stayed in his bed with a high fever, and hoarse breathing added to the running nose.

The doctor was sent for. He diagnosed pneumonia and prescribed medicines which Krystyna bought from the chemist on her way back from work. The next day Aunt Cecylia and Mamuska said that they would look after the patient, who seemed not to suffer but rather enjoy the attention that the three women gave to him. His amicable mood was inappropriate to the disease: it was as if the antibodies themselves did not realize the seriousness of the attack. His condition was not better after a week, and the doctor who had been so casual before, now creased his brow and even went a little pale as he listened to his patient's heart and lungs through his stethoscope.

The Count was ordered to hospital. His son and daughter visited him there every day and remained for an hour or two behind a screen in the paupers' ward. Then, one Saturday morning at nine, they saw at once that he was dying. Krystyna clutched at her father's hand as his breathing became laboured and slow. Stefan watched with fear and fascination. The minutes, then hours, passed. Doctors and nurses came and went; the Count fell into a coma. At ten past two his breathing stopped. There was a moment of quiet; then Krystyna collapsed over her father's body, her weeping rising to the tall ceiling of the ward, bringing the indifferent doctor and bored nurse, who

93

went through a routine of punching and slapping the corpse to bring it back to life.

Stefan stood still, paralysed by the sight of his father's face. The eyes had slipped round in the skull, but the features remained fixed in a distinct expression. It was the Kornowski grimace. And Stefan knew that he was watching not just the fate of his father, whose grizzled head lay on the pillow in front of him, but also his own destiny; for sooner or later it would be his face which would stiffen into the mask of the Kornowskis.

He was brought back out of his paralysis by a sharp look from the doctor. Without thinking, Stefan knew what role he had to play. He took hold of Krystyna's shoulders, pulled her off the bed and gently led her away – out of the ward and out of the hospital.

'He didn't suffer,' he said to her as they waited for a tram.

'How do you know?' she said, sniffing. 'How do you know what went on in his mind?'

'We did what we could,' he said.

The other people in the queue, waiting for the tram, looked awkwardly at Krystyna, whose face was still stained with tears.

'Let's walk,' she said.

They set off down the street towards the next stop.

'He had a sad life,' she said.

'He was happy when he was young,' said Stefan.

'I know.' She took out a handkerchief and blew her nose. Then she breathed on her fingers which were cold. 'Do you think . . .' she began. 'Do you think that people are mostly happy when they're young?'

'No,' said Stefan. 'I think that for some people life gets better and better.'

'I hope so, because . . . because I feel we haven't lived yet. Not lived to the full.'

'You've got Bruno,' said Stefan.

'I know, but still I feel trapped . . .'

'Well now you're free.'

'In a way,' she said.

'You don't have to look after Papa any more. You can give up Blomstein's. Make Bruno take a holiday. We can all take a holiday. We'll borrow some money from Aunt Cecilia and go to Paris . . .' Stefan's manner became excited; he waved his arms in the air. 'Why not, Krysia? In spring . . . in May, let's go to Paris.'

'In May, yes,' said Krystyna. 'But in May, you see, in May I shall be having my baby.'

Nine

Krystyna's pregnancy brought changes in her relationship with Bruno. Nature, it seemed, was more imperious, even, than the Central Committee of the Communist Party of Poland: he returned now in the evenings, and after their evening meal he would wash the dishes with Stefan and insist that Krystyna lie on the sofa with her feet up. Though a mild nausea would take her in the morning, she felt quite well at night, so she would protest, laughing, while the two young men fumbled with the pots and pans.

In some ways she looked better than before. A colour had come into the skin of her cheeks, as if she had been in the country; and the growing baby seemed to calm her nerves. She still felt a nagging sense of claustrophobia – she longed to get away from the flat, from Warsaw, from Poland – but knew that it would be imprudent to leave her well-paid job now that there would be another mouth to feed.

It was Stefan who, like an older child, felt jealous of the baby – even before it was born. He was shaken and isolated by the death of his father: and the happiness that was so evident in Bruno – and Krystyna's joy at her growing belly – seemed to exclude him. He therefore stayed away in the evenings, and spent still more time in the cafés.

He had already formed an unacknowledged liaison with Rachel – the Jewish student in the cell – whose neck and hair he had studied and admired in the dreary hours of their meetings. He had never spoken to her in particular, nor even met her eyes with any significant or suggestive expression in his own; but he knew that she could sense his eyes on her body –

time and again she had shuffled and squirmed in her seat, and then turned to try and catch his eye with a look that was half an inquiry and half an invitation.

She was pretty, kind and always smiling. There was therefore no reason for Stefan to be afraid of her. He even had some reason to suppose that she would not rebuff him if he asked her to have a drink in a café: she was, after all, his comrade already. On the other hand he had no experience of women whatsoever, and the older he became (he was almost twenty-one) the more difficult it became to commit himself to a course of action which might lead to an awkward situation . . .

The alternative, however, was to be trapped in Sluzewska Street, with its atmosphere of suffocating domesticity. At the next meeting of the cell, therefore, he managed to sit near the door and leave the flat at the same time as Rachel. As they set foot on the pavement outside he turned and asked her, in an indifferent tone of voice, whether she would like to meet him later and go to a film.

She blushed – whether from pleasure, displeasure or embarrassment, he could not tell – and said she would. They arranged to meet at a café near the university in an hour's time and then went their separate ways.

Rachel was late. Stefan sat looking out from the café across the street at the fading sun on the pastel-coloured houses opposite. As the shadows reached them, the occasional window would light up with electricity.

When Rachel finally entered the café, Stefan noticed at once that she was breathless and had changed her clothes. She wore a different skirt and blouse – both prettier and cleaner than those she had worn at the meeting: she had also tied back her hair, put lipstick on her lips and powder on her sallow, smiling face.

'I'm sorry,' she said as she sat down. 'I had to wait hours for a tram.'

'Where do you live?' asked Stefan.

She looked away. 'Not far, really.' She did not want to tell him.

'Perhaps she lives in the Jewish district and is ashamed of it,' Stefan thought to himself. He ordered a drink for her. 'Is there a particular film you want to see?' he asked. His own voice sounded pompous to himself, and he did not look at her.

'No, not really.'

He glanced at her. She looked shy but gave a small smile in return when she saw his eyes on her. He turned away. There was a moment of silence. 'I should be better at conversation . . .' he began.

'No,' she said.

'Why not?'

'You're good at writing.' She looked down at the table. 'And people who are good at writing shouldn't waste their talent on talk.'

'You're the only one who thinks that,' said Stefan.

'I like literature,' said Rachel. 'I don't think the others do . . . They're not sensitive to art. They judge it by other standards.'

Stefan nodded.

'But that's just bad luck,' she went on. 'The Party respects art. In Russia the artist is important. He's given every facility and he's admired . . . just for being an artist.'

'Have you been to Russia?'

A hazy look came into her eyes. 'Oh yes,' she said. 'I went two years ago to a Komsomol conference in Leningrad. It's wonderful, really it is. There's hardship, of course, and people have to make great sacrifices; but all the time they're building the first society the world has ever known based on justice and reason, and ruled by the proletariat.'

Stefan sipped his glass of beer. 'Let's talk about something more frivolous,' he said, smiling at her for the first time.

'I suppose we have had rather a lot of . . . well, Party talk for one day,' said Rachel.

'Rather a lot,' said Stefan, half-imitating the lilt of her voice.

'To tell the truth,' said Rachel, 'you've had rather more than me, because half the time I don't listen.'

'That can happen to anyone.'

'It's awful, isn't it? But it's sometimes so dull. Michael goes on and on, and Comrade Janusz and Comrade Andrzej . . . I liked Jan . . .' She stopped, hesitated, blushed, then went on: 'He was stupid that time about your story, but on his own he was interesting . . .' She blushed again.

Stefan said nothing: he ignored what she had said.

'Have you heard from him?' Rachel asked timidly.

'Why should I?'

She leant forward. 'You know he went to Moscow?' she whispered.

'Did he?'

'He used to write.'

'Was he your friend?' Stefan asked this in an abrupt tone of voice.

Rachel sat back and looked down. 'I used to see him . . .'

'I see.' Stefan made a (Kornowski) grimace.

'But I didn't love him. He was, well, a comrade.'

'Do you sleep with all your comrades?'

She blushed again and looked angry. 'I didn't say I'd slept with him.'

'Aha. Well, it doesn't matter.'

'But I did.'

Stefan shrugged his shoulders, as if he did not care, but a quick panic had taken hold of him. He scratched his cheek.

'Do you think it was wrong?' asked Rachel quietly.

'What?'

'To make love with Jan when . . . when I didn't love him?'

'My dear child,' said Stefan, 'I have no opinion whatsoever on that.'

'Why do you talk as if you were an old man?' she asked.

Stefan shrugged his shoulders, and then glanced at Rachel, who was looking at him with large, anxious eyes. He then wanted to look away again, to torment her for her infidelity, to be cold and strong; but he was held by the eyes, looking out with such timidity and warmth from such gentle, even features. Her hand came up to brush aside a strand of soft brown hair which had fallen over her face: she lowered her head as it did so, and Stefan had his chance to look away. He did not take it. He waited for her to look at him once again and she did; and in that second exchange of glances, everything was arranged and understood.

'I've wanted to be friends with you,' said Rachel (some minutes later), 'ever since you read your story.'

'I used to watch your neck,' said Stefan.

'My neck?'

'Did you notice?'

'I knew you were staring at me, but not at my neck.'

'Well I was.'

'And what do you think of it?'

'It's an exceptionally beautiful neck.'

'We can be friends, then, can't we? Since you like my neck and I like your writing?'

Stefan nodded. 'I like looking at your neck,' he said.

'You don't have to touch it,' she said.

'I might want to.'

'Then you can.'

This conversation was quick and intimate. In the cinema Rachel took hold of his hand and squeezed it. Stefan did not respond until 'The End' was on the screen: then he took his hand out of hers, put his arm around her shoulders, stroked the right-hand side of her neck, and then stood up. They left the cinema together. His face was without expression; hers had a smile.

'My father wishes he wasn't a Jew,' she said when they met next. 'That's what made me a Communist, I think – subjectively, that is – because he *is* a Jew. He can't be anything else. He slips back into the ghetto because he has nowhere else to go. And my mother is a real piece of dough. She clings to him like dough. She drags him back. He's a doctor, a really good doctor, so he could be anyone, but he has to be a Jew. His patients despise him, not because he *is* a Jew but because he behaves like a Jew who is despised by his Polish patients. He's grovelling and snivelling and greasy because that's the way Jews are with rich Poles and he can't think of any other way to behave. He's trapped. He needn't be a Jew. He doesn't want to be a Jew. But he chokes every time he tries to eat a piece of pork . . .'

'Do you eat pork?'

'Of course I do. I'm free, don't you see, because of the Party. You're the same, aren't you? If it wasn't for the Party, you'd still be a disgruntled, landless landowner – and you certainly wouldn't be seen with me. But you're free from those prejudices because you're a Communist. You stand side by side on an equal footing with Jews, Poles, Lithuanians, Byelorussians, Ukrainians, peasants, workers . . .'

'Can you feel my foot touching your foot?'

They were sitting in a café.

'Yes, why?'

'How do you react?'

'To what?'

'To my foot?'

'Well, I don't know. Am I meant to react?'

Stefan shrugged his shoulders.

'It's not erotic exactly,' said Rachel.

'Why not?'

'Because of the shoes. I mean, I could be the table-leg . . .'

'But I know that you aren't. I know that under the leather is flesh . . .'

'You're odd, you know.'

'If I tell you that my touching your foot with my foot . . .'

'My shoe with your shoe.'

'All right. If I tell you that it excites me . . .'

Rachel blushed. 'I wish you'd kiss me.'

'Impossible.' Stefan looked at her plump lips only four feet from his own. 'There is an abyss.'

'Where?'

'Between here and there.' He pointed to his lips and then to hers.

Rachel sighed and looked away at the other young couples sitting together drinking, talking and some exchanging quick kisses *à la Parisienne*.

'You look almost Indian,' said Stefan.

'I've got a straight nose and straight hair,' said Rachel. 'I'm afraid I must have some *goy* blood somewhere along the line. Or gipsy.'

Stefan leant forward on the table so that his face was only inches from hers. 'Did Jan kiss you?' he asked.

'I wish you wouldn't talk about Jan.'

'I'd like to know every detail.'

'That's unnatural.'

'Why?'

'I don't know, but it is.'

'You mean that I should be jealous because I'm supposed to love you.'

'I never said love . . .'

'Like then.'

'You asked to see me again.'

'I like your eyes.'

'Is that all?'

'No. Your neck.'

'Just my eyes and my neck?'

'No, your mind.' He laughed. She looked at her watch. 'Go on about your father,' he said.

'Oh, I'm sick of talking about him.'

'About being Jewish, then.'

'But I'm not Jewish,' she said. 'That's what I've been trying to tell you. There are no Jews or Poles in the Communist Party. For the first time a man is just a man, and a woman . . .'

'If I kissed you, where would I kiss you?'

'We'd find somewhere.'

'But would I have to kiss your lips?'

'It's normal.'

'I'd rather kiss the nape of your neck.'

'You can't do that here.'

'No.'

'But it could be arranged.'

'Did Jan ever kiss the nape of your neck?'

She smiled. 'No, never.'

When they parted that day at the street corner, Stefan kissed her hand in a quite formal way – but he had already arranged a meeting for the next day. When he returned home he made some tea for himself, and then withdrew into his room. There he sat down, sipped the tea and anxiously imagined what might be expected of him the next day. After a minute or two he went to his desk, took his pen into his hand, opened his notebook and started to write.

They stood together, mist rising from the cobbles. The stooped figures of Jews – the men with wispy beards and caps, the women with dank, dark hair in ringlets – passed them in the narrow street.

'Come in,' she said. 'The house is empty.'

'Where is your father?' he asked.

'He's out,' she said. 'They're all out.'

He followed her into the house, past the surgery, and followed her upstairs to the doctor's living quarters. There he was accosted by the strange atmosphere of the Hebraic household. There were signs and emblems on the wall, and a smell of incense, which conjured up an un-Christian East, and for a moment he felt afraid.

Then she turned and looked at him with her kind, brown eyes. 'What would you like?' she asked.

'What did you promise?'

She smiled. 'What *did* I promise?'

'A kiss.'

'Ah yes. On the back of my neck.' She laughed and came nearer to him and turned. 'Go ahead,' she said, lowering her chin to her chest like a martyr waiting for the excutioner's axe.

He took hold of her by the shoulders and slowly brought his lips down to touch the brown skin and wispy hairs which covered the mould of the bone, protruding at the top of her spine. Her hair tickled his nose. His lips touched the skin. She made no sound, but stood there with her head bowed. He kept his lips on her neck, then slowly moved them down, from vertebra to vertebra, unbuttoning her blouse which opened at the back as it became necessary, then pushing it forwards off her shoulders until it fell to the floor. He knelt: her skirt too was unbuttoned, and his lips continued their journey to the base of her spine. There . . .

Here Stefan stopped writing. He pondered. He chewed his pen. His imagination was inclined to leave it there, yet he knew that somehow he would be expected to continue. He should have turned her around, but he could not bring himself to do so. He thought of her breasts staring at him like the eyes of a fish, and of her ravening, bearded pudendum. Thus . . .

he kissed each buttock gently, then the back of her knees and finally, when he was lying on the floor, beneath her quivering body, he bit as hard as he could into the Achilles tendon of her left foot. She screamed and shook her foot. He clung to it like a terrier. She could not turn, but with her other foot she kicked at him until he let go. Then she ran sobbing to her room. He wiped his mouth and returned past the surgery to the front door and the street.

Stefan awoke the next morning with a feeling of dread; and some seconds later he recognized the cause, which was his meeting that day with Rachel. At breakfast he looked so depressed that Krystyna, who was putting on her coat to go to work, asked him what was wrong.

'Nothing,' he said. 'Nothing.'

After Krystyna had gone, Bruno sat at the table. 'You were seen yesterday with Rachel,' he said.

'Yes. We had a drink together.'

'You shouldn't really meet outside the cell.'

'Love knows no boundaries,' said Stefan sarcastically. 'And anyway, it's safer than going out with someone outside the Party.'

'Well, be careful,' said Bruno. 'She was friendly with Jan.'

'I know,' said Stefan. 'I know about that. But he wasn't diseased, was he?'

Bruno blushed. 'No, of course not. I didn't mean that. But, well, you mustn't tell her, but Jan was a spy.'

'A spy? What kind of spy?'

'An agent for Military Intelligence.'

Stefan laughed; then looked sober again. 'Are you sure?'

'He confessed in Moscow,' said Bruno. 'But remember, she mustn't know.'

'How extraordinary,' said Stefan. His eyes widened as if the cell was suddenly more interesting. 'What have they done with him?' he asked.

Bruno looked down into his cup of coffee. 'I don't know.'

'No wonder she hasn't had any letters.'

'Did she say that he wrote to her?'

'No. She said that he had once, but now he didn't.'

'Well, be careful,' Bruno said again.

'But the police know just what I am . . .'

'Not that you belong to the Party. And anyway . . .' Again Bruno looked down into his cup of coffee, 'it's not just the police. The Party too might suspect you.'

'Of what?'

'Well, of spying or . . . of opposition. Rachel's a Jew, you see, like Jan and Deutscher and all the others. You can't really trust them now. She may be in touch with Trotsky's people . . .'

'But is there any evidence . . .'

'Don't be naïve,' said Bruno. 'If we wait for evidence, the damage is done. This isn't a court of law. Reasonable suspicion is enough for the Party.'

'But that's preposterous. Rachel would die for the Party.'

'I know,' said Bruno. 'And I don't say that she's a spy. But you must understand that the fascists are ruthless, and we must be ruthless in return. If Dzerzhinsky had not been cruel, the Bolsheviks would have been beaten. He always thought it better to arrest nine innocent men if one spy was caught in the same net. That way, he saved thousands of real revolutionaries from the effects of one man's treachery.'

She remained seated as he approached her (in the café) but looked up with an expression that was timid, affectionate and amused all at the same time. Stefan glanced at her with no particular expression, sat down, ordered a drink and then stretched out his neck like a turkey because his collar was too tight. He had greeted her, but then for some minutes after that he did not talk to her. He sat staring straight ahead with her image on the periphery of his retina.

In this way he studied her without looking at her. He saw that she had bought a new dress – or was wearing one that she had never worn before. It was striped, and had buttons which went down the front; and at the bodice a button which might have been fastened was undone, so that a little of the curve of her bosom could be seen before it disappeared into darkness under the cloth. Her hair too had been arranged, and she had put on some scent which reached his nostrils and reminded him for a moment of the *demi-mondaine* with Onufry . . . and indeed her appearance was altogether more similar to that girl than to the sensible Party member who had turned up at the cell.

'If you like,' she was saying – in her soft voice with its Yiddish inflection – 'we could go back and eat at home.'

'Would your parents be pleased to see me?' he asked, still facing away from Rachel.

'They're not there,' she said. 'We'd be alone.'

104

Stefan felt a spasm in his stomach – a spasm of panic – but felt at the same time, 'the writer is a prophet' – and he clenched his teeth as if they were already sunk into her Achilles tendon.

They left the café and took a tram – but not towards Nalewki.

'Where do you live?' Stefan asked Rachel.

'Near the Lazienki Park.'

'The writer is not a prophet,' Stefan muttered inaudibly, thinking of the expensive villas in that part of Warsaw.

'Isn't your father a doctor?' he asked.

'Yes. Well, a surgeon . . .'

'You told me he lived in the ghetto.'

She tapped her head. 'In his mind.'

The house was that of a rich man – a villa of the turn of the century – with railings around the garden and a gate. A shallow flight of steps led up to the front door; there were lights on in the basement beneath. 'It's only the servants,' said Rachel, opening the front door with her own key. 'They won't bother us.'

The light was on in the hall, and Stefan was immediately assailed by the atmosphere of the house, not because it was Jewish – there was no sign of anything Judaic – but because it was modern and luxurious. The drawing-room into which Rachel now led him had thick, fitted carpets. The pictures on the wall were abstract and had special little lamps attached to their frames. The furniture was all Italianate and well made; the sofa and armchairs were cubic, and the tables had black tops with legs that were loops of stainless steel. Stefan had never set foot in a house of this kind before.

Rachel glanced around the room as she took off her coat. 'Good,' she said, seeing a plate of sandwiches and a bottle of wine with two glasses placed on a tray on the table. She took off her coat, turned to take Stefan's, which he had also removed, and then went back to the hall to throw them onto an inlaid ivory chest.

'I'm afraid it's completely bourgeois,' she said to Stefan, who was still stunned by the opulence of the room around him, 'but I can't help that.'

She crossed to the tray and sat down on the white leather

sofa next to it. 'Will this be all right?' she asked, making a gesture towards the tray.

'Of course,' he said, coming nearer and sitting cautiously on an armchair made of the same white leather, and with the same square arms.

'I told them to leave it out . . . in case we decided to eat something here.' Rachel looked a little confused at her own arrangements: she handed the bottle of wine and a corkscrew to Stefan. 'Would you like some vodka?' she asked. 'There's some over there.'

'This is fine,' said Stefan, taking the bottle and starting to uncork it.

The house had changed them both. Stefan was aware of a certain gaucheness in his behaviour, while Rachel was a little petulant – frowning when she discovered that there was no salt on the tray.

'Have you any brothers or sisters?' Stefan asked her.

'No,' she said.

'And don't your parents mind, or don't they know, that I was coming here this evening?'

'They let me do what I like.' She looked at him and smiled. 'Of course they'd want me to marry a Jew, but since I don't believe in marriage, the question doesn't arise.'

'Perhaps they hoped that you'd marry Jan?'

'They never met him. He refused to come into the house. His parents were poor: his father was a cobbler. He thought that Jewish capitalists were the worst.'

'This doesn't seem . . . well, I hadn't imagined a Jewish household to be like this.'

'I told you, my father wishes he wasn't a Jew. So do I, for that matter. But he can't escape it, whereas I have escaped it. I may have certain features which are from my Jewish origin, but so far as I am concerned, they're as irrelevant as someone else's Lithuanian ears or Estonian nose . . .'

'Of course,' said Stefan, looking at his sandwich before opening his mouth to eat it.

'Papa would become a Catholic if he thought it would make him acceptable in Polish society. Poor Papa. He'd be a Communist, too, if he didn't have so much to lose.' She waved generally at the room and its contents.

'You'd be prepared to lose all this?' Stefan asked.

'I hate it,' she said, drinking from the glass, and then wiping the crumbs off the rim. 'It suffocates me. I want to share the conditions of the working class . . .'

Stefan smiled.

'I know. No one believes me. But I do. I'd like to work in a factory and live in a slum, but the Party wants me to finish my studies . . . and while I'm at the university, it's easier to live at home.'

'Does your father's money come from his work?'

'And from textiles in Bialystok. That's where we come from.' She stood up and came to sit on the arm of Stefan's chair. 'I hope you're not put off by my origins. I'm afraid I'm a child of surplus value, but I can't help it, and when his capital comes to me, I shall pass it on to the Party.'

Stefan looked up. She raised her hand and brushed back a strand of his hair which had fallen over his eyes in a gesture that was almost maternal. 'Are you put off?' she asked.

'Off what?'

'Off me.'

'By this?' He rolled his eyes around the carpeted room. 'No, not at all.'

'It's still the same neck.'

'The same neck?'

'You've forgotten already. You said you liked my neck.'

'I still do.'

'Here, then . . .' She slid off the arm of the chair and sat on the floor in front of him, her back against his knees. She bowed her head, and brushed the hair away from the nape of her neck. Stefan leant forward with the terror of a man diving off a cliff, until he found that his lips were on her skin and the smell of her hair in his nostrils.

Rachel reached round with her hands, took hold of his arm by the cuff of his coat, and drew it down to press his hand to her breast. Thus Stefan sat embracing her from behind, just as he had imagined; and he started to move his lips down her vertebrae, just as he had planned. But no sooner was his mouth beneath the line of her shoulders than she stood up and walked away towards the door.

He thought for a moment that she was flying from him; but

at the door she stopped, listened and then locked it. She turned back towards him, smiled and returned. She took his hand, drew him to the sofa, sat on it and had him sit beside her; she took off her shoes, and then her stockings, while he watched her with a look of terrified fascination on his face which Rachel must have mistaken for love.

When she moved towards him Stefan opened his arms; and then his thin, aristocratic lips did what they could in response to the sensuous cushions of flesh that fastened upon them. With disbelief he felt her hands on his buttons, then on his flesh; then he resigned himself to the necessary experience, as if he was at the dentist, and after some twisting, puffing and the final, unmistakable ejaculation, he realized with inexpressible disappointment that the whole thing had happened as it should have done – that he and Rachel were lovers.

About a week later, Stefan ran into Bruno in the street and they went into the Café Ziemianska. It was not often that they met outside the flat where their old camaraderie had been inhibited by the presence of Krystyna. Now, as they sat in the warmth of the café, it seemed to return like an unexpected spell of winter sunshine. For a while they even forgot that they were Communists, and talked about films and girls as if they were students once again.

'How are you getting on with Rachel?' Bruno asked – smiling at his friend.

Stefan grinned back. 'Not bad.'

'I don't see her as a prude.'

'A prude? No, she's not a prude.'

'Where do you go, then?'

'Her father's house. They have a thick pile carpet.'

'She's rich, is she?'

'Textiles in Bialystok.'

Bruno shook his head.

'And she's the only child,' said Stefan.

'Be not tempted, comrade,' said Bruno.

'Not a chance,' said Stefan. 'She's going to give it all to the Party.'

A small frown came onto Bruno's brow and then left it again. 'Are you in love, then?'

Stefan shrugged his shoulders. 'In a way . . .'

'Krystyna was beginning to worry,' said Bruno with a grin.

'It took *her* long enough.'

'She had to wait for the right man.'

Stefan glanced earnestly at Bruno. 'She knew at once, didn't she? And so did you.'

'Aren't you so sure?'

Again Stefan shrugged his shoulders. 'I like her, certainly. I'd even say I loved her, but then I love every pretty girl I see, and Rachel is just one of them.'

'It's a dangerous condition,' said Bruno. 'You'll be perpetually unfaithful and perpetually unfulfilled.'

'I feel it's unreal, too. The house, the carpet, the parents who are never there, the servants who live under the floorboards . . . I feel I have stumbled into a story which I can no longer write because I am one of the characters. I feel I have no business to be there, but then I feel just as unreal in any other role – as a lawyer, as a Party member . . .'

'Which shows that you are a writer,' said Bruno. 'You live through invention. Your lust is transposed into curiosity. No wonder you feel ill at ease in the arms of Rachel: you are being unfaithful to your muse.'

'But I'm not a monk: and even a writer has to have experience. And anyway, I am in love with her . . .'

'And the other pretty girls . . .'

'There was once a girl – a prostitute, more or less – with a friend of mine, in a café. I didn't talk to her but I loved her. I still do, you see, so I can't love Rachel in the way you love Krysia.'

'We all have our fantasies . . .'

'But to have one night with that girl – that prostitute – I'd give up Rachel, I'd give up anything . . .'

'You'd better start saving,' said Bruno with a laugh, 'because all you'll have to give up are a few zlotys.'

Stefan shook his head. 'She'd never have me. I know. I haven't got the knack.'

'A professional is a professional . . .'

'No, you see, I'd make her feel ill at ease.'

There was a pause. Then Bruno, who was looking out at the street, said to Stefan: 'Have you noticed that half the men in the street are in uniform?'

'I know,' said Bruno. 'All paid by the state. And who are they meant to fight?'

'The Germans, or the Russians.'

'But we have non-aggression pacts with both.'

'Even so . . . the Germans might attack the Corridor.'

'And if they did?' asked Bruno.

'Well, we'd defend it.'

'For a week, perhaps.'

'Not longer?'

'What could our twenty-seven regiments of Lancers, and ten of Chasseurs à cheval, do against the tanks that Hitler is building now? It's a charade, performed by a quarter of a million men at a cost of eight hundred million zlotys, while the children can't go to school because they don't have shoes to wear.'

Bruno's face had gone mottled as he spoke, and it seemed for a moment as if tears of chagrin might come into his eyes.

'But why should you care?' asked Stefan. 'It's their fiasco, and it'll bring on a revolution . . .'

'It makes me ashamed all the same,' said Bruno. 'It's always been said that we aren't a real nation; that we can't run our own affairs. Even our own people thought that – Luxemburg, Radek, Warski. None of them really believed in an independent Poland. If it hadn't been for Lenin, the Party might still be against the idea.' He emptied his glass of beer.

'You do love Poland, don't you?' said Stefan.

'I love the Polish workers, and the Polish peasants,' said Bruno. He hesitated; then he added: 'Yes, I love Poland.'

'I can't, you see,' said Stefan – looking away from his friend towards the door which flapped to and fro as the waiters passed in and out.

'Why not?' asked Bruno.

'I don't know. We seem so foolish, so hopeless, so superstitious, that somehow we don't deserve to be a nation. When a German or a Frenchman looks at me with contempt, I feel contemptible. The Russians despise us – even the Bolsheviks – because we are despicable. We aren't strong or brave. We're poseurs, voyeurs, the lackeys of the French. Just look . . .' He pointed towards two ladies eating cake. 'They think they're elegant and fashionable, but they're just two sowish Slavs stuffing themselves, growing fat and gossiping . . .'

'You must love your country,' said Bruno, looking into Stefan's face. 'It's like a wife or a pair of shoes. They must fit, and if they pinch, you must wear them until they do.'

Stefan's face twisted into the Kornowski grimace. 'I dare say you were right,' he said. 'That's why I shall always be unfaithful, and always unfulfilled.'

Ten

On 12 May 1935 Marshal Pilsudski, the dictator of Poland, died from cancer in his stomach. The whole nation went into mourning. Cinemas and theatres were closed; dinner parties were cancelled; women changed into black dresses, men put on black ties; newspapers were printed with deep black borders. Full-page pictures went on sale, showing the Marshal on his deathbed with a hollow face and three days' growth of beard. One event, however, could not be postponed out of respect for the dead leader – the birth of Krystyna's baby. Her contractions started two days after the dictator's death.

There had been an argument in the family as to where the baby should be born. Krystyna and Bruno had thought that their flat would be good enough, with a doctor in attendance and Mamuska acting as nurse; but Aunt Cecylia had insisted that her niece go to a hospital, just to be on the safe side, and in the end Krystyna had agreed. Aunt Cecylia had found the money to pay for it, and it was Bruno who took her there in a taxi on the morning of 14 May.

The hospital had a reputation for being the best of its kind in Warsaw, but the facilities were all old-fashioned: there was no running water in the wards – nurses had to bring it in pails from the end of the corridor; and there was no lift, so that when Krystyna was admitted she had to be helped up two flights of stairs to the delivery room. But the midwife was a heavy, middle-aged peasant woman who reassured Krystyna because she was so like the peasant women at Jezow. She came in and out of the delivery room during the long hours of labour, squeezing Krystyna's hand and coaxing her to push and breathe; and when the baby boy was born it was the midwife who had the look of triumph and delight. Krystyna was dazed with exhaustion.

It seemed too for a time that Krystyna was less attached to the baby than others. When it was brought to her she held it, but without a curve in her arm and body. Bruno, on the other hand, cradled his son with such joy in the expression on his face, that the nurses giggled and (among themselves) called him 'the mother'.

Of these nurses, the one who looked after Krystyna was less brisk than the others. She had a grey face and once, when holding the baby, she swayed so much that Krystyna thought she might faint. The girl righted herself and took the child back to the nursery: but when the doctor came on his rounds, Krystyna told him that her nurse seemed unwell.

The doctor laughed. 'You're probably stronger than she is,' he said.

'Then why isn't she in bed?'

'No work means no pay. She may have children or parents to look after.'

'But that is absurd.'

'Absurd, certainly. But she is better off here than she would be elsewhere. She has four hours free out of twenty-four: some only get two. She has a bed in a dormitory; some nurses are expected to sleep in an armchair.'

'Why don't they protest?'

'They would be dismissed.'

'It's scandalous.'

The doctor shrugged his shoulders. 'It's certainly paradoxical that many of the nurses who dedicated themselves to the care of the sick don't themselves last more than ten years. They usually get tuberculosis of the kidneys . . . but there are always plenty more. So what can you do? One can't change the world . . .'

All this made Krystyna angry and ashamed. She said nothing more to the doctor, but when her nurse returned she attacked her for accepting such conditions, which made the girl go paler still for fear that the matron might overhear and imagine that she had been complaining. Then Krystyna announced that it was intolerable to exploit the nurse, and that she would discharge herself forthwith from the hospital; whereupon the poor nurse showed surprising energy in begging her to stay, saying that she would be blamed if she left, and that she would lose half her pay, which she needed to keep her own child alive.

Krystyna was trapped. She remained, but in a state of great indignation, never losing a moment to 'politicize' her nurse in fierce whispers, while the nurse swayed and snivelled, whispering 'yes, ma'am' when she agreed and 'yes, ma'am' when she did not – all of which meant that the baby had little attention from anyone apart from his father, who made daily visits to the hospital.

They called the child Teofil because they liked the name: and two weeks after he was born he returned with his mother to Sluzewska Street. There he was put into the hands of Mamuska and Aunt Cecylia so that Krystyna could go back to work at Blomstein's. The two old women had him secretly baptized by the parish priest: this was discovered by Krystyna, who was annoyed, and then by Stefan, who was amused. No one told Bruno.

Krystyna had fed her baby herself for the first week of his life; but then the child had been weighed and it had been decided that what she provided was not enough. Since she intended anyway to go back to work Teofil was put onto boiled cow's milk which was given to him by Mamuska, Cecylia, Krystyna or Bruno: especially at night, Bruno would give him his feed because the two older women slept below and Krystyna had not fully recovered from the ordeal of childbirth.

The first months of Teofil's life were a trial for those who lived with him. He slept in a small, wicker cot, in his parents' bedroom or in the living-room after they had gone to bed. But when he woke at night and cried, his screams went through the thin walls and woke not only his parents but his Uncle Stefan too. Stefan at least could roll over and thank God that it was not his responsibility: but the parents were eased out of their sleep by that exquisite combination of anxiety and exasperation; and then ponder the advantages of going to him or leaving him alone. And because he was a lighter sleeper, it was usually

Bruno who rose from the bed and went through to his son, picked him up, held him over his shoulder and patted him on the back to try and bring up some bubble of air which was tormenting him.

Bruno did this without complaint, and the next morning he would let the baby grip his fingers, or tickle him under the chin, with no trace of resentment for the broken night. Then, reluctantly, he would part from his son and go off to whatever business was at hand: because he was busy that year and would leave the house early in the morning in order to return at a reasonable hour at night.

With the advent of a new reactionary constitution and electoral law, the Party had resumed its call for a Popular Front. This had been rejected by the Socialists; the Party had therefore decided to go over the heads of the Socialist leadership and appeal to all opposition parties and trades unions for a general strike against the forthcoming elections.

Bruno was one of the small group which had been told to communicate this appeal to the mass of the workers in Warsaw. Pamphlets had to be prepared. The copy sometimes came from Belgium or France, where the Party leaders lived in exile; the printing presses were clandestine; and the network for distribution had to be such that a spy could not betray the whole organization. On top of this, Bruno now had a front 'profession' – he taught at a school in the suburb of Ochota; and though the headmaster was a Party member (so he could come and go as he pleased), some teaching had to be done if the job was to serve its purpose as a cover for his real activities.

In the summer a further burden was laid on his broad back. He was told to act as a courier on certain specified occasions between the Party organization in Warsaw and the Party leaders in exile. He would occasionally disappear for up to two weeks at a time, travelling with forged papers by Sweden. The leaders had their reasons for choosing Bruno: he was a direct link to the grass roots of the party – and lines of communication at that time were of particular importance. This meant that Bruno could himself influence Party policy; and certainly it became more consistent with his own ideas. For example a resolution of the Sixth Plenum of the Central Committee read

'We, the Communists, respect the independence of Poland . . . We, the Communists, are heir to the best traditions of the nation's struggle for independence and democracy . . . We, the Communists, are deeply attached to our homeland . . . We will not allow our homeland to become the bridgehead or marching ground for the Hitlerite generals . . .' For some, such sentiments were opportunistic attempts to attract the 'social-patriots': for Bruno they came from the heart.

Bruno never told Krystyna where he was going, nor did she ever ask. She knew that the drawer in which he kept his socks had a false bottom under which were concealed the forged passports and foreign currency, but she behaved as if she did not know they were there. She thought the loss of her 'night nurse' a small sacrifice for the undoubtedly important work he was doing for the Party; nor did she envy him his journeys in Western Europe so long as she thought of them as hurried and uncomfortable visits to the working-class suburbs of Brussels.

Then, one evening, after Bruno had been away for longer than usual, she returned from work to find him lying on their bed asleep. He still wore his clothes, and from the stubble on his cheeks and chin, it seemed that he had not shaved for some days. Beside the bed lay the battered leather bag in which he took his pyjamas, toothbrush and a clean shirt whenever he went away, and Krystyna crossed quietly to unpack it. She took out the dirty socks and underclothes, and then a dirty shirt which was wrapped around something hard. For a moment she hesitated; she was sufficiently disciplined to check her curiosity for a moment – a Party member must know only what she is meant to know – and certainly, if it was a gun . . . But then the shirt had to be washed, so she unrolled it and took out a bottle of Coty Eau de Toilette.

She stood for a moment, still with astonishment. It was as if she had found Bruno in the arms of a powdered prostitute. There in her hands, with its solid glass, pale colour and luxurious label – in most appalling contrast to the dirty shirt – was the evidence of some profound if incomprehensible infidelity.

She glanced at Bruno with a look of such fury that even in his sleep he seemed to notice it. There was some movement in the heavy legs and hips which lay sprawled on top of the covers. He stirred and then, with a sudden start, he awoke.

For a moment his face was tense, as if he did not know where he was: then he recognized the bed, the window – and finally he saw Krystyna and the bottle of toilet water which she still clutched in her hand. Her expression had changed: the fury had gone, but she did not smile at Bruno.

'When did you get back?' she asked.

'This morning,' he replied, sitting up and leaning on his arms stretched out behind him. Then he noticed the bottle. 'Aha,' he said. 'That was meant to be a surprise.'

'It was,' she said severely.

'It's for you,' he said – misunderstanding her expression and blushing at her suspicions.

'Where did you get it?'

He smiled again, but this time with slight shame. 'Paris,' he said.

'Were you in Paris?'

He held his finger to his lips. 'You shouldn't know.'

'Anyone would know who had opened your bag.'

Bruno swung his legs off the bed. 'If you don't want the stuff,' he began.

'If I wanted French scent,' said Krystyna, 'there are customers who would buy it for me.' Having said this, she put the bottle on the chest of drawers, gathered together Bruno's dirty clothes and went out into the kitchen.

Bruno simply shrugged his shoulders, and when he found her sobbing at the table he tried to comfort her: but she would not say what she felt because her sentiments were petty, selfish and the product of a bourgeois consciousness.

Eleven

Stefan returned late at night from Rachel's house with an air of mysterious achievement. He met her on the whole three times a week, on evenings when Rachel's parents were out.

They then always went back to the house near the Lazienki Park, ate their picnic on the thick pile carpet and made love. They made love in a dishevelled, half-undressed way. There was always the possibility that the servants might come in, or her parents come back early: thus Stefan saw only glimpses of Rachel's body – a breast poking through her bodice, or pubic hair in the shadow beneath her skirts.

He did not want to see more. He watched himself copulate with equal horror and fascination. Years of sexual speculation had estranged his mind from his genitals. He observed his own sensations with the same detachment as he watched her body quiver, her mouth loll open, her eyes grow glazed. He recognized, in his loins, a venereal sensation which was not unpleasant – they liked the thrust well enough, and her hands clutching his buttocks – but their pleasure was distinct from his own, and while they were at it, he was watching – his eyes gleaming with fascination as she rocked and moaned; and the joy for Stefan was not in his own ejaculation but in her body bucking, then the cry, the moan, the sigh. She was totally humiliated and Stefan, as a result, was triumphant.

And yet (as he returned on the tram late at night) what was her humiliation? What was his triumph? She was driven into ecstasy while he never lost control. He then was a man (consciousness) and she a beast (instinct). Yet the beast was satisfied: the man was not. Her happiness suffused her whole body: his was confined to his penis. And so while he triumphed in his mind, he was defeated in his body. He suffered still from rancid frustration.

Habits, once formed, are hard to break. If Rachel did not drive him to oblivion, she was still an honest, intelligent, amusing and pretty girl who laughed at his jokes and admired his writing. Since his previous companions, Bruno and Krystyna, were now so sour, he spent less of his time with them and more with Rachel. Together they agreed that children were a mistake – they interfered with love, sex, Party work and going to the cinema – and both agreed that if either happened to marry, they would not have children, or not until much later.

'After all,' said Rachel one evening when they had been to see the German film about a child murderer, *M*, and were walking together down the street, her arm through his, 'marriage is nonsense, isn't it? A bourgeois institution making women the property of men . . .'

'Of course.'

'But if one did decide to *use* it for its practical advantages, then one could have a private contract within the public one . . .'

'What practical advantages?' asked Stefan.

'Well, if one wanted to live together, say . . .'

'One can do that anyway.'

'Yes, but it causes scandal and as Party members we should avoid that. We should not "confirm their worst suspicions", as Comrade Janusz puts it . . .'

Stefan shrugged his shoulders, which had the effect of loosening his arm from hers. She flexed her elbows to take a firmer grip.

'I don't know,' said Stefan. 'I think one should defy society, all forms of society, like the murderer in the film; but not in a snivelling cowardly way like Peter Lorre. I'd like to make a film about a handsome, heroic child-murderer who rapes and murders little girls with audacity and style . . .'

'There are other things too,' said Rachel, not listening to what he said, but drawing him by the arm to the window of a shoe-shop and running her eyes over the display while talking. 'Parents come up with money, for one thing, which means you can rent a flat . . .' She hesitated, as if considering a pair of shoes. Stefan said nothing. 'Which means you can live together.' She turned and smiled up into his face. 'It would be nice, wouldn't it?'

Stefan said nothing, and as they walked on Rachel changed the subject. They went to the Café Ziemianska, where Rachel amused him with stories of Jews trying not to be Jews, and then he amused her with stories about Poles trying not to be Poles, one or two of which were about and against himself.

Teofil was teething and woke him three times that night; so when Stefan next saw Rachel, he questioned her closely about how much her parents would provide if they were to get married, and by the end of the evening they were engaged.

It became quite clear as soon as they told their families that they were the only two to be happy about their marriage. Stefan's Uncle Max and Aunt Cecylia were appalled that he was marrying a Jew – and Rachel's uncle and aunt in Bialystok were equally horrified that she was marrying a Gentile. Bruno and Krystyna were doubtful for reasons of their own; and it was only Rachel's own mother and father who were neutral. They only asked their daughter that they should be allowed to meet Stefan before voicing their opinion, and Stefan was summoned out to the house near the Lazienki Park for lunch on a Sunday.

Rachel opened the door, smiling as she did so. She kissed him quickly and then led him into the drawing-room. Stefan saw at once that the woman whom he took to be Rachel's mother was sitting on the exact spot on the sofa where he first had her daughter. The lady rose and turned, and he saw a decayed version of the same face as his fiancée's – Rachel with powdered wrinkles and hair so artificially coloured and waved that it looked like a wig.

She stood, smiled and then turned apologetically towards her husband, who came striding towards Stefan from the other end of the room. He was quite unlike his daughter, being squat and ugly, almost a gnome; but he greeted his future son-in-law with the warmth and suavity of a cosmopolitan. 'Have a drink, my dear boy. A glass of vodka now, yes, before I even introduce you to my wife. It's a difficult moment for us all . . . There, drink that. Now. We should have met you before . . . Rachel, why didn't you bring him here before?' Without waiting for an answer he took Stefan towards his wife, whose wrinkled hand he kissed. She smiled weakly, stretched her scrawny neck, and looked anxiously over Stefan's shoulder at her husband. '*Ecoute, chéri,*' she said. '*Ne donne pas trop à boire. Il n'aime pas ça.*' She then looked at Stefan, smiled again, and explained in awkward, halting Polish that she hardly spoke Polish at all. '*Je viens de Poznan,*' she said. '*Sprechen Sie Deutsch, zufällich?*'

'*Nur wenig,*' said Stefan. '*J'aimerais mieux parler français.*'

'Absurd,' said Dr Zamojski, Rachel's father. 'We are in Poland. We are Poles. We shall speak Polish.'

His wife smiled weakly again, and moved away. Stefan's arm was gripped once again by his host and he was led across the room which he knew so well to an armchair. Rachel watched.

'This isn't an inspection,' said Dr Zamojski, 'so you can relax. We are modern people, you know, and have brought up Rachel to make up her own mind. I have always said that she should choose: now that she has chosen . . .' He waved his arms in a vaguely dismissive gesture. 'So let us move onto other things. Politics, now. Will there be a war? Sooner or later, sooner or later, don't you agree?'

'I don't think . . .' Stefan began, but he was interrupted by his host, who had not been expecting an answer.

'Germany is strong. She is getting stronger by the hour. I was in Berlin last week. They're not against Jews when it comes to a difficult operation. I was called in by Professor Müller – a most delicate business . . . She is strong, and France and Britain weak. Decidedly weak. Democracies will always be weak.'

'But Poland isn't a democracy, Papa,' said Rachel, 'and Poland is weak.'

Dr Zamojski nodded. 'True.' He turned to Stefan. 'Are you a socialist like my little girl?'

'I . . .'

'I hope not, but I dare say you are. *La folie de jeunesse.*' He looked at his wife and repeated, '*La folie de jeunesse. La politique révolutionaire. Les jeunes gens . . . les deux . . . socialistes.*'

Mrs Zamojska shrugged her shoulders and raised her eyes to heaven.

'But you will see,' Dr Zamojski went on. 'When you are married now, with little children, property . . . have you property? I gather you had some. Are you a count? Rachel tells me that you are, but that you don't use your title. Well, I understand. *Qu'est-ce que c'est qu'un comte sans comté?* Now we too have an aristocratic name – Zamojski – but that was a joke of the Tsar to humiliate our nobility . . .'

Mrs Zamojska leant forward with an interrogatory expression on her face.

'*Monsieur est un comte, mais sans propriété,*' said Dr Zamojski.

Mrs Zamojska nodded.

'Of course I can give you something,' said Dr Zamojski. 'I can settle something on Rachel, but it will not restore your family fortunes. But then I am sure you are not marrying for that . . .'

'Of course not,' said Stefan.

'Not, certainly, if you are a socialist.'

When Stefan left, after lunch, Rachel came with him for a walk in the park. 'Did you like them?' she asked.

Stefan hesitated.

'They're a little absurd,' she said – answering for him like her father. 'But they'll do, won't they?'

'We aren't responsible for our parents,' said Stefan. 'My father was a lunatic and my mother was a fool.'

'But they'll do, won't they?' Rachel repeated.

'Of course,' said Stefan.

She squeezed his hand and then they walked through the trees towards the palace.

For one who regarded marriage as a regrettable practicality, Rachel prepared for it with unusual enthusiasm. She signed a lease on a small, light, elegant flat on Piekna Street, not far from Sluzewska Street. She had it decorated and furnished with the speed and assurance of a girl who had had the colours and patterns of curtains and upholstery running through her mind for some time. She knew just what carpets she wanted on the floor, and just where to buy a double bed which was larger than the usual size. And when her relations asked her what she wanted as a wedding gift, she told them down to the size of the saucepan or the colour of the blanket.

Rachel would consult with her future husband, but he rarely had an opinion; and if he expressed it she might well move onto something else. He was, in any case, well looked after. There was a small room in the flat, intended for a servant, which Rachel had prepared as a study. Bookshelves were fitted to one wall: a fine desk set against another – and on the desk, as her wedding present to Stefan, a brand new typewriter.

By the end of their engagement Stefan was impatient to be married – not so much for the desk, the typewriter or the large-sized double bed, as for the peace of a home not shared by a sulky sister and her squawking child. He had also discovered that among Rachel's qualities was a talent for cooking: occasionally she would 'try out' their new kitchen by preparing borsch or stuffed cabbage, which turned out much better than the same dishes cooked by Mamuska or Krystyna. They also 'tried out' their double bed and, for the first time, Stefan could see and examine her flawless, olive body with its fresh skin and graceful limbs. He knew now that he had the ingredients of happiness and so decided that he was happy.

If any inner voice told him that he was not, he shut it out of his mind – especially if Teofil was crying: and when Krystyna obliquely criticized his choice of a wife, he dismissed it as snobbishness or antisemitism.

'I don't see why you have to marry her,' Krystyna had said.

'Why not?' Stefan replied.

'One doesn't usually marry because one can't think of a reason not to.'

'I love her,' said Stefan flatly.

'Are you sure?'

'I love her as much as I'm likely to love anyone . . .'

'How do you know?'

'I'm old enough.'

'If she was killed by a tram tomorrow, would you care? Would you really care?'

Stefan smiled. 'Of course,' he said.

'There you are,' said Krystyna. 'You smile at the idea.'

'I may not be starry-eyed about her,' said Stefan, 'but I am not the sort to be starry-eyed about anyone: and it is quite respectable to believe that marriages are happier if you go into them with a sense of practical advantage.'

He glanced at Krystyna. She blushed. 'You'll get bored by Rachel,' she said.

'I'd probably get bored by anyone.'

'Quite.'

'In which case, should I marry at all? Is that what you mean?'

'I think . . . perhaps . . . you shouldn't.'

'Isn't that a little unfair? After all, most husbands get bored by their wives.'

'You might meet someone who would never bore you.'

'The Queen of Sheba doesn't live in Warsaw. I have to take what I can get.'

'It needn't be a doctor's daughter . . .'

'A Jewish doctor's daughter. Isn't that what you mean?'

'No. It's not that. But her family are capitalists . . .'

'So was Engels's.'

Krystyna looked at him in the eyes. 'Look,' she said. 'I'm not trying to persuade you not to marry her. Do, if you like. But I know you better than anyone else, and so I felt I should say what I felt. Well, now I've said it, and you can make up your own mind.'

'I've made it up.'

'Good.'

There was a silence. Then Stefan asked: 'What does Bruno think?'

'About Rachel?'

'Yes. And about my marrying her?'

'He hasn't said anything. I think he likes her, and he's glad. But he doesn't know you as well as I do.'

Now that Stefan was on stage as an ardent, if cynical, lover, he faltered in his lines both as a writer and revolutionary. In his own mind he was not really Stefan Kornowski, a penniless Pole, engaged to Rachel Zamojska, the daughter of a Jewish surgeon, but Raymond de Tarterre, an urbane young Parisian, about to marry a Mademoiselle de Rothschild. The world of Proust or Montherlant (whose books he had been reading) was more real to him than Warsaw: and it irritated him that Krystyna should try to spoil his fantasy. He dismissed her behaviour as possessiveness, or rancour at the bad patch in her own marriage. After their conversation he ignored her, avoiding her eyes, and returning to the flat only to sleep. It annoyed him that she did not lose the sour expression even at the wedding, which took place in November 1935, nor attempt to ease the awkwardness among the Jewish and Catholic relatives of the bride and groom.

It went well enough in spite of Krystyna. Aunt Cecylia chattered in French to Rachel's mother, while Uncle Max found unexpected common ground in a political discussion with Dr Zamojski. Bruno too was jovial, and Stefan himself was a great success as he kissed the hands of Rachel's aunts and great aunts from Bialystok as if they were duchesses and princesses from *À la recherche du temps perdu*. Then he left with Rachel for the Tatra mountains and was a married man.

They stayed in the best hotel in Zakopane, which did much to make Stefan happy in the first day of his married life. He took less pleasure in the ever-present and compliant body of his young wife than in shouting a command and having breakfast brought to his bedside by a polite young maid in a starched apron. Rachel noticed his good mood and high spirits and imagined that it was she who made Stefan so happy; and certainly he liked her well enough, but it was the French wine at dinner that really gave him joy; and if the clumsy orchestra which played was particularly Polish, it was not difficult for Stefan to block it out and imagine that he was in St Moritz, because he had never been to St Moritz and so could not know how it differed from Zakopane. Surely that too was a little town filled with peasants from the surrounding mountains wearing round, black hats and thickly embroidered woollen jackets which, in spite of the cold, they carried over their shoulders with the sleeves hanging free.

These he observed as they drove in a sleigh towards a lake known as the Sea's Eye. 'They're taller than the peasants at home,' he said to Rachel.

'Where?' she asked.

'In the Maulopolska, where we used to live. They're taller here, and they look less apathetic.'

Rachel smiled without interest.

'And they keep to the right-hand side of the road. There they'd drive in the middle, usually asleep.' He paused. 'It must be the mountain air.'

'It's because we're near Czechoslovakia,' said Rachel. 'Czech peasants are less stupid . . .'

She looked away and did not notice Stefan's expression of annoyance; then he too looked away. And in a moment the lake came into view, a flat and frozen dish surrounded by mountains. Beyond it, on the side of the mountain, there was a large wooden cross.

'Wherever there's a view,' said Rachel, 'they ruin it with a cross.'

Once again Stefan frowned, and this time Rachel noticed. 'I mean,' she said, 'that if they believe in God, they shouldn't try and improve on what he has created.'

The hotel, when they returned, was filled with red-faced people in long, blue trousers carrying skis. The lobby smelt of wet woollen clothes which had been hung up to dry in the boiler room below. It might have been the same in St Moritz but somehow Stefan did not think so, and the claret he ordered at dinner tasted less delicious than it had the day before.

That night they went down to the town again to watch an outdoor skating competition. Wrapped in their coats, and stamping the ground to keep their feet warm, they stood on the edge of the rink watching the graceful movements of the competitors. Little boys with trays of hot tea passed up and down among the spectators; a scratching waltz came out over the loudspeaker. Rachel clasped Stefan's hand and smiled happily up at him, but Stefan was still gloomy because Zakopane was not St Moritz.

The next morning, as they ate their breakfast in bed, there was an awkward conversation about what they should do on this, the third day of their honeymoon. Rachel wanted to ski but did not dare admit that she could do so because she knew that Stefan could not. Stefan, on the other hand, was finding the perpetual presence of his wife an unexpected strain, yet did not want to suggest that they separate for an hour or two in case she should misunderstand his motive. He therefore lay in bed while she rose, went to the window and then stretched her long, strong body while looking at the snow. 'It's such a wonderful day,' she said. 'We must go out into the mountains.'

'The trouble is,' said Stefan, 'that the sun and snow give me a headache . . .'

'We could get you some sunglasses or goggles for skiing.'

'Yes, well, we could: but, you see, I'm not used to all this fresh air. Why don't you go?'

'Without you?'

'You're a married woman. You'll be quite safe.'

'It's not that.'

'What, then?'

'Well, I like being with you.'

'Of course,' said Stefan.

'But if you'd like to stay here and write . . .'

'I could try . . .'

'Then I'll get out of your way. I might even go skiing.'

'Why don't you?'

'All right.'

She went to the wardrobe, took out her clothes, and started

125

to dress; and Stefan lay feebly in bed, wondering once again why the desire which gnawed at him at the sight of that body should have been so little satisfied by all that they had done on that bed the night before.

When Rachel had gone, and after he had shaved and dressed in a leisurely way, Stefan went for a walk through the town, glancing at the trashy bric-à-brac in the shop windows. Then he returned to the hotel and their room. The bed had been made, their clothes tidied, and there was no excuse for him not to sit down and write, as he had said he would. There was a table and chair, paper and pen; he was a writer and had nothing else to do. Even the novel he was reading he had finished the day before; and the newspaper he had read at breakfast.

The difficulty he faced with the white sheet of paper was not that he had no ideas, but that he no longer trusted his ideas to keep their shape as he gave them expression. After his experience with 'The Man Who Knew Lenin' and 'The Dustman of Warsaw', Stefan looked on his own creations with mistrust. He was most afraid that they would mock him – that they would scoff at his Communist ideals. For even though he lived the life of a 'rootless cosmopolitan' in his fantasy, Stefan still thought of himself as a committed Marxist, and this for one reason – that if he was not a Marxist, he was nothing, and if he was nothing . . .

Nothingness frightened him, just as the dark frightens a child. If Stefan had no objective values by which to judge and guide his own behaviour, then he could only go whichever way he was blown. *Das Capital*, like the Bible, was a chart on which he could measure his progress towards a given goal. But without either sanctity or socialism as a home port, his life would have no purpose whatsoever. Passion would take him one way, whim another, or perversity suck him down like a whirlpool.

He sat looking out at the mountains, chewing the end of his pen, and he cursed his speculative intelligence which had led him into this cul-de-sac. Why was he not like a peasant, dozing on a cart, letting the horse find its own way home? He envied them their superstitions – their simple choice of Heaven and Hell. 'The man who thinks is a fool,' he wrote at the top of the piece of paper, then added: 'said Raymond de Tarterre . . .' He paused, chewed his pen, and went on:

as he watched his mistress lying in her bath. Her breasts floated in the water. His eyes admired her body.

'*Donc, fay ce que vouldras,*' she said.

She lay naked on the carpet. Her lover painted her nipples with blood-red nail varnish. It dried and then cracked as the brown, pigmented flesh wriggled in the cold air.

'*Fay ce que vouldras,*' she murmured.

He tied her legs and arms with his dressing-gown cord, and bound them together so that she lay uncomfortable like a shackled antelope. Then he watched her; he watched her until it was dark. At eight he knelt and kissed her flanks. 'You are lovelier than a shaven pig at the abattoir,' he said, 'and more delicious.' He took a carving knife, cut a *tranche*, but lost his appetite at the sight of blood.

'But what shall I tell my husband?' she asked as he cut her loose.

'Just what you said to me – *fay ce que vouldras.*'

'But he will kill me,' she whispered.

'The law is more lenient towards husbands,' he replied.

'And tomorrow?' she asked as she dressed, the blood already showing through her skirt. 'Will you go to hear Thorez?'

'Of course.'

'You agree with the Party line?'

'Of course. Why not?' said Raymond de Tarterre. 'The man who thinks is a fool.'

This little story took Stefan ten minutes to write and an hour to polish. He then ate alone in the restaurant of the hotel; and in the long spaces of time he had to wait between the courses while his waiter slouched in the corner, gossiped, and bit his nails, Stefan stared into the middle distance. 'It's absurd,' he said to himself; and then again, 'It's absurd'; and if anyone had been sitting at his table, or had passed behind him, they would have heard what he said and assumed, perhaps, that he was a foreigner, unfamiliar with Polish ways, and that the absurdity lay in the length of time it took the waiter to bring a plate of borsch to the table. What such a stranger could not know would be that these words were but the small, audible part of a longer dialogue which was taking place behind the grimace.

It went something like this. 'It's absurd that my conscious mind is quite unable to control my artistic creation. I accept Marx. I accept Lenin. I accept the Central Committee of the Communist Party of Poland; but my muse mocks at them all. She is irony, undiluted irony. It is absurd. Absurd.'

'But perhaps, *mon cher Stefan*, you are not a Marxist at all, but have merely persuaded yourself that you are.'

'Why should I do that?'

'Fear of the void.'

'Nonsense. I accept absolutely that my purpose and fulfilment lie with history, with socialism, with revolution.'

'But that, my dear fellow, is the absurdity. For you know as well as I do that without God, there is no obligation. Each man is sovereign. Even if he sees a pattern in history, why should he follow it?'

'Because of his fellow-men.'

'But what does he owe his fellow-men? They are usually either villains or fools. The only possible reasons for loving them is that Christ commanded it, and that his commands should be obeyed because Christ was God. But Christ was not God, and so his commands are no more interesting than anyone else's.'

'But there must be some bond between men . . .'

'Certainly, it may be in your interest to combine with others against other groups of men, or against nature; you may even invent a moral ideology to strengthen the bond – patriotism, say, or socialism: but please don't take them seriously. You know as well as your muse that the Poles are no better than the Czechs, or the Czechs better than the Poles. And the same is true of the social classes. The poor are no better than the rich or the rich than the poor. Both are covetous and greedy; and the theory of socialism is only a cudgel picked up by the poor to threaten the rich, and if necessary beat them until they disgorge some of their wealth.'

'But this is absurd,' said Stefan to his imaginary *alter ego* (Raymond de Tarterre). 'I see the poor. I see them suffer – children dying for want of proper medicine, women unable to feed their babies for lack of food. And beside them the rich, skiing in Zakopane, dancing in Cracow, stuffing themselves with caviare and larks' tongues (if they can get the waiter to bring them). What is wrong with my impulse to change all this so that everyone has something, and no one has too little or too much?'

'Nothing, my dear Stefan, nothing. So long as you recognize your impulse for what it is – a matter of taste, and not a matter of right and wrong.'

'A matter of taste?'

'Precisely. You like justice for its symmetry, just as you prefer Classical architecture or the music of Mozart.'

'But this is absurd . . .'

'What you must not do is confuse your aesthetic preference for an ethical value: or talk in terms of right and wrong about someone like your friend Onufry, who is quite content to spend his money on whores and champagne, while the peasants starve on his estate. Shoot him, by all means, in your revolution: but don't call him a bad man just because he is a White; or consider yourself better than he is because you are a Red. For really the issues are as arbitrary as the colours which represent them.'

Twelve

About a month after their return to Warsaw, Rachel invited Krystyna and Bruno to dinner one evening, together with two other friends – a student of political economy and his girl friend who designed dresses. It was unfortunate that this girl – the designer – came in one of her own creations, and that Rachel had changed into an elegant black frock, because Krystyna came in the skirt and blouse she had worn that day at work, and without any of the touches of lipstick and powder that the other girls had applied to their faces for the occasion.

'I'm sorry,' said Krystyna, in a tone of voice that contained both contempt and embarrassment – though more of the former than the latter – 'I didn't realize that this was a dinner party.'

Rachel blushed. 'It's not really a dinner party,' she said. She glanced in confusion at the napkins and candlesticks on the table. Krystyna's eyes too went in that direction, seeing all that was neat and new. 'How elegant,' she exclaimed – her tone now pure contempt. 'Well, Stefan, what a change from the old slum in Sluzewska Street.'

Stefan's only reply was a grimace.

Bruno looked around. 'It's very nice,' he said to Rachel. 'Stefan's a lucky man . . .'

'And you're so unlucky,' said Krystyna; but before Bruno could answer, she had turned away to be introduced to Jola, the dress-designer, and to allow Paul, the student of political economy, to kiss her hand.

Since Stefan made no move to do so, Rachel poured each of their guests a glass of vodka and then brought in hors-d'oeuvres on a tray – blushing at the delicacy with which the little canapés had been arranged. And Krystyna, sniffing the embarrassment of her sister-in-law, began popping the little pieces of bread with fish, egg and cucumber into her mouth with gestures of exaggerated elegance.

Stefan turned back from the window. He began to attend to the others as if he had just arrived in the room, filling their glasses, then his own; then his own again; then his guests' glasses and his own . . . and so on, in a ratio of two to one. He did not talk, and of the others, only Bruno conversed in a normal way. Krystyna waited like a snake, ready to sting with some sarcasm; the other couple were confused by the atmosphere; and Rachel seemed close to tears. The atmosphere only improved when they sat at table, and hot food followed the cold down their gullets. Then they got onto the subject of the war in Abyssinia and the League of Nations, with Paul arguing that the League was the best chance for peace, Bruno taking the view that it would never be effective because it had no popular backing 'but was an invention of diplomats'. 'No one will die for the League of Nations,' he said. 'It is not an idea that fills anyone with enthusiasm, except French and British liberals who want to keep the world as it is.'

'Oh no,' said Paul. 'I must disagree. I mean to say, if we're to have peace – and we all want peace – then we must have some institution for ordering the world.'

'I am in favour of some sort of collective security,' said Bruno, 'but there will be no order in the world while there is injustice and there will always be injustice while we remain with the status quo.'

'The League can bring moral pressure . . .'

'What moral pressure? Can anyone really say that Mussolini has behaved worse than the British and French? It is not Italian imperialism that is the enemy but imperialism itself . . .'

While Paul and Bruno continued this conversation, Krystyna leant across the table and said to Rachel: 'You cook so awfully well.' She spoke in a tone of voice which could have been ironic and could have been sincere, and totally confused Rachel, who did not know whether to smile, glare, or look away.

'And the wine,' Krystyna shouted across to her brother. 'Real, French wine, Stefan. What style!'

Stefan stretched his neck in his collar.

'I do like French wine, don't you?' Krystyna said to Jola, the dress designer.

'Oh yes,' said Jola. 'I love it. Especially champagne.'

'Champagne, yes.' Krystyna turned to Rachel. 'Perhaps we can have champagne next time?'

Rachel blushed and scowled at the same time. 'I don't approve of champagne,' she said.

'You don't approve of champagne?' asked Krystyna, her eyebrows raised in an expression of mock-innocence and surprise. 'Is it the bubbles you disapprove of, or the colour?'

'The price,' said Rachel.

'But everything's relative, isn't it?' said Krystyna, turning to Jola. 'To some people – workers and peasants and tramps and people like that – wine from Bordeaux is just as exotic as wine from Champagne.'

'Is it?' asked Jola.

'Oh yes. They drink vodka, you see, and beer – but above all vodka. They're all drunk, always, all the time. That's why they don't do any work, and *that's* why they're poor.'

'Really,' said Jola. 'I always thought . . .'

'Lies, lies. Bolshevik propaganda. If a working man was sober, like my brother here, or hard-working, like Rachel, then he too could give dinner parties with French wine and candles . . .'

Krystyna spoke in a rapid, sharp voice which could not but be heard by the three men who sat among them; but Bruno persisted in his discussion of the League of Nations as if he did not want to hear what his wife was saying.

'And how do you know,' Rachel said to Krystyna, 'that the workers and peasants and tramps would want to drink wine?'

'Perhaps they wouldn't.'

'Then no harm is done by our drinking it.'

'None at all, except of course that the price of one bottle could buy a child a pair of shoes, and if that child had a pair of shoes he could go to school . . .'

'To acquire a taste for French wine,' said Stefan.

'To broaden his horizons,' said Krystyna.

'To acquire a taste for French wine,' Stefan repeated, 'which he could then not satisfy, and so would make him in time a good socialist . . .'

'Like you!' Krystyna almost spat at him as she spoke the two words.

'We may drink French wine,' said Rachel, 'but at least we don't have a servant.'

'Who does?' asked Paul, who had broken away at last from Bruno and the League of Nations to listen to the other more dramatic conversation.

'Why Krysia, of course,' said Rachel, with an elegant gesture towards her sister-in-law.

'What servant?' asked Krystyna.

'Mamuska.'

'She doesn't work for me. She works for Aunt Cecylia.'

'You may not pay her,' said Rachel, 'but you can't pretend that she doesn't work for you, cleaning your flat and looking after your child.'

Krystyna went red in the face. 'I shall start to pay her,' she said; and then added, 'now that I don't have to pay for Stefan.'

'And will you give her his room?' asked Rachel, 'instead of that cupboard in the kitchen? Or is that for the baby . . .'

Krystyna looked down at her food. 'She can have Stefan's room if she wants it,' she said.

'I think she probably prefers to live downstairs with Aunt Cecylia,' said Bruno. Then, after a strange look at Stefan, he turned to Paul again; and the whole company escaped into happier chat about plays and films and novels.

It took more than a month for Mamuska to forgive Krystyna for offering to pay her for looking after Teofil. Aunt Cecylia was offended too, and when Krystyna explained that it was only for the sake of her principles that she had done so, it only confirmed (in Aunt Cecylia's mind) that the principles were without any sensitivity to human feelings.

The two old ladies were upset because the offer seemed to taint what had become the most precious thing in their lives – their love for the baby Teofil. He was now over one year old, and though he could neither walk nor talk, was showing such spirit and humour that he charmed everyone who saw him – even Uncle Max who normally detested children. The old man was to be found on Sunday mornings after Mass, lying on his stomach on the floor of Aunt Cecylia's drawing-room, speaking to Teofil in his own language of gurgles and coos, and beaming at any little laugh that came as a reward.

Bruno too spent any time he had to spare with his son. Every morning, when he rose, and every evening when he returned from work, he went into the baby's room (Mamuska had remained in her cupboard), hoping that Teofil would be awake, and if he was he would crouch by the cot, put his finger through the railings and like Uncle Max make childish sounds to express his affection.

He would also pick him up and gently hug the boy, resting his cheeks on the baby's head; or press his lips against his cheek and tickle his ear with a whisper. He would have been happy to go on all morning, laughing into the little sparkling eyes; and might have done had not Mamuska come in, puffing from the climb up the stairs, and snatched Teofil from him with a jealous, angry gesture. For she had decided that she owned the child, and that Bruno and Krystyna were incidental adjuncts to the baby's existence.

It was Krystyna who was least sentimental about her own child, performing her maternal duties every now and then, playing with the child every now and then, but delegating her duties on the whole with open relief. Aunt Cecylia explained this detachment with the maxim that the bond between mother and child 'went underground'; but privately she was a little surprised that the mother seemed so insensitive to the charms of her son. She was tired, of course, when she came home from Blomstein's, and Aunt Cecylia muttered to Mamuska about Bruno's principles which kept his wife at work.

The 'quarrel' between Rachel and Krystyna was soon forgiven. No one mentioned it, and when Stefan and Rachel came to lunch with Aunt Cecylia the following Sunday, Krystyna went out of her way to be civil to her sister-in-law, as if she was somewhat ashamed of her behaviour; and after lunch the two girls – both so pretty in different ways – chased Aunt Cecylia and Mamuska out of the kitchen and washed the dishes together.

It was forgiven but not forgotten. Some weeks passed before Rachel gave another 'dinner party', and when she did, Bruno and Krystyna were not invited. Nor did the four meet at Party meetings any more. Bruno was transferred to the cell at the school where he taught, and Krystyna had been excused from most Party activities because of the child. Rachel still went to the same cell at the university, but Stefan had stopped going altogether.

One afternoon, in the spring of 1936, Stefan ran into Bruno outside the Royal Palace on Zamkowy Square. The two friends walked together along the Krakowskie Przedmiescie, past the Bristol Hotel and, when they reached the gates of the university they went through them to escape from the noise of the traffic. It was one of the first warm days of the year. Both wore overcoats but had unbuttoned them to let in the air. They walked down past the classical buildings of the university until they came to the benches which overlooked the Vistula. There they sat down and breathed in the scented air as if they were animals which had just emerged from hibernation.

'Do you remember how we used to sit here and talk?' asked Bruno.

'Of course,' said Stefan. 'Like Herzen and Ogarev on the Sparrow Hills. Liberty, justice, revolution . . .'

'We had quite clear ideas in those days.'

'You had the ideas.'

'But you accepted them.'

'I swallowed them whole.'

'And now?'

Stefan glanced at Bruno. The thought suddenly entered his mind that their meeting had not been accidental. 'Now,' he began; he paused, then said: 'Now, I have my doubts . . .'

'About what?'

'About the Party. That's to say, not about the Party as such, but about Communism.'

Bruno looked anxiously at Stefan. 'Are they doubts that I could help resolve?'

'Perhaps. I don't know. I'll explain them, if you like, but . . .' He turned and smiled at Bruno. 'I don't want to corrupt you.'

'Don't worry about that,' said Bruno. 'I'm in a better position than most to understand certain decisions of the Central Committee and the Comintern . . .'

'It isn't a matter of decisions, or of the Central Committee, or the Comintern,' said Stefan. 'I don't doubt, given the premises, that the decisions are right. I do not even doubt the Marxist analysis: history may well evolve in the way Marx said it did. Feudalism, capitalism, socialism – they may all be necessary to historical development just as compression, explosion and exhaust are to a petrol engine. What I doubt now is my obligation to take part in this development: for if it is inevitable, then my choice is anyway illusory; and if it is not, then what moral imperative obliges me to swim with the tide rather than swim against it?'

Bruno joined his hands together and clenched them tightly. 'But if you have seen the wretched conditions of the workers and peasants,' he said, 'and if you have understood that it is capitalism which is responsible, then you must work to change such a system for something better.'

'Why? Why must I? What does their condition matter to me?'

'But men are brothers . . .'

'They are not. And even if they are, am I my brother's keeper? Only Christ says that I should be; only He insists that men must love one another; and if Christ was God, then I might pay some heed to what He said – if only to protect my own interests in the next world. But there is no next world; Christ was not God; there is no God. And because there is no

God, there is no obligation. There is only force, and a calculation of interest . . .'

'And compassion,' said Bruno.

'And compassion, should you happen to feel it. And certainly, if you hate the sight of suffering, and conclude that a Communist system of society will remove the offending spectacle, then be a Communist: and if you think that the elevation of the Communist method into a religious belief will assist in the re-arrangement, then elevate it, by all means, and see how many people you can persuade that way. Quite a lot, I should think, because a need for faith of some sort seems to be a feature of human nature. But I am not convinced that your distaste for suffering is any different from mine for Stravinsky; and I do not see any argument which could convince a man who for whatever reason is indifferent to the sufferings of others, and does not suffer himself, that he should feel any obligation to join in your cause.'

Bruno looked down at the gravel below the bench. 'Unless you could convince him,' he said, 'that it was in his enlightened self-interest to work for a just society.'

'But it isn't, is it? For the bourgeois, or the Sapiehas or the Radziwills, or for Rachel's family who own factories in Bialystok. Or even for the man with a shop who dreams of making it a department store. Anyone who has more, or who dreams of having more, than the equal share will have less under socialism . . .'

'But it isn't a matter of money,' said Bruno. 'It is not material equality which will add to human happiness, but the abolition of exploitation and injustice . . .'

'But how can you know what will add to human happiness? The whole notion is elusive and paradoxical. Men strive for security, yet danger exhilarates them. They have soldiers and police to protect them, then climb mountains, or travel to the North Pole to escape from their suffocating safety. You can say that men are brothers, yet whenever they can they compete, just as animals compete, in games and races and tests of endurance and skill. You want a world where all the lions are tame, where the stags have a single doe; where the squirrels share their nuts – or best of all, are spared the burden of collecting them, but are given a sufficiency by the state.'

'It's not that,' said Bruno, in a voice that was unusually flat. 'But I do want to civilize man – to change his nature for the better. I don't wallow in the savagery of life . . .'

'And do you know why?' said Stefan – his voice shrill and persistent. 'Do you know why you and all other Communists want to civilize man, and change nature? Because you still believe in God, in original sin, and in the perfectibility of the soul. Your mind is moulded by twenty centuries of Christian belief, and though you say you are atheists, your whole philosophy is shaped by Christian beliefs and has no justification without them. The Soviet Union is not a new development in the evolution of human history; it is Holy Russia under another name – the same old nation of monks and mujiks in the thin disguise of those philosophical speculations which Karl Marx, the Rabbi's son, sold to the world as scientific truth.'

They continued their discussion until it was dark and lights blinked at them from the other side of the river. They shook hands when they parted, but nothing had been resolved.

Part Two

One

In July 1936, events occurred far from Poland which threw Europe further into turmoil. General Franco and his Moorish legions crossed from Africa onto the mainland of Spain in a direct assault on the Republican government.

At once all those with liberal or democratic convictions were outraged – among them Stefan Kornowski: and as the Civil War established itself in Spain, he was drawn back into active work for the Party. His doubts were put in abeyance; he accepted without hesitation the Party slogans which, in a more logical frame of mind, he might have picked to pieces – 'The fight for Spain is a fight for Poland'; 'For your freedom and for ours'.

The agitation for support for the Loyalist cause brought all four together – Stefan, Bruno, Rachel and Krystyna. There were no more dinner parties. Any spare food and money went to Spain. Even Aunt Cecylia gave moral support to their efforts, and only Uncle Max mumbled his support for Mola and Franco.

They were happy months – a return for Krystyna to the early days of her marriage, not just in their unselfishness and sense of purpose but in the sexual bond which renewed itself too with their reanimated commitment. But their very joy contained a contradiction: and as more and more Poles, some not Communists nor even Socialists, went off to fight for the Republicans in Spain, Krystyna could see on the face of Bruno the evidence of a terrible struggle. When he played now with Teofil, an expression of doom came onto his face; and at meals he could not concentrate on what others were saying but looked vacantly at nothing and left his food.

Bruno felt that he was nearing thirty – an age which seemed to him to mark the end of youth and the beginning of middle age: and though to anyone else his life of clandestine agitation for the Party might have seemed dramatic enough, to him all the discussions and slogans seemed irrelevant to the real battle for the future, which was with guns in Spain. He felt this particularly because he was a Pole. 'People scoff at us,' he said to Stefan, 'because they think we're cowards and poseurs. I'd like to show them that we're sincere, and that we can fight . . .'

'If you go,' said Stefan, 'I shall come with you.'

'To fight?'

'Yes, to fight.'

Bruno hesitated: his eyes seemed glazed as if he was looking back into himself. Eventually he turned to Stefan. 'Why?' he asked. 'Why would *you* want to fight in Spain?'

'I still hate the fascists,' said Stefan.

'Our wives wouldn't like it,' said Bruno.

'They would accept it,' said Stefan. 'They know how important it is . . .'

'It's so difficult,' said Bruno, 'to judge one's own motives.'

'But the motive is simple, isn't it?'

'What is it, then?'

'To fight against fascism,' said Stefan – this without a trace of irony in his voice.

'I know. To fight, and possibly to die. And when I think of Krysia, I feel that though she would weep . . . well, she wouldn't weep; she would be sorry, but she would understand.'

'So would Rachel.'

'I know. But there is Teofil.'

'Of course.'

'He is the only reason I hesitate. Because if I am killed, he loses a father; and if you are killed, he loses his uncle too. He grows up among women with only a vague memory of me, and perhaps a shrine in the corner of the living-room. You see . . .' – he turned to face Stefan – 'You see I can accept my own loss of my own life, because I would have died for some purpose; I can accept Krysia's loss of a husband – she might well find another, a better man than me. But Teofil's loss of his father – another man with my child . . .' He shook his head and pursed his lips.

Stefan studied Bruno, fascinated by this phenomenon. 'How strange,' he said. 'You love your son so much.'

'There, you see? That's what I tell myself. I can contemplate leaving Krysia but not Teofil. Does that mean that I love her less? And it's true. I do love her less. I do want to escape from Sluzewska Street – from the monotony of that flat, and the school, and the Party work . . . and perhaps that is my chief motive for wanting to go to Spain. The heroism and the self-sacrifice is a façade. I want the sun and the wine and the danger – just like an English gentleman who goes tiger hunting in Bengal.'

'He has more chance of coming home.'

Bruno shrugged his shoulders. 'Well, as you can see, I'm in a fine muddle.'

Stefan leaned forward on the table. 'I think we should go,' he said, 'because we are what we do. Action defines us. And if we shrink from this opportunity, there will always be the doubt in the back of our minds that we did so from cowardice; and Teofil will have a father, but a father who is frightened and disappointed and always regretting that he did not go . . .'

Stefan continued to hiss in his ear like the serpent in the Garden of Eden. For Stefan the International Brigade had become like the Tree of Knowledge – and action the Fruit. For months now he had felt restless and frustrated because he could not write; he could not write because he did not know what to say; he did not know what to say because he did not know what he believed; and he did not know what he believed because (following his own diagnosis), he thought too much and did too little.

Action, he thought, would clear the arteries of his inspiration. Courage, endurance and suffering would teach him more surely than intellectual speculation what was true and what was not. It would cut the knot in his mind; it would extricate conjecture from conviction.

It was not suitable that he should present these arguments to Bruno as a reason for going to Spain. Quite the contrary, he sought to persuade his friend that his own doubts were the promptings of some fascist demon who wanted him to stay at home. 'Think,' he said (on another occasion in another café), 'of the men, money and arms that Hitler and Mussolini have sent to help Franco. What chances have the Republicans unless they can draw on us – and on our convictions? And what respect will our children have for us when they grow up if we say: "Europe is fascist, my boy, because I couldn't bear to leave home . . ." '

'I hardly think that I will tilt the scales one way or another.'

'But you, and then me, and then a million others . . .'

Bruno was easily persuaded; and without telling Krystyna or Rachel, he and Stefan applied to the Party for permission to volunteer in Spain. It was given, and plans were made for their departure from Poland.

One evening Krystyna returned from Blomstein's. It was raining, her feet were wet, and she shook her umbrella in the street before starting up the four flights of stairs with the groceries she had bought on the way home. She came into the flat to see through the open door of her bedroom Teofil with her lipstick, drawing patterns on the carpet.

She shouted at him, dropped the groceries, and ran into the bedroom. Teofil looked up; then, from shock, guilt and the bedraggled appearance of his mother, began to cry. She picked him up into her wet arms and carried him into the hall, where she saw Bruno wearing slippers, holding a book and smoking a cigarette.

'Where's Mamuska?' she asked.

'She went downstairs.'

'And left Teofil?'

'She left me in charge.'

'Then for God's sake why didn't you watch him?' She pushed past her husband, trying to comfort her child, then she put him down and took off her mackintosh. She glanced at her face in a mirror – her sharp nose accentuated by the scarf holding her hair.

Bruno shuffled into the bedroom, looked at the scarlet marks on the carpet, and returned to the living-room. 'I'm sorry,' he said. 'I'll clear it up.'

Krystyna did not reply, so Bruno went into the kitchen for a brush, bucket and cloth. Then he shuffled through to the bedroom again and started to scrub at the marks on the carpet, while in the kitchen Krystyna gave Teofil a biscuit to keep him quiet and started to unpack the groceries.

'Why are you home, anyway?' she shouted from the kitchen. 'Why aren't you teaching?'

'I've stopped at the school,' Bruno shouted back.

'Why?' asked Krystyna.

Bruno did not reply. He looked down at the carpet: he had only blended the streaks of lipstick into a large red patch like blood.

Krystyna came and stood in the doorway, wiping her hands with a dishcloth. 'Are they putting you on to something else?' she asked.

'Yes,' he said. 'I'm going to Spain.'

Krystyna stopped wiping her hands. She stood stock-still; and Bruno remained with his back to her, staring at the red stain on the carpet.

'They can't send you, can they?' she asked – her voice and face a little tight.

'No,' said Bruno. 'You have to volunteer.'

She turned away and went back to the kitchen. Bruno stood, picked up the bucket and followed her. 'I should have told you,' he said, 'but I thought you might be against it.'

'And if I was?' asked Krystyna in a tone of voice he could not interpret.

'It would have made it more difficult to decide.'

'But you have made up your mind?'

'Yes.'

She said nothing, but started to peel off the outer leaves of a cabbage.

Bruno emptied the bucket into the sink. 'I must go,' he said.

'Of course,' she said. Then she added: 'I knew you wanted to go.'

Her tone of voice was still neutral – enigmatic. For years he had lived with her, but he could not tell what she was thinking. Then she suddenly looked at him and said: 'Don't leave me here' – and in that look and those words there was panic and despair which made him turn away: and before he could answer, she looked down and cut the cabbage in two.

Later they discussed everything – the advantages for her and for Teofil in remaining in Warsaw; the kind of clothes he should take with him; and much higher things. 'It's vital that the Party should lead the way in Spain,' said Bruno. 'The Polish battalion in the International Brigade could well be the nucleus of a People's Army in a Socialist Poland.' And Krystyna agreed, and took out his socks from the drawer with the false bottom to look for holes and darn them. Only once did she laugh – half with scorn, half with particular and private amusement – and that was when she heard that Stefan was going too.

Rachel did not laugh: she cried when Stefan told her and clung to him, and they made love without the proper precautions, which was how she became pregnant. But she did not know that at the time, and afterwards determined that she too would go to Spain as a nurse. It was only with some difficulty that Stefan persuaded her not to. 'There are plenty of nurses already,' he said. 'But very little food. You would serve the cause better by staying here and raising money . . .' He went on and Rachel was convinced: but he was not and he wondered (to himself) why it was that he decidedly did not want her to come. 'Perhaps Bruno is right. The cause is an excuse – an excuse to travel to Paris, Barcelona and Madrid. Certainly, I don't want to go with her. What adventure or excitement could there be for a married couple? How absurd! A family holiday with death at the other end – her brawny embraces in hot hotels, taking all my strength, and talking, talking, talking . . .' And he made a grimace (Kornowski) which turned into a smile when he saw that her loving, glistening eyes were on him – a smile which she misinterpreted and so embraced him and lay back and drew him to do again what went so well with these emotions of love, loyalty and sacrifice.

The two volunteers left separately. Bruno could not apply for a passport, and so prepared for his journey with forged papers, secret addresses, code names and passwords which would take him across frontiers and provide him with false identities on different legs of the journey.

Stefan's departure was different. Rachel, Krystyna and Aunt Cecylia all came to the station to see him off on the Paris express; and he was dressed quite smartly in a new suit of English tweed. He had a berth in a sleeping-car: altogether he was more like a young man setting off to study abroad, than a recruit on his way to war.

He felt like a tourist too as the train set off, and the weeping, waving women were left behind amid the steam and trolleys of the station platform. He sat by the window, his face fixed in no particular expression; but his eyes showed his ruthless excitement at the thought of the different frontiers, languages and policemen; the new smells, tastes and sensations; the streets and the buildings – the Champs Elysées, the Tuileries, the Left Bank . . . His mind, it must be said, was fixed more on Paris than on Madrid; and he wondered how long he would have to wait for Bruno and, once Bruno had arrived, how long it would take to enlist in the International Brigade.

He was expected at the Hôtel de Beaune and was told that 'Thiéry' (Bruno) had not yet arrived. Stefan registered under his own name and behaved like a tourist as he had been told to do – though everyone in the hotel seemed to know why he was there, were themselves East Europeans of one sort or another and hovered in a conspiratorial way around a Jugoslav called Broz.

It was not difficult for Stefan to pretend to be a tourist. For years he had dreamed of Paris; and like all his fellow-countrymen his upbringing and education had hung on France and French civilization. From morning to night, in the days he spent waiting for Bruno, he wallowed in the sights and smells of the city. The bread, the coffee, the boulevards, the buses, the women in the streets, the bookshops – they all intoxicated him far more than the wine he drank with his lunch or the aperitif he sipped at the Deux Magots or the Brasserie Lipp. He basked in Paris like a cat in the sun, and it was only in that short moment each morning when he was half asleep and half awake that he felt more like a mouse trapped between the Nazis behind him in Germany and the fascists in front of him in Spain.

Bruno arrived six days after Stefan. He was tired and unshaven, and after eating some food he slept, and awoke only at six in the evening. Then he shaved and dressed in some well-made but ill-fitting clothes which Broz, the Jugoslav, provided for him. 'Let's have an evening out,' he said to Stefan. 'Tomorrow, for all we know, we may be confined to barracks.' He smiled, and together they went out into the little streets of the Left Bank, and then walked up towards Montparnasse.

Bruno, who had been so tired, now strode ahead and Stefan – panting to keep up – suddenly realized how physically strong Bruno was. 'He'll make a good soldier,' he thought to himself.

'Shall we go to the Moulin Rouge?' Bruno shouted back to him.

'We're going in the wrong direction,' said Stefan. 'And anyway, it's expensive.'

'What shall we do, then?' said Bruno, pausing by a pillar to read the posters of plays and films.

'What do you want to do?' asked Stefan.

'You decide,' said Bruno. 'You're the Parisian.'

'Oh, I've done nothing yet,' said Stefan. 'I just sit and watch.'

'Then let's sit and watch,' said Bruno.

They walked up the Boulevard Raspail to the Boulevard Montparnasse and then went into the Dôme to eat and drink and watch others eat and drink – all talking, laughing and dressed in varied, exotic clothes.

'I wish Krysia was here,' said Bruno. 'She'd love it so.'

'She'll get here one day,' said Stefan.

'It feels wrong, somehow, to be here without her.'

'We're only on our way through,' said Stefan.

'I know.'

'When do you think we'll move on?'

'I don't know. We'll find out from Walter tomorrow.'

'Who's Walter?'

Bruno glanced around to see if he could speak without being overheard. 'Karol Swierczewski. He's head of the *bureau technique* in the Rue de Chabrol. He'll probably send us on to one of the *Maisons des Syndicats* – and from there we'll go down to Albacete . . .' He stopped, and looked anxiously at Stefan. 'Tomorrow will be your last chance,' he said.

'To do what?'

'To get out of going to Spain.'

'But that's why I'm here,' said Stefan.

'I know,' said Bruno. 'But remember what I said – that we often don't know our real motives for doing things. And if you have any doubts about fighting – about killing other men and quite possibly being killed . . .'

'But what would I do if I didn't go?'

'You could sit and watch,' said Bruno. 'Sit and watch and judge . . .'

'Do you think I am a coward?' asked Stefan – quite mildly and with real curiosity.

'What is a coward?' asked Bruno. 'Perhaps I would be a coward if I had imagination and detachment. What do brave men do but destroy each other, while the cowards survive . . .'

'It would be despicable, now, to back out.'

Bruno shrugged his shoulders. 'You would look after Teofil, wouldn't you, if you got back and I did not?'

'Of course,' said Stefan. 'But I'm no more likely to survive than you are. We'll go together, and live and die together . . .' And then, to cover his confusion at this extravagant phrase, he straightened his spine and craned his neck to catch the eye of the waiter and order two more glasses of cognac.

They returned early to the hotel to get a good night's sleep, and after breakfast the next morning they set out on a bus with their suitcases. They walked up the Rue de Chabrol, looking for the right number like two immigrant labourers who had been promised a job. When they found it the door was open; they went into the passage which led from the street into the courtyards beyond. Bruno tapped on the window for the concierge: an old man looked through and directed them towards a staircase on the far side of the courtyard.

The door of the flat on the second floor was opened by a middle-aged woman. Bruno asked for 'Walter'. They were invited in. The woman explained that 'Walter' was at that moment at the Rue de Lafayette, but that he was expecting 'Thiéry' and would be back shortly.

Bruno and Stefan were shown into a barely furnished room which smelt of polish, and sat on a sofa made of imitation leather. Stefan was nervous: he longed to smoke. He had no cigarettes in his pocket; nor had Bruno. 'I'll go and buy some,' said Stefan. 'I'll be back in a minute.'

'Don't be long,' said Bruno. 'We may have to move on as soon as "Walter" arrives.'

Stefan let himself out of the flat, went down the stairs, crossed the courtyard and went under the arch and into the street. Within fifty yards he found a *tabac*, bought five packets of cigarettes, and went back towards the flat where Bruno was waiting for him.

He had got halfway across the courtyard when he saw, standing by the doorway he had to enter, a dog. Stefan faltered. He took some steps forward but the dog growled, its hackles rose and Stefan stopped again.

The dog was large and black – a retriever of some sort crossed with a gutter mongrel. It had a crazed, delinquent look in its orange eyes, and looked at Stefan as if it were a lion about to leap on a sheep.

'This is absurd,' Stefan said to himself. He took a step forward. The dog growled again. He took a step back. 'I am not afraid of a dog,' he said to himself, looking back over his shoulder to see if the concierge could be called to his assistance. There was no one there. He looked back at the dog . . . at its teeth. Their eyes met – the dog's and the Pole's. The dog's were implacable. Stefan turned and went back into the street. He went to a café opposite, ordered a cup of coffee and paid for it. He thought to himself that he could wait for 'Walter' to enter the house: when he did, he could run after him. But ten minutes passed, then a quarter of an hour, and no one went in to the door opposite. A woman appeared carrying her shopping: she rang the bell to open the door. Stefan leapt up, crossed the street and entered through the door just in time to see the woman turn away from the courtyard and go up the first flight of steps.

He went into the courtyard. The dog still sat at the foot of the stairs. He looked up towards the sky and the flat where Bruno was waiting for him, then at the dog. He opened his mouth to shout, but no sound came forth. He turned, went back to the street and walked away towards the Opéra.

Two

On the same day that Krystyna received a letter from Bruno in Albacete, Rachel received one from Stefan in Paris; and since the letter from Spain had taken longer to reach Warsaw, it was evident to them both that Bruno and Stefan had parted company.

Both letters referred obliquely to this separation but neither explained it. Bruno said merely that 'Stefan has stayed in Paris for the time being, which I think is best'; and Stefan wrote to Rachel that: 'For the moment the writer has conquered the soldier. *Vive l'imagination: à bas la réalité*' – which made Rachel feel odd and stupid, because she had knitted him woollen gloves with a hole in the right hand to leave the trigger-finger free.

She was also enough of a literary critic to realize that though the letter was witty and affectionate – with elegant vignettes of Parisian life interspersed with personal reflections and avowals – it was all to dress up a request for money which came in the penultimate paragraph – money which she sent together with the news that she was pregnant.

All these things brought Rachel and Krystyna closer together. With feminine pragmatism they forgot that they had recently detested one another, and now met almost every evening when Rachel would help Krystyna with Teofil, and Krystyna would reassure Rachel about the baby she was expecting in seven or eight months' time. 'Of course Stefan will come back,' she said to her sister-in-law, 'and in the circumstances, it's probably just as well that he didn't go to Spain.'

'You don't think he'll stay in Paris?'

'He can't, can he, if you're having a baby?'

'Unless I joined him there . . .' Rachel said this with little conviction, and Krystyna, by not making any rejoinder, confirmed what Rachel knew quite well – that it would not be wise for her to go to Paris.

'Stefan was always funny,' said Krystyna – as if Rachel's thoughts had been spoken. 'Of course Papa was funny too. It's in the family, I'm afraid.'

'But you're so normal,' said Rachel.

'I had to be,' said Krystyna, without taking her eyes off the child's clothes which she was smoothing with a new electric iron.

When Mamuska was released from her duties downstairs to look after Teofil, Krystyna would go with Rachel to the Committee for Relief in Spain. As the Nationalists advanced towards Madrid, their agitation redoubled – and because it passed for a liberal cause, Krystyna even asked for and received contributions from her colleagues at Blomstein's – including Mr Blomstein himself.

She felt a special pride, and exercised a particular authority, among the other ladies on the Committee because it was known that Bruno was fighting in Spain. Indeed news leaked back that he had been made adjutant to Tadeusz Oppman, commander of the Polish Dabrowsky Battalion, which at that time was moving to the front in the siege of Madrid.

And because he was away and a hero, Bruno changed in her mind. She forgot his heavy body with its smell of sweat and importunate demands; she forgot the pedantic way in which he argued little points of domestic dispute; she forgot even, that he had left her in the dull pit of a monotonous life, and accepted the image that others projected of the courageous comrade who had sacrificed his happiness to fight in Spain.

But such is the paradoxical nature of women, that just as she forgot his body, she became aware of her own; and just as she idealized his image in her mind, the idea of another man slipped in beside it – not a specific man but the idea. She had never previously been particularly conscious of her body – indeed she was quite exceptional in combining such a graceful figure and lovely face with so little self-admiration. There was no full-length mirror in the flat, but only a looking-glass in the hall; and, above the basin in the bathroom, a mirror which Bruno used for shaving and Krystyna to tidy her hair or make up her face in the morning before going out to work.

She was almost wilful, too, in the way she refused to notice the glances of men in cafés or in the streets: and in the total contempt she directed at flirtatious customers at Blomstein's. It was extraordinary, then, that one evening, when she was changing after work into the slightly more casual clothes she wore for the Committee, she stopped while removing her stockings. The feeling of her own fingers on the inside of her legs produced a sudden and strong sensation all over her body. The stockings dropped onto the floor, and her hands came back to her legs – the fingers trailing up her thighs in a gesture that made the tingling, itching feeling in her groin mount to an intolerable pitch. She looked down and saw and admired her long legs: her hands became those of a man – a lover. They smoothed her stomach and went under her bodice. She lay back on the bed and inexorably her hands crept down her body to the mound of her pudenda, which was covered by the greying wool of her underpants, and kneaded that area of flesh – continuing rhythmically until she achieved the orgasm she had induced in herself.

It was only a day or two before she repeated this self-satisfying exercise of body and hands – and it might have sufficed as consolation for a woman whose husband was at war, had not other things happened – the first being Rachel's casual remark that she was glad she was pregnant 'because you feel less like it, don't you? Otherwise I'd go mad without Stefan.'

It was not a remark which called for any rejoinder – and Rachel had not intended to apply to anyone but herself: but having made the observation, she seemed to realize that it could equally well apply to Krystyna, so she glanced at her with a frank, feminine expression of sympathy and curiosity, but received only a blush in return. For a time, therefore, she said nothing more, but the curiosity grew and became so imperious that she did turn to Krystyna and asked her, in a particular tone of voice, whether she missed Bruno.

'Of course I miss him,' said Krystyna.

'No, I mean in *that* way.'

'Well,' said Krystyna – blushing and hesitating – 'yes, I suppose I do.'

'They're so lucky, aren't they, because they've got their fighting to distract them; or in Stefan's case, well, God knows what he's up to in Paris: probably visiting every brothel there is. But we're just stuck here with the same old life and no, well, love – if you see what I mean.'

Krystyna said nothing.

'Did you find that being pregnant put you off?'

'Yes, in a way.'

'I don't know how it happened, at least I do, but I'm glad it did because if it hadn't, I don't think I could have stayed faithful – not even with the best will in the world. I mean before I did it I never thought about it – at least not much – but once you get used to it, you really need it, don't you? I think so, anyway.' She glanced at Krystyna and giggled. 'Poor you,' she said. Then she added, with no pretence at disguising the connection: 'What do you think of that boy Jerzy at the Committee? He's pretty awful, isn't he, but rather nice. I mean, he's handsome, don't you think?'

Krystyna wrinkled up her nose. 'Not my type.'

'Well, if I wasn't pregnant, I promise you I'd find it difficult to resist him.'

It was true that this Jerzy – a conceited student of philology – was not the kind of man Krystyna found attractive. She considered herself to be as fastidious now as she had always been: and if it had taken her years to find an acceptable mate in Bruno, she was unlikely casually to accept a lover from among the idealistic youths on the Committee. She was unlikely, indeed, to accept a lover at all, since she was dedicated to her hero in Spain and more shocked than she appeared to be by Rachel's casual notion of fidelity.

On the other hand the idea had entered her mind like a worm into an apple. Her prudish purity was nibbled at each day and sometimes she smiled to herself, imagining a flirtation – only a flirtation – with someone or other – a customer, perhaps, or the student Jerzy or Michael M., the lecturer in mathematics who called on her one Sunday afternoon.

Krystyna was at first surprised and then flattered by his visit. Though he explained that Bruno had asked him, as an old friend from the days of the cell at the university, to make sure that she was well ('and what a charming duty to perform for such a brave man'), she knew that he was now an important person in both the Party and the Faculty of Science – an assistant professor and a candidate for the Central Committee of the Communist Party of Poland. She also wondered about the 'security aspect' of one member of a cell visiting another (for she still belonged to the same cell), which had once been considered so important: and then she worried suddenly about her own appearance and the tidiness of her living-room.

Assistant Professor Michael Mikolajczyk (to give him his full name) was dressed in a new grey flannel suit and as he sat down on the sofa he tweaked the crease of his trousers so that the cloth would not stretch at the knees. He seemed most self-assured: he never stopped talking, yet he never alluded to the Party or to the cell. Had a government agent been hiding behind the sofa, nothing whatsoever would have aroused his suspicions. Michael Mikolajczyk was so plausibly just an old friend of her absent husband.

The baby Teofil tottered across the room and the assistant professor took hold of his little hand and spoke soothingly in toddler's talk, while talking at the same time to the mother, Krystyna, about his own two children 'who are now almost grown up.' Krystyna made tea and brought that, together with some biscuits and some vodka with cups and glasses on a tray. She too played her part correctly and made no allusions to the cell or the Party, though they did talk about Spain and the threat to Madrid.

'So brave, Bruno,' said Michael Mikolajczyk, 'but hard for you too, isn't it, alone with the child?'

He looked at her and she intercepted the look, which was bland but calculating, and she blushed without understanding why. He was an ordinary man in appearance – small, plump and balding, with smooth skin on his cheeks and an aroma of pomade: but he had, all the same, some sort of physical presence. His suit was a little tight and he seemed in the fading light to bulge in many different places; and from these bulges there seemed to come some strange, hypnotic energy which Krystyna had never felt when she had studied him in the cell. He did nothing – nor did he say anything that he could not have said to her Aunt Cecylia – yet he gave a signal of some sort which was both invisible and obscene. She sensed it without seeing it; like pollen or musk it entered her body and made it heavy yet restless, and it was not until he rose to go – politely and properly – that she realized what it was: for as he took her hand to kiss it, he turned it and pressed his lips to her palm – and held them there; and she shyly let him taste the moistness of her skin.

That night she was alone. She went to bed early to read a book, but the hands which unbuttoned her clothes became once again a lover's hands, and then his hands – the hands of the plump, middle-aged Michael Mikolajczyk – and she rolled her head from side to side, and imagined that his bulging body was there on top of her. She smelt his pomade, which reminded her of incense, an incense of churches and the Virgin Mary, and for a moment she stopped but her body begged her hand to return and her hand obeyed. And as it did its work she longed for his fat, hot flesh to lie on top of her; and she imagined that it did, wriggling like a severed worm until it was over.

And when Michael Mikolajczyk invited her to go with him to a concert on the following Saturday night, she accepted – knowing quite well that when the music was over, and when they had been to a restaurant, he would take her somewhere and make her his mistress.

Three

In Paris Stefan had abandoned his socialist convictions just as a reptile sheds its skin. He had not betrayed them: he had simply stepped out of them as he walked away from the Rue de Chabrol thinking to himself: 'How can I fight in Spain if I can't face a dog?'

He reached the Jardin des Tuileries. It was a warm October morning – the sun, the leaves, the gravel, the sky all seemed to blend into a delightful setting for this moment of supreme liberty, which made Stefan suddenly so giddy that he had to sit down on a bench. He was free. He had achieved at last, in time, in space and within his own mind, what he had waited for all his life – one moment of total freedom. He was not hungry, he was not curious. He had no itch or ache to spoil the purity of his liberation.

Then all at once he wanted to write. He needed paper, a pen, a desk, a room, a hotel. He had left his suitcase with Bruno: but that was a detail. He took out his wallet to see how much money he had: it was enough. He walked out of the Tuileries, crossed the river, and went along the Left Bank to the Boulevard St Michel. There he bought a suitcase, then a pair of pyjamas, two shirts, underclothes, a toothbrush. After that he bought three student's notebooks, pen and ink and then found a cheap hotel where he took a small room under the roof.

What he wrote was nonsense. Chaos tumbled out of his mind; everything that had been held back by the dam of his Communist convictions now flooded out – pretentiousness, absurdity, obscenity, snobbery . . . Some of the longer pieces started coherently, but sooner or later they all 'degenerated' into nonsense, as if sense itself was slavery. And even his manner of writing was undisciplined. He carried his notebooks everywhere and scrawled in them in restaurants, on buses, or even in the middle of the night, standing to piss into his bidet.

He combined this inner chaos with a surface pose and some charm, so that the concierge at the hotel and the waiters in the restaurants and cafés all accepted him for what he was – a young Polish writer of aristocratic origins in reduced circumstances. And indeed when it came to writing a letter to Rachel (for some money), he showed again that he could communicate in a language understood by others when it was necessary.

He even made friends. There were other Poles everywhere, and somehow or other he ran into them: by the end of October he was part of a circle of young intellectuals – some Polish, some French – which met at the Deux Magots, and talked about God, Art, Love, Reality and Revolution.

'You are *there*,' Stefan liked to say to some timid young girl, brought by a Jerzy, Jan or Tadeusz, while pointing to the far side of the café.

'I beg your pardon?'

'You are not here, sitting beside me, but *there* by the bar.'

'I am not there. I am here.'

'No, you are there.'

'How can I be there when I am here?'
'You may think you are here, but you are there.'
'I *know* I am here.'
'Delusion.'
'You can see that I am here.'
'Mirage.'
And so on late into the night.

There came a time when Stefan became the centre of the group. He entertained them with the outrageous absurdity of his non-convictions. He made mincemeat of the Marxists; and the more serious revolutionaries sat at a rival table on the other side of the café. As October came to an end and November started, Madrid became besieged by the fascists and emotions rose in the Deux Magots. The Leftists would send their champions to challenge Stefan, but with the arguments he had used against Bruno in Warsaw, Stefan would repel them and each would retire to his own camp, scarlet about the ears at his mockery of liberty, justice and the proletariat.

After a time he ran out of money. He did not care to ask Rachel for more in case it arrived, as had the first, with news like that of her pregnancy. He therefore took a job teaching Polish history and literature to the son and daughter of some rich émigrés who lived in the Bois de Boulogne.

For a time no one knew that he was married, and he seemed to have forgotten it himself. His friends were mostly students, and he was normally assumed to be a student himself. He was, after all, only twenty-three years old and he behaved sometimes as if he were younger. It was as if he had caged maturity in his unconscious, for it was only in dreams that he was anxious – anxious about Rachel, Krystyna and his unborn child: and he awoke occasionally with the image in his mind of Bruno's blood-stained body lying in a gutter in Madrid; but 'dreams are dull' was one of his *bons mots* at the Deux Magots, and he would not bore his friends or himself with a re-run.

Four

News seeped through Europe about events in Spain. One third of the XI International Brigade had already been killed in Madrid: a whole company of Poles from the Dabrowsky Battalion died defending the Casa de Velazquez in the University City, but Bruno was still alive. Krystyna knew this from Michael Mikolajczyk, who had news through the Party.

At the beginning of December she received a letter from her husband which was stained with dirt and sweat. 'I dream of Christmas in Poland with you and little Teofil – of good, crisp snow and proper cold – not the nasty wind which torments us here. I long for you: if I had known how painful it would be, I would never have gone, but now I cannot return until it is over. So many friends, so quickly made, have already gone – not home, but into the ditches we dig for graves. They are dead but we cannot leave them . . .' Krystyna read this letter with dry eyes and put it into a little drawer in her dressing table: the photograph of Bruno which she kept under the glass top of the dressing table was obscured by her powder compact.

In mid-December news came of a new Nationalist offensive around Madrid. Mrs Mikolajczyk, the wife of Krystyna's lover, had already left Warsaw for the Christmas holidays, and Krystyna stood in her slip in the bedroom of the flat where she had come so often for the meetings of the cell, studying a map of Spain with Michael's arm around her shoulders and his hand holding her breast. His map was better than the one at the Committee: it showed the village of Villanueva and the Corunna road. Michael described how the Dabrowsky and Thaelmann Battalions had taken the town of Boadilla – his plump finger left her breast to point to it on the map – and then lost it again, leaving a hundred men dead: 'but not Bruno. He escaped. They say he has been fighting extremely well. They want him for the new XIV Brigade but Oppman won't let him go.'

Michael spoke about Bruno as if Bruno was her brother, and she listened with the same detachment until she felt his thighs press against her buttocks, and his hand roam from her breast.

It was late that night when Krystyna got back to Sluzewska Street. She let herself into her flat where Mamuska was dozing in an armchair, and touched her arm. 'I'm back,' she said.

The old woman started, and then looked cross. 'It's a fine time to come home . . . been politicking, have you? That's right. Save the world, but don't think of an old lady who has to get up at five . . .'

'I'm sorry,' said Krystyna in a tone more penitent than usual – which led the old peasant to dart a suspicious look at her.

'Or something else, was it, that you've been doing?'

'No,' said Krystyna. 'Politics . . .' But as she spoke, she knew it was useless, that the combination in old Mamuska of strong, accurate intuition and prurient suspicion led her straight on the scent to Krystyna's adultery.

'Politics, politics,' said Mamuska, shuffling towards the door. 'If you ask me, it's an excuse for Godless behaviour by un-Christian people . . . Oh, you laugh at me, an old lady who can't read or write, but I know right from wrong, yes I do, and you don't go to Mass on Sunday but you stay up all night doing sinful things . . .' She left the flat and slammed the door.

Krystyna sat back in the chair. She was tired, and she shrivelled up inside to think that Mamuska might realize—or her Aunt Cecylia. She did not even want Rachel to know: in principle she might be sympathetic but she would be shocked that it was Michael Mikolajczyk. Rachel had once remarked that his breath smelt, and then had wrinkled up her nose: so how could she understand . . . But then how could Rachel find out? How could anyone know? They were hardly ever seen together. And that hateful Mamuska was just a frustrated, suspicious old bag who sniffed sex everywhere because she had never had any herself . . . And anyway, why shouldn't she? She had been left in this dustbin by Bruno while he went off to perform heroics, so he had no right to condemn her. And who else could condemn her but Bruno? Not the Party, certainly, because Lenin had no views on adultery. And Michael was a Party member. And the Party was not the Church. No. She refused to feel guilty when she was doing nothing wrong – just because she had had a repressive Catholic upbringing with a fetish about purity and virginity . . . No, she must fight against guilt. Ignore it. Suppress it. Why shouldn't she fuck if she felt like it? And why not with Michael? He was not attractive but he was patient, he took trouble, he was kind. He never left her wanting more or wishing it had not happened – except that she did wish it had not happened, but that was different, that was guilt, and she fought against guilt; only now she was so tired, and when you are tired it is hard to fight, and she did feel guilty, she felt wretched and awful, and she wished she had never touched Michael or touched herself. She wished she had waited for Bruno, who was clumsy but good and kind and loved her sincerely and loved Teofil . . .

'I must go to bed,' she said to herself. She rose and went to look at her child. He had kicked off his covers; she leant over the cot to put them straight, and blinked away some tears to look at his little face – Mongolian in slumber. 'I'm so sorry,' she whispered. 'I'm so sorry.' Then she turned away and went to bed.

Five

Like his sister, Stefan felt free of all obligation, but did not exercise this freedom. He was sometimes taunted by the Leftists in the Deux Magots with his negative behaviour. 'You are not even a fascist,' they said. 'You are nothing but a bag of wind.'

Whereupon Stefan would reply that: 'Behaviour itself is slavery. Each act is a link in the chain which binds you . . . Pure freedom is pure idleness. And anyway, look at you, drinking coffee in the Deux Magots. Why aren't you out there, building Heaven on earth?'

Though able to construct theories like this to justify his own behaviour, it would have been more precise if Stefan had admitted to his friends what he knew himself – that all conscious acts require either necessity or will to inspire them; and that while Stefan had a small amount of the former to mould his day, there was none of the latter. Even his writing now subsided from futility. Only the image of Onufry's whore lingered in his mind to stimulate him.

Then, quite gradually, he became interested in the brother and sister, the children of the Polish émigrés, whose tutor he had been for the past two months. Though the children of a Polish mother and a Polish father, they both went to French schools – the boy to a lycée and the girl to a convent. Stefan was employed to come to their home in the evening, or on a Saturday morning, to teach them something of Polish history and literature. Later, with their parents' permission, they met Stefan at the Deux Magots: their father liked the idea that they move in a Polish circle of friends. It was difficult to see what benefit these quiet, sensitive adolescents could derive from the farcical conversation of their fellow-expatriates – but they came quite regularly two or three times a week and listened; and it was just this politeness and timidity which attracted Stefan. Their youth disturbed and excited him, and (increasingly) he ignored his other friends and talked to them.

The girl, Lise, was an excellent subject for his philosophical conversations ('You are there' 'Oh no, I am here') and the boy, Ladislas, listened to Stefan and laughed at him with irresistible deference. He was as delicate as his sister: their faces were both girlish but without the coquettishness of women. They were hermaphroditic, and their age too was ambiguous. In ways they were children, and in other ways grown-up. They were a riddle which interested Stefan, and then obsessed him. They were brother and sister and so a couple, loving one another, yet unaware of their bodies. Both were beautiful yet unconscious of it; and their beauty, though bodily, was unerotic.

Stefan's writing now became centred on Ladislas and Lise. He started a story in the style of the 'Blood of the Walsungs', and then wrote down questions in his notebook.

What does she think of his body? Would he be angry if someone kissed her? Or would he laugh (like a child)? When she is in pain, does she run to him? Or to her mother? Or to no one? How would she react to a sexual gesture? How would he? Is his penis delicate and fragile like his wrists? Or is it the only part of him which is monstrous and strong – like the genitals of a baby when it is born?

These thoughts of Stefan's were accompanied by an odd longing – not to do anything to Ladislas or Lise, but to have things done to them. He who had been freed from passions was now possessed by a prurient curiosity. He wanted to devour the brother and sister – devour, digest and spit out the skins. Without knowing what he had in mind, he planned to meet them outside the confines of the Deux Magots – to make an assignation in the Luxembourg Gardens and then take them to the room of some hotel – not his room but some other which he would take under another name. But before putting this plan into action he tried to imagine what would happen between the three of them. He took a pen and his notebook and wrote in the first person this fragment of narrative.

They are waiting on the bench; that is, they are there before me and I hesitate under a tree, watching them smile and laugh, before advancing to make myself known. Then I ask them what they would like to do. They shrug their shoulders, look at one another, smile, laugh, and say they do not care. We have a drink on the Boulevard St Michel and then find ourselves in the room I have reserved in a small hotel – a *chambre de bonne* on the top floor. The two of them sit on the bed. I sit on a chair. We talk and talk – about their father and then their mother: then, as the light fades, our talk becomes more personal, more intimate. Both pairs of eyes – young eyes – become wide and excited. They feel that something is about to happen to them – something adult. I ask them what they think of me. The boy says he likes me and that he would do anything for me. The girl agrees. 'Would you, for instance,' I ask the boy, 'would you take off your sister's watch?'

She holds out her wrist and gently he removes the watch and holds it to his ear to listen to the ticking.

'And you?' I say to Lise. 'Would you do something gross?'

'Like what?' she asks. 'Like this?' She sticks out her tongue – a little pink tongue.

'Worse.'

'Just say.'

'Then undo the buttons of your brother's trousers.'

She shrugs. 'Why not?' She leans across and undoes his buttons – quickly and casually. He lies back and watches her fingers.

'There,' she says.

'Now see what's inside,' I say.

Again, with a gesture that is *matter of fact*, she leans across, digs under the layers of cloth, and tries to bring out his penis; but it is erect. She needs her other hand to prise it out.

'There you are,' she says.

Ladislas looks at me with a smile. 'Is that what you expected?' he asks.

'Do you like your sister to touch it?' I ask.

'I don't know. It's never happened before.'

'Touch it,' I say to Lise. 'Touch it softly, there at the end.'

She does as she is told, tickling the red-blue skin, moving her fingers round and round, watching it bend and bulge until it spits out across the room.

'Look at that,' she says, wide-eyed. 'Did you see that? Look, on the wall. I never saw that before.'

Later . . . Later . . . She too is undressed. They are both naked. Only I wear my clothes – all my clothes. 'Take the knife,' I say to her.

'What for?' she asks.

'Are you no longer obedient?'

'I've done a lot already. And look, Ladislas has gone stiff again. Let's play that game where it hits the wall.'

'I have another one,' I say.

'I'll take the knife,' says Ladislas. 'What shall I do with it?'

'Cut a little hole in her skin.'

'In Lise's skin?'

'Yes.'

'But won't it hurt?' he asks.

'I don't want to be hurt,' she says.

'Only a little. Hardly at all. Like a vaccination.'

164

'But why?' she asks.

'Think, how pretty. A drop of red blood on your pale skin.'

'Where?' asks Lise. 'Here on my hand? Or my tummy?'

'Your tummy, yes,' I say.

She lies back and looks through her little breasts at her small stomach. 'Go on, then,' she says to Ladislas. 'Make a cut as he says.'

Ladislas takes the knife – a sharp, kitchen knife which I have bought at an ironmonger's. He jabs lightly at his sister's stomach.

'Ouch,' she says.

'Don't just prod her,' I say. 'Move the knife.'

He pushes and cuts and suddenly the knife goes in.

'Hey, now you're really hurting me,' says Lise, and she starts to cry.

'You've had your fun,' says Ladislas. 'It's my turn now.' He pushes and cuts again. She turns away. He stabs. I watch. He holds her by the hair and pushes the knife into her back above the kidneys. She screams. She clutches at the curtains: she turns back towards me. I watch. He stabs and stabs again, his eyes wide and excited, his penis erect until he screeches and arches and ejaculates over her and she lies twitching, cooling, gashed and dead.

Then he brushes back his hair with his blood-stained hands. 'But she is dead,' he says to me.

'I'm afraid so,' I say.

'I didn't mean to do that.'

'Of course not,' I say, 'but one thing leads to another . . .'

'I know.' He seems pensive. I am silent. 'But what shall I do now?' he asks.

'There isn't much choice,' I say. 'Prison. The mad house. The guillotine. Shame or . . .'

'Or what?'

I glance at the window.

'Yes,' he says. 'It would be better, I think. For Mama.' He stands, puts on his trousers and a shirt, makes sure that the buttons are secure and goes to the window. Before opening it he turns back to me and says: 'You were a friend of us both, weren't you?'

'Yes,' I say.

He pauses, laughs, then opens the window and jumps out. I watch: then I leave the hotel without being seen.

Six

The day after he had written this passage in his notebook Stefan started on his journey back to Warsaw. He travelled by Zurich, Vienna, Cracow – and as he crossed into Poland he saw his native country with a fresh eye; he saw how shabby it was, how incompetent and officious.

Rachel met him at the station, and at once he noticed her belly. She kissed him cheerfully and he felt it press against his stomach. He managed a smile before his face stared straight ahead and set in the Kornowski grimace.

Rachel's behaviour was firm, consistent, flawless. She had discussed it with Krystyna because it was not easy, after all, to deal with a warrior's return when he had not been to the war. 'It will be difficult for Stefan . . . psychologically,' she had said. 'I shall behave as if he has been skiing in Zakopane.' And this was what she did – like a mother whose son has just returned from his first holiday on his own. 'How was it? Goodness, I envy you Paris in spring. Quite right to have stayed. Who knows when you'll get another chance – if there's a war, as everyone seems to think, though I don't think there will be because the British and French will put their foot down sooner or later . . . Did you go to the Louvre? Every day? Every other day? I'd love to see it. I dare say I will . . .'

Rachel had developed a woman's knack of talking fast to conceal silence. She had also inherited her father's habit of asking questions – quite specific questions – without waiting for an answer. It suited Stefan, whose thoughts were on the shabbiness of Warsaw, the grotesque shape of Rachel and the image of Lise's body lying pale, slender, blood-stained.

And yet the friendly smell of cabbage and cigarettes, the old ladies carrying their bags, the self-important priests, the peasants shuffling ill-at-ease in the city streets – it all had a warmth and familiarity. Even Rachel's determined cheerfulness began to penetrate his icy mind, and by the time they had got back to their flat he felt quite well disposed towards her. He sat back in an armchair, sighed, smiled and even remarked that it was 'good to be home'. Whereupon Rachel looked at him for the irony in his expression and, seeing none, stopped talking for the first time since he had arrived.

'It must be awkward for you,' said Stefan.

'Why?'

'Because I didn't go to Spain.'

'Who cares? It doesn't matter. And what does it mean? It means you know more than others – Bruno said so in a letter. He said you knew how terrible it would be because you could imagine it; that imagination is like prophecy; that if he could have seen how it would be, he would never have gone.'

Stefan said nothing.

'He said it, I promise,' said Rachel. 'Krysia showed me the letter. She'll show it to you.'

'I'm sure he said it,' said Stefan. 'And I'm sure he meant it.'

'He has had a dreadful time,' said Rachel.

'Is he wounded?'

'No. But people have died all around him.'

There was a pause. Rachel clambered to her feet. 'I'll make some tea,' she said. She went into the kitchen. Stefan too stood to go and change out of the clothes he was wearing, which were sticky after so many days in a train.

When they met again, over the tea, Stefan looked at Rachel and asked her what she had been doing.

'Oh, this and that. Not much, really. One gets tired.' She glanced at her belly.

'I should have been here,' he muttered.

'No, you shouldn't. It's my business . . . It was my fault. After all, we weren't going to have children and now they say, well, it might even be twins.' She looked timidly at Stefan.

'That should be interesting,' he said, then stood and started to walk up and down the room. 'Have you been working for the Party?' he asked.

'The Committee For Relief in Spain,' she said. 'Officially it's not the Party, but that's what we were told to do.'

'And Krysia?'

'The same.'

'What about the cell?'

'Suspended, but we see Michael . . .'

'Mikolajczyk? Why?'

'Well, Krysia sees him.'

Stefan stopped. 'I didn't think she knew him.'

'She didn't. Only in the cell. But he came around. Evidently Bruno asked him to keep an eye on her.'

Stefan sniffed, then glanced at Rachel. Her expression explained. He sniffed again. 'And Teofil?' he asked.

'He's all right.'

'I'm leaving the Party,' he said abruptly.

'I thought you probably would,' she said.

'It may be awkward for you.'

'I'll leave too.'

'You don't have to.'

'I think I want to.'

'Why?'

She blushed. 'Do you remember Jan?'

'Of course.'

'He was killed . . . Not in Spain. In Russia.'

'I know.'

'As a spy.'

'Yes.'

'That's absurd, isn't it?'

Stefan shrugged his shoulders. 'It's unlikely.'

'It's absurd.'

'Good. Then we'll leave together.'

'What will happen?' asked Rachel.

'I don't know. We're not important. And if we have trouble . . .' – he grimaced – 'perhaps Krysia can use her influence with her new friend.'

That night, in bed, Rachel offered her bulbous body to her husband. 'You can, you know,' she said. 'It isn't bad for the baby.' But Stefan said that he was tired after the journey, then swallowed, and turned to face the wall.

After his return to Warsaw, Stefan went frequently – two or three times a week – to call on his Aunt Cecylia in Sluzewska Street, and then climb the three flights of stairs to Krystyna's flat – to talk to her and play with Teofil. In his absence the child had grown from a baby into a little boy who could both walk and talk, and flattered Stefan by remembering him. He called him 'Onka' because Krystyna had said that Stefan was his uncle: and whenever Stefan arrived at the flat, Teofil would rush to meet him shouting: 'Onka coming, Onka coming . . .' And then he would wait, beaming, for Stefan to grab him, hug him, twirl him and hold him upside down – small, everyday pastimes, but a joy for both the child and the man.

It was Teofil who reconciled Stefan to the idea of his own child, who would come into the world in a month or so. He was a boy of exceptional beauty – a blend of Bruno's strength and Krystyna's grace – with large eyes, long lashes and on most occasions a cheerful, trusting smile. Even Stefan, the reticent and mysterious uncle, found it impossible to ignore him: even in his most pessimistic moods Stefan was made to laugh by his nephew's mistakes of speech – by the way, for example, a hedgehog became a heg-hodge – or by the manner in which he emptied his mug of milk into his bowl of soup with such a deliberate and taunting smile.

Of course Teofil was not an angel. There were times when he flew into a rage and screamed and struggled with Mamuska or Krystyna; when he would not go to bed; or would not eat his food; or would not wear this or that shirt or pair of socks, and had to wear another. He missed his father – he missed him acutely – and could not understand why he was not there. 'Dadda's in Spain,' he would say: and 'Onka's come back from Spain. When Dadda come back from Spain?' 'Soon,' they would say, 'soon my little one,' and then look away to avoid his eyes, which the child, of course, noticed.

There was one aspect of Teofil's behaviour which was consistently bad. Whenever Michael Mikolajczyk came to the flat (as he did now on occasions) Teofil would turn sour. He refused to be dandled on the professor's knee: he would not even let himself be turned upside down. He would sulk, and cling to his mother's skirts, causing her to stumble with the coffee tray, lose her temper, slap Teofil which made him cry – in other words cause chaos and create an unpleasant atmosphere.

There was an occasion when Stefan was able to observe this. One Sunday he and Rachel had had lunch with Krystyna in her flat, had lingered afterwards and so had overlapped with Michael Mikolajczyk, who had called in around four. Rachel was overexcited that afternoon. She had talked and talked and (unlike Stefan) had failed to notice that Krystyna was fidgeting and distracted, and kept glancing at the door. When the doorbell rang, Krystyna glanced at Stefan and blushed. He looked away, pretending not to have noticed.

'Who can that be?' Krystyna asked Teofil in a baby voice. She stood to go to the door. Teofil did not answer her, but he seemed to have a good idea whom to expect. He went to the doorway of the living-room and, half-hiding behind the frame, waited and watched. Sure enough, they heard the door open, then a quick mumbled remark, then a loud, rich voice saying: 'I hope you don't mind my calling in. I was passing and thought I would see how you were getting along. Now, Teofil, my boy...'

Teofil turned and ran to his Uncle Stefan. Michael Mikolajczyk walked into the living-room: he nodded to Stefan and Rachel, and held out his hand to take Rachel's and kiss it, but could not conceal the irritation expressed in his eyes. 'How nice, comrades,' he said. 'What a pleasant surprise.'

Krystyna came back into the room – cringing slightly – and offered coffee to Michael Mikolajczyk in a formal, subdued way. Then they all sat around in silence, broken occasionally by a remark from Michael and a reply from Krystyna. Stefan was silent, and for once Rachel could think of nothing to say.

Eventually Michael turned to Krystyna and said, in a conspiratorial tone of voice: 'I have some news of Bruno.'

Krystyna raised her head. 'Is he all right?'

'Yes, quite all right,' said Michael. 'They're keeping him in Barcelona. They say he's as good at administration as he is at fighting ...'

'Thank God,' said Krystyna.

'What do you mean by administration?' asked Stefan – the glowering Teofil standing between his knees.

'I'm not quite sure,' said Michael, smoothing back the hair that grew at the sides of his balding head.

'I hope it isn't a euphemism for the NKVD,' said Stefan.

Michael said nothing.

'There are stories of torture and assassination . . .' Stefan began.

'For God's sake, Stefan,' said Krystyna. 'How can you say such a thing?'

'Only in the fascist press,' said Mikolajczyk, 'which I dare say you read now that you have left the Party.'

'How can you believe that propaganda?' asked Krystyna.

Stefan shrugged his shoulders, but Rachel suddenly blurted out: 'Why did they kill Jan?'

Michael looked astonished. His chin wobbled. 'Jan? Well, he was a spy . . .'

'He wasn't,' said Rachel.

'Do you know better than the Party?' asked Michael. He turned away from Rachel, and before she could reply he said to Krystyna: 'I was thinking of a visit to Wilanow and wondered if you would like to come with me.'

Krystyna glanced at Stefan, blushed again, then said: 'Yes, we'd love to, wouldn't we, Teofil?'

'Me stay with Onka,' said Teofil, gripping Stefan's knees.

'No, dear,' said Krystyna, crossing towards her child. 'Uncle Stefan's going home.'

'Me stay with Onka,' Teofil said again.

'Come on, Stefan,' said Rachel – her face still set in a scowl. 'We'd better go.'

Stefan did not move: he was caught in the tiny grip of Teofil.

'Come on, dear,' said Krystyna again, stooping to pick up Teofil.

'No, no, no, no,' he screamed as she lifted him into the air. 'Me stay with Onka. No, not go with that man.'

'Don't be silly,' said Krystyna, her voice quivering.

'No, no, no, not that man,' said Teofil, kicking his legs, his voice rising to a hysterical pitch. 'That man nasty. Me stay with Onka.'

And so it continued for a while, the mother firm on the surface but frantic underneath; the child ranting and wild in

171

his behaviour, but totally determined to stay with his uncle, who smiled disdainfully at the whole situation.

The assistant professor intervened. An idea seemed to enter his head, and he said: 'Why not leave the boy with Stefan? You could collect him later, perhaps?' And so it was arranged that Stefan and Rachel took Teofil to the park while Michael went with Krystyna to the palace at Wilanow.

It was a time when everyone read newspapers and listened to the radio – to the news, then to the lulling melodies of Kiepura, then to the news again – the change of government in Spain, the Nationalist offensive against the Basques, the shuffling of the non-intervention committee, the speeches of Hitler, the deliberations of the League of Nations, the pronouncements of the Comintern . . . and in everyone's mind there was the thought of war.

And yet everything has its opposite, and as the situation in the world at large grew more ominous, the literary and artistic circles in Warsaw grew more varied, frivolous and obscure; and Stefan, now freed from ideological restraint, became known as the most seriously frivolous and lucidly obscure of all young writers of the Polish avant-garde. His six months in Paris gave him a certain authority: 'But no one is writing that sort of thing these days,' he would say to throw some young adversary into confusion.

His own aesthetic theory was rambling and inconsistent, but then inconsistency was consistent with his theory. 'Art must express ideas, but then the ideas themselves must be works of art – freed from logic, sense, rationality. Artistic truth is too deep to be understood: it is absorbed by the subconscious . . .' etc. All this expounded at length in the Café Ziemianska while Rachel grew fatter and her father paid their bills.

It was typical of the times that Stefan's literary reputation grew while he wrote little and published even less. A short, absurdist story entitled 'Elizabeth Hoepner Takes an Aspirin with her Tea' was published in *Wiadomosci Literackie*, and he began to review for the *Kurier Poranny*; and indeed to the younger intellectuals – Gombrowicz's 'dishevelled thinkers, starving young poets, ragged dreamers' – he was quite a figure of the literary establishment.

Rachel kept out of his way: she was content that he came home each night and went with her to her parents' home at weekends. His story and his reviews were read at Sluzewska Street by Aunt Cecylia, who said that she did not understand them, and by Krystyna who made no comment at all. She was disturbed by Stefan's new role: she was even a little envious of his literary life, which she imagined to be more entertaining than the earnest gatherings of Party members.

One evening in early June she went with Michael Mikolajczyk to see a film, and as they came out of the cinema she said: 'Let's go to the Ziemianska and have a look at Stefan's bohemian friends.'

'Why not?' said Michael, taking her arm. 'It might be amusing . . . certainly it might be amusing, though I doubt that he'll be pleased to see *me* . . .'

'We've as much right to go there as he has,' said Krystyna. 'And we needn't sit down at the same table.'

They walked down the Nowy Swiat, arm in arm, assuming that people would assume that they were what they were not – friends, colleagues, ideological companions, but not lovers. They were recognized every now and then – by a student or a colleague of the professor's; and if they stopped, Michael would introduce Krystyna as: 'Mrs Kaczmarek . . . her husband, you know, is in Spain.' But everyone knew – everyone knows. Especially in a city like Warsaw.

They entered the Café Ziemianska. It was packed with people – their voices and cigarette smoke swirling around the waiters who swung to and fro between the tables, snatching up dirty glasses, taking money, giving change, disappearing, then reappearing carrying trays piled with tea, coffee, beer, cheesecake . . .

In the far corner the chairs around three tables had been formed into a semicircle like a small auditorium and there, in the centre, was Stefan. On a bench facing this literary circle there were places free, and Krystyna and Michael sat down – nearer to Stefan than they had intended but too far to hear what he was saying. Krystyna watched him all the same, amused by his gestures: he sat back, away from his table, with his legs crossed. He talked with a scornful expression on his face, gesticulating, grimacing, smiling, pointing, wincing . . .

Five or six others argued with him – his face darted from one to the other, and then suddenly he saw Krystyna. He stopped: his face and body seemed paralysed for a moment. One or two of the others turned to see what it was that had caught his eye: but by then Stefan had resumed as if nothing had happened.

In some circumstances it is worse to be ignored than insulted – or it amounts to the same thing – and it is more difficult to react. Krystyna felt furious and humiliated that her brother had chosen to behave as if she were not there; and Michael beside her felt embarrassed but talked as if nothing had happened. She replied to what he said in a half-interested, distracted way: she was shocked by her anger and shame, her disappointment and outrage; and while keeping up the talk about the leisure habits of the bourgeoisie – or whatever the subject of that particular impromptu lecture by the professor – she was frantically analysing her emotions and coming to realize that she had hoped to join in Stefan's circle because she was decidedly bored by her plump, conceited lover. 'And it is because of Michael that he ignores me; he is not ashamed of me, but he is ashamed of Michael because Michael is old and academic. And he's embarrassed because Rachel has told him that I sleep with Michael, but he's no right to think that because he can't know that I do, and it's wicked of him to assume it just because I'm seen with Michael in the Ziemianska. What malicious tongues people have . . .' And so on, with Michael's deflated voice going on and on about Veblen's theory of the leisure class and its relationship to Marx's theory of alienation – like a base accompaniment to her staccato tune.

They did not stay long in the café. They then went through the pantomime which was necessary when Mrs Mikolajczyk was in Warsaw. They returned to Sluzewska Street. They parted. Michael walked away while Krystyna went in, relieved Mamuska, waited for ten minutes, then went down again to open the door for Michael, who by this time had returned. Together they climbed the stairs to the flat. Then Krystyna, having reassured herself that Teofil was asleep, would go to the bathroom to prepare herself for the practised performance of Michael Mikolajczyk on her marriage bed. 'Perhaps,' she thought, as she looked in the mirror and removed her ear-rings, 'perhaps dull men make good lovers and interesting men make bad ones.'

At two in the morning Michael left Sluzewska Street: he had, after all, a wife and two children. At half past six, Krystyna rose as usual, made breakfast for Teofil and herself, then handed him over to Mamuska and left for work. When she returned at seven, she found Stefan with Teofil: Mamuska had gone downstairs.

'You saw me, didn't you?' she said to him immediately.

'Where?' he asked.

'At the Ziemianska.'

'Ah. There.'

'Didn't you?'

'I did.'

'But you pretended not to.'

A Kornowski grimace. 'I didn't know whether . . . with the professor . . .'

'I would like to have met your friends.'

Stefan waved his hands vaguely. 'They're not friends, really . . .'

'I should like to have met them.'

'Well come with me this evening . . .'

'I wanted to meet them yesterday.'

'But the professor . . .'

'What's wrong with him? He's been very kind to me. Or do you object to Communists now?' She put down her bag, took a precious (Jezow) saucer out of Teofil's hand, and sat down.

'Of course not,' said Stefan. 'But there's something about him . . . something fleshy, obscene . . .'

Krystyna blushed. 'I hope you haven't heard anything . . . about me and him. I know there's gossip.'

'Isn't it true?'

She blushed again. 'And what if it is? What right have you to criticize?'

'I didn't . . .'

'You swan off with Bruno and leave me stuck here – bored, bored to death, and alone. Can you imagine what it's like working all day at the same place – for seven years now I've

175

worked for Blomstein's – with only a child and two old women to keep me company in the evenings . . .'

'But you had the Party.'

'That's boring too. But Michael is . . . well, cultivated and he takes me to concerts and the opera and to restaurants . . .'

Stefan was silent.

'And what if I do sleep with him? Why shouldn't I? It's only bourgeois, Catholic morality which says that I shouldn't.'

Stefan opened his mouth to say something but Krystyna went on: 'You're a hypocrite, that's what you are. At least Mamuska is a Catholic, and by her standards I'm a whore. You're meant to be free of all that but you're not. You think I'm a whore too, don't you? Say so. Admit it.'

Stefan shrugged his shoulders. 'I like whores,' he said, 'but I don't like Michael Mikolajczyk.'

'Well I do,' said Krystyna, and she burst into tears. Teofil, the child, looked at her in amazement. She took out a handkerchief, wiped her nose, then said: 'I do like him. He's so kind and patient. I'd have gone mad without him. But sometimes I feel, well, guilty I suppose. I think of Bruno . . . but it isn't wrong, is it? Bruno would understand. We're all emancipated. How can it be wrong? Just two bodies? There's no God: society is corrupt. Right and wrong are political and historical concepts . . . That's true, isn't it, Stefan?'

Stefan shrugged his shoulders.

'But *you* told me.'

'What?'

'That God doesn't exist.'

'God? Of course God doesn't exist. That's certain, anyway. But as for all the rest – history, society, adultery . . .'

Krystyna sniffed. 'Don't call it that.' She sniffed again. 'It's love, not adultery.' She stood up. 'Has Teofil eaten anything?' She turned to her child. 'Have you eaten anything, my little darling? Would you like some of that lovely soup that Mama made yesterday?'

Rachel grew to an enormous size and, since she could hardly take care of herself, she moved to her parents' home near the Lazienki Park. Stefan remained in the flat, but he had lunch every day with Rachel and her mother. He was witty, solicitous and looked forward to the confinement with a curiosity that passed for excitement.

A little struggle was going on between Rachel and her mother about how long *after* the birth Rachel and the child or children (twins were now thought likely) would spend in the parental home. Rachel wanted to escape from her mother as soon as possible, and insisted that she could manage quite well in the flat if she hired a nurse. Mrs Zamojska begged her to remain for 'at least a month' where she was now – 'so much more comfortable with the servants – *les domestiques*' – she turned to Stefan – '*tout est si facile ici, tandis que chez vous . . . Et pense-toi, chérie, à ton pauvre mari . . . réveillé chaque nuit – et lui avec son travail si important.*' She too had seen his story in the *Wiadomosci Literackie* and had been immensely proud.

Certainly, Stefan did not look forward to the cries of his child in the middle of the night, so he did not press Rachel one way or the other. His thoughts were, more than anything, on his little nephew: his dreams were of a son like Teofil with a touch more Kornowski, perhaps, but the same charm and good looks: and when Rachel eventually went into hospital he had a place prepared for this son in his mind just as solid and real as the silk-lined cot in the house near the Lazienki Park.

Like most men he was indifferent to the atrocious sufferings of his wife as she produced first one, and then a second child. He went to visit her on the first day after the delivery, walking down the corridors of the hospital with springing footsteps, his nose out in front, seeking the scent of this new experience of paternity.

In the private room he kissed his wife – weak and yellow on her bed. Then he sat on a chair and waited while the nurse was sent to fetch the new-born babies.

'There is a boy and a girl,' said Rachel.

'Delightful,' said Stefan, staring out of the window – then glancing at the door. 'One of each . . . it couldn't be better arranged.'

As he spoke the nurse came in, shoving the door open with her hip and carrying a child in each arm. Stefan half-stood to greet his progeny. He looked into the two little faces under black hair which poked out from the two bundles – and then started back: for staring back at him were miniature replicas of his father-in-law, the surgeon.

'But which is mine?' he asked in confusion.

Rachel tried to lift herself up in the bed. 'Which is which?' she asked the nurse.

'Can't their own mother tell?' the peasant girl asked. 'Why this is the little boy . . .' she lifted one bundle higher than the other, 'and this is the little girl.'

Stefan looked again: his father-in-law, the squat, hideous, talkative Mr Zamojski, looked at him from one side of the nurse's bosom and then from the other. Stefan turned away.

'They don't look very nice when they're as young as this,' said Rachel, catching something of Stefan's disappointment from the expression on his face.

Stefan looked again: he wanted to strangle them both at once. His hands went forward but normality and convention asserted themselves. He chucked them under their chins – the one and then the other.

'What shall we call the boy?' asked Rachel timidly.

'Isaac,' said Stefan abruptly.

'Isaac?' said Rachel.

'Isaac and Rebecca,' said Stefan.

'They're both Jewish names,' said Rachel.

'And the boy must be circumcised,' said Stefan, his voice rather shrill. 'Above all, he must be circumcised.'

Rachel sighed and smiled. 'You are sweet,' she said. 'Really you are. I didn't know how to ask you about that, but Mama and Papa . . . well, it would make them happy, and I know it's nonsense to us, but to them it means so much and after all . . .'

The nurse carried the twins out of the room. Stefan leant over and kissed his wife with the purest, simplest, most exquisite irony.

Seven

For a month after the birth of the twins, Rachel remained at her parents' house. Then, in the middle of July, she announced that it was intolerable to be living apart from her husband and moved back to the flat with her twins and a nursemaid. All at once the quiet, untidy dwelling became a functional, chaotic inferno, with babies screaming, women shouting or singing at their round of loving chores. The curtains became impregnated with the pungent smell of damp nappies; the covers with the sickly-sweet odour of mother's milk. All horizontal surfaces were piled with cots, towels, clothes, pots, bottles and the nursemaid's knitting; and Rachel, the nursemaid and Rachel's mother who called every day all beamed at Stefan and one another with a fixed, self-important, self-satisfied smile.

This feminine conceit and dominion drove Stefan into the street. He might have borne it better if the two babies had made him feel anything but repugnance: but the more he looked at them, the more clearly he saw the features – even the mannerisms – of his father-in-law. He was tormented by the thought that neither his son nor his daughter would grow into elegant, debonair Kornowskis but would both become squat and hideous Jews. He felt totally swindled – swindled by his fate, by women and in particular by Rachel.

If he smiled at her now, it was only a smile of irony. His behaviour towards her was formal, and it proved the success of his deception that she did not seem to notice – or if she noticed, she did not seem to care. He had served his purpose like a drone bee, and was packed off every morning to the cafés with a little money to buy coffee and his lunch.

His financial dependence upon his parents-in-law made his situation particularly humiliating, and Stefan determined to take some work which would make him independent. He let it be known in the Ziemianska that he was 'on the market', and within a week was approached by the editor of the *Kurier Poranny* to write a series of articles on the Czarniecki trial.

Or so it was called. The accused was in fact a young Army officer – a lieutenant in the Chasseurs called Stanislas Brec-Zwolenski – a rich elegant, aristocratic young man who served on the General Staff. The charge was treason – or, more specifically, that he had conveyed certain details about the Polish armed forces to a French newspaper which had used them to prove that Poland was no match for Germany.

What made this trial so particular – the very obverse of the famous Dreyfus affair – were the Lieutenant's connections: not his family connections, which were impeccable and obscure, but his friendship with the family of Prince Czarniecki – in particular with the Princess.

The Princess Czarniecka was an exceptional woman. She was young, beautiful and married to one of the richest and most distinguished men in Poland. The Prince was fifteen years older than she was – a remote man who had supported Pilsudski and now devoted himself to the building of the new race-course in Warsaw. He had always allowed his wife to do as she pleased, and as a result she had built up a salon frequented by the rich, the cultivated and the powerful. Ministers, cardinals, composers and writers all mingled together in the Czarniecki Palace on the Ujazadowski Avenue – and sprinkled among them were young men and women who were neither rich, powerful nor cultivated but had elegant figures or pretty faces. Such was the Lieutenant Brec-Zwolenski.

Stefan accepted the assignment with enthusiasm. For some time he had been curious about the Princess, and about 'society' in general. He had unobtrusively resumed the use of his title, and affected the mannerisms of an 'English gentleman'. It amused his friends: no one took it seriously. But combined with his literary talents and his knowledge of law, it led the editor of the *Kurier Poranny* to see him as a suitable correspondent for the 'Czarniecki trial'.

Stefan was there when it opened. He chose not to sit among the journalists but in the public gallery, and shortly after the trial had begun his decision was shown to have been correct, because the door opened at the back of the gallery, the public prosecutor faltered and the Princess Czarniecka entered the court.

Stefan knew it was she – he had seen her picture in newspapers and magazines: and even if he had not, it was quite clear from her demeanour. In her own mind she was doubtless 'slipping in unnoticed' – but by the extravagant simplicity of her costume, the bright gold of her hair and the triumphant look in her eyes, it was quite apparent that she was the most important presence in the whole court.

She sat down only a few feet from Stefan and leant forward, resting her chin on her hand with an expression now anxious and pensive. The prosecution continued to outline its case – the military secrets in the French newspaper, the meeting between the Lieutenant and that newspaper's correspondent in Warsaw; the Lieutenant's admission that he had met the correspondent; that he had brought facts and figures into the conversation; that he had received money in return.

In the dock Stanislas Brec-Zwolenski sat with an expression of amused disdain on his handsome, cherubic features. Only once did he glance towards the gallery – a glance which Stefan, so near to the Princess, could intercept, understand and use in evidence . . . The mouth of the Princess moved in half a smile.

In the days which followed Stefan was able to study her closely, for she came every day, always about twenty minutes after the proceedings had begun, and always in a manner to cause the lawyers to falter, hesitate, and then go on. Her appearance – her famous 'beauty' – was completely Slav. She was not tall, had a plump figure and a wide face with fleshy lips. Her eyes were blue and expressive – expressive above all of confidence in her beauty and her righteousness. They were at times scornful, at times defiant: she laughed as the prosecution tried to avoid the use of her name. But by then it had been proved that the facts and figures in question – the secrets that the Lieutenant had 'sold' to the Frenchman – had not been available to the General Staff in Warsaw, upon which the Lieutenant served, but came from Army Headquarters in Poznan. How then had they come into the Lieutenant's hands? They had been given to him, said the Lieutenant, by a friend whose name he could not reveal, with the clear understanding that they were not secret but were available in any work of reference.

This threw the prosecution into confusion. Juniors scuttled out of the court to find the statistics, as published by the Ministry of Defence, while counsel lamely insisted that the general availability of a set of figures did not preclude the possibility of treason. After all, had not the Lieutenant taken money like Judas?

'I never asked for payment,' said the Lieutenant proudly. 'It was sent to me, and when it arrived I paid it straight into the National Fund.'

A murmur of approval arose from the court. A sneer came onto the face of the prosecutor. Could this fine gesture be proved? Were there witnesses? Or was the court to accept the word of the Lieutenant? Not at all, replied the Lieutenant. Prince Czarniecki had been with him at the time.

A gasp from the court. The Prince, but not the Princess? Would he really give evidence to save the man who – rumour had it – was his wife's lover?

The Lieutenant returned to the dock. The Prince was called. He walked majestically to the witness box. The presiding judge was deferential: the public prosecutor stuttered his apologies.

'Ask your questions,' said the Prince.

'Were you, by any chance, Your Excellency, were you with the accused when he received a certain payment from a French journalist, M. Martin . . .'

'He came to lunch that day. He showed me the letter of credit . . .'

'And what did you say?'

'I gave him the name of a horse . . .'

Laughter.

'And what did he say?'

'That he would pay it into the National Fund.'

Murmurs.

'Do you know, Your Excellency, how Lieutenant Brec-Zwolenski came upon the lists of military dispositions?'

'Yes.'

'I wonder if you might tell the court.'

'My wife gave it to him.'

Gasps and confusion. The prosecuting counsel blushed scarlet.

'And how did your wife . . .'

'I gave it to her.' A majestic pause. 'So if Brec-Zwolenski is a traitor, then so am I and so is my wife.'

The wretched lawyer stood without anything left to say. The Prince, however, continued his explanation in a tone of dignified contempt: 'The facts were not secret. They were available to anyone who took the trouble to read the estimates published by the Ministry. I came upon them, in concise form, and thought they ought to be known. That is all.'

The case was dismissed. The court-room was in turmoil. Stefan's eyes flitted from one face to another and then glanced back at a third. The Prince looked tired, and because he looked tired he looked old. He pushed his way through the crowd of lawyers, journalists and spectators and left the room: but the Lieutenant, still in the dock, was in ecstasy. The cherub was indeed in its heaven, with hands reaching up on every side to shake his in congratulation; and every now and then he would look up to the public gallery to catch the eye of his divinity.

And she smiled down, her face illuminated with a modest and benevolent joy that the outcome was as it should be – but betraying no excitement that might be considered improper. With a last look at the Lieutenant she stood to go. Stefan looked away: he did not want her to notice that she had been studied. Then suddenly he heard a voice by his ear: 'Count Kornowski?'

He looked up. It was the Princess. She smiled down at him with the correct measure of aristocratic familiarity. Stefan got to his feet and kissed her hand.

'I am the Princess Czarniecka,' she said.

He nodded.

'They tell me that you are writing about the trial.'

'I am.'

'I am so glad,' she said. 'You write so well.'

'Thank you.'

'It is not a compliment. But why don't you come and meet the leading actors?' she said.

'I would love to . . .'

'Come tonight. We're giving a little party to celebrate.'

This was how Stefan entered the Czarniecki Palace. He went that night in a mood of grotesque elation – not just because he had gained admission, but because the Princess had heard of him – she had said: 'You write so well.' And at the reception she followed up her judgement by taking him around the actors, editors, princes, generals, introducing him as the 'talented Count Kornowski who is writing about the trial'. Even when she left him and attended to her other guests, Stefan followed her with his eyes – besotted not with her person but with her position and the glittering spectacle around him. He felt like Frédéric in the drawing-room of Madame Dambreuse. All around him were silver dishes, sparkling glasses, champagne, vodka, cold geese, boars' heads, different coloured icecreams and sherbets; sumptuous dresses in scarlet and blue, marble bosoms, curving necks, wisps of hair covering emeralds and eyes which were curious and excited.

He wandered around in a daze. His glass was continually refilled by the liveried servants and he became drunk like everyone else. He joined one group, then another, watching the shouting, flirting faces. The Prince alone looked mournful and exhausted. He stood under a portrait of an ancestor, a young girl at his side. Stefan lurched in their direction but by the time he reached the portrait the Prince had gone. The girl was still there. She smiled at him. 'Who are you?' she asked.

'Count Kornowski . . .' He bowed and clicked his heels.

'Oh, yes, the writer.'

'And who are you?'

'I'm the daughter.'

'Whose daughter?'

'Your host and hostess's daughter.'

'The Princess is your mother?'

'She isn't as young as she looks. She dyes her hair.'

'How old are you?'

'Fifteen.'

Since he knew no one else, Stefan remained with the young Princess. She gave him witty little sketches of the various guests – her relatives, and one or two self-made millionaires. 'Mama is always so delighted,' she said, 'when people make money who aren't Jews.' She pointed next to the Lieutenant. 'You know him, of course?'

'Brec-Zwolenski . . .'

'The star of the show.'

'He must be glad to be free.'

The young Princess laughed. 'Do you think he might have gone to prison?'

'Why not?'

'Things don't happen like that. Why, this party was planned a month ago.'

'You were so sure.'

'Don't say that in your article. It wouldn't look good.'

'And tell me,' said Stefan. 'Was it really true that the Lieutenant gave the money to the National Fund?'

The girl laughed. 'Of course not,' she said. 'I was there when he showed them the cheque. "Five hundred zlotys," he said. "Let's see if we can spend it all at the Europejski . . ."'

A week later Stefan was asked to lunch at the Czarniecki Palace. His article had appeared in the *Kurier Poranny* and the Princess told him how much she had liked it. 'You are quite right,' she said. 'My husband is a "modern patriot". What an excellent phrase.'

There were ten at lunch – including Lieutenant Brec-Zwolenski, who sat near his mistress like a Saluki. Stefan sat between the wife of a general and an old aunt of the Prince. He talked first to one and then the other about his life: neither seemed aware that he was married, and for a while he forgot it himself. He savoured once again the food, the footmen, the silver goblets, the porcelain . . .

At the other end of the table sat the Prince – silent but amiable – with his daughter beside him. He seemed possessed by a mild boredom, and spent most of the meal watching his wife not as if he was suspicious but as if he admired her more than anything else in the world. As he did so, a footman placed a golden bowl in front of him, then poured water from a silver jug into a crystal goblet. The Prince took a drink of the water, swilled it around in his mouth, and then spat it out into the bowl. It was a sign that lunch was at an end.

Stefan stood back to allow the Princess to lead the way into the drawing-room; but as she walked past him she took his arm, guiding him out in front of any of her other guests.

'How do you write?' she asked Stefan.

'How?'

'Do you wait for inspiration? Or do you set yourself certain hours?'

'Sometimes I am inspired,' said Stefan, 'but on other occasions I sit down with an empty mind and a blank piece of paper . . .'

'And which method produces the best work, do you think?' She sat down on a sofa and gestured to Stefan to sit down beside her.

Stefan shrugged his shoulders. 'It's hard for a writer to judge his own work.'

'Well, your story *The Son of Man* . . . How did that come about?'

'That was a matter of opportunity. My wife and the children . . .' He hesitated, blushed, but the Princess did not react. 'They went away for a month. I was on my own. The dining-room table was cleared. I took paper, pen and sat down . . .'

'Is that where you normally write? On the dining-room table?'

Stefan shrugged his shoulders and smiled. 'Or the Café Ziemianska. I used to have a study but the nursemaid sleeps in it now.'

'But that is absurd,' said the Princess. 'Here we have twenty empty rooms. You must use one of them. Would you like that? You could come and go as you liked . . .'

When half the guests had gone, Stefan was taken by the Princess and her butler down the corridor of the Palace – then up some stairs until eventually they came to a musty room with closed shutters. These were opened by the butler, and the light came in to reveal a large bed, an ornate chest but also a heavy desk and chair.

'There,' said the Princess. 'Will this do for you?'

'It would be magnificent,' said Stefan.

'You can leave things here. We never use it. We don't, do we?' She turned to address the butler.

'No, Your Excellency,' the silent man replied.

'No one will disturb you or your papers here. The drawers even have a key. You can lock things up if you like.'

Stefan went to the window which looked out over the Palace gardens. 'I think,' he said, 'that working here I would start a novel.'

'Then it's settled,' said the Princess. 'No more need be said . . .'

'Your kindness . . .' Stefan began.

'Don't think of it. It's an honour to help an artist. You are the true aristocrats. *Nous sommes les faux*. And remember, there's always lunch if you want it. You have only to tell them to lay a place for you.'

It was here, in this disused bedroom of the Czarniecki Palace, that Stefan Kornowski began a full-length novel with only the muffled cries of the Princess's younger children in the garden to distract him.

The plot was to be this. A young Frenchman, a pilot like St-Exupéry, makes a forced landing near a farm in Brittany. He breaks his leg. The farmer's daughter (Matilde) and her brother (André) help him to their father's house. There they set his leg, but the pilot (Raymond) remains to recuperate. He has fallen in love with Matilde. She seems to respond to his affectionate glances, but 'looks over her shoulder' at her father, brother . . . After a while, Raymond begins to suspect that there is some secret, some sin, which brings together the inhabitants of this remote farmhouse.

Matilde, the daughter, suddenly makes a gesture (while dressing his wounds) which confirms that she returns his love. She sees Raymond as a symbol of liberty: he flies. Yet his leg is broken. The bonds which keep her to her family – a blend of licit and illicit love – represent both slavery and security. The one is the other. Raymond too is shackled – first by his broken leg, then by his affection. His leg mends; but he pretends that he is still lame so as to remain at the farm. Indeed he pretends to be worse. Matilde must bring him his food. She must nurse him. She must wash his body. Bonds must be forged between Raymond and Matilde which are more intimate even than those between Matilde and her brother . . . Matilde and her brother? What happens between them each night when they retire?

Raymond starves himself to seem sick. Matilde grows

stronger, healthier. She shines. The brother broods. The father and mother are silent, even when grasping the banknotes which Raymond now presses into their hands. No one speaks about the situation; but everyone knows what the situation is. The leg is mended: he could walk. But he is afraid to walk because then he would no longer need Matilde, he would be free again, he could fly . . .

Suddenly the situation reverses itself. One afternoon, as Matilde bends over him to tuck in the blanket of his sickbed, Raymond notices (or thinks he notices) that her belly protrudes: she is pregnant. Who can have fathered the child? Her brother! Raymond is horrified. He wants to escape but is too weak. He wants to be strong again. He eats as much as he can but he grows paler, weaker . . . His cheeks are hollow: he can barely hold a cup to his lips.

He suspects that he is being poisoned. But why? And by whom? By Matilde? Has she guessed that he knows her secret? Does she fear that if he is well, he will denounce her and her brother?

Certainly, Matilde is poisoning him, but not because she fears exposure. She is not pregnant. She has no incestuous liaison with her brother. But Raymond, the symbol of liberty, has disappointed her and she is sick of looking after him. A true farmer's daughter, she decides that if he will not mend, he had better go. She puts rat poison into his milk and sure enough he dies.

This summary of the plot may seem to give the dimensions of a story rather than a novel; but the style was heavily descriptive – each gesture had a paragraph, each object a page – and there were elaborate evocations of the Breton countryside in the changing seasons (taken from encyclopedias) which were woven into the symbolism of the character and plot.

The novel, entitled quite simply, *The Crash*, was started in the middle of October, 1937. By the end of the year Stefan had reached Chapter Three: the pilot, Raymond, had reached the farmhouse. Progress, then, was not swift: but the writer had many delightful interruptions in the reception rooms of the Czarniecki Palace. The novel, after all, could be written at any time, but the tea from the Princess's samovar would not stay warm for ever.

The Princess by then had become his close friend but not his mistress. There was never any question of that because the Lieutenant Brec-Zwolenski was always in attendance. He was, however, an imbecile, and the conversation which he could not provide flowed abundantly from Stefan Kornowski; and it was repaid by confidences, gossip, *bons mots* about the literary world, and an earnest approval of his work. This approval meant much to Stefan. In some moods he was self-confident, arrogant – but in others he was uncertain of himself. His notebooks are full of contradictory attitudes towards his own work. 'I write because I am too lazy to do anything else, and too bored to do nothing' (February 1937). 'The writer ties up the loose ends left by the politicians, historians, scientists, priests and poets; he makes sense out of the nonsense of life – or nonsense out of the sense, whichever seems most urgent at the time he puts his pen to paper . . .' (March 1937). The Princess, by her flattery, her interest in his opinions, her close attention to anything he said – and by forcing anyone else at her salon, whether a prince, a politician or an army officer – to treat him with respect, seemed to confirm Stefan's higher estimation of his vocation. If someone who was so much admired should admire him, there must be something worth the esteem.

Rachel was never invited to the Czarniecki Palace and no one expected that she should be. When Stefan had told her about his 'office', she was a little anxious that he would be enticed away – perhaps by the Princess herself. For a week or two she made a special effort to cook what he liked to eat; she showed an interest in his work and affected an erotic delirium. But Stefan's lizard eyes watched each move she made, and knew the reason for it. And sure enough, when it became clear that Stefan was not about to leave her, Rachel relaxed into the mood of domestic contentment which had possessed her since her children were born.

She had by now regained her tall, attractive figure but not her former personality. There was now no trace of the racy, radical independence. Conservative instincts and values had risen in her mind as surely as the milk in her bosom: and opinions flowed from her like breasts beset with uncontrollable lactation – expressed in her own voice but with meaning and intonation indistinguishable from her mother's. It was her mother, after all, with whom she spent most of her time.

Stefan was not unconscious of her attitude towards him. She faced a dilemma which was common enough. She had little use for him as a lover because her body, once so shrill in its erotic demands, was now fulfilled by the minor pleasures of sucking, sleeping and eating. There was no sexual current at all. Nor was Stefan a breadwinner: her father provided her allowance. He was only necessary in a formal way as the father of her children, and as such she was fond of him, though she realized now that a steadier man would have been a wiser choice.

The twins grew plump on her rich milk, and their faces lost the appearance of two little old men which had led Stefan to see them so clearly as his father-in-law. But if they grew less like the surgeon, they did not grow more like Stefan. It was generally agreed by Rachel's relatives that they both took after their great-uncle Isaac who ran the family business in Bialystok.

Eight

Four days before Christmas, Krystyna returned to Sluzewska Street at about eight in the evening. She had been shopping after work, and while one arm was stretched by a string bag filled with groceries, the other clasped a number of packages containing presents for Teofil and the other members of her family.

Because she did not want Teofil to see what she had bought – and because her hands were full – she went past Aunt Cecylia's flat where Teofil was waiting for her and went on up to her own. She put down the bag of groceries to take her key from her handbag, opened the door, picked up the groceries again and went in.

It was dark, and her hands were too full to switch on the

light, but after seven years she knew her way around the flat. She crossed the hall, pushed open the door into the living-room and went towards the table, intending to lay down the presents before proceeding with the groceries into the kitchen.

Suddenly she stopped and stood still. In the dim light which came in through the windows from the street below, she could see a figure slouched on a chair in the corner of the room. For a moment she thought it was a burglar who had fallen asleep: but two wide-open eyes were watching her from the semi-bearded face, and she suddenly sensed that the man was a murderer.

'What do you want?' she asked, backing towards the door.

'Where is Teofil?' asked the man in a flat tone of voice.

'Downstairs . . .'

He did not move, but she now knew it was Bruno.

When she switched on the light he blinked, but did not smile, and Krystyna approached him cautiously as if he was still a dangerous intruder.

'When did you arrive?'

'This afternoon.'

'I would have met you.'

He shook his head. 'I came in the back of a lorry. I smell of cabbage.'

'You must have a bath, and something to eat.'

'I'd like to see the boy.'

'Yes, of course. I'll fetch him.'

Krystyna turned towards the door; then she looked back at Bruno. In appearance he was hardly recognizable, as the man who had left more than a year before. He was thinner, especially in the face. His cheekbones protruded so that his eyes seemed sunken in their sockets, and their expression was unlike any she had seen before – a mixture of callousness, despair and exhaustion.

The beard too made him look sinister; and as he stood his movements were different – slow and careful, as if his limbs ached. He stood but did not come towards Krystyna. He went instead to the window. She watched him, because he seemed unaware of her presence until she heard him say: 'The boy . . . you were going to fetch Teofil.'

'Yes, of course.'

She went into the hallway, turned on the light, and then

went down the flights of steps to Aunt Cecylia's flat. Teofil was sitting at the kitchen table, a napkin around his neck, laughing while Cecylia put pieces of bread soaked in egg into his mouth.

'Come on, my darling, come upstairs,' said Krystyna, wiping his mouth with the napkin. 'I've got the biggest surprise . . .'

'Is it Christmas?' asked Teofil.

'Not yet, no. But you can have a lovely present *now* . . .'

Teofil's eyes widened and he pushed his great aunt aside. 'I want a present,' he said. He walked towards the door, then turned to his mother. 'Carry,' he ordered. 'Carry me.'

'No, just a hand,' she said, clasping his little fingers with hers. 'You're too big now to carry up all those flights of stairs.'

Step by step they climbed to their own flat. Krystyna began to be anxious that Teofil might be shocked by Bruno's appearance and so started to prepare him. 'The present isn't a toy, darling . . .'

'Is it a surprise?' asked Teofil.

'Yes,' said Krystyna. 'It's a surprise person . . .'

Teofil stopped and looked at her. 'A person . . .'

'Yes. You'll see.'

She had left the door open, and now let Teofil go in first. He ran on his little legs through the hall and into the living-room. In the doorway he stopped. There, standing by the window with his back turned, was a man.

'Papa,' said Teofil.

Bruno turned. He saw his child. 'Teofil,' he said. He crouched, opened his arms, and waited with a great smile on his face. Teofil began to walk towards him with a shy, embarrassed look on his face; but then at the last minute he rushed and sprang into his father's arms. Bruno wrapped them around the little body, and from the callous, despairing, exhausted eyes came tears.

For days after his return Bruno remained in the flat in Sluzewska Street playing with Teofil. When he had shaved off his beard and changed into some clean clothes he looked more like his previous self, though his face was still haggard and the clothes were baggy because they were now too big.

The child was delighted. He hardly had a word or a glance for Cecylia, Mamuska or his mother. All his attention was on his father and the father's attention was on his son. He built arches and bridges with wooden bricks – then stared for hours at Teofil, who drove his toy cars through the arches and over the bridges. Like Teofil, Bruno seemed hardly aware of Mamuska, who brought them lunch muttering under her breath about this and that; or of Krystyna when she returned in the evening.

At night Bruno slept on his marriage bed, but facing away from his wife. Since his return he had not so much as kissed her hand, and for a time Krystyna was afraid that he might have heard rumours . . . But his manner was not that of a jealous husband. No flicker of emotion of any kind appeared in his eyes when his glance happened to fall on her face. All he saw was his son. He seemed not to notice the difference between Krystyna's presence and that of Mamuska.

Krystyna, in her behaviour towards him, was paralysed by inescapable feelings of guilt. She rejected them but felt them all the same. She was tormented by the idea that Bruno might have returned when she lay in bed with Michael Mikolajczyk, and her first impulse had been to find Michael and tell him that they must never meet again. She could not ring him at home; and the next day, when she telephoned him at the university during her lunch hour, he was not there. Her dread was then that he would call in at Sluzewska Street before she returned: and so she pretended to have a headache and left Blomstein's early.

Michael had not been there by the time she returned, and he did not come that evening, nor the following evening. Christmas came without any word from him: and Krystyna realized that he must know through the Party that Bruno had returned. She felt relieved at this demonstration of Michael's wisdom and tact, and hoped that their affair would lapse just like that. It terrified her to think that Bruno might ever know.

She tried to behave towards Bruno as she would have done had everything else been normal. Once, when he was sitting on the sofa, she sat down beside him, put her arm around him and asked him if he felt better.

'Better?' he asked. 'I wasn't ill.'

'No, but you were so tired and thin.'

He laughed in an unpleasant way. 'We were all tired and thin.'

'Was it terrible . . . the fighting?'

'No . . .' He did not elaborate.

'But in Barcelona you must have seen the dead and wounded.'

Bruno stared into the middle of the room, and did not answer. Krystyna said nothing more.

On Christmas Eve, Stefan, Rachel and the twins came in the late afternoon to Aunt Cecylia's flat, where they crowded in with Uncle Max, and Krystyna, Bruno and Teofil from above. They stood around the tree which Cecylia and Mamuska had decorated with tinsel and candles, and sang carols. Since this always reminded her of Jezow, Krystyna sang with tears in her eyes, but her voice was loud and firm: so too were the voices of Stefan, Rachel and Uncle Max. Mamuska sang with a peasant wail, and Cecylia's voice was lost because as always she presented the profile of which she was so proud. It was only the children who were silent, their mouths open in amazement at the spectacle, and Bruno whose mouth was tight shut.

His attention was always on Teofil – the wide eyes sparkling with the reflected candlelight. He showed no sign of interest or even recognition towards the others with the exception of Stefan who, as he entered the room, had provoked a flicker of interest and a slight smile.

When they finished singing carols, the packages were taken from under the tree and handed around. Only the gifts which everyone had bought for Bruno at the last moment lay in a pile unopened. He was with Teofil opening his presents, fetching him the chocolates hanging from the tree, and peeling off the silver and gold paper in which they were wrapped.

At the traditional Christmas Eve meal of soup, carp, baked potatoes and a paste of poppy-seed, Bruno was silent, his eyes fixed on the clay crib in the middle of the table. The others – the Kornowskis – jabbered happily and talked about the old days in Jezow. At eleven Stefan and Rachel prepared to go home, and the two old ladies – Cecylia and Mamuska – put on their coats for Midnight Mass. It was then that Bruno astonished them all. He lifted up Teofil, who was asleep in his arms, and handed him to Krystyna. 'Take him up,' he said. 'He should be in bed.'

'Where are you going?' asked Krystyna.

Bruno turned to Cecylia and Mamuska. 'I'll go with you, if I may. I'll go with you to Mass.'

Christmas passed, and then the New Year. Krystyna waited for Bruno to resume some sort of work for the Party but he remained in the flat, playing with Teofil, washing dishes, cleaning the floor. He looked less thin, and his mood was better – continually better. But there remained something strange about him. The hard look on his face did not soften: it merely cracked like a plate. He twitched: and his expression would sometimes collapse into shapeless, wobbling panic. At night too he would wake with a cry and cling to Krystyna's body like a child, smelling and squeezing her, and hiding his head in her bosom.

In the middle of January, Krystyna stood at the counter at Blomstein's, placing a necklace in its case, when Michael Mikolajczyk entered the shop. He looked at her, at first anxiously, and then when she inadvertently smiled, he approached and asked about a ring.

'A ring for a young lady?' asked Krystyna, feeling suddenly quite cheerful at playing this game with the professor.

'For a young lady, yes, aged around twenty-seven . . . Beautiful, very beautiful, with green eyes . . .'

'An engagement ring, perhaps . . .?'

'No, alas. She is married.'

'Tch, tch.'

'Well, you know how these things happen . . .'

'Of course.'

'And her husband has just returned from abroad.'

'Yes.' She glanced at Michael under her lashes – a glance which said much to him; and revealed a certain amount to herself. For it expressed complicity; and beneath the clean cotton and wool of her clothes she felt a longing for his stubby touch, his preposterous lechery, his flabby flesh, his scent of cigarettes, pomade, chocolates, sweat and ink.

'I kept away,' Michael whispered. 'I didn't know . . .'

'Can you meet me after work?' she said quietly, holding a ring up to him as if they were discussing it.

'Yes. I'll be waiting for you.'

'Then we can talk.'

'Yes.'

'This ring,' said Krystyna, her voice a little louder, 'is seven thousand zlotys.'

'A little beyond my means, I am afraid.'

'You mean the young lady is not worth it?'

'Oh no. She is worth far more.'

'Perhaps she should find a richer admirer?'

'Indeed.'

Michael was waiting for her when Krystyna left Blomstein's that evening, standing looking at some galoshes in a shop window.

'I can't be long,' she said.

'Of course not,' he said. They walked down the pavement in silence, for a moment, jostling past the others: then Michael said: 'Zofia is away. We could go to the flat . . . if you had time.'

There was another silence: then Krystyna said: 'All right, but we'd better take a taxi.' Which they did – both silent, almost shaking; and in the flat with no words they fell upon each other – sniffing, licking, whimpering – frenzied with frustration. On the dingy Mikolajczyk marriage bed they made love again and again until her legs dangled lifeless and he gasped like a landed fish.

'I can't live without you,' he said.

'I know,' she said. Then she added: 'But you can't leave Zofia, can you?'

He sighed.

'And I can't leave Bruno. Not now. Especially not now.'

Her life became a nurse's round. So many men depended on her – Bruno and Teofil for their breakfast, then Blomstein, then Michael, then Bruno and Teofil again: and at night, after washing the supper dishes, she would take a bath and go straight to bed, read a book perhaps while Bruno remained in the sitting-room listening to the radio, and then switch off the light and go to sleep.

From Michael, Krystyna had a rough account of Bruno's reasons for returning to Warsaw. He had evidently been involved in 'unpleasant but necessary Party work in Barcelona – the liquidation of Anarchists and Trotskyists, and had probably been kept too long at the same job'. He had lost his nerve and had deserted.

The Party, according to Michael, was taking no action against him for the time being. It was recognized that he needed a rest. 'They look upon it as a nervous breakdown,' said Michael, 'not as an act against the Party . . . though for how long they'll take that attitude, I don't know. There have been arrests in Moscow. Several comrades are suspected of spying – Krajewski, Warski, Walecki . . .'

'But that's impossible,' said Krystyna.

'You never know,' said Michael, putting on his earnest, pompous Party face.

Their conversation was in a café. Zofia Mikolajczyk had returned to Warsaw and there was now nowhere they could go to be alone – unless it was a hotel, which was elaborate and expensive for the half hour or so which Krystyna could spare on her way back from work.

There was no question of going out together at night. If she wanted to go to a concert or a film, Bruno would now come with her: indeed he never went out alone. He waited for her like a patient for his nurse. And gradually the frustration built up again in Krystyna and Michael Mikolajczyk and both longed for the old days when they had been free to lie for hours in the same bed.

Nine

In March 1938, the Nazis marched into Austria. In Warsaw people walked along the wet streets with dejected expressions on their faces. Blomstein did even better business than usual; and Stefan reached Chapter Five of his novel. Progress had been slow. He found it difficult to live in his Breton farmhouse in his imagination with all the fascinating distractions of the Czarniecki Palace going on under his nose.

The particular distraction at that time was the daughter,

Tilly, whom he had first met at the party after the trial. Her tutor had gone back to Paris for the Easter holidays and she was therefore at a loose end. She would come along to his room, walk in, say: 'Am I disturbing you?' and without waiting for an answer, settle down on the bed.

'What are you writing?' she asked on her first visit.

'A novel.'

'I know. Mama told me. But what is it about?'

'A man . . . a woman.'

'Huh. Very original.'

Tilly had myopic eyes and her hair in ringlets. Having been brought up in a seasoned circle of society, she concealed her *naïveté* behind a brash manner *à l'Américaine*.

'What would you like me to write about?' asked Stefan.

'Pain.'

Stefan started and looked sharply at Tilly, but her eyes were on the hangings of the bed. 'Why pain?' he asked.

'Because I think it's interesting. I mean, everyone's so afraid of it, aren't they? Just the thought of it. Look at the Austrians. Running like sheep.'

'Aren't you afraid of pain?' asked Stefan, chewing the end of his pen.

'I'm training myself not to be.'

'How?'

She sat up, blinked at him, and held out her finger. 'Look. Do you see that sore? I did that with a match. I held it in the flame for ten seconds. You feel the pain and you detach yourself from it, so you conquer it and have nothing to be afraid of.'

'I don't see the point of it all.'

'If you aren't afraid of pain, then you needn't be afraid of the Germans.'

'Are you afraid of the Germans?'

'Yes, I am. They'll bomb us and march in. I know they will.'

'But we have an army.'

Tilly laughed. 'That won't be much use. Not if they're all like Stanislas. If he's going to defend us against Hitler, we would do better to surrender now.'

'But your mother must feel he has qualities . . .'

'She likes his looks, that's all. He bores her to tears, though. That's why she likes you. You keep her amused . . . And also she thinks it's smart to patronize the arts. And it flummoxes all the old monsignori and brigadiers. You make them feel stupid and philistine; and they're meant to make you feel small. That's her idea, anyway. Divide and rule.' Tilly glanced at Stefan, gave an artificial smile, shook her locks . . .

Stefan said nothing but wrote 'Strindberg' on a piece of paper: and under it, 'Miss Katasia: a play in one act'.

By the end of March, Michael and Krystyna became desperate. Perhaps it was just the spring which pushed their blood like sap to press upon the nerves and brain; or it was the feeling of anxiety and urgency which followed the Anschluss. 'It's impossible,' Krystyna said to Michael, 'I can't go on. He's like an invalid, hovering around, useless, eating . . . He goes out a little on his own. He takes Teofil for a walk. But otherwise he clings to me. He is normal for a while and in a way, but shrinks from the traffic. Oh God . . .' She hid her face in her hands. 'I had an invalid father for five years, and now an invalid husband.'

'You have become his mother,' said Michael, sipping his glass of beer with his thin, professorial lips.

'I don't want to be his mother,' she said. 'I want . . . I want you.'

'He should be weaned,' said Michael.

'If only he was still in Spain,' she said.

'Somewhere, at any rate.'

'Couldn't he be sent abroad, as a courier? He used to be.'

'He is not to be trusted in his present state.'

They were silent, thinking: then Michael looked shiftily at Krystyna and said: 'Of course the police would like to entertain him. They're always a little out of date.'

And Krystyna cocked her head, blushed and looked innocent. 'The police? Would they arrest him?'

'If they knew who he was, and where he was.'

'That would be dreadful, of course. He'd go to prison.'

'Only for a while.'

'And they say conditions aren't so bad these days,' said Krystyna. 'But, well, we could never do that – denounce him. There are limits . . .' And then she stopped and looked up at Michael with limitless longing. No more was said. They paid the bill, finished their drink and left.

Stefan and Bruno met for lunch on odd occasions at a small restaurant in the middle of town. It was almost the only reason for Bruno to leave the flat alone. 'Krystyna encourages me,' he said to Stefan. 'She used to complain that I was never at home. Now she thinks of any excuse to get me out of the house.'

'She says you've changed,' said Stefan, watching his brother-in-law for his reaction to what he said. 'They say you had a breakdown in Spain.'

Bruno made a movement with his mouth which might have been a sour smile. 'A breakdown? Is that a psychological term? Well perhaps I did suffer from a breakdown.' He leant forward and whispered to Stefan: 'That dog. The one which frightened you?'

'Yes.'

'Could you shoot it in cold blood?'

'Yes.'

'In the back of the neck?'

'Without hesitation.'

'Because you hate dogs.'

'Yes.'

'But why do you hate dogs?'

'Because they bite.'

Bruno nodded. 'Yes. They bite. And sometimes they have rabies. All good reasons. So you shoot your dog, but there are other dogs. And you shoot them. Day after day, you shoot dogs, and sometimes you torture them because they know things you must know – it must be done. You are the midwife of history. Birth is a messy thing . . .'

His hand was shaking: he hesitated. 'But then you cease to be afraid of dogs. They don't bite. They just whine and die.'

He paused, then looked at Stefan. 'In the end, I couldn't take it. They mistook me for a stronger man. I felt like Sholokhov's Bunchuk. I kept thinking of Teofil . . . I dreamt he was in danger. I had to see him so I made some excuse and left. I knew the route, the contacts. It took me a week to get from Barcelona to Warsaw. Only a week. I wish to God I had left before.'

'Don't you believe any more?'

'I neither believe nor disbelieve. I watch Teofil. I kiss his fat little cheeks and hug his body and tickle him to hear shrieks of joy. I tickle him until he begs for mercy . . . for mercy. Then I stop.'

'And the Party?'

'Don't you know what is happening to the Party? It is disintegrating. Every day they uncover a new spy in the leadership. Bobinski, Ryng, Ciszewski and Henrykowski – they've all disappeared in Moscow. Jasienski and Wandurski too. As fast as we were liquidating Anarchists and Trotskyists and fascists in Spain, they were liquidating Polish Communists in Moscow . . .'

'Perhaps they were spies . . .'

'Perhaps. Perhaps I am a spy without knowing it. Everything is in the melting pot. Only one or two things are certain. The first is that I am safer a lunatic living at home, than sane in the streets. The second is my son. All my judgements and feelings are in confusion except for my love for him. And it is on this rock that I shall build whatever future there may be.'

'What a burden for a child . . .'

'He does not feel it. He's happy to have me to play with.'

'And Krysia?'

'Krysia? You tell me. Is it true what I was told? That she consoled herself with Michael Mikolajczyk?'

'Who told you?'

'Comrades in Spain. Gossip travels faster than telegraph.'

'Yes. It is true.'

'And he is right in the centre of the Party. If he thought that I was sane, I would be called to Moscow and . . .' He drew his fingers across his neck.

'Things can't be as bad as that.'

'If Lenski and Bronkowski could not save themselves, what chance would I have?'

Stefan shrugged his shoulders. 'Is it hard to pretend to Krysia?' he asked.

Bruno hesitated: he looked down at his hands. 'It is hard, yes. I thought of her too. I regretted so much what she had suffered. I was going to make it up. But now, for Teofil, I must survive and Krysia can't be trusted.'

His face hardened, and Stefan – realizing what thoughts had

hardened it – said: 'She was lonely and bored. And he took her to the opera.'

'One day,' said Bruno, 'I will strangle Michael Mikolajczyk. For the moment I shall need all my wits just to survive.'

The conversation changed. Stefan described the Czarniecki Palace: he tried to amuse Bruno but could rarely provoke more than a feeble smile. Bruno's eyes flitted around the restaurant – a cheap one used by students and writers: they alighted on two men who looked out of place; then returned to Stefan and his stories.

They finished their compote, then their coffee. They smoked cigarettes, paid the bill and then rose to go.

'Would you like me to talk to Krysia?' asked Stefan.

'I can't risk it,' said Bruno. 'Tell her that I'm a broken man. Moscow mustn't know that I'm well.'

Stefan and Bruno left the restaurant. In the street they parted – Stefan to return to the Czarniecki Palace, Bruno to be arrested at the corner of the Krackowski Przedmiescie by two officers of Polish Intelligence.

Krystyna behaved perfectly as a prisoner's wife. She went each weekend to Lodz, where Bruno was held, with a parcel of food and clean clothes. She complained about the injustice of it all – losing her husband just when he had returned – and almost imperceptibly resumed her excursions to concerts and vernissages with Michael Mikolajczyk.

Never did the two of them allude to their conversation in the café, except once on a Sunday when Michael met Krystyna upon her return from Lodz. Then she said: 'It is true, you know. They are quite well treated. He says his cell is dry, that he's allowed books, paper and pencil. And to talk to the other prisoners.'

'And how is he taking it?' asked Michael a little anxiously.

'Oh, he's fine, darling, really he is.' She smiled. 'Much happier than he was in the flat. He looks quite relaxed. And quite sane.'

There was now no impediment to Michael and Krystyna spending part of the nights together as they had before; but this freedom did not last for long, because Michael Mikolajczyk was summoned to Moscow.

He told Krystyna as they lay in bed together. 'There's been a big change in the leadership,' he said.

'Don't go,' she said. 'They may arrest you.'

He smiled. 'No, no. They don't associate me with that lot. They need fresh men at the top – men they can trust.'

'Will they trust you?'

'Of course. I'm not an agent . . .'

'Nor was Jan.'

'We can't be sure about that.'

She ran her hand over his heavy, hairy stomach. 'But what shall I do without you?'

'Wait,' he said softly into her ear. 'I won't be gone long. They haven't sent for Zofia or the children. That means I am to return, probably as a member of the Politburo.'

'Take care,' she whispered, 'I need you.'

In his room in the Czarniecki Palace, the little princess, Tilly, held up her putrefying finger for Stefan's inspection. 'I can hold it in the flame for twenty seconds now,' she said. 'Twenty seconds over a candle. I keep it bandaged, though, because Mamma says the sight of it puts people off their food.'

'Pain is only half of it,' said Stefan, sitting cross-legged, facing away from his desk.

'What is the other half?' asked Tilly, lying back on the bed.

'Pleasure.'

'True.'

'People run from pain, and pursue pleasure.'

'But I don't pursue pleasure,' said Tilly. Then she thought for a moment and said: 'What is pleasure, anyway?'

'Music, swimming, food, the sun . . .'

'I could do without all of that.'

'It's harder than you think.'

'I'll prove it to you. I'll say I feel sick and do without lunch.'

'That isn't the only pleasure.'

'I hate music, swimming, the sun . . .'

'There may be pleasure you aren't aware of . . .'

'Love, do you mean? Grown-ups always mean love, don't they? You think that when the time comes, I won't be able to resist a lieutenant like Stanislas.'

Stefan shrugged his shoulders. 'Will you?'

'Of course.'

'But you don't know . . .'

She blushed. 'Those nuns don't teach you anything.'

'What about your tutor?'

She laughed. 'Monsieur Lambertin? He goes the colour of a beetroot if you excuse yourself to go to the lavatory. No, you'll have to teach me all about that . . .'

'What? About . . .'

'Pleasure. *Les plaisirs d'amour*, to be specific. Come on now. What do I do?'

Stefan passed his tongue around his dry lips. 'Well, first my little princess . . .'

'You may call me Tilly.'

'First you lock the door.'

She jumped down from the bed and pushed a brass bolt into its socket. She then came and stood next to him. 'And then I sit on your knee, don't I?' she said. 'And you kiss me and then do things – rude, disgusting things, and try and make me like it.' She sat on his knee. 'Come on, then. Lesson One.'

'Lesson One,' said Stefan, 'is called "Holding Hands".' He took her hand in his and for half an hour or so they tried to discover what pleasure could be derived from this pastime. When it was time for the samovar, they concluded there was none.

At the end of May Bruno along with twelve other Communists was moved from Lodz to Poznan by train. Six of them escaped from the coach, but Bruno chose to remain. In Poznan they were put in with four other Communists. Of these, one had been arrested as he crossed the frontier from the Ukraine. He brought the news that the Communist Party of Poland had been dissolved; that almost every Polish Communist in the Soviet Union had been arrested and liquidated as an agent for Polish Military Intelligence; and that those who were still in Poland or abroad were being lured back to Moscow. 'Stalin never forgave us for standing up to him,' said this particular comrade, 'and he won't stop now until he has got us all. I tell you, Kaczmarek, we're safer here in a Polish prison than we would be anywhere else.'

There was further, furtive talk about the purges in Moscow. 'And that idiot Mikolajczyk. Condemned by his own conceit.

He thought that they were going to make him Party Secretary. Instead he was arrested as he stepped off the train.'

At lunch at the Czarniecki Palace, Stefan and Tilly behaved as if they hardly knew each other. She always sat next to her father: he always sat next or near to the Princess at the other end of the table.

The Princess, now that she had secured Stefan as a pet intellectual, gave him less of her attention; but when she bestowed it, it was total, powerful and benign. 'Is the novel going well?' she asked once, leaning towards him in front of the bishop to her left.

'I've laid it aside for the moment,' said Stefan. 'I'm writing a short play.'

'How exciting. What sort of play?'

'A parody on Strindberg.'

'Well, when you've finished, let me know. We'll get Edelmann to put it on.'

'It may be a play to be read rather than performed,' he said.

'Well, just as you like; but in my experience something can be made of anything with the right director . . .'

'I shall show it to you when it's finished,' said Stefan, 'and you can decide.'

The butler appeared with the golden bowl of water for the Prince to wash out his mouth.

'I hope Tilly isn't distracting you from your work,' said the Princess with a slight, involuntary frown. 'I gather that she interrupts you . . .'

'Such a charming child . . .' said Stefan.

'But quite insensitive,' said the Princess. 'If she disturbs you, just tell her to go away.'

'Of course,' said Stefan.

'After all, you come here to work, not to amuse an adolescent girl who has nothing better to do.'

In July Rachel and the twins (Isaac and Rebecca) went to stay with her parents in the Tatra mountains, where they had rented a chalet. Stefan was invited too, and Rachel begged him to come in a timid and unconvincing manner – not expecting him to accept and feeling relieved that he did not.

Stefan was delighted to see them go because he was short of money and thought he could make some by staying in his Aunt Cecylia's flat (she was also away) and letting his flat to some visitors to Warsaw. When Rachel had gone he spent a whole day tidying it as best he could. He put clean sheets on his marriage bed, and then went to the Ziemianska to ask if any-one knew of anyone who would like to rent a flat for a few weeks.

'For a few weeks, no,' said a youth called Leon. 'But for a few hours . . .'

He laughed. Others laughed. Stefan laughed and said: 'A few hours? So much the better. As long as they pay. I need the money.'

Leon ran off, and in half an hour came back with a ten zloty note. Stefan gave him the key: and in the days which followed, after word had got around, he did a brisk business letting his home by the hour to different people – students, government officials, even a girl produced ten zlotys and bashfully asked for the key. All Stefan had to do was return every now and then to change the sheets.

And at the Czarniecki Palace he continued as Tilly's tutor. They had progressed from Lesson One to Lesson Two. 'Does this produce a sensation?' Stefan asked Tilly, running his fingers up and down the inside of her leg as she lay half-clothed on the bed.

'Yes,' she replied. 'It tickles.'

'Nothing else?'

'No.'

'And is tickling painful or pleasurable?'

'Well . . .' She giggled. 'Both . . . neither. I don't know.'

'Do you like it?' he asked – gently moving his fingertips on the soft skin, brushing the bristling little hairs.

'I like it, yes, but it still tickles.'

'Half pleasure, half pain. Neither. Both. Ambiguity . . .'

'But when you move your hand up, there, yes . . .' She clutched it. 'I like that . . .' She tried to direct his hand but he withdrew it.

'That, Princess, is for Lesson Five. And we are only on Lesson Two.'

'Can't we go straight to Lesson Five?'

'No. One at a time.'

'How many lessons are there?'

'Ten.'

'What's Lesson Three?'

'Tongues.'

'Why tongues?'

'Look at your tongue.'

Tilly sat up, propped herself up with her arms and stuck out her tongue. She bent it round towards her nose and squinted. 'I can't see it.'

'Then look at mine.' He opened his mouth and stuck out his tongue.

Tilly studied it. 'Ugh,' she said.

'Describe it,' he said; then opened his mouth again.

'It's red and white with spots on the top, and blue shiny veins underneath . . .'

He shut his mouth. 'Precisely. It's disgusting. And my lips?'

She peered closer. 'They're all cracked.'

'And your lips,' said Stefan, 'even though they are pink and soft, have a little line of white slime at the edges; and your tongue . . .' – she opened her mouth and he looked into it – 'your tongue has a yellowish white moss at the back, and those same bluish veins, and yet . . .'

'People kiss,' said Tilly.

'People kiss. Their tongues touch and intertwine: they suck each other's spittle and lick the rotting mucus from the roof of their mouths . . .'

Tilly's face was screwed up with disgust.

'Would you like to try it?' asked Stefan.

'What?'

'A kiss.'

'No. It's disgusting.'

'But love is disgusting. Disgusting, painful, absurd – yet people not only do it, they are obsessed with it. You'll see. And why? To pursue pleasure? To avoid pain? Or is it the other way around? To avoid pleasure? And pursue pain? That is what is interesting . . .'

Tilly watched him, fascinated.

In his notebook Stefan wrote:

. . . the continuous conflict between control and ecstasy. How to analyse rapture without destroying it? My hand is held by Tilly Czarniecka. She draws it to her pudendum. She is young, pretty – her blouse is unbuttoned, her skirt hitched to her hips. I think of that early piece of prose – the Princess and the jester – and find myself in the real situation which years before I imagined. And I think again (always) of Drieu la Rochelle: 'I promised myself I would be faithful to my youth . . .'

My passion is curiosity, but unlike all other passions it can have no moment of rapture. The saint, the sensualist or the huntsman – they all have their moment of total concentration – the orgasm of the kill: but for me the moment never comes. It is destroyed by the thought: 'Is this oblivion?'

Something dark and deep to smother my curiosity. Blood, sperm, death. Is this why I flirt with Tilly? To squeeze her neck until her pretty, misty eyes pop out of their sockets? And then remember nothing – so great was the ecstasy?

Some days later:

Since there is no God and no after-life, no good, no evil, no Heaven, no Hell – then ecstasy is everything. It is what we should pursue – ecstasy prolonged – indefinite ecstasy. Then Heaven would exist on earth in each one. For Rachel: to suckle forever, a child at each breast. For Tilly: perpetual defiance of her mother. For Bruno: to serve – the atheist monk. For Krysia: indignities – cheap orgasms from the truffle-tongued Marxist professor – to be what she resisted for so long. For me: to be God – to provide immortality by fusing perfect pleasure (orgasm) with perfect pain (death). To die in that way myself.

And the last entry for July:

Even as a sadist I am a Pole. De Sade, a Frenchman, carried his inclinations to their logical conclusions. I too would like to whip the soft, pink flesh of adolescent girls – their crystal tears, their pleading eyes. I dream of the life of a pasha, lying on a bed of budding breasts and buttocks, eating *pâté de clitoris de jeune fille*, washed down with a glass of their tears:

but I am a Pole – a poseur, a voyeur, an absurdity. I tickle the thighs of a silly Slav who calls herself a Princess: in Paris she would be sent to the scullery.

Krystyna waited to hear from Michael Mikolajczyk in Moscow. When a month had passed and she had heard nothing, she had a day of panic in which she did not go to work but telephoned first to the university, where nothing was known, and then to Zofia Mikolajczyk herself. She pretended to be a student, and asked after the professor; and the wife believed her because she sobbed and said that Michael had disappeared. 'It is dreadful, dreadful,' she said. 'I fear the worst.'

Krystyna now rushed to a woman she knew – a Party member – who worked on the Committee for Relief in Spain. She asked her, begged her, for news of Michael. The woman was embarrassed – doubly embarrassed – and of course she had no news. No one had news of those who disappeared.

Krystyna then returned to her flat, cried on the bed and fell asleep. When evening came she awoke, fetched Teofil from downstairs and fed him in such a normal way that only the blotched skin of her face was evidence of her earlier despair. The next morning she told Blomstein that she had been suddenly sick and, since it had so rarely happened before, he believed her.

At the end of July she took Teofil to spend a week with Rachel in the mountains. The little twins loved Teofil, and Teofil – even at the age of three – was generous enough to be kind to his younger cousins. He had few other friends of his own age and liked the space of the chalet in the Tatras – the space, the green grass, the fresh air.

The friendship which had grown up between Krystyna and Rachel while their husbands were abroad had persisted. They stuck to each other with feminine practicality which overcame fundamental incompatibility. They both had children: they both had difficult husbands – absent in one way or another. They both loved Stefan – and Krystyna had reason to think that Rachel did not condemn her for her affair with Michael Mikolajczyk. It was never discussed – they talked more about where to buy cheap clothes for the children; or which butcher left too much fat on the meat. They sometimes even turned (conversationally) to the Czarniecki Palace, and discussed the Princess and her relationship with Stefan.

'Do you think they are having an affair?' asked Rachel, as if Stefan was a casual acquaintance.

'Wouldn't you mind if they did?' asked Krystyna.

Rachel blushed and shrugged her shoulders. 'I don't know. Not really. I'm not really a jealous person.'

'I can't see them doing it, can you?' asked Krystyna.

Rachel laughed. 'I can see her, but not Stefan. He doesn't like that sort of thing much.'

'He may not like it with you,' said Krystyna smiling.

Rachel shrugged her shoulders again. 'Well, good luck to him.'

When Krystyna was not talking, her features relaxed into an expression of melancholy and bitterness. Rachel noticed this and asked her (disingenuously) whether Bruno's imprisonment made her unhappy.

Krystyna's face tightened into a happier expression. 'Oh well,' she said with a sigh. 'I'd almost got used to living without him, you know. But he was sweet with Teofil. *He* misses him, don't you, Teofil?' She leant forward and talked to her child. 'Poor Papa, gone away, hasn't he?'

Teofil just looked at her and said: 'Yes, Papa's gone away but he's coming back soon.'

'Of course he's coming back soon.'

'And Onka's coming back soon.'

'We'll soon see Onka.'

Then Teofil shook his head gravely. 'Michael *not* coming back soon.' Whereupon Krystyna blushed scarlet and went into the kitchen for fear that she would start to cry.

That evening the two women talked about politics – about Hitler and the Sudetenland, the war in Spain, and the chance of a war between Germany and Poland. 'I dread it,' said Krystyna, huddling over the fire which had been lit to warm them in the cold evening air. 'Yet if it's going to happen, I wish it would happen soon. I hate this waiting – the threats, the stupid diplomatic shilly-shally . . .'

'I'd prefer that to war,' said Rachel. 'At least we're safe and comfortable . . .'

'I know,' said Krystyna without enthusiasm. 'You are, and I am. But what about Bruno . . .'

'He's better off in a Polish prison than he would be in a Russian one.'

'Yes, I dare say,' said Krystyna with a sigh.

'I do see it must be awful for you,' said Rachel. Then she added timidly: 'Perhaps you ought to change your job . . . just to do something different?'

'Who'd pay me as well as old Blomstein?' asked Krystyna. 'And anyway, I'm used to it. It's become a habit. I don't have to think about it.'

There was a silence. The lamp spluttered. 'Do you still feel at all . . .' Rachel began: then she hesitated.

'Go on,' said Krystyna.

'Do you feel any commitment to the Party?'

'No,' said Krystyna in a dull voice.

'Neither do I,' said Rachel. 'I feel . . . now . . . that only the children matter . . . I live for them, and I don't care if Poland is Communist or capitalist so long as they are well-fed and safe and happy.'

'You should be ready to leave,' said Krystyna. 'It would be difficult for you if the Germans came.'

'We've already made plans,' said Rachel. 'If war is declared, we're going to Bialystok, to my uncle's house in the country.'

'Would you be safe there?'

'Oh yes, surely? They only want the Corridor.'

'I suppose so.'

'What would you do?'

Krystyna thought to herself. 'I don't know,' she said. 'There probably wouldn't be much I could do. I might go back to Jezow. There are peasants there who'd look after me. And Teofil.'

'At least you'd have food if you were in the country.'

'But sometimes I wish I could get right away . . .' Krystyna spoke in a slow, soft voice, staring into the embers of the fire. 'Away from Poland, from Europe even, to Babylon or somewhere like that.' She stopped, laughed and then turned to Rachel. 'It's silly, isn't it? A dream. I don't even know where Babylon is.'

'That way, I think,' said Rachel, waving towards the south. And both girls laughed.

Stefan wrote in his notebook:

Today we reached Lesson Five. We sat opposite one another on the floor, Tilly with nothing on under her skirt. Her knees were raised. So were mine. The faint scent of her adolescent genitals disgusted me: nevertheless I removed my shoe and placed my left leg between her thighs. I inserted my stockinged toe into her cunt and softly moved it against her clitoris. We both watched the big toe as if it was a worm, both for some minutes with detachment. Then Tilly admitted that the venereal sensation was not unpleasant, and eventually that it was enjoyable. She leant back and rested her torso on her elbow. I continued to wriggle my toe until her buttocks moved in a kind of rhythm: then I started to press harder with the toe so that its pressure would produce pain as much as pleasure. 'No,' she murmured. Her hands came down to ease the pressure from my foot, but when I started to withdraw it she said, 'No,' much more emphatically, clasped it between her legs and had it dig into her until she bounced with a silly little orgasm.

She agreed afterwards that it was extraordinary, but that she did enjoy it and would like to do it again.

That night I dined at the Palace, invited by the Princess who placed me on her left. Tilly gave me a 'look' from the other end of the table. I ignored it. Opposite me sat the impresario Edelmann whom the Princess has decided will put on my plays. He said that he had read them both and would like to put them on in September. 'I hope they aren't too long,' said the Princess. Edelmann laughed. It was quite clear that he slavers after the Princess. 'If anything they are too short,' he said. 'A play can never be too short,' said the Princess. The impresario laughed again; and afterwards offered me three hundred zlotys for the option. I accepted.

Ten

Stefan's double bill – *Miss Katasia* and *Scenes from the Class
War* – opened in the small Prodski theatre on 1 October 1938.
The audience for the first night was invited, and besides the
critics it consisted chiefly of the friends of the Prince and
Princess Czarniecki. They were all dressed in elaborate, magnificent evening clothes, and before the curtain went up they
chattered wildly about Chamberlain, Czechoslovakia and the
astonishing, scandalous absence of Lieutenant Brec-Zwolenski
from the Princess's entourage. Some said that he had been
mobilized; others that he had been dismissed; and a third party
maintained that he had absented himself to protest against the
Princess's 'patronage' of Count Kornowski.

Stefan himself sat in the circle near to but not next to the
Prince and Princess. His Aunt Cecylia, Uncle Max, Krystyna
and Rachel had seats in the stalls. Rachel herself had said she
would prefer to sit there rather than next to Stefan. 'I couldn't
bear to be the "writer's wife"', she had said. 'I'd much rather
be an anonymous spectator.' So she sat in the stalls while
Stefan, in the circle, sat between Edelmann and the director,
who talked to one another over his knees. He sat silent watching
the curtain, his face fixed in a permanent Kornowski grimace.

The lights were lowered: the chatter stopped. There was a
hush. The curtain rose for *Miss Katasia* to show the porch of a
church with the pulpit just visible beyond the door.

(An EDUCATED STABLE BOY is sitting on the bench in the
porch trying to compose a letter. He is picking his teeth.)

STABLE BOY: (to himself) Katasia. You are too natural. You
disgust me. How can there be anything of any value between
us? I shall never see you again. (He examines the toothpick.)

213

Dear Katasia. If ever I ran my fingers over your teeth, it was not a gesture of affection or endearment. It was merely that at the time I had mislaid my nailfile . . . (He looks at his toothpick again) and knowing this . . . (He shifts his position) you will never want to see me again. (He stands up, paces up and down, and sits down again.) My darling Katasia: my confessor, Father Paul, refuses me absolution unless I pledge never to see you again. We must be brave. Adieu.

(He is interrupted by the entrance of another man, dressed in a fantastic fashion, like a South American Savage.)

STABLE BOY: Who are you?
SAVAGE: I am just an aimless wanderer.
STABLE BOY: I see.
SAVAGE: Yes, I am just an aimless wanderer.

(He peers into the church and then leaves the stage.)

STABLE BOY: Katasia. I always hated you and now I am leaving you. My aim was to humiliate you, and that done I am free to pursue my destiny. (He sits down, evidently satisfied with the final version. A few moments later a sturdy young woman enters the church porch and he jumps up. It is KATASIA.)

KATASIA: What are you doing here?
STABLE BOY: I was just waiting for Mass, Miss Katasia.
KATASIA: Well, you will hardly have time to stay for Mass.
STABLE BOY: No, Miss Katasia. Miss Katasia . . .
KATASIA: What is it?
STABLE BOY: Well, I wondered . . .
KATASIA: Get along. Remember to be in the hay loft at eight tonight. (The STABLE BOY leaves the stage: the SAVAGE reappears.) Who the devil do you think you are?
SAVAGE: Just an aimless wanderer.
KATASIA: Well that just won't do, you know. You can't just turn up here and announce that you are just an aimless wanderer. Oh no. This is the twentieth century, you know.
SAVAGE: Yes.

KATASIA: And this extraordinary costume. You are surely ashamed?

SAVAGE: Yes.

KATASIA: What is it then? Why are you just an aimless wanderer?

SAVAGE: Well, I am no Christian.

KATASIA: No Christian?

SAVAGE: No Christian. I am no Christian at all.

KATASIA: I see. Perhaps you would like a job on the estate? Is there anything you can do?

SAVAGE: One or two things.

KATASIA: I am sure there will be something. I will talk to the bailiff.

SAVAGE: That would be very kind.

KATASIA: You could train to be a lawyer or a diplomat or something like that. How would you like to be a lawyer?

SAVAGE: A lawyer? A judge, perhaps?

KATASIA: Yes. A judge or a politician. You will make plenty of money and rise to some great social position.

SAVAGE: It would certainly give an aim to my life.

KATASIA: Yes, it would give an aim: and who knows, when you are qualified we might get married?

SAVAGE: Oh yes.

KATASIA: We would live in a house and have children. Think of that.

SAVAGE: Oh yes. Oh yes. Now I have an aim in life.

KATASIA: Well, I must go to Mass now. It has been very nice to meet you like this.

(KATASIA goes into the church. The SAVAGE peers curiously into the church. Enter the THREE BROTHERS of Katasia.)

FIRST BROTHER: I never would have known it was a Sunday if Katasia had not kicked Jola down the stairs.

SECOND BROTHER: She always does it, every Sunday.

THIRD BROTHER: I never know why.

SECOND BROTHER: It's as good a day as any.

FIRST BROTHER: She is jealous.

SECOND BROTHER: Why?

FIRST BROTHER: Jola is prettier.

THIRD BROTHER: I prefer Jola.

SECOND BROTHER: So do I.

FIRST BROTHER: Me too.

SAVAGE: And me.

FIRST BROTHER: You don't know Jola. She is never allowed out of the house and you have certainly never been in it.

SAVAGE: That is true, but she sounds nicer.

SECOND BROTHER: She is.

THIRD BROTHER: Even though she cannot join in games.

SAVAGE: Why not?

THIRD BROTHER: She can't run or walk.

SAVAGE: She can't run or walk?

SECOND BROTHER: And she is fourteen years old. Doesn't that shock you?

FIRST BROTHER: You see, every time she tries to walk, Katasia pushes her down on the floor.

THIRD BROTHER: The stairs on Sundays.

FIRST BROTHER: And now there is a permanent maid to do it.

SAVAGE: You should stop them. Why don't you stop them?

FIRST BROTHER: She can crawl very well.

SECOND BROTHER: And she can swing and hop and rolls around in the sweetest way.

THIRD BROTHER: If she could walk, she might become just like Katasia.

FIRST BROTHER: It would spoil her nature.

THIRD BROTHER: The doctor once said that it was quite natural for the elder daughter to be jealous of the younger one.

SAVAGE: Poor Jola.

THIRD BROTHER: You have never met Jola. How can you say poor Jola when you have never met her? She is perfectly happy. She has plenty of books. She reads like anything.

SAVAGE: It is a scandal.

FIRST BROTHER: She really is happy. You must believe us.

SAVAGE: It is a public scandal.

SECOND BROTHER: Happier than most girls of her age, I should say.

FIRST BROTHER: She has no problems. None of the usual sort.

SAVAGE: No problems?

SECOND BROTHER: Not of the usual sort – the sort Katasia has.

FIRST BROTHER: Jola will never marry.

THIRD BROTHER: Who would want to marry a wife who could not walk?

SAVAGE: I don't see why not. I might want to marry her.

(A priest enters. He nods to the BROTHERS, looks the SAVAGE up and down and enters the church.)

FIRST BROTHER: (after a pause) Were you serious in saying that you might want to marry Jola?

SAVAGE: Well I might be. But I have never met her.

SECOND BROTHER: We could arrange an introduction.

THIRD BROTHER: You have to crouch down when talking to her.

SECOND BROTHER: And smile. She thinks people are always smiling.

SAVAGE: Would she have to crawl up the aisle? Would it be a crawling wedding, with everyone crawling?

SECOND BROTHER: Jola gets very giddy when she is propped up.

SAVAGE: But how would she be as a lawyer's wife?

FIRST BROTHER: So you are a lawyer, are you? What a strange costume.

SAVAGE: Tradition.

FIRST BROTHER: I see.

SAVAGE: Or a politician's wife.

SECOND BROTHER: She'd sleep with anyone.

THIRD BROTHER: Yes, anyone at all.

SAVAGE: What do you mean?

THIRD BROTHER: Well, she is rather like that.

SAVAGE: She's still quite young.

SECOND BROTHER: Yes, of course. I mean later.

SAVAGE: When she was my wife?

SECOND BROTHER: Yes, by then. Certainly.

SAVAGE: I don't want to marry that sort of girl.

SECOND BROTHER: You wouldn't mind it in Jola.

THIRD BROTHER: When you saw her crawling around there, you would forget any grudge you had against her.

SECOND BROTHER: She's enchanting.

FIRST BROTHER: Pretty.

THIRD BROTHER: She's one in a million.

217

SECOND BROTHER: One in ten million.
FIRST BROTHER: Quite unique.
SECOND BROTHER: Kind.
THIRD BROTHER: Gentle.
FIRST BROTHER: Considerate.
SAVAGE: Then it's settled. I'll marry Jola.

(In the background the PRIEST mounts the pulpit.)

PRIEST: I read from Isaiah.
FIRST BROTHER: It will cost you something.
SAVAGE: Much?
FIRST BROTHER: For Jola, it will seem like nothing.
THIRD BROTHER: One of those feathers would suit me.
SAVAGE (taking one from his head dress): Here.
PRIEST: 'Day of desolation . . .'
SECOND BROTHER: I would rather like that medal you have there.
PRIEST: 'Seven women take hold of one man . . .'
SAVAGE: This one?
SECOND BROTHER: Yes, if it's all right by you.
PRIEST: 'Saying "we will eat our own bread and wear our own apparel . . ." '
SAVAGE: I am rather fond of this one myself.
SECOND BROTHER: She has fine legs.
SAVAGE: Jola?
SECOND BROTHER: Yes, Jola has the finest legs I have ever seen.
PRIEST: ' "Only let us be called by thy name to take away our reproach." '
SAVAGE: All right. Here is the medal. And for you?
FIRST BROTHER: I am the breadwinner. Money for me.
SAVAGE: Thirty zlotys?
FIRST BROTHER: Fifty.
SAVAGE: Forty.
FIRST BROTHER: Forty-three.
SAVAGE: Forty-two.
FIRST BROTHER: Forty-three.
SAVAGE: Forty-two.
FIRST BROTHER: Forty-three.

SAVAGE: Forty-three zlotys it is.

PRIEST: 'Seven women catching hold of one man . . .'

FIRST BROTHER: You have struck a good bargain.

PRIEST: ' "to be saved from the reproach of barrenness" '.

FIRST BROTHER: But there is one thing. Katasia will have to be consulted.

SAVAGE: I suppose there is that.

PRIEST: 'But the Lord has his doom waiting for them.'

(KATASIA walks out of the church.)

KATASIA: I cannot stay there a moment longer.

FIRST BROTHER: You always take the sermons personally.

KATASIA: They are meant personally. Anything can happen on the day of desolation.

SECOND BROTHER: It is only Sunday today.

KATASIA: Did I remember to throw Jola down the stairs?

FIRST BROTHER: The maid did it.

KATASIA: As long as it's done.

FIRST BROTHER: Have you a busy day?

KATASIA: A very busy day. I have to teach this savage how to be a lawyer, and meet the stable boy in the loft at eight.

FIRST BROTHER: I meant to tell you. The stable boy has gone.

KATASIA: Gone?

FIRST BROTHER: He left this note for you.

(KATASIA opens the letter and reads it aloud.)

KATASIA: 'Miss Katasia. I must do what I cannot say. I have fled with Jola.'

THIRD BROTHER: How fantastic.

FIRST BROTHER: Why Jola, I wonder.

KATASIA: He is used to four-legged creatures.

FIRST BROTHER: What are we to do?

KATASIA: Well, there is still the savage.

FIRST BROTHER: He has just contracted to marry Jola.

KATASIA: Idiot. Jola has just run off.

SECOND BROTHER: You could marry him, Katasia.

THIRD BROTHER: And be a lawyer's wife.

KATASIA: We had considered that.

219

FIRST BROTHER: (to the SAVAGE) How about it?

SAVAGE: She can walk.

THIRD BROTHER: And sing.

SAVAGE: Jola couldn't sing?

THIRD BROTHER: She was tone deaf.

SAVAGE: Then I'm much better off with Katasia.

KATASIA: You always would have been.

FIRST BROTHER: Then it's settled at fifty.

SAVAGE: Fifty it is.

PRIEST: 'And the Lord has his doom waiting for them.'

The curtain flopped down. There was a short pause – a moment of complete silence: then someone shouted 'Bravo' and the clapping began. It began; it continued; it rose to a crescendo; it was sustained. Then it subsided and the scramble began to get into the foyer to buy the icecreams before they sold out and to see the Princess or the Minister of this or that who was in her party. Everyone's face was smiling. 'Delightful' was a word which wafted over the heads of the crowd. Then 'succinct' – and 'succinct' seemed to triumph over 'delightful' as a wittier epithet to describe the play – wittier, and with a prudent touch of double meaning. 'Succinct,' they shouted – even 'delightfully succinct'; and an old general was heard to say that it was the first time a play had not sent him to sleep.

Then Czechoslovakia, Chamberlain and peace in our time. There was an atmosphere of mixed hysterias – relief, terror, disgust, bravado, patriotism . . . and the fascinating riddle of the Lieutenant who was not there and the Princess who was – standing with a straight spine, her lips in a permanent pout. People paid their respects. She smiled, nodded, listened, smiled and moved on like a royal barge on choppy waters. The author was seen to introduce her to three women who stood out from the rest by the drabness of their dresses. Some said they were his mother and two sisters: others that this could not be so because one of the girls looked Jewish and the other did not.

'But Kornowski isn't a Jew?'

'Then she must be his wife.'

'But is he married?'

'Well, if he is he keeps her well out of the way . . .' Etc.

The interval was extended, yet when the bell rang for the

nd half of the programme the audience had only been in the theatre for three quarters of an hour. Slowly they moved back into the auditorium – shuffling, chatting, laughing and once again sat in the plush seats of the small theatre, waiting for the lights to go down and the curtain to go up for the second of Stefan Kornowski's plays – *Scenes from the Class War*.

Scene One. A Drawing-room. The COUNTESS X is sitting on a sofa doing nothing. The doorbell rings and a few moments later the MAID shows in an elegantly dressed GENTLEMAN.

GENTLEMAN: (crossing and kissing the COUNTESS's hand) Dear Countess, I must tell you about something that happened to me yesterday . . .
COUNTESS: (turning to the maid) Molly, bring us some coffee will you?
MAID: Very well, madam. (She curtseys and goes out.)
COUNTESS: Well, James?
GENTLEMAN: I bought a striped shirt at the market. A tramp came up behind me and asked me for it. I looked at him with contempt. He swore at me. I spat in his face. He hit me. I gave him the shirt to confuse him.

(The COUNTESS remains silent for a moment as the MAID enters with a silver tray, silver coffeepot and spoons, porcelain cups, milk jugs, and plates covered with petit fours. The MAID goes out.)

COUNTESS: Why, John, what a strange thing to happen.
GENTLEMAN: It was, wasn't it?

Scene Two. The Kitchen. The MAID is baking. A scruffily dressed man, THE TRAMP, is leaning against the table watching her.

THE TRAMP: What are they, then?
MAID: Oh, cakes and tarts.
TRAMP: For you?
MAID: For madam, though I may take a few.
TRAMP: And I may get some?

MAID: Wait until they're done, greedy.

TRAMP: (after a silence) I asked a man at the market for a shirt. He looked at me with contempt so I swore at him. He spat in my face so I hit him. He gave me the shirt. I only wear it on Sundays.

(The MAID laughs and wipes her hands on her apron.)

MAID: Well, wear it now for a quick moment.

(Both exit arm in arm.)

Scene Three. The COUNTESS's bedroom. The COUNTESS is seated before her dressing table, studying herself in the mirror. The MAID is brushing her hair.

COUNTESS: I'm dining out this evening, Polly, and I simply cannot decide what to wear . . . pass me the talcum powder . . . Polly, yes, and leave the hair alone but dust me there, yes, and there . . . George told me that it is a carnival ball, but I am sure it is meant for the young. All my costumes are so old-fashioned . . . Ah, you may bring me my clean underclothes from where they are warming by the radiator, Polly, surely they will do, whatever I wear over them. But better the lower one . . . and rub my shoulders a little, will you? If I am to caper around this evening, they must be supple. Do you think I could simply go in an evening gown?

MAID: I think madam would do better to do something bizarre.

COUNTESS: Bizarre, Polly, yes, but what?

MAID: Something even a little audacious, madam?

COUNTESS: Audacious, yes, Polly, but dare I?

MAID: And something amusing, madam . . .

COUNTESS: Yes, yes . . .

MAID: Madam could go as a chorus girl.

COUNTESS: Yes, yes, but I don't like people to see my tattoo.

MAID: Madam should be proud of her tattoo.

COUNTESS: And I have no costume.

MAID: Would madam consider dressing up in a sheet?

COUNTESS: A sheet? Oh, a sheet. What an amusement. Yes, what fun. But then, Molly, they would see too little. I have no wish to be smothered.

MAID: What, madam, what about . . .

COUNTESS: Yes?

MAID: And I have one if madam has not . . .

COUNTESS: What, Polly, what?

MAID: A gentleman's striped shirt, madam.

Scene Four. The Drawing-room. The COUNTESS is not there. The GENTLEMAN is shown in by the MAID.

GENTLEMAN: So, Polly . . .

MAID: So, sir . . .

GENTLEMAN: It is wet today.

MAID: Yes, sir, and the Countess will be down in a moment, ready to go with you to the Carnival Ball.

GENTLEMAN: This humidity is tiresome, Polly. It cramps one, you know.

MAID: It gives the cramp, does it sir? I wouldn't know, you see. I don't leave the kitchen.

GENTLEMAN: You should leave the kitchen, Polly. To take the fresh air. I know you don't understand about such things, but the body is thwarted by such confinement.

MAID: Oh, I'm not thwarted, sir, I can tell you that.

GENTLEMAN: (eyes widening) Aren't you thwarted, Polly? No, perhaps not; but your children. Think of your future children . . .

MAID: Children, sir? Poof.

GENTLEMAN: Have you no interest in children, Polly? Doesn't your female organism cry out for them?

MAID: Well, I wash the linen, sir, and that's as much thought as I give them.

GENTLEMAN: You wash the linen, do you, Polly? Your own clothes? The Countess's clothes?

MAID: And your clothes too, sir, if you'd care to leave them here.

GENTLEMAN: My clothes. Oh, I would have to think about it. Would you wash them with your hands, Polly, in the same water as your own? Would my gentleman's shirts and collars swill in with your intimate garments?

MAID: Yes, sir. And with any old striped shirt.

(The COUNTESS enters, wearing the striped shirt.)

223

COUNTESS: Look, John. How do you like my costume?
GENTLEMAN: Well, it's . . . Oh God. What the Devil. By Jove . . . (He collapses expostulating.)

Scene Five. The Kitchen. The MAID and the TAMP are sitting arm-in-arm listening to the radio.

TRAMP: Now I am without a shirt for Sundays.
MAID: But you never get up on Sundays anyway.

Once again the curtain fell; but this time there was no moment of silence before the audience burst into vehement applause. It had got the hang of this 'theatre of brevity'. There were waves of clapping, cries of 'bravo', then shouts for 'author', 'director', curtain calls, more cries, laughter, applause – only the critics remained inscrutable, clapping just as much as politeness demanded. Yet even they could not escape the atmosphere of triumph which filled the theatre like stage smoke. As the audience roared, clapped, shouted, judgements were born. The play was a success. A *succès de scandale* (because they were short and had references to dirty linen); a *succès d'estime* because they were absurd. The actors and actresses embraced. Bouquets of flowers were thrust into their arms. The director appeared on stage, then Edelmann the impresario; and finally, for no apparent reason, the Princess was there in front of them all, her arms filled with flowers. She smiled with her plush lips and beckoned as best she could to the balcony for the author who was now the only missing pillar to this triumphal arch: but the lights shone in her face and she could not see him: and indeed he was not there, but had left the theatre to walk in the streets alone.

The inscrutable critics gave the play the same reception as the audience on the first night. 'Short, sharp, shattering,' wrote Nienaski. 'A vindication of absurdity as a means for expressing the kernel of truth. In *Miss Katasia* – all that need be said about women: in *Scenes from the Class War* – all that need be said about Society.'

Schwartz, in *Kurier Poranny*, officially declared the birth of 'the Theatre of Brevity'. 'Now a play is like a poem – its meaning distilled into minimal dimensions so that each sentence each gesture, becomes a scene in itself . . .' Only one critic (in the *Express Wieczorny*) was ironic in his praise. 'At last a playwright who understands what a Warsaw audience loves in the theatre – an opportunity to dress up beforehand, and eat and drink afterwards. With two plays lasting at most a quarter of an hour each, last night's audience at the Prodski Theatre was totally enthusiastic. No wonder Count Kornowski is acclaimed as a genius.'

One member of the audience who was not entirely delighted with the previous evening was the Princess – but this only because Stefan had not appeared at the reception she had given after the play. Indeed for several days after the first night he skulked in his own home, and read the reviews with a dismal expression on his face. Rachel, who had bought the papers, and read the reviews out loud in an excited voice, could not understand his reaction to this success: but she could not understand the success either, and when Stefan asked her, point-blank, what she thought of the plays, she just answered: 'But they were frightfully good, weren't they? Everyone says so.'

When Stefan asked Krystyna the same question she said, with an ambiguous smile: 'Well, no one else could have written them.'

The plays were a success with the public as well as the critics, so that Stefan, for the first time in his life, had money to spend and was taken up by aristocratic circles which wanted to seem literary and literary circles that wanted to seem aristocratic.

The Princess forgave him for running out on her reception – but made him do penance by attending many more. He was, after all, her discovery: and she claimed her rights by standing with him arm-in-arm as her guests filed past. Stefan put up with it all, though he knew what was assumed now that the Lieutenant was no more to be seen. He put up with it, but with a bad grace. He did not enjoy his success. He felt the whole thing was a fraud, a charade, a dance, a polonaise of silly Slavs – while others marched.

His mood was made by the mixture of private and public events pressing on his mind. Hitler crouched like a panther with blazing green eyes – his purpose to pounce on the silly chickens, the Poles, of which Stefan was one – the chickens which scratched in the dirt and called it art or life. Stefan was not only aware of Hitler; he was obsessed by him. In some sense he envied him his fanaticism, his power, his ruthlessness. He saw him as an artist, achieving with whole nations what Stefan could not achieve with words. His art was bad, but this force and ambition were incontestable. He was a man who lived his thoughts, who imposed his pattern on life, while others were shaped by whatever came along.

I promised to be true to my youth (wrote Stefan), and in my youth I promised my life to my mind. I swore that I would never subject it to instinct or inheritance: that I would not roll through life posturing, drunk, absurd – a Pole! I would be a man, distilled into his essence, obedient to the dictates of thought. For this I became a writer, for at least in his imagination a writer is sovereign and free. And what am I now? A fashionable success! The protégé of a Princess, the author of two pseudo-plays whose artistic merit lies in their mockery of art. The theatre of brevity: the music of silence; the school of blank canvases. What a triumph of my Polishness over myself!

This line of thought brought Stefan into a hidden state of panic. The more time he spent with the Princess and her friends – with their silly posturing and fruitless décolletages – discussing art, his plays, Hitler, Chamberlain, the weather, the new race-course, as if they were taking truffles out of chocolate boxes and popping them into their mouths – the more terrified he became that he would die as one of them. 'Here lies Stefan Kornowski – dilettante, littérateur. He amused Warsaw for a week.'
There were occasions when he told himself that it was ridiculous to write his own epitaph when he was not yet thirty years old; yet he knew that at thirty the die is cast, and that in these precious years he was becoming the man he would always be.
Life at home had nothing to console him. Rachel's domesticity was in its way more irritating than the falsity of the Princess's salon. Like a cow sensing a storm, she had settled down on her dry patch of grass and chewed cud with her calves. She was

protected from anxiety by the kind of complacency which maternity engenders: nothing outside her family circle could threaten her because nothing outside her family circle was real. So besotted was she with her children, she could not conceive of anyone who might want to do them harm. And Stefan, as he watched her busy herself in the kitchen, gaily whisking eggs or lovingly wiping the mouths and noses of the twins, was moved to an even greater state of depression. 'Here lies Stefan Kornowski, beloved husband of Rachel Kornowska, father to Isaac Kornowski, tailor . . .'

It might have been that this self-disgust would have sent him back to his writing with greater determination – to leap out of his Polishness into the Olympian heights of world genius. He did look once again at his novel, but every word of what he had written disgusted him. It reeked like an old cheese of affectation and pose. There was not a phrase which was serious or sincere. Its aspirations were only to be clever: its achievements so far were only artificial.

But what was art but artificiality? It was a fraud – a concoction of ersatz emotions and experience which gave the illusion of life. It was a hallucinatory drug for those without the courage to live – they could love, suffer, be cowardly, be brave in one novel after another, all the while sitting in an armchair.

Only action was real. Bruno had understood that, and Stefan now envied him – envied him even in his prison cell. For even if he were to be executed tomorrow, he could be sure that his life had been what life should be – action directed by reason and conviction.

Of course Bruno had advantages. He was brave. His convictions were simple and his body was strong. Stefan had the matching disadvantages. His convictions were negative, his body weak – and he was a coward. But there was time.

In the wet, dark days of November, Stefan's life was dedicated to introspective contemplation of this sort. He went each day to the Czarniecki Palace and lay on the large bed in his room, staring at the tall ceiling, rising every now and then only to write down his thoughts in his notebook. The Prince and Princess were shooting on their estate in Lithuania, and Tilly was in Paris; so he was undisturbed and could lie for hours more comfortably but substantially in the same way as he had in the summer house in Jezow. And as in Jezow he began at the beginning.

I think therefore I am, therefore my thought is my being. And what is my thought? When the impurities of trivial, transitory preoccupations have been extracted, and only the distilled essence remains it is:

1. There is no God. My senses do not perceive Him: nor does my reason suggest that He must exist.
2. Since there is no God, reality is what is real to me. Heat, light, truth, love, longing exist only in my brain and body. If my head is removed from my shoulders, everything ceases to exist. In other words, the individual is sovereign. He is the Lord and Master of Creation because Creation exists only in him.
3. What is to be done with the power and freedom? To pursue pleasure. To attain 'happiness'. Pleasure being what is enjoyed; happiness being a state of contentment on one level, and ecstasy on another.
4. But what if (like Hitler) I could only be content if all Jews were removed from the face of the earth, and all Slavs reduced to servitude? Good luck to you.
5. But what if (like a Jew or a Pole) I could only be content if I was protected from Hitler's antagonism? Good luck to you. Form an army. Invent a morality in which men are equal and nations have a right to self-determination.
6. But what if (like Stefan Kornowski) you hate health, nature, wholesomeness? What if copulation is repugnant and ecstasy attained only through pain and degradation? Good luck to you.
7. But what if (like Tilly Czarniecka) you are silly and young and present your body to your mother's friend because you want to seem adult and defy your mother, only to find yourself strangled, gashed and dead? Hard luck.
Conclusion: I think therefore I am, therefore I am my thought. My thought dictates ecstasy and contentment. I search for it in culture, patriotism and family life but all

bore me, disgust me; and boredom and disgust are pain. I search for it in sexuality but I remain frustrated. I ask my imagination to project actions which will relieve the frustration: and into my mind comes the form of a fatuous adolescent (Tilly), her face beatific as simultaneously she attains death and orgasm. That for me would be the moment of triumph, ecstasy, oblivion – a victory of truth over habit, convention, Polishness . . .

By the spring of 1939, Stefan Kornowski was calm again. He became noticeably benevolent, playing with his children, talking to Rachel and being quite witty at the Princess's parties. Everyone had a different explanation for this changed mood. The Princess said that it was because his work was going well: 'a writer's mood always depends upon his work'. Rachel thought it was because his plays had come off at the Prodski Theatre. Krystyna put it down to the spring weather. Tilly Czarniecka was quite sure that if Stefan looked happier it was because she had returned from Paris and was eager to resume their lessons in life.

Eleven

In March 1939, the Germans moved into Memel and Prague, while the Western powers decided that there was nothing to be done but reassure the Poles and temporize with the Russians.

In May, quite arbitrarily, Bruno was released from prison. Krystyna received a telegram a few hours before he arrived in Warsaw and was able to meet him at the station. The train was crowded, some of the passengers already fleeing from the west towards the east. Krystyna stood at the barrier and saw Bruno long before he saw her. He stood out from the crowd because he was tall, and because he walked in an unhurried way, his head high, his hand carrying a small bag containing his few belongings.

When he reached the barrier, he looked down – not searching for a face but to give his ticket to the ticket-collector. His hair was cropped short and his face was thin. When he recognized Krystyna he smiled – though again without any anxiety or surprise.

They embraced like old friends and walked arm-in-arm towards the trams.

'Why did they release you?' she asked.

Bruno shrugged his shoulders. 'I don't know. We aren't the danger now.'

In the streets there was evidence of mobilization. They passed columns of young recruits, their peasant faces unmistakable under their berets. On the pavement, officers who before had sauntered elegantly now walked with a brisk pace and a still more self-important expression on their faces.

'For twenty years,' said Bruno, watching these military activities from the window of the tram, 'they have taken the wealth of Poland. Soon we shall see if it was all worthwhile.'

He walked into the flat in Sluzewska Street ahead of Krystyna. Teofil sat at the kitchen table, his face covered with jam. His mouth dropped open when he saw his father. Bruno dropped his bag and whisked his son out of the chair into his arms. He twirled him around in his embrace and kissed him with such strength that the jam was wiped off onto his stubble moustache.

Later, when Teofil was in bed, and Mamuska had returned to the flat below, Krystyna served supper for her husband – soup, sausage, black bread and beer – which he ate carefully down to the last crumb. They hardly talked. Bruno asked about Teofil, and Krystyna told him stories which made him smile – an unnatural, inscrutable expression for his melancholy face. And she gave him news of Stefan and Rachel. 'Stefan's so perverse,' she said. 'When everyone was optimistic in the autumn, he was depressed. Now, when we're all worried, he has become quite cheerful . . .'

'He always goes against the tide,' said Bruno.

While Krystyna cleared away the dishes and washed them, Bruno read the paper and then switched on the radio to listen to the news. Krystyna came and sat beside him, and when the news was over, and the radio switched off, she looked at Bruno and asked him: 'What will you do now?'

He looked into her eyes. She looked away. 'Perhaps you don't know,' she said.

'In prison,' said Bruno, 'at least you have time to think.'

'Have you . . . have you reached some conclusions?' Again she glanced at him and again, when he met her gaze, she looked away.

'For myself, yes,' he said. 'But you . . .'

She laughed. 'Me? Don't . . . I mean to say, treat me how you like.'

'Haven't *you* reached any conclusions?'

Krystyna shrugged her shoulders. 'I suppose there'll be a war.'

'Inevitably.'

'For the Corridor?'

'Goebbels will think of some excuse . . .'

'And what will happen?'

'The fascists will win.' Bruno looked straight ahead at the window, speaking as though he was reciting something he had learnt by heart. 'It will be a matter of months – perhaps weeks. The Polish army will be obliterated, all those regiments of Chasseurs crushed by German tanks. France and Britain will do nothing. Britain has no army: France has only the Maginot Line, which you cannot move to Poland. There is the Soviet Union, but their forces are disorganized and demoralized . . .'

'You can't think, surely, that the Germans will get as far as Warsaw?'

'Almost certainly . . .'

'But they only want the Corridor and Silesia . . .'

'Hitler does not stop. Look at Czechoslovakia. Read *Mein Kampf*. He has designs on the whole of Europe . . .'

'And on us?'

'On us? Certainly. We will be slaves unless, of course, we are able or intelligent. In that case it will be the concentration camps . . .'

Krystyna looked at him now full in the face. 'I thought we might escape . . . to Jezow. The peasants there would hide us.'

Bruno smiled. 'Nine out of ten might hide you, but the tenth would be a spy. A Ruthenian or a fascist would denounce you. They'd smoke you out.'

'Then what can we do?'

Bruno looked at her with no particular expression. 'The drawer in the bedroom,' he said, 'the one with my socks and handkerchiefs. It has a false bottom . . .'

'I know.'

'In it I shall leave an address in Lvov – a cobbler's shop. The man was in the Party. He is also a friend. He can get you into Roumania, and give you addresses in Bucharest of others who will help you . . .'

'But you . . .'

'I shall stay. That is what I decided in prison.'

'But the Party has been dissolved . . .'

'I know. I will not stay for the Party.'

'Then for what?'

'For Poland.'

Krystyna looked down at her knees and said, in a low voice: 'Haven't you fought enough?'

Bruno took her hand. 'I have fought too much,' he said, 'and I have killed too many men – men who were not guilty in the name of ideals which were unsound. But now . . .' He hesitated. 'Now, even if I don't know what I believe, I know what I am. A Pole. And I will not run from the Germans. Never. I am not a coward, and my son will not be a slave.'

Those months of early summer were strange but happy. Only Teofil was untroubled: he could not see the signs of war, but just his father's presence – peaceful, benign, returning each day from a job in a timber yard to play with him – often with a new consignment of wooden bricks which made castles, towers and viaducts. At weekends all the grown man's time was spent with the child – taking him on expeditions by bus into the country, or by boat down the Vistula to the castle of Bielany. Krystyna would come with them, and away from the city she too would look happier. The mother and father would walk arm-in-arm: on a picnic she would lie back on the grass and Bruno would lie next to her on his stomach, his face close to hers, his hands moving wisps of her hair that had fallen over her face.

They did not talk about anything substantial. The lines of melancholy on their faces showed what they had suffered: the cautious, tentative smiles showed what they had forgiven. They could now look into each other's eyes, unafraid of what they might see in their expressions. Yet every once in a while, each looked away, glanced at the horizon and set his or her jaw in a hard expression as if waiting for a wind that would blow them both in different directions.

Stefan knew that Bruno had been released – and he saw him once or twice with Krystyna – but he made no attempt to see him alone and Bruno, in his turn, felt estranged from the fashionable, outrageous young writer who was so welcome in the drawing-rooms of the Ujazadowski Avenue. In a sense they avoided one another, or they avoided finding themselves alone together. They had much in common in their past, but nothing in the future.

Stefan was preoccupied with his Grand Design, his *acte gratuit*, the sacrifice of Tilly Czarniecka on the altar of logic and amorality. Now that he had made up his mind to kill her, only two problems remained. The one was to bring Tilly to a point where death and ecstasy would be one: the other was to arrange things so that he would not get caught. It was not at all part of the 'logic of his existence' that he should be put down by society as a mad dog.

There was a third problem, less precise than the other two, and that was a faltering will. Murder was easy enough seated at a desk with pen and notebook – but in reality it seemed grotesque and improbable. Stefan had no real Sadistic drive, and his expectation of ecstasy was speculative: he knew quite well that the imagination was unreliable.

But these doubts were dismissed as the product of his Polishness – the trait in the national character which lives in fantasy and never follows anything through. He was determined to succeed, if only to show that he was not pliable stuff, moulded from without by national character, but was himself the mould: and, more specifically, to prove to himself that he was more than the difficult, idiosyncratic child that the soft women around him believed him to be.

In July a friend of the Princess who was also a director of the Baltic Steamship Company offered Stefan a return ticket, first-class, on the maiden voyage to America of the *Jagiello*. The

233

gesture was part of a publicity stunt – an actor, an opera singer and a champion skier had also been invited, together with numerous journalists: it would involve making the return journey across the Atlantic, with only three days in New York in between, but everything would be at the expense of the company, including 'a reasonable consumption of alcohol'.

Stefan accepted without hesitation. He liked the idea in itself; he wanted to get out of Warsaw; and he saw it as an opportunity to meet Tilly Czarniecka somewhere outside the city.

The boat was to sail from Gdynia at mid-day on 20 August, and Stefan promised Tilly that she should go with him. He would smuggle her on board, he said, as his secretary, with a forged passport and a false name. To Tilly, who was just sixteen, this adventure 'with the man she loved' was a fulfilment of her most ambitious, romantic, defiant, unlikely dreams – and she too accepted without hesitation, and agreed at once that the whole thing must be a deadly secret between them.

Together in Stefan's room in her parents' home they planned her escape. It would be unwise, said Stefan, for them to travel together to Gdynia. The best plan would be for Stefan to go there alone and establish himself in a hotel, while Tilly took a different train to Bydgoszcz, a town between Gdynia and Warsaw, take a room and wait for Stefan, who would meet her there on the night of the 19th. Then, on the morning of the 20th, they would travel to Gdynia and board the *Jagiello*.

As they sat together, making these plans, Tilly was alight with love and prettiness. Her eyes promised joys which no man had dreamt of; her lovely, girlish body trembled with surrender. Stefan was not unaffected by this aura of erotic promise, and the longing in her myopic eyes, 'but Rachel too was like that,' he said to himself, 'with a body just for me. I have been swindled once: I will not be swindled again.'

He turned and smiled at Tilly. She squirmed and clutched at his arm like a child. 'I'll do anything to make you happy,' she said. 'Anything at all.'

Stefan was to be away less than a month – and for most of the time he would be on a ship: there were therefore no great preparations to be made. All the same, Stefan passed by

Sluzewska Street to say goodbye to Krystyna and Bruno. He went with Rachel who, in the days before his departure, seemed to cling to him even though she thought the trip 'a good thing for Stefan'.

This ritual farewell to his relations was one of the few functions she could share with him, and she had him hold her arm not only as they walked in the street but also as they climbed the stairs to Aunt Cecylia's flat, where they were to look in before going to the fourth floor for the evening meal.

Aunt Cecylia gave them little thimbles of vodka which they drank sparingly. Stefan was affable, joking with his aunt – remembering the old days.

'You're a changed man now,' said Cecylia – her head in profile. 'So elegant, so successful . . . I hardly recognize you.'

'But in my heart I am the same,' said Stefan with just enough irony in his tone of voice to make Cecylia glance at Rachel before smiling at her nephew and then turning away again.

'Be careful in New York,' she said to Stefan. 'There will be many temptations . . .'

'I shall only be there for three days, with the whole staff of the Baltic Steamship Company to keep an eye on me . . .'

'Well, I hope we'll all be here when you get back,' said Cecylia with a despondent glance at the window.

'Nothing so terrible can happen in a month,' said Stefan, smiling, laughing, and helping himself (with great charm) to some more vodka.

Krystyna and Bruno were waiting above, and Teofil had been allowed to stay up to see 'Onka' whom he loved so much. And for twenty minutes or so they all looked at and talked to Teofil not just because he was demanding and endearing, but because he saved them from talking to one another. So much of what they had been through – of what they knew and could not say – blocked avenues of conversation. All that had brought them together before – which had kept them talking late into the night – was now too dangerous to talk about. Politics had been poisoned by the ignominious dissolution of the Party in Poland, and the liquidation of so many of their former friends. Love was haunted by the spirit of Michael Mikolajczyk, whose obese sensuality remained like pus in a wound. They could not even gossip about people they knew, for what friends could they have in common from Rachel's kitchen, Krystyna's jewelry shop, Stefan's drawing-rooms and Bruno's prison?

Thus, when Teofil was eventually sent to bed, and they sat around the table, they were tongue-tied. Bruno and Stefan quickly drank more vodka, proposing numerous, lugubrious toasts to one another – 'our past', was one; 'our future' another. At that Krystyna interrupted them and said: 'I'll drink, but not to the future.'

'Oh but you must,' said Rachel. 'You must always hope for the best.'

'Come on, Krysia,' said Stefan. 'A toast is like a prayer – an atheist's prayer.' He filled up her glass, and then held up his own. 'To the future.'

They drank, the two men throwing back their heads and emptying their glasses in one gulp; the two women sipping them with more caution.

'If a toast is a prayer,' said Bruno, 'then I think the future needs another one.' He reached for the bottle of vodka and filled first Stefan's glass and then his own.

'We'll say a novena,' said Stefan. 'The future . . .'

They drank again, and filled their glasses again.

Krystyna glanced anxiously at Bruno and her brother. 'One thing is certain,' she said. 'We shall have more chance in the future if we are sober than if we are drunk.'

'On the contrary,' said Stefan. 'The only brave Pole is a drunk one. If they equip the army with vodka, they will have a better chance against the Germans than they will with guns.'

'You are all so pessimistic,' said Rachel. 'I don't believe we shall be defeated so easily. We have an army, after all . . .'

Krystyna glanced at Bruno, who looked into his glass with a more serious expression on his face. 'In the end we shall win,' he said, 'but it will be a long fight . . . and a lot of us will suffer.'

The others were silent.

'If we are to be a nation,' he said, 'then we must fight until the last German, the last . . .' He hesitated for a moment, then went on: 'the last foreigner of any sort is on our soil.'

'You sound like Pilsudski,' said Rachel.

'Bruno is patriotic now,' said Krystyna with the air of a

woman describing to another woman her husband's latest hobby.

Bruno filled his glass and drank again without waiting for a toast. The others were silent.

'Well, I shall go back to Bialystok if it looks like war,' said Rachel. 'The Germans won't get as far as that . . .'

'Unless they move in from East Prussia,' said Stefan.

'But they wouldn't, would they?' Rachel asked Bruno.

Bruno looked up, as if about to answer: but then seemed to decide that it was not worth it.

'And what will you do?' Rachel asked Krystyna, giggling because she was drunk.

'How do you mean?'

'To get away from the bombs?'

'I don't know,' said Krystyna.

'Well I shall go to Bialystok and Stefan can come if he likes . . .' Again she giggled and looked at Stefan. 'Though I dare say you won't like it, with Mama and Papa and Uncle Isaac . . .'

'I shall become a war correspondent,' said Stefan, 'and send back surrealist dispatches for the *Kurier Poranny*.'

And so they went on, with fear, vodka and forbidden topics producing this frivolous, aimless conversation. At the end of the evening they said goodbye as if they were only parting for a day or two.

Stefan was equipped for his journey with new clothes packed in a new suitcase. He also had a letter of credit for three hundred dollars, and one hundred more in two fifty-dollar bills. Rachel had provided him with some of this money, together with a list of purchases he was to make in New York. 'Above all clothes for the children,' she said. 'They have those waterproof coats which you can't get in Warsaw.'

Stefan took the list and put it in his wallet. He crouched and kissed his children, stood up again, said goodbye to the girl who looked after them and then carried his case and bag down to the street. Rachel came with him to the station, and in the taxi she clutched his hand in hers with a kind of benevolent possessiveness. Stefan's mood was in suspense. He felt ill-at-ease in his new suit – and apprehensive.

'I hope you have fun,' said Rachel. 'But watch out for the ladies on the boat. A long voyage is meant to make them, well, suggestible . . .'

'I shall lie back on a deckchair sipping beer,' said Stefan, 'observing the weaknesses of human nature . . .'

She squeezed his hand. 'And then you'll come home, won't you? I don't like being without you, especially with all this talk of war.'

'Of course I shall come back,' he said. 'My ticket is only valid for the maiden voyage.'

'You might meet a fascinating negress . . .'

He screwed up his nose. 'Unlikely,' he said. 'And then,' he added, 'what about my career as a war correspondent?'

She smiled, kissed him, squeezed his hand: and then sat in silence – what she would have called 'an intimate silence' – and Stefan squeezed her hand in return with ferocious tightness, as if it was the neck of Tilly Czarniecka.

The Gdynia Express waited on the platform. They found his reserved seat in a first-class compartment, saw the suitcase safely on the rack and paid the porter who had carried it. Then they waited on the platform, saying little. It was hot. Rachel kept brushing back her thick locks which fell over her face, and Stefan noticed that other men who passed them on the platform glanced at her face, then at her figure, then at him. 'Go ahead,' he almost called after them. 'She's all yours.' Then he looked at her face (she smiled) and her figure, saw that she was still a beautiful woman and yet wondered how he had ever been able to caress her. 'Now I could not do it,' he thought to himself. 'Not even with a knife.'

Rachel, intercepting his glances, and suspecting that there was a more complex emotion behind them than the simple affection of a husband taking leave of his wife, smiled at him quizzically; but his eyes gave nothing away. His expression once again became bland.

The whistle blew. Other passengers entered the train, and Stefan climbed on behind them just before a passing porter closed the door. He stooped through the open window and gave Rachel a last kiss. She held on to his hand, even as the train was moving away.

'Write,' she said.

'I'll be back before the letter,' he said.

'Take care,' she said.

The train went faster: their hands parted and Rachel stopped, but remained there; and Stefan stayed at the window until she was out of sight.

He went to his seat and looked out of the window at the suburbs of Warsaw, then at the flat valley of the Vistula, the peasants' houses with painted walls and whitewashed railings. 'When I come back,' he said – addressing the Vistula as much as himself – 'When I come back I shall be a God. I shall have eaten of the Fruit of the Tree of Knowledge. Good and Evil will have been made subject to my will. An unnecessary creature with bulbous breasts will be dead – a young sow sacrificed on the Altar of Reason.'

The train clattered on, over bridges, level crossings, through villages, past more wooden houses and a shrine to the Virgin Mary. 'And you,' said Stefan, speaking now to the statue of the shrine. 'Do your worst. Put a dog at the door of her room. It won't stop me. You can't. My will is virulent and invincible. And Tilly too will shriek blasphemies at the extremity of her pleasure and pain.'

He looked at his watch. The train would be late into Gdynia but Stefan had allowed for delays. He had six hours to go to his hotel, establish himself, make himself noticed, have a drink, dine, before sneaking back to the station to catch the midnight train back to Warsaw. At Bydgoszcz he would get off the train, and walk to the hotel where Tilly would be waiting for him in room 313. An hour later he would leave again, catch the morning express for Gdynia and at mid-day embark upon the *Jagiello* with the maximum *éclat*.

The plan was not flawless. There were people who might notice him when he returned to the station – porters or ticket-collectors – but the third-class compartments of the trains were filled with soldiers, there was confusion: he could count upon the Polishness of the Poles to cover his crime.

Twelve

Everything in Gdynia had been built since the First World War, but the Grand Hotel had already established a certain style. The porters opened the door of Stefan's taxi with a flourish. There was a thick carpet on the floor of the foyer; and the reception desk was polished and clean. Behind it an elegant girl was speaking passable French to a Frenchman; and when Stefan announced himself she nodded and even smiled to acknowledge that Count Kornowski was an important guest.

His room looked out towards the sea. The horizon beyond the confines of the bay mingled in a haze with the sea. To the left were the cranes and warehouse roofs of the harbour, with one or two ships' funnels poking through – one of them, perhaps, the funnel of the *Jagiello*. Stefan looked at his watch. It was six.

He unpacked his suitcase, hanging his suits in the wardrobe, placing his shirts and underclothes in the chest-of-drawers. Next he took a bath because he felt grimy after his journey. Then he lay on his bed to rest. At seven he changed into a dark, double-breasted suit and went down to the foyer of the hotel. He went to the restaurant to inquire about dinner and booked a table for eight o'clock. Then he went to the bar and ordered a bourbon, both to prepare himself for America and to ensure that the waiter would remember him. The drink was brought: he sat back on the plush seat at the small glass-topped table, sipped his drink and every now and then popped an olive into his mouth, and then spat the stone out into his hand.

Later he ordered a second whisky. The unusual alcohol in his blood made him feel brave and benign – both at the same time. He was excited at the thought of the adventure before him: he looked forward to meeting Tilly, her eyes sparkling with intrigue, her body warm from sleep yet ready for the last lesson in the art of love . . . Or so he imagined. He smiled, and looked vacantly at an empty chair on the other side of the room. A strong but pleasant smell of a woman's scent entered his nostrils which, for a moment, he took to be part of his fantasy: but then a lilting voice beside him stuttered his name. 'Count Kornowski?'

He looked round and up and recognized her immediately.

'Count Kornowski?' she said again. 'I hope I'm not disturbing you. You won't remember me, but we met once with Jan Onufry . . .'

Stefan got to his feet. 'Of course,' he said. 'In the Café Ziemianska.'

The girl – for she was indeed the girl, the *demi-mondaine* who had been with his friend Onufry in the café – smiled at him with a kind of practised, deliberate modesty. 'I saw your picture in the paper,' she said. 'Aren't you going on the *Jagiello* to New York?'

'That's right,' said Stefan, gazing at her in some confusion.

'You know it must be five years since we met . . .' She blushed, but again a practised blush – 'but I remembered you from that one occasion. Of course I have read about you, and I saw the plays . . .'

'Won't you sit down?' asked Stefan.

The girl – more a woman now – glanced over her shoulder, then looked at Stefan and laughed. 'I'd love to, if I'm not disturbing you . . . just for a minute.'

She sat down opposite Stefan: Stefan too returned to his seat and beckoned to the waiter.

'What would you like to drink?' he asked.

'What are you drinking?'

'Whisky, bourbon.'

She laughed again. 'To prepare yourself for New York?'

'Exactly.'

'And they have bourbon?'

'Certainly.'

'Then I'll have one too.'

The waiter came and took the order. Stefan leant forward and said: 'I don't think we were ever introduced . . . formally.'

'Valeria,' she said. 'Valeria Kotkowska.' She smiled and straightened her skirt over her crossed legs.

'I am . . . well, you know who I am.'

She smiled again. 'Everyone knows who you are.'

'I hope not,' said Stefan, affecting modesty but thinking of the train he was to catch incognito at twelve o'clock that night.

'I remember,' said Valeria, 'Onufry used to say that you were exceptional – that everyone at your school knew you would make a success of your life . . .' There was no trace of irony in her voice: and she looked into his eyes with the same warmth and clarity. The effect of this expression from such a poised, elegant and beautiful woman was to make Stefan for a moment confused.

'I haven't seen Onufry for some time . . .' he began.

'I see him from time to time,' she said. '*Comme ça.*' She shrugged her shoulders. 'Now, of course, he has been mobilized.'

'Yes, of course.'

'They say a war is inevitable.'

'They've said it before.'

'I know. But I have this friend who thinks one should go . . .' She blushed. 'That is, if one isn't going to stay.'

'Are you going?'

'Yes. He has business in Sweden. We are going to Stockholm.'

Stefan looked towards the bar.

'He isn't here,' she said. 'He's coming tomorrow.'

Stefan looked back at the girl – Valeria. There was no particular meaning in her expression. She just looked at him with her large eyes, a charming smile. Her face was made up with powder and lipstick; not, however, in the smudged Polish manner, with a smile painted on lips in thick lipstick, but with all the artistry of the French – the powder, rouge, mascara and lipstick applied so skilfully and sparingly that one could barely discern their presence.

The reason Stefan looked at her so closely was to guess her age. She looked younger than he was, but then how old had she been six years before?

The waiter brought her bourbon and a third for Stefan. She took it, then smiled and made the gesture of a tentative toast which, from the way it happened, was intimate and conspiratorial. Stefan, with the help of the imported whisky, began to be disturbed by her presence. The slightest movement of her

242

body made him aware of its proximity – her stockinged legs, the skin of her throat, her ear half-covered by a lock of hair. She combined simplicity with sophistication, innocence with allure; and all with a touch of vulgarity like a pinch of spice in a stew.

'I envy you going to America,' she said. 'And all for nothing, isn't it? But you deserve it, if anyone does . . . After all, you're getting them publicity, aren't you?'

'And your friend?' asked Stefan. 'Who is he?'

She blushed and then giggled. 'Well, he's older,' she said, 'and if you must know . . .' she leant forward and her voice became a whisper, 'he's got a wife and children in Warsaw.'

'Are they going to Sweden too?'

She grinned. 'Not that I know of. They think he's just going for a business trip.'

'Will you enjoy it there?'

She shrugged her shoulders. 'I'll be safe.'

At that moment a waiter from the restaurant came into the bar and crossed to where Stefan was sitting. 'Your table is ready whenever you are,' he said; whereupon Stefan, without thinking, told him to add a second cover.

'I hope you will join me for something to eat?' he said to Valeria.

This time she did not blush or look around but said that she would.

They moved through into the restaurant – a huge room lit by one large chandelier. At one end there was a raised platform for a band; and in front of it a space for dancing. No players were on the stage, but a trumpet and a saxophone lay waiting on two of the chairs.

It had been unnecessary to book a table since most of them were empty. Stefan and Valeria were led across the room by the head waiter, who then left them to study the menu. While Valeria was absorbed in this, Stefan glanced at his watch: it was still only ten past eight – plenty of time, he thought, to dine with this charming woman before catching the Warsaw Express.

They ordered their food, and he chose some French wine; then she started to chatter about Onufry, telling funny anecdotes about his behaviour which flattered Stefan by their indiscretion.

She started each story: 'I know I shouldn't tell you this, but I know I can trust you' or: 'I swore I'd never tell anyone, but then you aren't anyone, are you?' or: 'Telling a writer is like telling a priest, isn't it?'

She was also most candid about her relationship with Onufry. 'He was dreadfully mean . . . not in public, of course . . . it was always champagne – but in private. Phew. Mean as a Jew. I put up with it because I liked him. Quite a bit, anyway. More than the old bird I'm with just now. But then he isn't mean. Far from it . . .' This candour, coupled with the indiscretion, heightened the sense of intimate conspiracy which existed between them. They were in it together . . . but in what? How could she know what Stefan had once felt for her? And how could she guess that he had a commitment to the thoughts and emotions of his youth?

For this was what obsessed Stefan as he sat opposite Valeria – not Valeria herself but the image of the girl he had seen six years before, drinking champagne with his friend Onufry. If now her shoulders, her wrists, her nose all enchanted him so that he longed at once to possess them, it was less from an immediate desire than from a homage to his earlier emotions. He was like an older brother wishing to indulge his younger brother – the younger brother was himself six years before. 'What I would not have given to be sitting here with Onufry's whore!'

The service was slow. When the band started to play, the waiters seemed to decide that no one would want to eat so they stood by the door to the kitchen, watching the dancing couples. By half past nine they had only eaten a first course of radishes, cucumbers and carrots chopped up as *crudités*, and a second course of soup. At a quarter to ten the venison which they had ordered was set before them, and another bottle of claret. And Stefan by now was intoxicated – not only by the wine and the whisky, but by the conjunction of so many events, emotions, excitements – the whore, the *Jagiello* and the thought of Tilly in Bydgoszcz.

'Do you know what?' said Valeria when she had eaten half her venison.

'No. Tell me.'

'I should love to dance.'

The music had started again: four or five couples were shuffling around the polished wooden floor. Stefan got to his feet reluctantly. 'I hardly know how . . .' he began.

'It helps the digestion,' she said with another of her radiant smiles.

They moved across the dining-room and suddenly Stefan found himself with his hand holding her hand, and his arm around her waist. This proximity overwhelmed him: he could smell her, he could see quite clearly her unblemished skin; he could feel the weight and consistency of her body.

The blouse she wore was made of silk. His hand slid on it until he held her with more force; then he felt, through the silk, the thin layer of soft flesh over her muscles which moved like orchestrated sinews in time to the music. She sensed the rhythm perfectly and, without in any way leading him, drew him into the music too.

When it stopped she did not let go of his hand, but looked into his eyes with an expression of childish happiness and excitement which could only flatter him. The music started again. The dance was slow and Valeria's limbs became heavier. They moved closer together so that he could feel the faint jostling of her legs and breasts against his body. He now not only smelt the scent she wore, but the warm smell of her skin. Her head moved nearer to his head; her hair, then her cheek, brushed against his face. He was intoxicated, isolated, trapped . . .

The music stopped. The band laid down their instruments. Stefan and Valeria returned to their table. Valeria began to eat again and Stefan glanced at his watch: for even in his elation he was conscious of his mission and the night-train to Warsaw. It was twenty-five minutes past ten: he had time to finish his dinner and then make his excuses – go up to his room, perhaps, and then walk out 'for a breath of fresh air'.

With a sigh, Valeria abandoned her venison. Stefan called the waiter to remove the plates and they ordered icecreams. 'I love icecream, don't you?' said Valeria. 'Even when I'm full, I can always manage an icecream . . .' She smiled with that smile – that smile of a child and a whore combined. 'That is her attraction,' Stefan thought to himself. 'To be innocent in her depravity and depraved in her innocence . . . with the slim body of a child and a child's delight in icecream, yet exuding the scent of musk and French perfume . . .'

She was quieter, too, not with the hesitation of someone who cannot think of what to say, but with the sultry silence which says that a mood had gone beyond words. The waiter brought the icecream, and in a fit of folly Stefan ordered champagne to go with it. Valeria's eyes sparkled, then glowed. Stefan looked into them. The champagne arrived and frothed into their glasses. He raised his glass: she raised hers. An unspoken toast.

They danced again, and this time the proximity was un-equivocal: their bodies touched when and where they could, moving against each other, only two thin layers of cloth separating skin from skin. Valeria's hair touched his cheek; then she lowered her hand so that it rested on his shoulder. 'Stefan . . .' she whispered into his ear – nothing more. Simply his name.

They returned to the table. It was eleven o' clock. They drank more champagne. The waiter brought the bill. Stefan wrote down his room number and signed it. Valeria's elbows rested on the white tablecloth: her head was bowed. She was looking at the bubbles in her glass.

'Shall we go now?' said Stefan.

She looked up. 'Yes,' she said.

Outside the restaurant, in the foyer, he turned to her and said: 'I must go to my room . . .'

'Does it look out to sea?' she asked.

'Yes.'

'Can I come and see the view?'

They went up in the lift. 'Half an hour to the station,' thought Stefan. 'That leaves half an hour for her.' And then: 'What will I have to give her? A fifty dollar bill? Or will the price of the dinner be enough?'

They entered the room. His hand went out to turn on the light, but it was intercepted by a hand of hers which gently led his hand away from the switch. She closed the door. They were in darkness. She let go of his hand and crossed to the window, finding her way in the dark like a cat. Then she drew back the curtains and there was the view of the Gulf of Danzig – the grey sky and black sea with the little lights of ships and stars.

To the left were the brighter lights of the docks, and from

below came the dim, greenish light of the street lamps. It all threw back into the room a pale illumination of their forms and faces. Stefan went to stand beside her – the tall, thin figure of Onufry's whore. For some time they stood side by side, both staring out to sea: then she turned and looked up into his face with her clean, angelic features, open and trusting. He took her hands: they embraced. Their lips met and then kissed – hers trembling and moving only a little, like those of an uncertain girl. From her mouth came a little whimper. He looked into her eyes to see if he had hurt her: they were closed. He breathed in the scent of her skin, then kissed her lips again, then her eyelids, then her hair, then her neck. She whispered imprecise words, and all the while he wondered if she was pretending or if it was real. A clock struck in the distance. 'I must hurry,' he thought. 'I must hurry or I shall miss the train.'

They were both naked. 'Now,' he thought, 'now I must finish with her.' But her gentle, childish hands directed him to wait. She sat up facing him, staring at him as if marvelling at his flesh. Then, slowly, like drifting leaves, her hands began to stroke his skin, moving around his body while her pouting lips pushed forward to give him small kisses on the lips. He did as she did, his lips kissed hers and his hands caressed her body – but Valeria was always ahead of him, and all she did had a rhythm. She raised him to a state of acute excitement only to let it subside, then rise again with wave after wave of erotic pleasure. Sometimes she was beside him, whispering into his eyes and ears: sometimes her lithe body would be over him, her head travelling down his body, her lips kissing each inch of the journey, her long legs gripping his body, her velvet thighs smothering his nose and lips until, in delirious pleasure, he lost consciousness of what he was doing or what was being done to him.

He lay beside Valeria. She was still. Slowly his consciousness returned. Her hair was in his mouth – her face, glistening with sweat, lay inches from his eyes. His hand came up to move the hair: the clock struck twelve. He heard the chimes but did not move. She stirred. She opened her eyes, smiled, looked fleetingly, modestly aside: then back into his eyes. She kissed him and sighed. They closed their eyes. She slept, her arms

247

still clutching Stefan. He remained awake. He thought he heard the whistle of the night-train to Warsaw. Then he too closed his eyes and slept without dreams.

Thirteen

On 23 August 1939, V. M. Molotov, the Soviet Commissar for Foreign Affairs, and Joachim von Ribbentrop, the German Foreign Minister, signed the Nazi-Soviet pact of non-aggression. War, which had been probable, was now certain.

Rachel rushed round to Sluzewska Street that evening to find Bruno and Krystyna bent over the radio. They switched it off when she came in – there was no fresh news – and sat quietly while she told them that she was leaving next day for Bialystok. 'We're going to live in my uncle's country house,' she said. 'Mama is coming too and Papa will follow later.'

She was flushed, and spoke in a breathless voice. 'I do wish Stefan hadn't gone,' she said. 'But none of us knew it would come as quickly as this . . . but when he gets back, will you tell him to come and join us?'

'Of course,' said Krystyna. 'You must leave the address.'

They gave Rachel a pencil and a piece of paper: and both watched in silence as she wrote out the name of the village near Bialystok.

'But what will you do?' asked Rachel, as she handed the piece of paper back to Krystyna.

'I don't know yet,' said Krystyna, glancing at Bruno.

'Well, you can always come to us,' said Rachel. 'Mama told me to tell you that.'

Krystyna smiled. 'If there really is war, and a danger of bombs on Warsaw, I'll probably go to Jezow.'

'Of course,' said Rachel. 'They'll look after you there.'

Rachel's visit was short. She still had not packed her children's clothes. She embraced Teofil, Bruno and Krystyna, and repeated that they were to send Stefan to Bialystok as soon as he returned.

After she had left, Krystyna went to the kitchen to prepare something to eat. The little boy, Teofil, played quietly with his wooden bricks; Bruno sat on the old sofa watching him.

Eventually Krystyna called from the kitchen and father and son went through for their evening meal. The two grown-ups ate in silence; only Teofil chattered on, apparently oblivious to their mood.

When he had finished his food, Krystyna lifted him from his chair and took him to the bathroom to be washed. Then he cried, but only because he did not want to go to bed. Dressed in his pyjamas, he was allowed back into the kitchen to kiss his father goodnight. There was a book to be read at his bedside, but finally he was tucked in and the door closed to his room.

Krystyna returned to the kitchen. Bruno sat at the table, staring at his plate and tracing lines in the sludge that lentils and gravy had left at the bottom of his plate. Briskly and in silence, Krystyna began to wash the dishes and Bruno rose to help her. There, with the dishcloth in his hands, he told her that the time had come.

'For what?' she asked, without looking at him.

'I must go into the army,' he said.

She turned and looked at him with startled, mocking eyes. 'The army? The Polish army? Why, you yourself have always said that their sabres and epaulettes will be smashed in a week?'

'I know,' he said, looking away from her. 'But I can't just stand by and watch . . .'

She continued to stare at him. 'But won't the Soviets march on us too? Surely now is your chance to build a socialist Poland?'

'No,' he said, shaking his head. 'I won't work with them.'

Krystyna let out the dirty water, dried her hands and removed her apron. 'Why not?'

'Because they're Russians.'

'I thought the Working Class was international?'

Bruno was silent. Krystyna moved through to the sitting-room and sat down on an armchair. She had nothing to read, and her back was straight like a mother preparing to scold a child; and like a guilty child Bruno followed her and sat down on the sofa. 'You must understand,' he said. 'I can't just wait and watch . . .'

'The army won't take you.'

'Yes. Quite a few comrades are now in the army.'

'And what about us? What are we meant to do while once again Don Quixote sets off to save the world?'

Bruno turned pale. 'Not the world,' he muttered. 'Only Poland.'

'Ah well, at least your causes are coming closer to home. Last time it was humanity . . .'

Bruno said nothing.

'Perhaps one day you will think of your home itself, of your wife and child, waiting in Warsaw for the bombs to drop.'

'You needn't wait . . . You could go to the country – to Jezow, or with Rachel.'

Krystyna gave a kind of exasperated snort. 'But you said yourself that they'd find me there – that sooner or later the Gestapo would round up past and present Party members . . .'

'Yes, but by that time I would be with you . . .'

'Unless you were dead.'

'Unless I was dead.'

'How will I live? What will I live on?'

'You could stay at Blomstein's . . .'

'It's always Blomstein's. I've worked there for ten years because you were too idealistic to feed your wife and child . . .' Tears of frustration came into her eyes.

'What do you want me to do?' he asked.

'I want you to take us away – to Roumania or Turkey or Paris. I have never been to Paris . . .'

Bruno shook his head.

'You say yourself there are ways . . .'

'I can't,' he said. 'I can't leave Poland now.'

'Go, then,' she said. 'Go and fight for the Polish fascists against the German fascists, and leave us to die.' She stood, went to their bedroom and slammed the door. Bruno went to the door and listened to hear if she was crying; but no sounds of sobbing reached his ear. Later when, he crept into the bed, he thought she was asleep, but she turned under the quilt and hugged him in a fierce and desperate embrace.

The next morning, Krystyna prepared breakfast for her husband and son in the usual way. Then she went into the bedroom to prepare herself for her day's work at the jewelry shop. She straightened her grey skirt and white blouse, and tidied her hair in front of the mirror.

'Will you be in this evening?' she asked Bruno, as she always did, so that she would know what food to buy on the way home.

'I don't know,' he said.

'Well, if you won't be back, you had better tell Mamuska.'

She stooped and kissed Teofil, as she always did before leaving; then she embraced Bruno in a more impersonal way and left the flat.

There was no business at Blomstein's. One or two old ladies came in trying to sell their jewelry, but Blomstein would not buy – and some sleek and well-dressed men came in to buy, but Blomstein would only sell for gold or foreign currency.

Krystyna stood at the counter with no expression on her face. The other girls whispered in the corner with frightened faces, occasionally lapsing into nervous, almost hysterical giggling. Their future was uncertain. Blomstein himself sat in his office, brooding over little notebooks. Krystyna, who was the only one permitted to enter his office, caught a glimpse of the numbers and figures in the notebooks: they meant nothing in themselves, but she knew that they referred to different sums in different bank accounts abroad.

'When and how will he go?' she asked herself.

On the way home she tried to buy food for their supper, but at most of the shops there were long queues, and some had already run out of supplies.

'People are hoarding, Countess,' the old man told her, who normally sold her lentils, sugar, rice, salt . . .

'Some of us don't have time,' said Krystyna.

The shopkeeper gave her most of what she needed 'just for you, Countess, from my own supplies'. And at another shop she managed to buy some sausage. All the same, it was late when she returned and Mamuska was angry because she too had to go out and buy provisions. 'And the war hasn't even started,' she said. 'Mother of God, what will life be like then . . .' She shuffled out of the flat and closed the door.

Krystyna unpacked the groceries and then saw that she had forgotten to buy milk. She cursed under her breath. Teofil came into the kitchen and nagged at his mother to build him a castle. She snapped at him: he started to cry. She picked him up, kissed him, and went with him into the sitting-room. His bricks and toys were scattered all over the floor. She sat on the sofa, picked up a book and started to read it to him. He put his thumb in his mouth and half-closed his eyes as his mother repeated the familiar story.

Then the door of the flat opened and Bruno came in. Teofil sat up, took his thumb out of his mouth and opened his eyes. 'Look, Mama, Papa is a soldier.'

There indeed was Bruno dressed in the uniform of an ordinary soldier. He leaned over his wife and child to kiss them, but avoided Krystyna's eyes. 'They accepted me,' he said. 'I have to report to barracks tonight.'

'How long have you got?' she asked.

Bruno looked at his watch. 'About an hour.'

Krystyna stood up and went back to the kitchen to cook the food she had brought back. Bruno remained in the sitting-room and finished the story for Teofil.

When their supper was ready, Teofil was put to bed and they sat silently together in the kitchen. 'There are queues and shortages already,' said Krystyna.

'People panic,' said Bruno.

'You can't blame them.'

'No.'

Bruno opened a bottle of beer, poured some into Krystyna's glass and then emptied it into his own.

'I think Blomstein's going to get out,' said Krystyna.

'Why?'

'He's got money abroad. He's been sending it out for years – to London and to Zurich.'

'Will he close the shop?'

'I suppose so.'

They both ate in silence for a time. Then Bruno said: 'If you leave, let me know where you are.'

'Of course,' she said.

'In any case,' said Bruno, 'it won't last long.'

The hour passed. Bruno went into the bedroom and packed

his pyjamas and shaving kit into a bag. 'I'll try and let you know what happens to me,' he said to Krystyna, who stood watching him.

'Yes.'

He went into Teofil's room and kissed the sleeping child. Krystyna followed. 'Look after him,' he said.

'Of course.'

'If there's bombing,' said Bruno, 'go down to the cellars.'

'Yes.'

They went into the hall.

'It won't last long,' he said again.

They kissed, their arms around each other's bodies.

'God bless you,' she said.

He smiled. 'Take care.'

On her way to work the next day, Krystyna bought one adult ticket and one child's ticket to Lvov. She also made seat reservations for the night-train on the following Saturday. In her lunch hour she went out to see if it was easier to buy food in the centre of the city but found that there were just the same queues and shortages. On her way home after work she went into a department store, bought a cheap suitcase, a large leather bag and four plastic shopping bags.

She ate that evening with her aunt and told her that she was going to leave Warsaw.

'Perhaps you're right,' said Cecylia with a sigh. 'It would be best for Teofil . . . and those awful queues in the shops. But where will you go? And what about your work?'

'I don't think that the work will last much longer anyway.'

'But how will you live? Of course I shall give you what I can . . .'

'I'll manage. Everything's much cheaper in the country . . .'

Krystyna stood up to clear away the plates: Mamuska was on the fourth floor with Teofil. 'What will you do, Aunt Cecylia?' she asked.

'Me? Oh, I'll be all right. I've been through a war before.'

The next day was a Friday and almost no one came into the shop. At four in the afternoon Blomstein called Krystyna into his office and asked her to sit down. He sat at his desk, his little notebooks open in front of him, pressing the tips of his fingers together, then clenching his fists and unclenching them.

'I don't think,' he said, 'that it will be necessary to open the shop tomorrow . . .'

Krystyna nodded.

'You could have the day to yourself.'

'It would be no trouble,' she said.

'No, no. I know how hard it is just now. Queues in the market, shortages . . .'

'Very well.'

There was a knock on the door of the office. One of the younger girls looked in, glancing first at Krystyna and then at Mr Blomstein.

'There's a customer, sir,' she said.

'To buy or sell?'

'To buy, sir. A gentleman . . .'

'We cannot accept zlotys.'

'I told him. He wants to pay in English pounds.'

Blomstein gestured to Krystyna. 'See to it,' he said.

Krystyna rose from the chair, returned to the shop. She recognized at once the kind of customer – a sleek but furtive businessman – and she served him as if the purchase of precious stones to the value of seven hundred pounds sterling was a normal thing for anyone to do.

She took the bundle of white five-pound notes straight to Mr Blomstein. He took them, fingered them, held them to the light. 'Good,' he said. Then he glanced at Krystyna. 'Open the shop tomorrow as usual,' he said. 'But remember. No purchases. And no zlotys. Only pounds, dollars, or Swiss francs.'

'Very well.' She nodded to her employer – again as if his instructions were all in a day's work. And as usual, on a Friday night, Blomstein gave her the keys because the next day was the Jewish Sabbath, when he would remain at home.

That night Krystyna packed the suitcase she had bought with some clothes of Teofil's and some of her own. As she took two blouses from the chest-of-drawers, she glanced at the drawer in the top in which Bruno kept his socks. She opened it. Some of the socks were gone. She removed those that remained and then lifted up the thin piece of plywood that acted as a false bottom to the drawer. There was her passport, and beneath it the name and address of the cobbler in Lvov.

She replaced the false bottom, closed the drawer, finished packing and went to bed.

The next morning she went to Blomstein's as usual, but carrying a shopping bag stuffed with the three others. She unlocked the shop, opened the office and put her shopping bags down behind the desk. She then went to the drawer of Blomstein's desk, unlocked it, took out the second set of keys and unlocked the safe.

Two of the other girls arrived, and together they took the rings and necklaces out of the safe, placing some of them in the window, others in the display cabinets inside the shop. By nine they were ready for business.

Again there were few customers. A young man came in, pretending to be interested in a ring: it soon became clear that his real interest was one of the girls, and Krystyna allowed her to serve him. At eleven another man came in with a bag full of Polish currency. He wanted to buy what he could, and when Krystyna told him that they could not accept zlotys he became enraged. He shouted at them – 'filthy Jewish profiteers' – but eventually left them. The girls giggled. Krystyna remained impassive.

She did not go out in the lunch hour. One of the girls bought a sandwich for her, and she sat on a chair in Blomstein's office to eat it – not on his chair, of course, but on one placed against the wall. She read a fashion magazine, drank mineral water and straightened the seams of her stockings on the calves of her slender legs.

At three Blomstein looked in, which had never happened before. Krystyna told him about the blustering Pole who had tried to buy jewels with zlotys.

'But you didn't sell?' said Blomstein.

'Of course not,' she said.

'Good,' he said; and with a furtive look out of the shop window, he went towards the door. 'I'll see you on Monday,' he said.

He left. The shop was quiet and empty. People rushed past in the street, and in and out of the Europejski Hotel at the corner. One of the assistants asked Krystyna what would happen to the shop when war broke out.

'I don't know,' she said. 'Mr Blomstein might close it.'

'And what will we do?'

She shrugged her shoulders. 'Find another job.'

'It's all right for you to say that, but it isn't that easy. You'll be looked after because you're beautiful . . . Nothing's too much trouble for men if you're pretty. But I'm not, and I need my pay because my mother's sick . . .'

The girl whined on. Krystyna did not listen. She looked at her watch. Time passed. At six she told them that they might as well close the shop. 'No one will come in now,' she said.

The girls began to take the jewelry out of the windows and display cases and return them to the safe. Krystyna watched them, as she always did: she checked that nothing had been forgotten, then locked the safe.

One by one the three girls picked up their handbags, straightened their hair, put on a little lipstick, powdered their faces and then left the shop. The last one asked Krystyna if she wanted her to help lock up.

'No, you go on,' said Krystyna.

When she was alone she lowered the blinds and went back into Blomstein's office. There she opened the safe again and began methodically to put all the jewelry it contained into the four shopping bags she had brought with her that morning. It took some time. The necklaces were in cases; the rings in little boxes or on trays. With the care and skill that she had acquired in the course of ten years at Blomstein's, Krystyna picked them out, wrapped them in tissue paper and dropped them into the shopping bags.

In three quarters of an hour every single stone, every scrap of precious metal – Blomstein's entire stock – was packed away. All that was left in the safe were some bundles of foreign currency collected in the course of the previous week – including the seven hundred English pounds. These too she wrapped in tissue paper and put in the bags.

At a quarter past seven she left the shop, carefully locking it behind her. She carried the heavy bags to the tram and returned home in the usual way. She climbed the four flights of stairs to her flat, and when she relieved Mamuska she told her to tell her Aunt Cecylia that she and Teofil were leaving that night.

'Then it's just as well that I've fed the boy,' said the old lady, shuffling towards the door.

Krystyna did not reply. She kissed Teofil and then went straight into the bedroom. There she packed the contents of her shopping bags into the large leather bag that lay open on the bed. When it was done she covered the contents with a layer of her clothes, closed it and bound the bag with leather straps.

She went back into the sitting-room and crouched in front of Teofil. 'We're going away, darling. We're going on a nice train.'

'To see Papa?' he asked.

'No,' she said. 'Not now.'

She stood up, went into the bedroom and crossed to the drawer with Bruno's socks. She opened it, removed the false bottom, then her passport and the address. There was some foreign currency too which she took and put in her passport. In its place she put a piece of paper on which she had written the words: 'I have never seen Paris.' She replaced the false bottom, closed the drawer, took the leather bag and the suitcase, and herded Teofil in front of her towards the door.

At her aunt's below she looked in just to embrace her and say goodbye. 'I'll let you know where I am,' she said.

'But you'll be in Jezow, won't you?' said Cecylia.

'I expect so.'

She kissed Mamuska and asked her to see that everything was switched off in their flat. 'I don't know when I'll be back,' she said, 'or when Bruno will get away.'

Mamuska looked sulky; then she suddenly kissed Krystyna and enveloped Teofil in a great embrace, while tears trickled down her leathery, wrinkled cheeks. 'God protect you, my little one, God protect you.' She let go of them just as suddenly as she had hugged them, and with Krystyna and Teofil went down to the street, where they found a taxi. It took the two travellers to the station, and the night-train to Lvov.

Fourteen

The first days of the maiden voyage of the *Jagiello* passed without incident. The passengers were relieved to have escaped the atmosphere of crisis – so relieved indeed that a hysterical gaiety infected them. On the first night out from Cherbourg, where they had picked up more passengers, there was a fancy-dress ball which degenerated in certain areas into an orgy. Respectable wives of decent Polish citizens danced without their shoes: some were seen to disappear with sailors. The blame the next morning was fixed firmly on the celebrities who had not even paid for their berths. The writer and the actor, above all, had incited the passengers at their table to improper excesses – plying them with vodka and setting an example of frenzied, unprincipled behaviour.

The Polish passengers felt all the more ashamed when that very day the Captain gave them the news of the Nazi-Soviet pact. For the remaining days of the voyage there were no festivities, but small groups of crestfallen passengers crowded around radios which had been set up around the ship.

On 1 September the engines suddenly stopped. For the first time in eleven days there was no vibration, but only the hiss of the ship floating through the water. The passengers rushed on deck and looked west; for there, rising from the water, was the Statue of Liberty and beyond it, the towers of Manhattan.

Then the loudspeakers called the passengers to the dining-room, where the Captain addressed them. He told them that war had broken out between Poland and Germany, that bombs had fallen on Warsaw, Gdynia, Cracow, Lodz. He said that he and his crew were determined to return to Poland as quickly as possible and fight in the Polish navy. They would therefore be grateful if passengers would have their baggage ready before they docked, and be prepared to leave the ship as soon as

258

possible. Those who were returning on the *Jagiello* could go on shore, but only for the day.

The meeting broke up in confusion. The passengers returned to their cabins like frightened chickens. Only the celebrity writer Stefan Kornowski remained in a flippant, mid-Atlantic mood. He was seen to pinch the backside of a widow from Lublin as she bustled towards the lower deck.

Nor was anyone particularly surprised to see him walk down the gangplank carrying his suitcases, his face twitching with an unusual grimace. The actor was with him, but returned in time for the voyage back to Poland. He reported to the Captain that they were not to wait for Kornowski.

Part Three

One

In the late 1950s, when it was still thought vulgar in certain English circles for girls to work or train for a profession, the daughters of the rich would invariably be sent abroad to learn a language. This was the course of action chosen for Annabel Colte, the twenty-two-year-old daughter of the Earl of Felsted, who was pretty and intelligent but, because of her education, quite unprepared for ordinary life. She had dark hair, pale skin and looked four or five years younger than she was – a shy adolescent who hunched her shoulders to hide her paltry bosom.

She was thin – noticeably thin – but far heavier now than she had been; for since the age of fourteen she had suffered from that disease of the mind – *anorexia nervosa* – through which food becomes repugnant; and the journey to France was the last step in a painstaking cure recommended by a Harley Street psychiatrist. 'She must now learn to stand on her own two feet,' this Dr Ebermann had said to Annabel's mother. 'The worst thing in the world would be to keep her at home.'

The mother and daughter returned for Christmas to Mulford Park, the huge gloomy house on the North Cornish coast which looked out over the Atlantic and was their home. There Annabel waited while her mother telephoned her acquaintances to ask about Paris. She waited and she wandered around the house, hiding from her weak and apologetic father, smiling sadly at the servants and cringing from memories of childhood.

The sound was always of the wind, until every now and then the corridors would echo with the sharp, bossy voice of her mother. 'Anna, Anna? Where are you? There's a course at the Sorbonne which people say is good. You don't have to have exams to get in. You would do that, wouldn't you?'

'I could try . . .'

'You must take a more positive attitude, darling.' The mother spoke to her daughter but their eyes never met.

'Where would I live?'

'Do you remember Sarah Graham?'

'Yes.'

'I know you didn't like her much, but it would be useful to be with someone you knew.'

'Is she in Paris?'

'Yes. She's doing this course and living with a French family.'

'Would they have me?'

'Mrs Graham says that she's sure they would. She's given me the address. I'll write to her . . . I might even try and telephone . . .'

It was arranged, and ten days later Lady Felsted returned to London to see her daughter onto the boat-train at Victoria Station. The pale child was installed in a corner seat of a first-class compartment like the heroine of a story by Henry James. She wore a fur-trimmed coat and had brand-new baggage: the Felsteds were so rich that they did not even indulge the traditional snobbery of shabby suitcases.

Annabel's face had no expression. She watched her mother look anxiously at the other passengers – the students wearing jeans and carrying knapsacks, who walked past them towards the second-class compartments. She saw the relief in her mother's expression as a genteel, middle-aged couple came into the compartment and she listened as her mother asked them to 'keep an eye on her'. When Lady Felsted was on the platform, the mother and daughter exchanged a cold kiss through the window.

'Sarah is going to meet you at the Gare du Nord,' said Lady Felsted. 'And if you miss her, just go to a taxi and give the driver the address of Madame de Pincey.'

'Don't worry, Mother.'

'Get a porter at Dover . . .'

'Yes.'

'Those people in the compartment said they would help . . .'

'Yes.'

'Take care.'

'I'll be all right.'

The train drew away from the platform. Even now the mother did not meet her daughter's eyes. She waved while glancing vaguely aside. Annabel returned to her seat, smiled at the middle-aged couple, and opened a magazine. Every now and then she looked up and out of the window at the grimy houses which back onto the railway line, wondering what her life might have been like if she had been born there instead of Mulford Park.

Sarah Graham, a girl wearing a tweed skirt, a tweed coat, a cashmere jersey and a string of cultured pearls, was waiting at the barrier of the Gare du Nord. The two girls embraced as if they were old friends, and walked behind the porter towards the taxis. Sarah, the big, tall girl, gabbled to her frail, shy companion: she told the driver where to take them in abominable French, and was angry when he did not understand. Annabel looked at her with a dazed distaste.

'It's awfully jolly here,' said Sarah once the car was underway. 'Frightfully expensive, of course, but that shouldn't bother you.'

Annabel smiled but said nothing.

'Madame de P. is awfully nice – a bit strict, but nice. And old Monsieur is a dear. He doesn't do anything – nothing at all. Just sits and makes flirty remarks . . .'

'Do they speak English?'

'Madame de P. does, and Monsieur does a bit. And there's a son who went to school in England.'

'Is he there?'

'Not now. But he's coming.' She wriggled and giggled. 'He looks smashing from the photos.'

'What does he do?'

'Something in the City.'

'And what is he called?'

Sarah hesitated. 'They told me but I can't remember. Some funny name.'

Monsieur and Madame de Pincey lived in a large flat near the Etoile. There was a small, old-fashioned lift which carried the two girls to the second floor while the suitcases were left to the concierge. The door was opened by a middle-aged maid. 'This is Marie,' said Sarah, leading the way into a dark vestibule. Annabel followed. She saw a door open down the corridor. A tall woman pushed back a lock of hair from her forehead and came towards them.

'Are you Annabel?' she asked in an English spoken with an unusual but attractive accent.

'Yes,' said Annabel. She held out her hand to shake that of Madame de Pincey, but the older woman took a firm grip of her shoulders and kissed her on both cheeks – one after the other.

'Welcome to Paris,' she said, 'and the Château de Pincey.' She waved her hand around the small vestibule as if it was the hallway of a palace.

'It is very kind of you . . .' began Annabel.

'My dear,' interrupted Madame de Pincey. 'There is only one good thing about the fall in the fortunes of our family, which is that we take in paying guests and have charming young women like you and Sarah to brighten up the lives of us two old codgers . . .'

She pronounced the word 'codger' with a deliberateness as if she had learnt it that morning from a dictionary: it was also ironic because Madame de Pincey was not yet fifty.

'Sarah, my dear. Will you see that they bring the suitcases? I'll show Annabel her room . . .'

She took Annabel by the arm and led her down the dark corridor. 'We will talk English for a day or two, don't you think?' she said. 'It is bad enough being in a strange city without having to speak a strange language. And then, when you have got used to us a little, we will speak French. *Nous ne parlerons que du français.*'

'That would be kind. My French isn't very good . . .'

'By the time you leave,' said Madame de Pincey, 'you will be fluent. I can promise you.'

She opened a door and led Annabel into a small room which had pretty, flowered wallpaper and a tidy bed with a bright patchwork cover.

'This is lovely,' said Annabel.

'It is small,' said Madame de Pincey, 'and there is not much of a view. But at least it is quiet – you will be able to sleep at night.' She looked out into the courtyard, and for a moment stood quite still as if watching a beetle on the windowsill. Annabel studied her face. In the light she could see the wrinkles in her skin, the blue of her eyes. Then Madame de Pincey focused her attention once again on the English girl.

'The bathroom is across the corridor,' she said. 'You share it with Sarah, and my son will probably use it when he comes. You can have a bath whenever you like. There's plenty of hot water. Dinner is usually at eight.' She smiled. 'I'll leave you to unpack. When you're ready just come along to the drawing-room and meet Alain.'

Monsieur de Pincey was a small man with a moustache. He was around ten years older than his wife and had a bumbling, jovial manner which was a contrast to her severe kindness. He spoke some English, and what he said was accompanied by a wink or a nudge which made Sarah giggle but had quite a different effect on Annabel. The first remark addressed to her ('You must let me show you the sights, my dear. I am an expert on the Eiffel Tower') made her blush scarlet. Tears came into her eyes. She looked down at her glass of Dubonnet and then sipped it to cover her confusion.

Madame de Pincey glanced furiously at her husband, who looked embarrassed and turned back towards the buxom Sarah.

On the second day after her arrival in Paris, Annabel started the course in French Civilization at the Sorbonne. She went with Sarah Graham on a bus to the Boulevard St Michel, bought ballpoint pens and exercise books and hurried to catch the lecture by what Sarah described as the 'smashing Maurice Duverger'. She understood only half of what he said but took in his wiry, gesticulating hands and intelligent, Gallic features as part of the whole landscape of exotic sights and smells. Words and phrases such as 'Marxism' and 'existentialism' wafted into her mind, as did the smell of coffee, croissants and French tobacco in the Boulevard outside.

At mid-day they came out into the street. 'Where would you like to have lunch?' asked Sarah.

'Where do you usually go?'

'There are some cafés where you can get something to eat, or one or two restaurants, or the university canteen . . .'

'I'm not very hungry.'

'I'm starving.'

'You choose, then.'

'The canteen. It's cheaper.' Sarah again looked enviously at Annabel, whose family's wealth was well known.

'Good,' said Annabel. 'I'd like to have a look.'

They crossed the Boulevard St Michel and walked down towards the Odéon. 'It's full of scruffy students,' said Sarah.

'I don't care,' said Annabel. 'I've had enough of well-dressed people.'

On the afternoon of her fourth day in Paris, Annabel and Sarah had lunch together as usual but then split up – Sarah to go to a film with an English boy she had met doing the same course, Annabel to go to the Louvre. 'And remember,' said Sarah, 'we're meeting Madame de P. at five in the Rue des Saints Pères.'

'I've written down the address,' said Annabel.

'Don't tell her that I've been to the flicks,' said Sarah.

'I won't.'

Annabel walked down the Boulevard St Germain, alone in the streets of Paris for the first time. She felt strange, almost giddy, after so many months – so many years – closeted in boarding schools, hospitals and Mulford Park. Now she was among ordinary people who seemed to her extraordinary – their movements, their faces, their clothes, their behaviour. She saw people slouching, others arm-in-arm. The students seemed to wear what they liked, and it was Annabel, in her uniform of tweed skirt and twin set, who was out of place.

The mixture was too rich. She could feel herself cowering from life in the street. Paris gorged her soul, and she rushed to the banks of the river to fix her eyes on the water where no human faces could be seen. Then she walked along the *quai*, crossed the Pont Royal and entered the cold and lofty halls of the Louvre Museum.

At a quarter to five she set off back towards the Left Bank. It was a cloudy January afternoon and was almost dark. The passers-by who had seemed so flamboyant earlier on now scuttled past, wrapped in their overcoats and mackintoshes.

Annabel reached the address in the Rue des Saints Pères where she had been told to meet Madame de Pincey. She rang the bell: the door opened automatically and an old lady peered through a half-open door.

'*S'il vous plaît*,' said Annabel in halting French. '*L'appartement de Monsieur Kornowski.*'

'*Troisième, à gauche*,' said the concierge.

She climbed the dark, slightly smelly staircase until she came to the third floor. She looked at the door on the left. There was no bell, so she knocked.

The door was opened by a man. Annabel was startled by his appearance not only because it was in such contrast to the elegance of Madame de Pincey. He was thin, had a balding head of hair and wore baggy black trousers. His brown cardigan was covered with the grey stains of cigarette ash, and there was a hole in the right elbow.

He smiled weakly, and stood back to let her in. Annabel took a sharp breath of air and walked past him into the flat. That too was quite unlike the apartment near the Etoile. The paintwork was old, and there were no pictures on the wall. Three doors led off the hallway: through one she saw a cramped little kitchen with dirty plates piled onto a stained, wooden draining-board; and through another an equally confined bathroom with a bidet, a hip bath and a torn, cream-coloured shower curtain. The taps had lost their lustre.

The third door – the door through which the man directed her to go – led to a larger room, one end of which was lined with books. Other books stood in piles beneath them. The walls were cream-coloured; the room smelt of cigarette smoke. It was ill lit, and so for a moment Annabel could not make out the figure of Madame de Pincey sitting on a chair in the corner.

'Where's Sarah?' she asked.

'She is coming on her own,' said Annabel.

269

'Weren't you together?'

'No. I wanted to go to the Louvre and she . . . she went shopping.'

Krystyna nodded. 'Have you introduced yourselves?' she asked.

The man shook his head.

'This is Annabel Colte,' she said. Then she added something swiftly in a foreign language – neither English nor French.

'I am delighted to meet you,' said the man in an odd accent.

'This is my brother, Stefan Kornowski,' said Madame de Pincey.

Annabel shook his hand but Madame de Pincey must have noticed her perplexed expression for she said: 'I am Polish. Didn't you know?'

'No,' said Annabel, 'but . . .' She hesitated.

'But it doesn't matter?' said Madame de Pincey, finishing her sentence for her with a sardonic smile.

The man turned to Madame de Pincey and said something in Polish.

'Stefan wonders if you would like some tea,' said Madame de Pincey to Annabel. 'He could perfectly well ask you himself,' she said. 'He speaks excellent English, or he should do. He has lived for nearly twenty years in America.'

'I can speak English,' said Stefan to Annabel, 'but I am very shy.' He smiled. 'However,' he went on, 'I can offer you some tea with lemon – I am out of milk – and some biscuits.'

'That would be very nice,' said Annabel and she too smiled.

Sarah, the boisterous Sarah, was late. It was six before she arrived at the flat, and then she lied about losing her way. It was obvious to everyone that she was lying, and Stefan Kornowski, with a scornful smile at Madame de Pincey, said: 'You had better be careful. She has been meeting secretly with Alain.'

Madame de Pincey did not seem to be amused. 'You must try and be punctual,' she said to Sarah. 'I do not like worrying.'

Two

There were one or two occasions when Krystyna arranged to meet her 'girls' at her brother's flat; and quite rapidly Annabel came to look forward to these encounters with the scruffy, smelly Pole. He never said much, but glanced at her every now and then with an expression of sympathy – intense sympathy – and something else – something which fascinated her but which she could not fathom. And one day, in the taxi driving back to the Etoile, she told Krystyna that her brother 'looked so interesting'.

'You should go and visit him,' said Krystyna. 'He's rather lonely and he'd probably talk to you more if I wasn't there.'

'What does he do?'

'Ah!' She shrugged her shoulders. 'He used to be a writer,' she said, 'but now, I don't know. He writes a journal, and he thinks . . .'

Sarah Graham had theories about Stefan Kornowski. 'I don't believe for a moment that he's her brother,' she said.

'Who is he, then?' asked Annabel.

'What do you think?' said Sarah with a leering look.

'You mean her . . . her . . .'

'All French women have lovers,' said Sarah.

'But she isn't French.'

'That makes it all the more likely. She misses Poland, I know she does. So she has a Polish lover. You can see that she and Monsieur P. aren't exactly *fesse à fesse* these days . . .'

'What does that mean?'

'Cheek to cheek.' She giggled. 'They have separate bedrooms.'

Annabel thought for a moment with a grave expression on her face. 'Then why did Madame de P. tell me to go and visit him?'

'To cover up her own visits.'

'Perhaps I'll just get in the way?'

'I should go,' said Sarah. 'It's not as if you know anyone else in Paris. I mean to say, you've done the Louvre and the Musée de Cluny, and you aren't going out with anyone the way I am . . . I say, you didn't tell Madame de P., did you? I don't want her writing to Mummy.'

Annabel shook her head gently.

On the first occasion that Annabel went alone to visit Stefan Kornowski she took an apple tart which she had bought at a baker's in the street. He made tea and again apologized because there was no milk but only lemon; and these two things – the apple tart and the absence of milk – became little traditions, for soon she went there three or four times a week to talk with Stefan Kornowski. Tea with the Pole took the place of those visits she had made to Dr Ebermann in Harley Street. Stefan Kornowski had the same curiosity about her life; the same patience with her quiet, tentative answers; the same tact in not pursuing his inquiries into forbidden areas. When he asked about her father, for example, she made no reply at all but stared for a long while at her fingers.

At first Annabel did not show a comparable interest in him. She was fascinated but not curious. The small flat, like a monk's cell, with the bed in the living-room and the tea-cups always unwashed in the sink, was so far from the well-ordered household at Mulford Park that it became for her as exotic as the Sahara Desert or the jungles of Brazil. Even the books in Stefan Kornowski's flat – the piles of cheap editions in English, French, Polish and German – were of a different order from the vellum-bound volumes in the library at Mulford, which no one ever took from the shelves. Above all she was fascinated by his desk and the notebooks which sometimes lay open, exposing line upon line of sprawling handwriting in blue ink. Once, when Stefan was in the kitchen making tea, she glanced at an open notebook, but she could not understand the words. They were Polish.

'Has anything you have written been translated into English?' she once asked him as he poured out the tea.

He made a funny face (the Kornowski grimace). 'No,' he said. 'At least not that I know of.'

'It's a pity,' said Annabel. 'I should like to be able to read something.'

272

'It may be just as well,' he said.

'Why?' she asked.

'You might find them boring,' he said.

She smiled. 'I doubt it.'

'Or improper,' he said.

She blushed savagely and withdrew into herself. Stefan Kornowski went from the room to fetch hot water for the tea pot. 'It is presumptuous of me to call myself a writer at all,' he said when he returned, 'since nothing of mine has been published for twenty years.'

'Why not?'

'I couldn't write in America. The people or the landscape did not inspire me . . .' He hesitated; then added: 'And I couldn't look back.'

'Then what did you do?'

'I worked in a bookshop in Chicago – a Polish bookshop.'

'All the time.'

'No. At first I went West – to get as far from Europe as it was possible to go. I wanted to work as a cowboy or a lumberjack, but I was told that I had a weak heart so I returned to Chicago.'

'And why did you come back to Europe?'

'As I said, I couldn't write in America.'

'And can you write here?' she asked.

'When I find a plot.'

'What sort of plot?'

'It must have a happy ending.'

'Is that difficult to find?'

'Yes it is,' said Stefan, 'because art depends on life and in life there is no ending.'

'When the prince and princess marry . . .'

'That may be the end of one story, but it is usually the beginning of another.'

'Death,' said Annabel. 'Isn't that a kind of ending?'

'Of course,' said Stefan Kornowski. 'At death I may know how to end a story, but by then it will be too late to write it down.'

Stefan Kornowski would describe his childhood to Annabel – and Jezow, the house where he was born, became in her mind another Mulford Park. Some of his experiences she could not equate with her own because they were beyond the scope of her imagination. She could not conceive of her father going bank-rupt, and she did not understand what Stefan meant when he mentioned once that he had 'gone through a Communist phase'.

'And why did you go to America?' she asked.

'I went for a holiday,' he said, 'and stayed to avoid the war.' He gave another of his sardonic smiles. 'I am what is known as a coward,' he said.

Annabel blushed. 'And Madame de Pincey,' she said. 'Did she go with you?'

'No. She went first to Roumania, with Teofil, and then came to Paris.'

'Is Teofil her son?'

'Yes.'

'And is Monsieur de Pincey his father?'

'No. His father was a Pole. He was killed.'

'How sad,' said Annabel.

'Yes,' said Stefan. 'It was a pity.'

Annabel could now find her own way back from the Rue des Saints Pères to the de Pinceys' flat near the Etoile. She always returned in time for supper, and occasionally would go out again afterwards, either with Sarah to a film, or with Madame de Pincey to the Opéra, or the Comédie Française. By the end of her first month in Paris she had established a small, secure world of the two flats and the lecture halls of the Sorbonne. She felt safe – almost self-confident – and wrote letters to her mother and Doctor Ebermann which made them both feel that they had been right to send her to Paris.

Then, one evening at the beginning of February, she re-turned to the de Pincey flat and went as usual to her room to change out of her wet shoes and put her books on her desk. She might then have remained there, reading a book or writing an exercise in French grammar, but on this occasion there was a knock on her door and the voice of Krystyna de Pincey called out her name.

Annabel went to the door and opened it.

'Come into the living-room,' said Krystyna. 'I would like you to meet my son.'

She then went back down the corridor, leaving Annabel in a

minor state of panic at this breach in the walls of her world. She went at once to the mirror to look at herself – her pretty face which she thought so plain, her soft brown hair which she detested. If she had dared she would have hidden in her wardrobe, but Krystyna de Pincey had a way of making suggestions which one did not refuse. Annabel thus straightened her neat skirt, brushed a speck of fluff off her jersey and walked down the corridor towards the living-room as if marching to the scaffold.

She pushed open the door and entered the dimly-lit living-room as quietly as a cat. It was full of bric-à-brac, but she saw at once a long pair of trousered legs sticking out from an armchair. She saw too Krystyna de Pincey sitting on the sofa and Alain standing with his back to the fire.

'Come in,' said Krystyna.

Annabel remained by the door; then took a few steps forward. The legs uncrossed themselves: the feet came off the ground and a tall young man was suddenly standing in front of her. He advanced with pure, open features, held out his hand, took hold of hers, which she had unconsciously extended, and said: 'How very nice to meet you.'

She smiled feebly, and then looked quickly for refuge in the now familiar eyes of Monsieur de Pincey.

'A drink?' asked Alain uneasily: he was cautious now when talking to Annabel.

She nodded.

'A Dubonnet?'

'Yes please.'

'Come and sit down,' said Krystyna.

'You must excuse me for looking rather a mess,' said the young man, gesturing disparagingly at his elegant clothes, 'but I only arrived half an hour ago and haven't had time to take a bath . . .'

'Are you Teofil?' Annabel suddenly asked.

'Yes, indeed,' he said – clicking his heels with mock-Prussian formality. 'Teofil de Pincey at your service.'

'I have only one son,' said Krystyna, moving towards the end of the sofa so that Annabel could sit next to her.

'And I have only one mother,' said Teofil, stooping to kiss Krystyna like a little Lord Fauntleroy.

Annabel smiled.

'But two fathers,' said Teofil. 'One here . . .' he gestured towards Alain who approached Annabel with the glass of Dubonnet – 'and one who is dead, a certain Bruno Kaczmarek – rather a stranger to me, I am afraid.'

'You were very young . . .' said Krystyna.

'But I have this vague memory of a tall man who hugged me like a bear.' Teofil smiled wistfully to himself and then, with perfect politeness, he switched the smile to Annabel. 'But you have only one of each?'

'I am afraid so.'

'I know all about them – Lord Felsted of Mulford Park in the county of Cornwall. You have a cousin called Colin McCann whom I knew at Oxford. You probably don't know who he is, but he used to boast about his distinguished relations . . .'

Whatever the strange complexities of Annabel's anorexic mind, it still had that perfect pitch which could discern when someone tried too hard. Teofil's behaviour, like his English accent, was too good. 'I know whom you mean,' said Annabel with a reflex reserve – a reserve which kept her undistinguished cousin in his place and by implication, anyone who might know him.

Teofil felt a little of this chill. He stopped talking for a moment and when Annabel had seated herself beside Krystyna, he returned to his armchair.

'Teofil is going to live here for the time being,' said Krystyna to Annabel.

Annabel smiled. She looked across at Teofil and felt suddenly inexpressibly sorry at his crestfallen expression. 'What do you do?' she asked him.

'Oh . . . frightfully boring. I work in the City . . . merchant banking.'

'In London?'

'For the last couple of years. Now I'm going to do a stint in the Paris office. Make use of my French.'

'Why . . . I mean, how do you come to speak such good English?'

Teofil looked at Krystyna. 'My mother, in her infinite wisdom, sent me to an English school . . .'

'Which one?'

'A Catholic school called Downside. Have you heard of it?'

'Yes, I think so.'

'Not a bad place, really. They got me into Oxford.'

As he said this he glanced at his mother. So did Annabel, and she saw on Krystyna's face a set expression of satisfaction. 'I think the English public school education is the best in the world,' she said. 'In France it is all intellect . . .'

Teofil laughed. 'She thinks that rugby made me the man I am.'

Annabel laughed too – or she opened her mouth as she smiled, which in her amounted to a laugh. Teofil was so delicate and gentle in appearance that it seemed absurd to think of him in a rugby scrum.

'It got you into Oxford and it got you a job,' said Krystyna sharply.

Now Alain began to protest. 'You speak as if your son is a fool . . .'

Annabel leant forward and said to Teofil: 'Did you really play rugby?'

'Yes,' he said. 'I was a forward . . .'

'But also he is clever,' said Alain in his bad English. 'Very clever. A high degree at Oxford.'

'Of course he is clever,' said Krystyna with an affectionate, mocking smile at her son.

Teofil blushed. 'What about you?' he said to Annabel. 'Where did you go to school?'

'I went to several.'

'And what did you do after school?'

'Nothing very much,' she said. 'I wasn't well.'

Sarah Graham came back breathlessly just as Marie, the maid, shuffled in to say that dinner was served. She looked nervously at Krystyna, who frowned: but Teofil immediately began to tease her about her 'lover', which kept them all amused throughout the meal. After dinner they had coffee, and it was not until about eleven that they went off to their various rooms.

While she was reading in bed, Annabel received a visit from Sarah who came and sat on the end of her bed wearing a dressing-gown. She told Annabel that the English boy at the Sorbonne had 'made a pass' at her in the cinema – 'More than a kiss . . . you know . . .' – and that she did not know what to do. 'I mean, what would *you* do, Anna?'

'I wouldn't let him,' said Annabel severely.

'I know . . . I know I shouldn't. But men sort of need it, don't they? And I don't want him going off to some tart.'

'That's better than becoming one yourself.'

Sarah blushed. 'I suppose so,' she said: and not having heard what she wanted to hear, she went towards the door. Then she hesitated. 'What do you think of Teofil?' she asked.

'He seems all right.'

'Yes.' Sarah wrinkled up her nose. 'Yes, I suppose so.'

Three

Teofil came into the dining-room the next morning to find Annabel sitting there alone, eating her breakfast of coffee and a small crust of toasted bread. He too poured some coffee into a bowl, added milk, then sat down next to her and picked up *Le Figaro*. He had washed his hair, which made him look younger than he was.

'I gather that you've seen something of my uncle,' said Teofil.

'Yes. He's been very kind.'

'Would you take me along some time?'

'Of course. But haven't you met him before?'

'I did as a child, before the war. But then he went to America and we came here. I haven't seen him since then.'

'When did he come back to Paris?'

'About a month ago . . . just before you arrived.'

'I didn't realize that . . .'

'What's he like?' asked Teofil.

Annabel hesitated. 'I suppose he's odd,' she said. 'But I do like him.'

'I'd like to meet him,' said Teofil. 'He might tell me something about my father. Mama steers clear of that topic of conversation.'

'I'm going to see him this afternoon,' said Annabel.

'I've got to go to the office today,' said Teofil. 'But what about tomorrow?'

'All right,' said Annabel, 'I'll arrange it.'

That morning she went as usual to the Sorbonne, had lunch with Sarah in the students' canteen, and then went alone for the third time to the Louvre.

Her caution about life itself had made her particularly sensitive towards works of art. Though her parents were culturally philistine in the tradition of the English upper classes, she had grown up among beautiful painting, sculpture, furniture and tapestry collected in past centuries by more enlightened generations of her family. She loved in particular the paintings of the eighteenth century – those of Boucher and Watteau, for example. They had none of the menace which she saw in earlier depictions of Christ or the Virgin Mary; nor the earnestness of nineteenth-century art.

On this occasion she went straight to Watteau's *Embarkation for Cythera* and studied the figures of men and women in the landscape. The men were all whispering to the women, and were hovering over them; the women looked modestly pleased, and all the while a small dog scampered among them and a child looked on. Annabel spent some time on a bench in front of this picture: she liked it because it showed love between men and women as something gentle and innocent.

There was also a painting by Boucher – *Rinaldo and Armida* – which she sought out and studied. Here there was one couple, seated among swirling draperies, with a classical building behind. The girl was hardly clothed: her legs and breasts were bare. The youth wore armour of a sort, and a shield and helmet were at his feet, but his features were almost as feminine as the girl's; and though his eyes were only inches from the pink breast, he looked only with adoration into her eyes. Cupids – plump children with little wings sprouting from their backs – played among the draperies. The whole made love seem like a happy game and Rinaldo, the young man, she observed, looked something like Teofil de Pincey.

She glanced at her watch. It was time to go to see Stefan Kornowski. She gave a last look at Rinaldo and Armida and then hurried from one gallery into another, looking for the way out. She got a little lost and found herself among Lautrecs and Van Goghs, then Klimts and Schieles. She shuddered and walked on, looking neither to her right nor to her left.

She climbed the steps to Stefan's flat as fast as she could, just as she had done when she was late for an appointment with Dr Ebermann. She was flushed and out of breath when, clutching the apple tart, she rang the bell, but realized it only when a gleam of surprise came into the eye of Stefan Kornowski.

'I'm sorry I'm late,' she said.

'It doesn't matter,' he replied.

He went into the living-room and closed a notebook in which he had been writing.

'Am I disturbing you?' Annabel asked.

'Of course not,' said Stefan.

'You must say if I become a nuisance.'

'And you must tell me when you are bored of a lonely old man . . .'

'Oh no,' she said. Then she blushed; and to cover her embarrassment she sat down.

'I sometimes think,' he went on, 'that you visit me just for the tea, because at half past four an Englishman must have tea . . .'

'But tea with milk.'

'Precisely. And so subconsciously I ensure that there is never any milk – just to prove to myself that you come for more than the tea . . .'

Annabel laughed: a sound actually came from her open smile, and though she hardly noticed this herself it put a second quick gleam into the eyes of Stefan Kornowski.

'I could always have tea in a café,' said Annabel. 'There is even an English tea shop in the Rue de Rivoli.'

'Of course,' said Stefan.

'I don't just come for the tea. I like talking to you.'

'It is hard to see why you should.'

She hesitated. 'I feel that you know a lot.'

'A wise old man,' he said, smiling.

'You don't look particularly old,' she said with a frown.

'I am forty-four.'

'That isn't old.'

'You are as old as you feel. Isn't that an English expression?'

'Yes.'

'I feel old. I have lived through quite enough.'

'But you escaped . . .'

'In body. Not in mind.'

'Did you suffer?'

'In my own particular way . . .'

Now Stefan looked embarrassed. He rose and went into the kitchen to boil water for their tea.

Annabel waited in her chair; and as he came back into the living-room he said: 'Most girls of your age are more interested in younger men.' He sat down, watching Annabel for her reaction. She looked at her hands.

'I know,' she said. 'But that can wait, can't it?'

'Of course.'

'What can one learn from people of one's own age? Their experience is just as limited as one's own.'

'Perhaps,' said Stefan, lighting a cigarette.

'It's more difficult to understand,' said Annabel, 'why you should waste your time with me.'

Stefan made that peculiar expression (the Kornowski grimace). 'Ah,' he said with a vague gesture that meant nothing at all. Then he rose to go back into the kitchen to take the water from the stove and make the tea. It was not until they had drunk this tea, and Stefan had eaten the apple tart, that Annabel asked him if she might bring someone to see him.

He frowned. 'Of course, if you like.' He looked disgruntled, and Annabel smiled.

'It is someone who particularly wants to meet you,' she said.

'But who?' asked Stefan in an irritated tone of voice. 'No one else knows that I am here?'

'Your nephew,' she said. 'Your nephew Teofil.'

She had never before seen Stefan Kornowski seem shocked. He straightened his spine and craned his neck. 'Teofil? Is he here?' he asked as if his nephew might be hiding in a wardrobe or waiting outside the door into the flat.

Annabel smiled. 'No,' she said. 'He couldn't come today. But he would like to come tomorrow.'

'Of course, of course he can come,' said Stefan. 'I didn't know he was in Paris . . .'

'He's been sent here by his bank,' said Annabel as if she had something to do with the arrangement of his life, 'and for the time being he's going to stay in the flat.'

Stefan nodded. He seemed almost dazed.

'You've never met him, have you?' asked Annabel.

'When he was a child . . . But he won't remember me.'

'He's longing to meet you. He wants you to tell him about his father.'

'Yes,' said Stefan. 'I knew his father.'

Teofil was at dinner that evening, and Annabel reported that she had arranged for him to go with her on the following afternoon to see his uncle.

'And try and persuade him to come here,' said Krystyna, overhearing their conversation. 'Invite him for lunch on Sunday.' She smiled at Annabel. 'You don't know what a privileged person you are,' she said with a slightly mocking smile. 'You're the only one who is allowed to go in and out like that . . .'

Annabel said nothing, but for the rest of the meal her pretty features formed into an expression of mild self-importance.

On the following afternoon Teofil met her as arranged and they walked together along the Boulevard St Germain towards the Rue des Saints Pères. 'What time does he expect us?' he asked.

'Half past four,' said Annabel.

'Then we have plenty of time . . .'

Annabel glanced at her watch. 'I have to buy the tart.'

'What tart?'

'An apple tart. You know . . . *tarte aux pommes*. I always do.'

They came to a baker's shop. Annabel bought the tart as usual and they then walked on up the Rue des Saints Pères, Teofil walking next to the street and hovering over Annabel as if to protect her from the brusqueness of the passers-by. As politeness it was exaggerated and out of date, but Annabel seemed to appreciate his attentiveness. She was also proud to know so well the way to Stefan's flat. 'It's here,' she said as they came to the entrance to the building. 'Follow me.'

282

When Stefan opened the door she went in first. 'This is Teofil,' she said.

Stefan stood back. He watched his nephew enter with sharp eyes, then held out his hand to shake it. Then they gabbled in Polish and embraced. Annabel looked away a little confused. In a moment, however, Stefan was at her side. 'You cannot imagine,' he said in English, 'what a mixture he is, this boy, of his father and mother.'

He led them into the living-room. He seemed excited, and though he tried to talk in English for Annabel's sake, he would every now and then spill over into Polish. Teofil too seemed delighted to meet his uncle. They exchanged disjointed reminiscences, and asked questions without waiting for answers. 'But why did you go to an English school?' 'But why did you stay in America?' 'I remember when you first learnt to walk . . .' 'And I don't know if I remember you at all. Were you the big, tall man who hugged me?'

'No,' said Stefan. 'That was your father.'

'I knew it must have been him. Now you must tell me what he was like . . .'

And because they were so excited by what each had to say to the other, Annabel decided that this time she would make the tea. She went into the kitchen, boiled the kettle, emptied the old tea-bags out of the tea pot, washed the cups which lay dirty in the sink and returned with a laden tray.

The two men hardly noticed when she handed them tea and slices of apple tart. Annabel sat down to listen to them, half hurt by the way they were ignoring her, yet grateful that at least some of the time they remembered to talk in English.

'Your father was noble and brave,' said Stefan. 'Which is a nice thing to be able to say to a son.'

'He died in the war, didn't he?' asked Teofil.

'Yes. He was a partisan. Has your mother never shown you the letter?'

'What letter?'

'She told me that she had had a letter from one of his men which describes how he died.'

'She is odd about my father. She doesn't like to talk about him.'

'It's only natural,' said Stefan with a twist of irony on his lips. 'She is quite a different person now.'

283

'What was she like then?'

'She had no money, no money at all. She worked in a jeweller's shop.'

Teofil blushed, and for a moment was aware of Annabel's presence – glancing in her direction to note the expression on her face.

'Of course she was also a Countess,' said Stefan, as if sensitive to his nephew's embarrassment.

'What . . . a Polish Countess?'

'Of course.'

'And are you a Count?'

'Count Stefan Kornowski . . . the last of the line.' Stefan tilted his body forward in a mock bow.

'And my father?' asked Teofil.

'He was . . . a natural aristocrat.'

'Not a Count, or anything like that?'

'He was the son of a schoolteacher.'

Teofil blushed again. 'And what did he do?'

'Surely your mother told you?'

'She said that he studied law . . . and then that he too was some kind of teacher.'

'Yes, but that was just . . .' Stefan's voice faded as he spoke.

Teofil laughed nervously, and once again he glanced at Annabel. 'Everyone is so evasive about my father,' he said. 'He must have been a pimp or . . .'

'No, no,' said Stefan. 'He wasn't a pimp. Far from it.'

'What was he then?'

'A Communist.'

Teofil now went quite red in the face. 'How do you mean? A Communist?'

'A member of the Communist Party. So was your mother. So was I.'

'But Mama supports de Gaulle . . .'

'Times have changed.'

For the third time Teofil glanced at Annabel, as if she might indicate how he should react to this information: but she looked just as baffled as he did. She had only a vague impression of what it meant to be a Communist.

'So you see,' Stefan went on, 'he did not spend much of his time in the classroom. Communists were outlaws, liable to arrest at any moment; and your father was always travelling with forged papers, setting up secret printing presses, organizing cadres . . . and of course he fought in Spain.'

'Yes,' said Teofil. 'Mama told me that.'

Teofil now asked further questions and Stefan answered them. He described their childhood in the country, their father's bankruptcy, the move to Warsaw. He tried as best he could to give the two privileged children an idea of what it had been like without money in a poor country. He described his Aunt Cecylia, and the way she always kept her face in profile: he described her flat and the flat on the fourth floor; then Uncle Max and finally came back to Bruno – Bruno the young student of law, 'alive with a passion for justice'.

It was getting dark but no one switched on the light. Stefan was inspired by his own description of the past. His lean face was taut with the effort of transposing memories into descriptions; and the languid boy and girl listened like rabbits transfixed by a snake. Their feeling for Bruno as a secret revolutionary changed with Stefan's descriptions from a confused distaste to some sort of admiration. The image in Teofil's mind which had been vague now took the shape of someone like Robin Hood or the Count of Monte Cristo.

Eventually there was a pause and Stefan stood up to switch on the lights. Annabel glanced at her watch and saw that they must go.

'I hope that you will come again,' said Stefan.

'Of course,' said Teofil.

Stefan picked up the tray with the tea pot, tea cups and the remains of the apple tart. 'I'll get your coats,' he said.

While he was out of the room Teofil crouched to examine some of the books piled on the floor. 'It's quite a library, isn't it?' he said to Annabel.

'Can you read Polish?' asked Annabel.

'More or less,' said Teofil, standing again and going to the table, where there were other piles of books and magazines.

'And French and English?' asked Annabel.

'I find Polish the most difficult,' said Teofil, glancing at the notebooks which lay open on the table. 'And my vocabulary isn't as large as it should be.'

He started to read what was written on the paper in blue ink.

He read, and suddenly he blushed and looked away. Then he bent over the notebook again.

'What does it say?' asked Annabel.

'Nothing,' said Teofil, moving away from the table.

Stefan came back into the room carrying their overcoats. Annabel said nothing more, but at the door to the flat she reminded Teofil that he was to ask his uncle to lunch.

'Oh yes,' said Teofil, turning towards his uncle with a slight coldness in his manner. 'Mama hoped you would come to lunch on Sunday.'

Stefan seemed to hesitate.

'Madame de Pincey said we were to force you,' said Annabel.

'Very well,' said Stefan. 'I'll be there.'

They took leave of Stefan – Teofil still with an odd reserve – and then, because they were late, they hailed a taxi to take them back to the Etoile. Once seated next to Teofil on the back seat, Annabel turned to him and said: 'Go on, tell me. What was written in the notebook?'

'I couldn't possibly tell you,' said Teofil. 'It was . . . it was obscene.'

Four

No sooner had Teofil returned with Annabel to the flat near the Etoile, than he asked his mother for the letter.

'What letter?' asked Krystyna.

'Uncle Stefan told me that there was a letter about my father's death.'

'Your father?' She glanced at Alain, then at Teofil. 'Oh, you mean Bruno. Yes. There was a letter. I'll see if I can find it.'

After supper Teofil had to remind Krystyna before she went to a chest-of-drawers and from the bottom drawer took out a shoe box filled with papers. 'I'm not sure I have it still,' she said. 'I should have kept it. And you ought to see it, I suppose

... I wonder how Stefan knew about it? I must have told him. Yes, here it is.'

She drew out of the bundle an envelope. 'It took six months to reach me,' she said. She handed him the envelope.

Teofil took it and for a moment studied the old stamps, the many postmarks and the simple scrawl of the handwriting. Then he went into a corner of the drawing-room, and while the others drank coffee and made conversation in French, he read it over and over again.

When the conversational practice was over, Annabel came up to Teofil and sat down near to him on a chair. 'What did it say?' she asked.

'It just says how he died,' said Teofil. There were tears running down his cheeks.

'Can I see?' asked Annabel. She took the letter but stared blankly at the Polish writing.

'I could translate it for you,' said Teofil.

'I would love it if you would,' she said, 'unless it's private.'

'No,' he said. 'Not in particular.' He took up the pages again.

'It's from a simple man – a peasant. You can see that from the style. He seems to have dictated it to a priest. He probably couldn't write himself. It begins "Your Excellency . . ." You see, he didn't know how to address my mother.

Your Excellency. Through the will of God the duty has fallen on me to write through the hand of Father Ignacy the . . . tidings of your husband Colonel Kaczmarek who has died for Poland. He was commander of our unit of the AK operating near Bialystok and had killed more Germans than all the rest of us. He was a good commander and a good man and only once he took a risk, going to the village of B. when the Germans were just there to save a relative who was Jewish. Only three of us went with him and it was no use because they had already taken the Jews, including the woman he looked for and her two children and her other relatives. But while we were there a patrol of ss came into the village and we were reported by some villagers who were afraid. We had no chance. The cottage was surrounded and we went without fighting to save the villagers. They took us out of the village into the woods. They made us dig a ditch. Our Colonel your husband would not do it. They shot him dead. We three others dug the ditch. They shot us all the same and kicked us in and pushed earth over us. By the mercy of God the bullet went through my body but I was alive. I stayed still but when they were gone I could lift myself out from the ditch. We had not dug it deep. My comrades were dead and so was our Colonel. I was in pain but I wept for him. He had told us all often of you and his son Teofil. He prayed each night that God should keep you safe. Hoping that his prayers were answered, I am your servant Jan Podroski.

Teofil was now weeping again. Annabel said nothing but sat in stupefied silence. Krystyna, who had been out of the room, returned. She saw her son weeping and for a moment her face stretched into an extraordinary expression of mingled emotions – anguish, hatred, remorse. Then she composed herself. 'You had better keep it,' she said to Teofil. 'There is little else for you to remember him by.'

'Who was the woman?' asked Teofil.

'What woman?'

'The Jewish woman.'

'Oh yes. That was Rachel. Stefan's wife. She had twins. They all died.' She crossed the room, put the coffee cups on the tray and carried the tray out of the room.

Five

Because she was a guest in his mother's house, it would be considered only polite for Teofil to go out with Annabel. During the week they would go to the theatre or cinema, and at weekends he would take her on 'expeditions around Paris or outside to Versailles and Fontainebleau. There were certainly occasions when he went to see other friends, but he always made sure that he had an evening free for Annabel.

She too was happy to go with him – in those particular circumstances. When any other young men invited her out – and one or two English youths at the Sorbonne did try – she would refuse for fear of what might be involved: but since Teofil's attentions could be construed as just an aspect of his filial duty, nothing was involved – nothing except a little culture and entertainment.

It was Annabel who defended Stefan against Teofil's reservations 'There's something creepy about him,' Teofil had said after a second visit they had paid to him one Saturday afternoon.

'Maybe,' she said. 'But to me that makes him more interesting. I hate people you know all about as soon as you see them.'

'Such as young bankers . . .'

She smiled. 'No, not at all. As a matter of fact . . .' She blushed and leant towards Teofil to talk in a lower voice. 'As a matter of fact I was thinking of Sarah.'

Teofil laughed. 'She isn't very deep . . .'

'So many girls at school were just like that. The sort who were bossy and were made prefects. I hate them.'

'You can't hate Sarah.'

'No,' said Annabel. 'I don't hate her, but I'm glad I don't have to see her all the time.'

'Then it's just as well that she's got a boyfriend.'

'Yes.'

'And you've got me.'

Annabel blushed. 'I didn't mean . . .'

Teofil smiled at her. 'Nor did I.'

'I know it's an awful bore for you,' said Annabel.

'Not at all.'

'Of course it is. You wouldn't be here unless your mother forced you to come with me.'

'She may have suggested it,' said Teofil – now blushing himself.

'I could go by myself, you know.'

'I'd be sad if you did,' he said with such evident sincerity that Annabel stopped teasing him. They smiled at one another to seal the truce.

In this way Annabel and Teofil grew closer together – something which was watched with fascination by the ebullient Sarah Graham. She thought only of that sort of thing, and also had an interest: she had not forgiven Annabel for her prim reprimand about 'going too far' with her English boyfriend, Godfrey. Since Sarah regularly went too far in the flat which this Godfrey shared with another English boy, she was determined that everyone else must do so – that even Annabel who was so pretty and rich should give in to the demands of her sexual nature.

She waited and watched, but for weeks she waited in vain. Teofil and Annabel never stayed out late and they never went into one another's rooms. On a weekday they came straight back from the theatre or cinema; on a Friday or Saturday they might have a drink in a café before returning to the flat and retiring to their respective beds. At night Sarah would listen to the movements in the flat – hoping that she might hear Teofil creeping along to Annabel's room; but each footstep was explained by innocent movements of Teofil, his parents, Annabel or the maid.

Sarah was sure that Teofil and Annabel fancied one another. There were all the signs. Annabel blushed and smiled in a special way whenever Teofil came into the room; her expression became unusually animated, and it was quite common, now, for her to laugh in Teofil's presence.

Teofil, in his turn, behaved with a particular panache when Annabel was present. He would lay down the paper when she came in to breakfast, and stand to make sure that there was coffee in the pot – something, Sarah noted, that he never did for her. Even more convincing proof in her eyes was Teofil's refusal of an invitation to dinner with the Duchesse de R. just because he had half-arranged to go to a film with Annabel on the same evening.

The weeks passed and Sarah still looked for some secret glance between the two that would betray a guilty complicity. She was frustrated. Their glances became more affectionate, more amused – but there was no complicity. At last Sarah could bear it no longer. One evening, when Teofil was out and the whole household had retired early, she went along in her dressing-gown to visit Annabel in her room.

Annabel too was in a dressing-gown – one made of pretty, embroidered quilting. She was seated at her small desk writing a letter. She had brushed her long brown hair and even Sarah, who was now familiar with her appearance, was struck by how like a child she looked. Her belongings too were arranged like those of a little girl. On her desk were two framed photographs – one of her nanny, the other of her pony. There was a third photograph of her parents, which was placed along with her hairbrush on the chest-of-drawers.

This innocence did not deter Sarah. She shut the door behind her and went to sit on Annabel's bed. 'Did you go to the literature lecture today?' she asked.

'Yes,' said Annabel.

'Could I look at your notes? I missed it.'

'Of course,' said Annabel, opening a drawer of her desk.

'Not now,' said Sarah. 'Tomorrow will do.'

Annabel laid down her pen.

'Am I disturbing you?'

'Oh no,' said Annabel. 'I was only writing to Mother. She gets cross if I don't write.'

'So does mine. She even wrote to Madame de P. to ask if I was still alive. I got a real blowing up after that. "Teofil always wrote to me once a week." ' Sarah imitated Krystyna's comic English accent.

Annabel smiled.

'But then I'm sure he's a good boy in every way,' said Sarah, with innuendo in her tone of voice.

'How do you mean?' asked Annabel.

'Well, isn't he?'

'What?'

'A good boy.'

Annabel seemed to sense the innuendo but could not understand it. 'He's very polite,' she said. 'A bit too polite, really ...'

'He always asks you first?' said Sarah with a sneer.

'He always asks me if I want to see this film or that ...'

'When it doesn't really matter what you see?'

Annabel looked confused. 'How do you mean?'

'Well, you don't go out with him just to go to a film ...'

'No. I like his company.

'That's obvious.'

'There's nothing wrong with that.'

'Of course not. Nothing at all. Even if you . . . well, you know.'

'If what?'

'Hasn't he kissed you?'

Annabel blushed scarlet. 'Oh no. It isn't really like that at all.'

'Huh.'

'I don't think he thinks of me in that way.'

'Of course he does. All men do.'

'Perhaps.' Annabel stared ahead of herself as if pondering.

Sarah was suddenly afraid that her friend might start to cry. 'He's probably just too shy.'

'You see,' said Annabel suddenly, 'we're not really as grown-up as you are.'

Now Sarah blushed. 'Nonsense,' she said. 'You know the facts of life, don't you?'

'Of course,' said Annabel. 'But when I'm with Teofil, I don't really associate him with all that.'

'But you like him, don't you?'

'Yes. I think he's wonderful. I'm happier with him than I have ever been with anyone before.' She paused, then glanced at the photograph on her desk. 'Except Nanny,' she added.

'Well, then?' said Sarah.

'All the same, I don't think of him in *that* way. It's funny, isn't it? Because he's awfully handsome and attractive. But I can't imagine ever . . . touching him . . .'

'Have you ever imagined it with anyone?'

'Oh yes,' said Annabel.

'With whom?'

'You won't believe me.'

'Go on.'

Annabel looked at Sarah. 'With Stefan Kornowski,' she said.

Her imaginings concerning Stefan Kornowski were vague. As she lay in her bed each night, waiting to sleep, he came to her and enveloped her. She dreamed of him wrapping her in a rug which smelt of his cigarettes. He embraced her and hugged her; there were even kisses of a sort, but these came when she was semiconscious, drifting down into slumber.

During the day, when she went to visit him, she was only

conscious that she loved the smell and feel of his flat, which was small, warm and untidy. He was also kind and always interested in what she had done. She told him about her uneventful life – her excursions with Teofil, the lectures at the Sorbonne – and he would ask for more details – the plot of the film, the food she had eaten, what Teofil had said about Fontainebleau, and once whether he ever held her hand.

'My hand? No. Why?'

'If I was a young man, I would want to hold it.'

She smiled. 'It wouldn't occur to Teofil.'

'He may be too timid.'

'Why timid?'

'Perhaps he is afraid of your reactions?'

Annabel smiled again. 'What would they be?'

'Don't you know?'

Stefan sat at the chair by his desk: Annabel on the sofa. He leant against the upholstery; her body lay languid and relaxed. 'I sometimes think,' she said, 'that you know me better than I know myself.'

Stefan sucked the inside of his cheek.

'I feel,' she said, 'like a character in a book.'

Stefan looked at the wall behind Annabel.

'A book you are writing. The paper is blank. I am blank. I am waiting for you to put some life into me . . . to tell me what I would do if my hand was held . . .'

It was raining. There was the sound of wind which rose above the noise of the traffic below. Two dim lamps lit the flat. Her eyes were on Stefan Kornowski; then they looked down at her own hands.

'You see,' she said in a quiet, deliberate voice, 'what's been written already won't do. Someone must cross it out and start again . . .' She did not look at Stefan Kornowski, so that his eyes could creep down from the wall and study her – her soft hair falling forwards over her bowed head, her slim body conventionally covered in cashmere and tweed, her narrow legs in black ribbed stockings, slightly parted at the knee. There was a long silence. She waited; but Stefan did not move, and when she looked up he was looking away, his face twisted in the familiar grimace.

She rose to take the tea cups into the kitchen. She washed

them and came back into the living-room. He was writing in his notebook but laid down his pen as she entered.

'I'm sorry,' he said. 'It is rude of me to write when you are here. But at my age, with my memory, one forgets one's ideas five minutes after one has had them, unless one jots them down . . .'

Annabel rested her thin body against the arm of the sofa. 'I'll forgive you,' she said, 'if you tell me the idea.'

'Ah,' he said, glancing at his notebook. 'It was about the real and the unreal, the visible and the invisible . . .'

She waited.

'And disease,' he said.

'Why disease?'

'Think of a single malignant cell . . .'

'Yes.'

'Then of a complex of cells. A man. Can he be malignant, like the cell?'

'Of course. Destructive . . . like a murderer.'

'But with murder there is blood. What I wonder is whether a man can be invisibly destructive . . .'

'He could hurt someone's feelings,' she said. 'Then there would be no blood.'

'But there would be tears. What I wonder is if there are acts, or even thoughts, which produce no pain or sorrow, but in themselves are the workings of a cancerous cell . . .'

'I don't understand,' said Annabel.

'Imagine,' said Stefan, 'that a man hates a child – his own child. He never shows it. The child never knows . . .'

'But it's unnatural . . .'

'And are health and nature one and the same thing?'

'Yes,' said Annabel.

'But nature is cruel. When a stag grows old, his wives are taken by a younger beast: and when too many rats occupy the same hole, they fight a war to the death. Yet when human beings do the same sort of thing people say it is wrong . . .'

'We have higher standards.'

'Perhaps. But doesn't it show that it can be wrong to act naturally – that there is no necessary connection between health, nature and righteousness?' His question was fast and intense.

'No,' she said.

'So where do your values come from?'

'I don't know. I hadn't thought.'

'From God, perhaps?'

She hesitated. 'I don't really believe in God,' she said.

'There you are,' he said. 'We escape from God without much difficulty, but it is not so easy to escape from the Good.'

It was late – later than usual – and Annabel prepared to go. She put on her coat and gloves, and took her umbrella from the bath where she had left it to drip. She dawdled in the hallway. She could see that Stefan wanted her to go, that he was impatient to return to his notebooks, but still she fussed with her gloves as if there was something she had meant to take with her and had forgotten. But there was nothing: she would go out just as she had come in.

As soon as he had closed the door behind her, Stefan returned to his living-room and stood for some time looking down at the street below. He saw Annabel leave the building and walk away. Then he went to his desk and sat before his open notebook. He turned back to the passages which described Annabel when she had first entered his flat – the delicate face with unmistakably English features, the spindly figure in the drab clothes that the English upper-classes thought proper at that time. He had seen at once what she was – a woman desperate to be a child again, a frightened creature who carried around in horror and disgust the burden of her breasts and genitalia.

His first impulse had been to seduce her. It was this lust that Annabel had mistaken for sympathy and the fantasies it inspired that Teofil had read in his uncle's notebook. But that very visit had changed Stefan's attitude towards Annabel, and when now he tried to puzzle out his own behaviour – when he asked himself why he had been paralysed when Annabel had lain at his feet and had offered herself by her passivity – unable to draw her body towards him, or kiss her childish lips – it was the image of Annabel with Teofil which came into his mind. 'It was Teofil,' he muttered to himself. 'Teofil prevented me.'

But another voice in his mind, the voice of his alter ego, Raymond de Tarterre, whispered that it had nothing to do with Teofil – that it was his own cowardice which had paralysed him.

'It is just the same as it was with Tilly Czarniecka. You are indelibly a voyeur.'

'The two belong together,' Stefan said to himself.

A scoffing laugh came from Raymond. 'On the contrary, they belong apart. They are both empty and immature – two timid hermaphrodites waiting and longing to be depraved.'

'But Teofil . . .'

'He protects himself from life with a shell of dandyism. He shrinks from women and the mushy bog of their sex and affection.'

Stefan turned on his inner voice. 'Your cynicism is banal. If this was art and not life, what sort of plot would that be? Another *Lolita*. It would be more original to write about the love of two innocents . . .'

This inner dialogue continued. The whispering voice of Raymond de Tarterre accused Stefan of remorse: 'You feel a paternal responsibility towards Teofil because, here in Paris, twenty-two years ago, Bruno entrusted him to you should you survive. You think that Teofil loves Annabel, or could love her, and that if they married they would live happily ever after. The truth is, of course, that middle-age has made you impotent, gaga and sentimental . . .'

With increasing confidence Stefan defended himself against his alter ego. 'My heart is weak. At any moment I may drop dead. All that matters to me now is to write one book before I die, but for that I must have a theme. Depravity did not provide me with one, nor did the dull, dead years in America. Now I have a story of purity and innocence which will amaze the jaded and disillusioned world.'

Six

Both Annabel and Sarah went home for Easter, and it was then that Stefan and Teofil found themselves alone together for the first time. After lunch on Easter Sunday, Alain and Krystyna went to visit Alain's sister in the Bois de Boulogne, leaving the uncle and nephew in their sitting-room. Then Stefan suggested a walk to 'clear their heads' and they left the flat.

'Do you feel at home in Paris?' Stefan asked Teofil as they walked towards the Champs Elysées.

'Oh yes,' said Teofil. Then he added: 'As much as I do anywhere.'

'And England?'

'Not so much.'

'I wonder what you would feel in Warsaw.'

'Is it beautiful?'

'It was.'

'I'll go there some time.'

They walked a little further in silence, and then came out on the wide avenue of the Champs Elysées.

'And do *you* feel at home in Paris?' Teofil asked his uncle.

'More than in Chicago or New York.'

'Do you miss Poland?'

'Yes.'

'So does Mama.'

'In the Middle Ages,' said Stefan, 'exile was like a prison sentence . . . a punishment for treason.'

'Couldn't you go back?'

'No. They have long memories . . . and so do I.'

'And would I . . . do you think I would be in trouble?'

Stefan shrugged his shoulders. 'I don't know the people in power.'

'Were they friends of my father?'

'Some of them, perhaps. Most of his friends were killed by Stalin.'

'I wonder,' said Teofil, 'if he had survived, whether my father would have been a Communist now.'

'I doubt it,' said Stefan. 'He became disillusioned.'

'Why?'

'Some terrible things were done in the name of Progress.'

'I know. But now, perhaps . . .' He turned to his uncle. 'You may not believe this, but I am drawn to Communism. I've never told my mother because it would upset her, but it seems to me on balance that Communism has benefited the human race . . . Perhaps not in Poland, but in China and even in Russia.'

'It's a strange view for a merchant banker,' said Stefan.

Teofil blushed. 'I know. That's why I keep quiet about it. You see, I'm a late developer. My upbringing has been such an odd mixture that I've never felt any confidence in myself. I just tried to fade into the background – and going into the City seemed to be the thing to do. But now I'm inclined to drop the borrowed clothes, if you see what I mean, and discover my own personality . . .'

'I once wanted to do that,' said Stefan.

'And did you succeed?'

'No. And I gave up trying.'

'Why were you a Communist?' Teofil asked him.

'I also thought that on balance it would benefit the human race.'

'And did you change your mind?'

'I ceased to care about the human race.'

Teofil looked perplexed. 'I can see that if you don't care . . .'

'I came to realize that Communism is a morality,' said Stefan, 'and I did not believe in right and wrong . . . Whereas you, I can see, have something of your father in you. He had to feel that he was serving others. He suppressed the wild, idiosyncratic side of his nature and never doubted the absurd hypothesis that men are equal . . .'

'But why is it absurd?'

'Because men are not equal. In every perceivable way they are unequal.'

'Their souls are equal.'

'How do you know?'

Teofil blushed. 'Christ said so.'

'On what authority?'

'He was the Son of God.'

Stefan smiled. 'Yes, of course. I had forgotten that you were a Catholic. Well certainly, if Christ was the Son of God, and Christ said that men were equal, then you have something to build on . . .'

'And what do you build on?' asked Teofil.

'I don't build,' said Stefan. 'I abandoned philosophical speculation when I left Europe. And in America no one expects you to have a system: the Anglo-Saxons live quite happily without them.'

'Do you mean that for twenty years you have lived without any convictions?'

'For nineteen. Without convictions. Without principles. Without curiosity. Almost without needs or desires. I took what came my way – a cup of coffee, a job or a love affair . . .'

'But what were you like before then, when you were my age?'

'Callous, eccentric, conceited . . .'

'And what did you want out of life?'

'Freedom. Complete freedom from all extraneous pressures and influences.'

'And did you achieve it?'

'For a moment, yes. There in the Tuileries Gardens.' Stefan pointed in the direction of the gardens on the other side of the Place de la Concorde. 'Across there is a bench. We might go and see if it still exists. I sat there and felt I was free.'

'Why at that particular moment?'

'I had just kicked the last survivor off my raft.'

'Who was that?'

'Your father. I was going with him to Spain. Then I realized that I was a coward and I deserted him. It was the most glorious moment of my life . . .'

'And after that?'

'I went downhill. What I wrote was futile. I became social, snobbish and . . . well, I behaved badly. But at least I was free. I have always felt free, ever since that moment, detached from all obligations . . .'

'And do you still feel free?'

Stefan hesitated. 'Yes, more or less. There is just one commitment . . .'

'What is that?'

'An artistic matter. Something I must write for my own satisfaction.'

They entered the Tuileries Gardens and looked for the bench, but could not find it. There were others walking there, working off their Easter lunch, but it was getting late and Stefan and Teofil prepared to part, each to return to where he lived.

'You must come and have tea with me soon,' said Stefan.

'I should love to,' said Teofil.

'I miss our little English friend.'

'So do I.'

'She's very fond of you,' said Stefan.

'She's very fond of you,' said Teofil, smiling at his uncle.

'Perhaps,' said Stefan. 'But you are more eligible.'

Teofil blushed. 'I would feel more eligible,' he said, 'if I had a better idea of what I wanted to be.'

Both Stefan and Teofil now walked off in different directions – Stefan to cross the Pont Royal and walk to his small flat, Teofil to take a bus back to the Etoile and the larger apartment belonging to his mother and stepfather.

Alain and Krystyna had not returned, the maid was out and so the flat was empty. Teofil suddenly felt at a loose end. There were two possibilities for the evening – one lot of friends had suggested a film and another had said they would take him to a party – but the thought of both depressed him. Films were only enjoyable if you could forget that they were films, and the party in the 16ème would be full of youthful fanatics – apologists of *Jeune Nation* and the paratroops.

What he would like to do, he thought to himself, would be to see Annabel – to go with her to a film or a party. He wanted her face before his eyes, her voice in his ears, her quiet little laugh which came so cautiously to the surface of her features. In his mind he began to count the days before her return. There were twelve, and twelve days suddenly seemed an intolerable length of time – and then perhaps she would fall ill and not return at all. He knew about her anorexia, and though he did not quite know what it was, he believed it to be like malaria – a recurring disease.

He decided that he would write to her and went to look for some paper; but then he realized that even if she wrote back at once he could not get a reply for a week or ten days, and even that distance in time seemed unbearable.

There was the telephone. Though no one in the flat made calls abroad, it was done at his office and there was no real reason why he should not do it now – especially while his mother and stepfather were out. He did not know the number of Mulford Park but he knew the address and in ten minutes had the number. He dialled for the international operator, gave her the number and waited.

The call went through London and Plymouth; but he heard the tone which meant that the telephone was ringing in Cornwall. He imagined that some butler would answer, but the voice he heard was a woman's, with a harsh, haughty sound to it.

'Could I speak to Annabel, please?' he asked.

'Just a minute,' said the woman. Then, a moment later: 'Who is that?'

The line was faint but clear enough for Teofil to catch the note of suspicion. 'Teofil de Pincey,' he said.

'Oh yes,' said the woman. 'Just a moment.'

There was a short pause: then Annabel's quiet voice said hello.

'Annabel?' he said, feeling close to tears. 'Is that you?'

'Yes.'

'This is Teofil.'

'I know.'

'How are you?'

'All right.'

'I just rang to wish you a happy Easter.'

'Yes. To you too.'

There was a pause. Teofil almost panicked and put the telephone back in its cradle, but then Annabel said: 'Can you wait a minute? I'll go to another phone.'

He gripped the telephone and waited: he heard one click, then another, then Annabel's voice clearer against a quieter background.

'I'm sorry,' she said. 'There were other people in the room.'

'How are you?' he asked again.

'All right,' she repeated. 'Well, more or less all right.'

'Are you ill?' he asked.

'No,' she said.

'We all miss you.'

'So do I.'

'Paris isn't much fun without you.'

There was a pause: Teofil thought that he might have gone too far. Then Annabel said: 'Shall I come back earlier?'

'I wish you would.'

'All right.'

'Will your mother let you?'

'Yes, I should think so.'

'When will you come?'
'I'll send a telegram.'
'I'll meet you.'
'All right.'
There was a pause.
'You'd better ring off,' said Annabel. 'It's frightfully expensive.'
'Very well. But come soon.'
'I will.'
'Annabel . . .'
'What?'
'I . . . well, I'll tell you when I see you.'
'Goodbye, then.'
'Goodbye.'

Seven

Like all rapturous moments in life, the reunion of Teofil and Annabel at the Gare du Nord went unnoticed by the protagonists themselves. Since the telephone call on Easter Day the idea that they were in love with one another had grown in the mind of each one so that at the very moment when they might have been suffused with the grandeur of the event, their thoughts were all on the tiny details of behaviour – the cut of their clothes, the scent of their breath; and when they saw one another at the station, each thought only of crossing fifteen yards of the platform without making the other shudder. When they met they did not embrace; they did not even look into one another's eyes. Teofil shook Annabel by the hand, and then looked for a porter

In the taxi, when a little of the terror had subsided, he glanced timidly into her eyes, and seeing a sweet, shy look he took hold of her hand. It was covered by a woollen glove and lay lifeless in his.

'I'm happy to see you,' he said, wondering whether the taxi driver could understand English.

'I'm happy to be back,' she said.

'Was it difficult . . . to change your arrangements?'

She smiled. 'A little. My mother wasn't pleased.'

'But she let you come?'

'She couldn't refuse. Dr Ebermann was on my side.'

'Who is he?'

'A doctor.'

'Now I feel guilty. Perhaps you missed a ball or . . .'

'She did want me to go and stay with some people, but it wasn't that. I wouldn't have gone anyway.'

'So why was she against you coming back?'

'She was suspicious.'

'Of what?'

Annabel turned to him and looked straight into his eyes. 'Of someone ringing me from Paris. That's never happened before.'

Teofil had kissed girls before and had not taken much pleasure in it, which was why he had never gone further. For the same reason he dreaded the moment when he would have to kiss Annabel but knew that it had to be done; and rather than have it hanging over him, he decided to get it over with. After dinner with Alain and Krystyna he suggested to Annabel that they go out for their coffee to a café on the Champs Elysées. Annabel said that she would like to and went to fetch her coat.

'She's probably tired,' said Krystyna to Teofil in an irritated tone of voice. 'You might at least have let her go to bed early.'

'She could have refused,' said Teofil. 'And anyway, we won't be long.' He did not look at his mother for fear that she should see the hatred he felt towards her just at that moment.

And so, with the grumpy insinuating eyes of Krystyna boring into their backs, Teofil and Annabel left the flat and went down to the street. The anger which Teofil still felt made him braver than he might otherwise have been. While still walking in the dark sidestreet, he took hold of Annabel's hand; and a block from his home he stopped, turned towards Annabel and kissed her.

It was a definite kiss but quite unpractised. Both pairs of lips barely opened, but were pressed together in imitation of the older kind of film; but Teofil's arms went around her shoulders and Annabel's came up to clutch the coat on his back with the clenched grip of a baby.

'I love you,' he said awkwardly, like a boy playing a part he had not rehearsed.

'So do I,' she said. 'I love you.' And she spoke with just as little conviction; but they were both so delighted to have got it over and done with that for the rest of the evening they hardly let go of one another's hand or looked anywhere but into each other's eyes.

It did not occur to either of them that they would not get married: it was quite common in the 1950s to assume that the emotion would suffice for a lifetime. The moment when this assumption became a conscious proposal was another lost to them both in obliqueness. Teofil, with some inkling of what was involved in terms of class and property, had put the question into the distant future; but quite soon after her return to Paris, Annabel would drop remarks such as: 'I don't think that dogs should sleep in the house, do you?' or: 'We can live in France if we have to.' Finally, after this last remark which was made on a bus which was taking them to the river, Teofil said: 'And so we'll marry, will we?'

'Oh yes,' said Annabel. 'Don't you think so?'

'Yes.'

'Don't you want to marry me?'

'Of course I do.'

'I assumed we would.'

'So did I.'

They got off the bus by the river.

'What will your parents think?' said Teofil.

'I don't care,' said Annabel. 'I don't care what they think.'

'We could live on my salary,' said Teofil, 'but not in much style.'

She put her arm around his waist and hugged him. 'Don't worry about that,' she said. 'My father so hates to pay taxes of any kind that he's already made over most of his money.'

'To you?'

'Yes, to me.'

It was a spring evening. The air was warm. They walked arm-in-arm along the quai and felt sufficiently free, in this public place, to give to each other those simple kisses with pursed lips.

Eight

One morning in the middle of May, a few days after the revolt in Algiers against the government of Pflimlin, Krystyna telephoned her brother and asked him – or rather ordered him – to meet her for lunch. Since the only engagement he had that day was for tea with Annabel, Stefan agreed to do so.

He arrived first in the restaurant and saw on Krystyna's face as she came in through the door a look of irritable anxiety. She greeted him brusquely and started to study the menu.

'What are you eating?' she asked him.

'Soup. Liver. Salad.'

She wrinkled her nose.

The waiter came; they ordered their lunch.

'Why did you want to see me?' asked Stefan.

'Must there be a special reason?'

'You look worried.'

She frowned and avoided his eyes. 'Well I am,' she said. 'It's those children.'

'What has happened to them?'

'Teofil told me last night that they are going to get married.' She glanced sharply at Stefan and caught the gleam in his eye. 'Did you know?' she asked.

'I had an idea.'

'It's one of your tricks,' said Krystyna – hissing at him.

Stefan did not reply.

Krystyna began to pick at the ends of her hair as if forgetting that it had been set by a Parisian hairdresser, imagining it to fall to her shoulders as it had in the old days. Stefan studied her and saw her as the anxious girl from before the war – shorn of her elegance and mannerisms – for like all Poles she had aged well and was not really so different.

'You must stop it,' said Krystyna.

'Why?' he asked.

'They're not suited.'

'Can't you see your son as an English gentleman?' asked Stefan, with an expression of slight mockery on his face.

'No, I can't.'

'But that's what you brought him up to be.'

'You don't understand. They won't allow it.'

'Who won't?'

'Her family.'

'Can they stop it?'

'If they try.'

'Love thrives in adversity . . .'

She looked up and stared at him with her blue eyes. 'Please, for once, be serious.'

Stefan frowned and looked away. 'Why should I be serious?'

'Stefan,' she said. 'I know you despise me . . .'

'I don't.'

'I know you think that I'm a fool – that I've become false and snobbish . . .'

'I don't.'

She gave a snort of exasperation and sat back in her chair. 'Tell me, then. Tell me why I am worried and afraid, and why I have come to you.'

'You're frightened of losing Teofil,' he said.

The waiter came with their first course – soup and egg mayonnaise.

'Perhaps I am,' said Krystyna.

'You cling to him as your salvation . . . You're besotted with him . . . You're jealous of Annabel.'

She frowned. 'Do you really think that?'

He shrugged his shoulders. 'I was never able to tell the difference between what I think and what I really think.'

'That's why I asked you to be serious.'

Stefan took a noisy mouthful of his soup.

'Perhaps you are right,' said Krystyna. 'Perhaps I am just a possessive mother: but Teofil is so young and sensitive, and so is she. I always thought that a strong woman . . . Do you know, I don't think he has ever slept with a girl?'.

'Nor had I at that age.'

'Nonsense. You were married. And anyway, you aren't a good example for him to follow.'

'You are wrong about Annabel,' said Stefan. 'She is potentially stronger than all of us.'

'But the child is in and out of psychiatric hospitals . . .'

'Life has thrown her off balance; but now, by marrying Teofil . . .'

'She will be worse off than before; because her parents won't let her marry Teofil. The estates, the money, they have all been settled on her, and they won't let it pass to an expatriate Pole.'

'Fresh blood,' said Stefan.

'They don't think like that. You've been in America for too long. You've forgotten how hard and uncompromising these French and English families can be.'

'She will insist.'

'Who?'

'Annabel.'

'And if she does, who will suffer? Teofil. He will be the battle-field.'

The waiter came to clear away their empty plates and bring the next course. Stefan craned his neck to try and catch sight of his liver, as if that was immeasurably more important to him than their conversation.

'Listen, Stefan,' said Krystyna, seeing that she was losing his attention. 'Please listen now and then I'll shut up. You may be right, that I am possessive. I don't know. But Teofil is my life. He is all I have from those hard years and I must see him happy. I owe it to Bruno and Cecylia and to Mamuska – all those who are dead in Poland. I owe it to them . . .' She hesitated. 'And so do you, Stefan. You owe it to them – to the dead.'

She watched his face. His eyes stopped looking for the waiter and stared vacantly into the middle distance: and then he said, in a tone of voice quite flat and normal: 'There is no need to be concerned. I have it in hand.'

Annabel wrote a letter to her parents in which she told them baldly that she was going to marry Teofil de Pincey. Five days

307

later she received a telegram telling her to return to England at once. She ignored it. Then there came a telephone call. Sarah, Teofil and the de Pinceys talked about this and that, trying not to overhear Annabel in the hall. 'I'll come back in June . . . It's what we arranged . . . no, of course not. I want the wedding at home . . . No. I don't need to see Dr Ebermann. It's my own decision and I've made it . . .'

She rang off and came back into the drawing-room.

'Was it your mother?' asked Teofil.

'Yes,' said Annabel. There was a pause: then she added: 'She wants me to go home.'

'Perhaps you should go,' said Krystyna.

Annabel turned a cold eye on her hostess. 'Are you turning me out?' she asked quietly.

'Of course not,' said Krystyna. 'It's just that . . .'

'I'm very sorry,' said Annabel, interrupting her, 'that you are placed in an awkward position. But there it is. It has happened. And I won't give in.' She crossed the room and stood beside Teofil.

Alain and Krystyna exchanged glances but said nothing.

The next blow from Mulford Park was a letter from Lady Felsted to Krystyna. It accused her of misusing the trust they placed in her hands to insinuate Teofil into Annabel's affections – of exploiting the girl's psychological fragility to secure a fortune for her son. By the same post Sarah received a letter from her parents ordering her to return home at once.

Before leaving for the Sorbonne in the morning, Annabel had seen a letter to Mme de Pincey with an English stamp and addressed in her mother's handwriting. In the evening when she returned she saw that Krystyna's eyes were red from tears. She asked her at once if the letter had been from her mother. Krystyna said that it had. Annabel demanded to see the letter, which Krystyna took from her desk.

As she read it, Annabel turned white. Two angry eyes stared at Krystyna from her angelic face as if Krystyna was somehow to blame for having received it. Teofil returned just as she had finished the letter: he was ignored. This was a matter between women.

'Madame de Pincey,' said Annabel. 'We both know that everything she says is untrue.'

'I know, my dear, but . . .'

'I would like you to pay no attention to it.'

Krystyna started to sniff and shrug her shoulders like a bird flapping its wings. 'But you're children,' she said.

'I am twenty-two,' said Annabel. 'That's old enough to make decisions for oneself.'

'Oh, you may think so.'

'How old were you when you married?'

'I was . . . yes . . . twenty-two.'

'And was it a mistake?'

'No. No more than it ever is. You're right. You only seem young to me. Of course, if you love one another . . .' She suddenly gripped Annabel with both her hands and kissed her on both cheeks. Then she took hold of Teofil and hugged them together, one arm around each body.

She did not reply to the letter from Lady Felsted. She left it to Annabel. 'If you are so ashamed of Teofil,' Annabel wrote to her mother, 'without knowing him, without meeting him, then certainly it would be better if we were married in Paris . . .'

After this there was a pause – a silence in which Annabel, Teofil, Krystyna, Alain and Stefan Kornowski all waited for a telephone call, a telegram or a letter – or even the appearance in Paris of Lord and Lady Felsted. Teofil had a nightmare in which the British ambassador appeared at the door of the flat dressed in a gold and scarlet uniform shouting: 'Habeas Corpus, Habeas Corpus . . .'

Finally two letters arrived from Mulford Park – one for Annabel, the other for Krystyna. In both it was suggested that when the course at the Sorbonne was finished, and when it suited them all, Annabel should bring Teofil and his whole family to stay at Mulford so that they could all get to know one another and then decide what was best.

Nine

The end of the Fourth French Republic and the birth of the Fifth, which took place in the late spring and early summer of 1958, went almost unnoticed by Stefan Kornowski. For what interest could there be in a new constitution when his living masterpiece – the new *Paul et Virginie* – was taking shape before his eyes? The two innocents were engaged. There in his flat their two hands – those active extensions of their immature flesh – clutched one another: and timid, loving looks flitted back and forth across the room. And each glance and gesture was noted by Stefan and recorded afterwards in his notebook.

One problem preoccupied him: he sat for long periods at his desk, chewing the end of his pen, analysing it and looking for a solution. This was the persistent absence of any sign of lust in either of the two young lovers. Their love was immediately and undeniably apparent. Annabel had only to go into Stefan's kitchen with the tea cups for Teofil to look mournfully towards the door like a pining dog; and when he came to meet her there after a day at work, Annabel would greet him and take his coat with such a look of pride and admiration that he might have been a hunter returning from a month in the wild.

Their embraces, however, were chaste; and the way they held one another's hand seemed symbolic. Both had beautiful faces and graceful bodies, yet they behaved as if admiration was all that was required. For a time Stefan thought it was *pudeur* – that when they were alone a certain sensuality must arise in them. But when he asked Krystyna obliquely whether 'the children crept into one another's beds', she replied that she was sure that they had never even been alone together in their rooms. 'It's odd, isn't it?' she said. 'We weren't like that.'

In the middle of July they all travelled from Paris to London with a large amount of luggage. On Alain's advice, Stefan had bought himself a tweed suit, heavy brown shoes and a dinner jacket. He had also brought a bathing costume, because Annabel had told him that they often bathed in the Atlantic Ocean.

They spent two nights in London – Annabel in her parents' flat in Mayfair, the de Pinceys and Stefan Kornowski in the Piccadilly Hotel. No sooner were they in the city than Teofil became authoritative: he took Stefan to Jermyn Street to buy shirts and then to Simpson's in the Strand for lunch. Before returning to the hotel they walked around St James's, Teofil pointing out the various clubs to his uncle. As they passed White's Club Stefan said to Teofil: 'Perhaps you will be a member one day?'

Teofil blushed. 'I don't think so,' he said. 'It's not my style.'

That evening they had dinner in a restaurant in Knightsbridge chosen by Teofil. There they were joined by Dr Ebermann, Annabel's psychoanalyst, and his wife. He was a kindly-looking German who sat near to Teofil and talked to him while Annabel watched and Stefan talked to the wife.

When dinner was finished they went out into the street and walked up towards Hyde Park looking for taxis. Stefan found himself beside Dr Ebermann. 'I have heard a great deal about you,' the psychoanalyst said to him. 'I think you have done a lot for Annabel.'

Stefan did not look at Dr Ebermann for fear of his professional perception. 'We're all very fond of her,' he said – vaguely and pompously.

'You probably do not realize how important you are to her,' said the doctor.

'She seems to love my nephew.'

'If you will forgive me for saying so,' said Ebermann, 'it is not as simple as that. I think, when you have met the parents and seen the house, you will understand better. For the child – for Annabel – they are oppressive. She was crushed under them. Now she has escaped. Your nephew, you see, is the first and only decision she has made for herself. Otherwise she was trapped by her involvement with her parents, who are themselves not stable human beings . . .' He lowered his voice and went on: 'It is so often the case for a psychoanalyst that we are asked to cure children when it is the parents who are sick. But of course you cannot say so. Now Annabel has defied her parents, which is an excellent sign of her recovery. Of course it is dangerous too. There may be some hysteria in her determination, and if somehow she is frustrated she might withdraw again – perhaps for ever.

'I tell you all this,' said Dr Ebermann, 'because I imagine – from what Annabel has told me – that you have their happiness at heart.'

'Yes,' said Stefan. 'I should like to see them settled.'

Ahead of them, Alain had stopped a taxi and had opened the door for Mrs Ebermann. The doctor had a last word with Annabel: then he patted both Annabel and Teofil on the shoulder like a priest giving a blessing, and climbed into the taxi.

Krystyna and Alain continued walking towards Hyde Park: Stefan, Teofil and Annabel followed behind.

'Dr Ebermann liked you,' Annabel said to Teofil. 'He says that we are right to get married. He's on our side.'

'But everyone is on your side,' said Stefan.

Annabel frowned. 'I hope so,' she said.

They left the next morning from Paddington Station on the Cornish Express. As the train travelled west, Stefan felt increasingly alien. The fields were all bordered by plump hedges unlike any he had seen in Poland, France or America. The landscape was neat and trim, like a well kept garden. Annabel and Teofil seemed at ease, chatting together, their innocent hands occasionally meeting and then letting go again; but Stefan felt increasingly conspicuous in his tweed suit. He had hoped to disguise himself as an Englishman and had turned out a Pole in fancy dress.

It was in this frame of mind that he stepped out of the train at Plymouth and walked ahead of the others towards the ticket barrier. On the other side there was a small group of people waiting for the passengers – among them a woman with a sharp, well-powdered face. It occurred to Stefan that this might be Annabel's mother but he was not sure until the woman's eyes alighted on him and then looked away with a mixed expression of horror and embarrassment.

When they were face to face and Annabel – having given her mother a kiss which was no more than a gesture – was introducing them, Lady Felsted was forced to shake hands and smile; but Stefan could see what control was required to prevent the expression of distaste from returning to her features. He studied her brittle face as she shook hands with Krystyna, Alain and finally Teofil, when it finally betrayed a trace of contempt. Then it snapped back into a mask of impassive arrogance.

She led them to the two waiting cars – one driven by a rustic chauffeur, the other by Lady Felsted herself. And in convoy they set out towards the north coast and Mulford Park.

The distance they had to drive – almost fifty miles – and the nature of the roads which lay like ditches in the hilly countryside gave a proper impression that the house was inaccessible and remote. Even after they had passed through the granite gates there was a mile of driveway before the enormous neo-Gothic mansion appeared from behind a screen of trees.

The cars stopped on the gravel by the front door, which was like the entrance to a cathedral. Stefan Kornowski eased his legs from out of the back of the car where he had been sitting while the chauffeur danced around the vehicle to hold the door which Stefan had already opened. Stefan stood and stretched. He looked to the north-west and saw the sea a mile away and many hundred feet below. To the north-east, just visible, was the small fishing village of Mulford; further round there were courtyards, kitchens and the servants' quarters.

'Do come in,' said Lady Felsted, her thin voice empty of expression.

They followed their hostess into a hall which was as cold and as dimly lit as the crypt of a church. Even Annabel seemed changed by their new surroundings; her face took on a set expression.

A man appeared before them. Stefan was about to extend his hand, thinking him to be Lord Felsted, but realized just in time that he was a servant – a butler or a footman – for he walked straight past them and returned carrying Stefan's suitcase.

'If you will follow Mr Briggs,' said Lady Felsted, 'he will show you your room.' She then led Alain and Krystyna, followed by the chauffeur, down one passage while Stefan followed

the butler up the wide staircase which rose from the hall. Teofil
and Annabel had disappeared.

After a long journey down carpeted passages Stefan was led
to his bedroom. There the butler left the suitcase on a stand and
remarked mysteriously that tea was in the nursery. Then he too
disappeared and Stefan was left alone amid Edwardian furniture
and a view of the sea.

He started to unpack. He hung his dinner jacket in the wardrobe and put his shirts in a drawer. He took out his precious
notebooks and put them in the drawer of the dressing-table.
Then he heard a knock on the door. He stood quite still. There
was another knock and Teofil's voice asking for him. He went to
the door and opened it. There were Teofil, Alain and Krystyna.
'Are you ready?' asked Teofil.

'Certainly,' said Stefan.

'There's some tea downstairs,' said Teofil.

'English tea,' said Alain.

'In the nursery,' said Stefan.

'Where is the nursery?' asked Krystyna.

'I don't know,' said Teofil. 'I'll go and find out.' He started
down the corridor.

'Don't go without me,' said Krystyna to her son.

'Shall we take a different route?' said Alain to Stefan.

'By all means,' said Stefan: and together the two older men
went down a different corridor in search of crumpets and hot
buttered toast.

They came to the large staircase. 'Would the nursery be on the
ground floor?' asked Alain.

Stefan shrugged his shoulders. 'We shall have to ask for a
map.'

Together they descended the shallow flight of stairs and once
in the hall they stood for a moment wondering which passage to
take or which door to try.

'The nursery is sure to be at the back,' said Alain.

'What is this room, I wonder?' asked Stefan.

'Try the door.'

'After you,' said Stefan.

'Very well,' said Alain; and with Stefan covering his rear, he
opened one of the heavy doors which led off the hall.

The room they entered was large and faced south, so that for

314

a moment neither Stefan nor Alain noticed that four or five people were sitting on chintz-covered sofas and armchairs. They stood in the doorway like surveyors, studying the ornate woodwork of the bookshelves and mantelpiece, until Stefan saw the heads of two women around fifty peering at him like cautious chickens; then the lean figure of a man of around the same age. As he was studying the man looked up from his magazine: their eyes met. The man smiled and stood up. Alain and Stefan crossed to meet him.

'Lord Felsted?' asked Alain.

The man smiled again – the smile of someone who finds most things in life either amusing or absurd. 'As a matter of fact, no,' he said in a rich, deep voice. 'Jack Marryat's my name. Teddy was last seen in the gun-room.'

Alain excused himself and the man – Jack Marryat – still with a half-amiable, half-sardonic smile on his face, sat back in his armchair and returned to his magazine. The others in the room said nothing. The women watched in silence and Alain and Stefan left the room.

Out in the hall Alain hesitated again. 'Where now?' he asked.

'The nursery,' said Stefan, 'or the gun-room.'

They came to another door leading off the passage. It was half open, and through it Stefan – who now led the two men – could see rows of books on white shelves set against a red wall. He listened at the door and heard a mumbled remark in a man's voice. He pushed the door open and saw Annabel standing at the fireplace.

When she saw Stefan, her face lit up. 'Come in,' she said. Then she turned to the man by the window. 'Father,' she said, 'this is Teofil's uncle, Stefan Kornowski. And his stepfather, Alain de Pincey.'

Lord Felsted turned to face his guests. The light was behind him and for a moment Stefan could only see his stooped figure outlined against the window; but then he came into the room to meet them and suddenly he saw his face and in his face his weakness. He was handsome – Annabel resembled him, not her mother – and retained every advantage in the colour of his eyes and the structure of his bones; but the flesh sagged and the features were lined with the indelible lines of snobbery and dissipation.

He shook Stefan by the hand. 'How do you do,' he said. 'How good of you to come.' His eyes made no attempt to agree with the mouth: their expression was of boredom and distaste.

'It was kind of you to invite us,' said Alain de Pincey.

'I hope you'll find something to do while you're here,' said Lord Felsted.

'I am sure we will,' said Alain.

'Do you play tennis?'

'Certainly,' said Alain.

'And you, Mr er . . . Korniski?'

'Not since I was a child,' said Stefan.

'A pity,' murmured Lord Felsted.

'I'll teach him to play croquet,' said Annabel.

'Yes,' said Lord Felsted. 'That isn't difficult. And of course there's the beach . . .'

He now led them out of the library and up a narrow flight of stairs to a large, dark room with a rocking-horse and a linoleum floor. 'There should be some tea,' he said to Stefan who followed behind him.

'It's the nursery,' said Annabel. 'We always had tea up here when I was a child.'

'An old custom,' said Lord Felsted.

They sat down at the long table covered with patterned oilcloth, and a moment later a middle-aged woman came in with a tea tray.

'This is Nanny,' said Annabel; and the woman smiled with a benign expression on her face, but hurried on to put sandwiches and scones on the table.

Then, one by one, the other guests appeared from different corners of the house. Annabel went off to find Teofil and Krystyna; passed her mother as she went through the door. Lady Felsted came to the head of the table and introduced Alain and Stefan to the different people who seemed to be her sisters (the two women from the drawing-room) and her sisters' children. There were twelve at table, and some of the guests – like Jack Marryat – had not appeared.

'The house is quite full in summer,' Lady Felsted said to Alain. 'In winter no one comes near us.'

Stefan studied Lady Felsted as she poured out the tea. Any talent he had ever possessed for seeing into the minds of others, assessing their motives and intentions, was now operating on her. He tried from the look in her eye, the line of her mouth, the movement of her hand, to gain some impression of her character. He already possessed the evidence of the letters – the letters to Krystyna and the letters to Annabel, all of which had been shown to him. Their form and content suggested a woman who was so limited in intellect and imagination that she could only live according to her prejudices; and nothing that he saw now contradicted this impression. Her features were sharp and pinched; her voice hard and artificial. Any smile was contrived; even with her husband, her daughter, her two sisters and her sisters' children, her manner was cold.

The father, Lord Felsted, who sat at the other end of the table, was superficially more charming. He smiled and laughed and teased his nieces, and it was only his eyes that betrayed his boredom. Every now and then, while those around him were laughing at his joke, he would cast a quick look at his new guests; it was only Stefan's reptilian eyes which caught the flicker of calculated contempt in that hasty glance.

What was clear to him, there at the nursery table, was that the change of heart in the Felsteds could not be sincere. He could enter into their minds quite enough to realize how fully they must despise the Continental riffraff with which their daughter now proposed to unite their family; he could understand why they had not felt it necessary to see Teofil to know that he was unsuitable. It was enough that he was the son of a Polish adventuress, the stepson of an absurd Frenchman and the nephew of a writer whom no one had heard of.

Then why had they been invited? Perhaps the Felsteds imagined that Mulford Park alone would be enough to frighten Teofil away. And indeed it looked as if this might be so as he came into the nursery behind Annabel and sat down next to her, in the middle of the table. When he had first kissed her, when he had agreed that they should be married, he may have had some idea of what was involved; but now that he saw what went with Annabel – the huge house with its corridors and servants, the aunts and cousins, the guns and labradors, the priceless collection of paintings and sculpture, the framed photographs and painted portraits, the stuffed stags and leather armchairs – surely now he would look for a way to escape? Even

Annabel's determination would not be enough to keep him.

Stefan watched Annabel as she sat at tea, talking to her aunt with the slight disdain that the daughter of the house always feels for the poor relative. 'She will have to choose,' he thought to himself. 'Teofil will never bear the weight of it all.' And when tea was finished Stefan crossed the room to Annabel and asked her if she would show him around the house. 'Otherwise I shall get lost, and you will have to send out a search party before every meal.'

'Of course,' she said, and together they escaped, leaving Teofil and the de Pinceys in the hands of the Felsteds.

She took him from room to room, giving each one its title when opening the door, but lingering in none of them. 'This is the morning-room,' she might say or 'This is a sort of sitting-room which no one uses much.' And like this they wandered past the library, the gun-room, the billiard-room, the drawing-room and up the stairs to see a huge spare room with a four-poster bed 'where the Prince of Wales once spent the night'.

'And where is your room?' asked Stefan.

'At the other end,' said Annabel, 'up in a tower. Would you like to see it?'

They set off once again along the corridors. 'It was a pity,' said Stefan, 'that you had no brothers and sisters.'

'I know,' said Annabel. 'It would have been more fun. But my mother so hated having me that she wouldn't have any more.'

'How do you know?'

'Nanny told me.' She walked a few paces in silence. 'It was hard on my father,' she said. 'He wanted a son.'

They came to the end of the corridor where, at the corner of the house, there was a narrow opening to a small spiral staircase.

'This is where my kingdom begins,' said Annabel with a small smile. Then she led the way up the stone steps while Stefan followed, breathing in the faint aroma of scent and dust that followed in the wake of Annabel.

'That's a bathroom,' said Annabel as they passed one door; she did not stop but continued to climb up the staircase until they came out onto a small landing with two cloverleaf windows to light it. There she opened the only door and led Stefan into her bedroom.

It was a charming room – large, with the round walls of the tower. There were four windows looking in all directions, pale blue wallpaper and a four-poster bed with white hangings, white covers and white sheets. Everything about it was neat, small and virginal. A pair of velvet slippers were placed together on the rug by her bed; the embroidered, quilted dressing-gown hung from a hook from her door. There were none of the accoutrements of womanhood, such as hair-dryers or curlers, but small china statuettes and silver ornaments.

'What a pleasant room,' said Stefan.

'I used to feel safe up here,' said Annabel. 'Nanny slept down below.'

'Has this always been your room?'

'No,' she said. 'I used to sleep at the front.'

'Near your parents?'

'Yes.' She blushed – a blush which alerted Stefan like the scent of a fox to a hound.

'Why did you move?'

For some time she did not reply: she had heard but she did not reply. Nor did she look at Stefan. Instead she seemed to be pondering her answer as if it had to be dredged from some dark depths of her memory. Then, in a clear voice she said: 'My father tried to make love to me. I moved because of that.'

'And did he succeed?' asked Stefan.

'Not really, no. He just made a mess.'

'How old were you?'

'Fourteen.'

'And where was your mother?'

'In that bed I showed you.'

'With the Prince of Wales?'

She looked at him but did not smile. 'No. With someone else.'

'What did you do?'

'I came to sleep up here.'

'With your Nanny down below.'

'Yes.'

'And he never tried it again.'

'No. I think . . . I think he was ashamed.'

Stefan sucked at his gums and looked out towards the sea.

'Are you shocked?' asked Annabel.

319

He turned back into the room, and looked into her clear, interrogatory face. 'Yes I am,' he said. 'Which is strange.'

'Why strange?'

'Because I don't believe in morality.'

'You told me that once before,' said Annabel, 'yet in so many ways you are like a priest.'

'A priest?'

'What I told you just now . . . about my father. I've never told Teofil. I hope he never knows.'

'Does no one else know?'

'Nanny knows. And so does Dr Ebermann.'

'And your mother?'

Annabel turned down the ends of her mouth. 'Oh, she probably knows.'

Stefan looked out of another window – this time to the south over the garden and park. 'Don't you feel different here?' he asked Annabel.

'In a way . . .'

'Such a large estate . . . It must have seemed like a private kingdom, with you as the princess.'

'Yes.' She agreed flatly. 'But I was ill for much of the time.'

'Of course.'

'And I wasn't happy . . .'

'Not even before . . . as a child?'

'No. I was alone. My cousins came only in the summer; and mother was too much of a snob to let me play with the tenants' children.'

'And when your parents die? Will you live here?'

'No.'

'What will you do with it?'

She gave a cunning smile. 'Sell it. I like the garden, and I like the sea, but the house itself is grim – even without the memories . . .'

'Were you never happy?' asked Stefan.

'Yes,' she said. 'I was happy in Paris.'

They left the room and returned down the spiral staircase, this time with Stefan leading the way. Then they walked side by side towards the main stairs.

'You should tell Teofil,' said Stefan.

'What? About my father?'

'No. What you've just told me. That this house is not part of you . . . that your proper personality belongs elsewhere.'

'Don't you think he knows?'

'He may do, but it's always safer to spell things out. Otherwise he may feel . . . well, that it's more than he can manage.'

She bit her lower lip. 'I hadn't thought. Poor Teofil.' Then she smiled. 'He must love me, mustn't he, if he hasn't run away already?'

Stefan now went to his bedroom to take a bath and change for dinner; and while seated swathed in a towel, waiting to cool down before putting on his dress clothes, he wrote in his notebook.

Conversation with Annabel. Her father's gross act explains everything – above all her love of Teofil. But if her parents know how she feels about them, about the house and the inheritance, then they cannot be counting on it to suffocate her suitor. They must have other plans. Perhaps they imagined that he would look absurd at Mulford – a parvenu, a foreigner; that Annabel would despise him. Did they know of his English education which can turn even blacks into gentlemen? His clothes are correct; his manners impeccable. And he has charm. But if they did not know, why were they not 'taken aback'? They must have other plans.

Between half past seven and eight o'clock the whole house party assembled in the drawing-room, all dressed for dinner – the men in black dinner jackets or velvet smoking jackets, the women in long skirts or dresses. Stefan, like Alain, wore what was correct, and was conspicuous only in that his costume was so new. Teofil, of course, had a slightly shabby dinner jacket – a veteran of the debutante dances given for the sisters of his friends at school – as did Lord Felsted. Among the women, Krystyna was as conspicuous as her brother because of the superb elegance of her Dior gown: Lady Felsted and her sisters wore drab dresses as if to emphasize that it was just for form that they changed at all.

Almost the last to arrive was Annabel. She wore a simple skirt which she had bought in Paris and a white blouse with a lace bodice – but she had tied back her hair, which suddenly made her seem less a child and more a young woman of exceptional beauty. There was something in her manner, too – her flushed cheeks and strong movements – which gave the impression of a more formidable personality.

She took a glass of sherry from her father and then crossed to Teofil. 'How smart you all look,' she said, smiling at Stefan, Alain and Krystyna. Then, as she opened her mouth to say something else, she saw another guest enter the room. She hesitated, closed her mouth, and blushed. Stefan noticed this at once: he turned and saw that the other guest was the man he had mistaken for his host earlier that afternoon.

'Who is that man?' he asked Annabel.

'Sir Jack Marryat,' she said. 'He's a friend of Father's. I didn't know he was here.'

'What does he do?'

'Nothing. He's very rich.'

'Is he married?'

'Yes. He's got a wife somewhere.'

'But not here?'

'No. They lead sort of separate lives. He . . .' She hesitated.

'What?'

She turned to Stefan and smiled. 'Women are meant to find him irresistible.'

'And do you?'

'Of course not. And anyway, I'm not his type.'

Dinner was announced by the butler and they all filed through to the huge dining-room. There Lady Felsted, with the help of a plan drawn on a piece of paper in her hand, directed each guest to their proper place. Alain was on her right; Krystyna on the right of Lord Felsted. Stefan was placed between the aunts; Teofil between the cousins; and far from them both, at the other end of the table, sat Annabel with a twelve-year-old girl on one side of her and Sir Jack Marryat on the other.

Ten

The next day it was hot. Stefan rose at nine and found his way
down to the dining-room, where Teofil and Annabel were just
finishing their breakfast. Annabel, dressed in jeans, jumped to
her feet and took Stefan to the sideboard. She showed him the
coffee and milk, and pointed to the covered silver dishes on the
hot plate. 'You must have a proper English breakfast,' she said.
'There's bacon and egg in one and kedgeree in the other.
Remember, we'll all be going to the beach so there'll only be a
picnic lunch.'

She seemed in an excellent mood. She skipped back to Teofil
and took him by the arm. 'Come on,' she said. 'Let's play tennis
before anyone else gets the court.'

Stefan returned to the sideboard. He poured himself a cup of
coffee and cautiously removed the lids of the silver dishes. With
a dubious expression on his face, he lifted a piece of bacon, then
a sausage, then a tomato and finally an egg onto his plate. Then
he looked into the other dish, took a spoonful of kedgeree, held
it poised over his plate, shrugged his shoulders and sprinkled it
over the bacon and egg. He sat down at the table, nodded to
the aunts and cousins who sat eating and reading newspapers,
took a newspaper himself and set about his breakfast.

At eleven the whole party assembled for the beach. Two
Land Rovers, and a tractor with a trailer, were drawn up in
front of the house. The children all climbed into the trailer and
the grown-ups into the Land Rovers. Then the cavalcade set off.

'The best beach is difficult to get to,' said Annabel who sat
in the back of the first car with Stefan, Teofil and Krystyna.
'You can drive part of the way. Then there's rather a climb
down the cliff. But we always go there – and no one else ever
does. We have it to ourselves.'

The Land Rover bumped over a stony farm track which led

over the fields towards the sea. Lord Felsted was driving; his wife sat next to him on the front seat and Jack Marryat sat by the window. He kept leaning over towards his hostess and making remarks which the others could not hear, but which led to peals of her brittle laughter. Occasionally he would turn and repeat the joke to the guests behind.

They stopped at the top of the cliff and parked their vehicles on grass cropped close by sheep. Then each member of the party took a load – some the picnic, others bathing towels and rubber rings. The older children carried rugs, Lord Felsted a parasol and Jack Marryat came last holding a basket filled with six bottles of claret.

Stefan had been given a basket and he set off after the others along the path; but when he came to the top of the cliff he felt quite giddy. The edge was precipitous. Far below he could see the waves breaking on rocks and sand. The path was cut into the cliff but there was no fence or rail between Stefan and a sheer drop of several hundred feet onto the rocks below. He looked ahead at the children scrambling unaided down the precipitous path, quite unconcerned at the risk; the grown-ups too seemed indifferent to the danger, and Stefan saw no alternative but to follow.

This perilous descent was only the start of Stefan's lesson that day in the strange behaviour of the English. When the party had reached the bottom of the cliff it pitched camp. Baskets and bathing-suits were dumped on the rocks, and cousins and guests lay down on the jagged ground as if the stones and boulders were the softest sand. Then conversation started about the sea. It had seemed to Stefan that though the weather was warm, the water was altogether too turbulent for anyone to venture in: yet from the snatches of conversation he overheard between Annabel and her cousins, the sea was not rough enough. The waves were 'pathetic': it was 'hardly worth going in'.

All the same it was agreed that they would swim before lunch. Stefan, who like Lord Felsted and Jack Marryat sat on a rock on the fringe of the circle of women, looked around for bathing huts; and since there were none, for shelves of rock behind which the women could modestly change into their costumes. There were several suitable places, but when he looked back at the group he saw to his astonishment that rather than move away from the public view, each started a strange wriggling movement which developed into a kind of striptease. While continuing with the most banal conversation, the aunts and cousins, the mothers and daughters, all reached under their dresses to remove their brassieres and underpants and, still covered by their skirts and dresses – or in the case of Annabel, with a towel – replace these garments with their bathing costumes.

When he realized what was taking place, Stefan looked away in embarrassment; but he saw that no one else appeared embarrassed. Lord Felsted and Sir Jack remained facing the group of women and children as if nothing unusual was taking place. Marryat was smoking a cigarette. Even so, Stefan might have faced away from all the arms and limbs had not Annabel asked him if he was going to swim at the very moment she was disentangling her knickers from her feet.

'I haven't got a costume,' said Stefan.

'That's no excuse,' she said, reaching for the bottom half of her two-piece costume. 'We brought some spare trunks along. People always think that they won't swim, but they usually do.'

'I'll see,' said Stefan.

'You feel marvellous afterwards.' She pulled the bottom half of her bikini up under the towel which covered her hips. It fell away and Stefan caught a quick glimpse of a buttock before it was covered by the cloth.

His tongue went over his lips. He glanced around to see if he alone were agitated by this undressing on the beach. He looked back across the legs and slips and stockings to the two men opposite – Lord Felsted and Jack Marryat. Marryat was still smoking. His eyes were half on his host, half on the group. Stefan looked for Teofil: he was standing, looking out to sea. Then he turned and himself tied a towel around his waist and only a few feet from a cousin started to undress. Stefan looked for Krystyna: she lay back in the sun, her eyes closed. She had put on her costume under her dress before coming to the beach. Alain was climbing the rocks away to the right.

The fresh, damp air affected Stefan's senses. The waves, the clothes, the limbs, the rocks all blended into a whole. Only his astonishment was out of place; and even as he sat there his excitement at the turmoil of cloth and flesh, and his outrage at the contempt of the women's immodesty, were eroded by the salty breeze. His eyes went back to Annabel. She was stretching her hands behind her arched back to unhook her brassiere. It was stiff, and her face was twisted into an expression of effort. Then it became undone. She drew it down under her blouse and leaned towards a rock for the top half of her costume. As she did so, a perfect pink breast was quite clearly visible through the opening of her blouse. Stefan saw it, and for a moment it held him. Then he glanced at Marryat, just in time to see that he too was caught by the breast. Then Marryat turned his head. Their eyes met, and before either could look away again, there was a split second of complicity.

Annabel clipped the top of her bikini into place, took off her blouse and stood up on the stones. Both men looked casually at her lovely long body as it walked unsteadily towards Teofil. He too stood up in his costume, and the two young bodies jumped from rock to rock down towards the sea.

One beautiful day followed the next, and each was the same as the other. There was breakfast, tennis, croquet, the beach; then tea, croquet, tennis, a drink, a bath, the vesting of evening clothes, another drink, and dinner. After dinner the women would go through to the drawing-room while the men would remain at the dining-room table, moving up to sit around Lord Felsted. The butler, Mr Briggs, would bring a decanter of port to the table, and then hand around a box of cigars.

Stefan was almost seduced by these candle-lit evenings. The men had all the charm and wit which was absent in the women, and seemed to flourish without them. Lord Felsted and Jack Marryat had perfect manners and flawless charm. They always brought Stefan and Alain into their conversation, explaining a joke which had not been appreciated. Teofil was treated with a particular warmth, like a new member of an exclusive club. Indeed Alain was persuaded that Lord Felsted was treating Teofil 'just like a son-in-law'; and when Krystyna complained how dull it was with the women, Alain told her to suffer it for the sake of her son.

It was only Stefan who noticed the small details of behaviour which poisoned his port and dried his cigars – how, for example,

Jack Marryat was always placed next to Annabel at dinner; how, when the men rejoined the women, Lord Felsted always took hold of Teofil's arm and led him to talk to the aunts and the cousins; while Jack Marryat sauntered towards Annabel who greeted him with a blush.

Marryat was the joker in the pack of cards. He had an extraordinary effect on everyone in the house – the kings and queens and lesser cards of all the different suits – through a combination of qualities, but above all by his vitality and charm. He could turn a room full of sullen cousins into a gaggle of giggling, good-natured girls after two minutes' conversation; he made Alain feel that he was witty, Krystyna feel that she was young; and even Lady Felsted laughed at what he said when she rarely smiled at anyone else. Only Stefan was not conquered by the mildly mocking deference which Marryat accorded him.

His attraction was all the more powerful for being so unobtrusive. He was not obviously handsome, witty or charming; indeed his most engaging quality was his modesty. Yet it was known that he was more than a millionaire; that except for some excursions into Conservative politics he did nothing; that he had a wife and six children who waited patiently for his occasional visits on his estate in Yorkshire.

Stefan learnt all these details of his life by listening to the aunts and cousins gossip on the beach. There were twittering arguments about Marryat's mistresses. One cousin knew someone who had seen him at a party with a Cynthia X – 'and they went off upstairs'. Another swore that another woman – 'the wife of Bertie Brown' – was his permanent mistress.

'And he gets girls from Madame Claude,' said a third.

'And what's so amazing,' said the first – the supporter of Cynthia X – 'is that no one minds. Even when he drops them, they adore him. There are a dozen girls in London who would leave everything for a night with him . . .'

There were giggles at this mention of 'a night'. Stefan looked out to sea.

'I don't quite understand,' said an aunt, 'what he's doing here.'

'He used to be a friend of Uncle Teddy,' said a cousin.

'I know,' said the aunt. 'But they haven't seen much of each other since they married.'

'He must find it a bit dull,' said a cousin. 'It's not as if he fancies any of us . . .'

'None of you, no,' said the aunt – pressing her thin lips together and glancing across to the rocks where Jack Marryat was with Annabel collecting shrimps from a pool.

Eleven

Stefan was now alarmed. Whenever he saw Annabel, Marryat's stooping figure was beside her, the whiskers which sprouted from his cheek brushing against her ear as he whispered some witticism about the other guests. At dinner he was always sat next to her while Teofil was placed at the other end of the table. To Stefan the conspiracy was clear.

His anxiety for his two characters, and the happy ending to their story, was mixed with other emotions which he recognized and analysed in his notebook.

Am I jealous? She now hardly talks to me but saves all her private conversation for him. Once I could have had her. She stood in my flat inviting me . . . And now, what I gave up – for the story or for Teofil – ripens for a beast of my own species. He seduces her with my tricks – the skills of the priest, the psychoanalyst, the novelist, the rake. He is kind and funny. He flatters her obliquely; or ironically, so that she wriggles with the uncertainty of whether he means it or not.

Most skilful of all, he is charming, flattering and flirtatious with Teofil. He never excludes him, but always treats him as the 'proprietor' of Annabel. Teofil responds as expected. Like Bruno, he is naïve and good-hearted: he cannot cope with cunning. His eyes light up whenever Marryat enters the room. He wants to be liked by Marryat: Marryat is the man he would like to be – rich, titled, intelligent, a master of all the mystic details that make up an English gentleman.

With the kind of adoration that younger children feel for an older boy, Teofil and Annabel were drawn to Marryat. On expeditions to the beach they would always contrive to sit in the same Land-Rover while Stefan and the de Pinceys were left to travel with the aunts: on the rocks they would sit around Marryat and swim when he went swimming. In the evening, when Teofil came into the drawing-room before dinner, he would go straight to Marryat's circle, never to his uncle or mother. Annabel too would go to Marryat, whether Teofil was with him or not: and if he was, they would sit side by side, linked by the baronet who stood with his back to the fire.

The Felsteds, the de Pinceys, the aunts and the cousins would all make conversation in a flat tone of voice which was an admission of its banality. They all half-listened to the wittier, livelier talk on the other side of the room; and one by one would desert their group and move towards the fire as if they were cold – when burning logs on those evenings in July were quite superfluous.

Only Stefan remained apart – silent, impassive, watching each movement, each change of expression in the others. He studied them like a snake, feeling with panic that he might be too late. The strings of his puppets were now held by another man who, every now and then, glanced at Stefan with a look of amused mockery.

With growing desperation Stefan looked for a flaw in Marryat's game, but there was no flaw because it was not a game but:

the natural process of decay, the inexorable movement of the immature towards the mature, of perfection towards decay. Three apples – one rotten, two sound: the sound apples are corrupted, not the rotten apple made good again. Marryat needs only time. Nothing can be done against him.

Behind his Kornowski mask, Stefan was unhappy and this unhappiness confused him. Since childhood he had protected himself from painful emotions by analysing them out of existence – by dismantling them in his mind so that each component was isolated and ineffective. Now he floundered in misery and could not discover what caused it. Was it envy and chagrin, that he was not the seducer? Was it solicitude for Teofil? Was it his happy ending? Or was it the memory of Bruno who, on the night before leaving for Spain, had entrusted his son to Stefan?

To each of these raw emotions he applied his solipsistic philosophy of amoral egoism, but the balm was ineffective. He saw or thought he saw what would happen if Marryat should succeed. Annabel might withdraw once again into a childish paralysis of will; or make a marriage of convenience to a suitable Englishman and join the sorority of Marryat's girls in London.

And Teofil would turn away from women. He would wait for a Marryat from Sodom: in two years he would stand at one of those bars in Paris, clean tight trousers stretched around his buttocks, his eyebrows plucked into lines of wide-eyed depravity . . .

But what is this? I think and feel like a Jesuit from St Stanislas Kostka. I have become the apologist for Natural Law – for chastity, conjugality and procreation! The champion of innocence! The enemy of sin! Am I so old and gaga that I should revert to the ethics of the Catechism?

His reason was no match for whatever it was that drove him to save innocence from corruption. In the end he excused himself to himself as an artist. Righteousness was the theme of the work in hand. He was committed to a happy ending in the conventional style: Teofil and Annabel were irrevocably the models for his hero and heroine; and so in spite of the disadvantages – in spite of the Englishness of Mulford Park and all the inscrutable details of talk and behaviour – he would fight to the finish.

His first thought was that Teofil should go out, like David against Goliath, and slay the giant Marryat with the pebble of his love. And so that evening he wandered into Teofil's bedroom while they were changing for dinner and asked him for a stud.

Teofil, of course, had several studs in reserve and could provide one for his uncle at once: but even after he had put it in his pocket, Stefan waited in the room, watching his nephew tie his bow-tie.

'How do you like this life?' he asked.

Teofil turned and looked at him. 'What do you think?' he asked.

Stefan shrugged his shoulders.

'Was it like this where you lived?' asked Teofil.

'When?'

'As a child. At Jezow.'

Stefan shook his head. 'No. Much simpler.'

Teofil seemed relieved. 'I don't really like it,' he said. 'It's too complicated. But then Annabel doesn't like it either. She says that when her parents die she'll sell it.'

'Good,' said Stefan. 'Otherwise it might possess you.'

'That's what she said,' said Teofil, brushing his hair. 'She thinks that traditions are only good if they are useful.'

'And do you agree?'

'Yes I do. I don't want to become a sort of Prince Consort . . .'

'No.'

'In fact . . .' Teofil hesitated and looked at his uncle. 'I had quite a talk with Annabel. You see, I told her that I wanted to change my name. Change it back, that is, to Kaczmarek . . .'

'Why?'

'I like Alain, all right, but I don't want his name. I'm not a Frenchman. I'm a Pole, an expatriate Pole.'

'Like me.'

'Yes. Like you. And . . . well, this is what I told Annabel. I don't think that one should get married pretending to be what one is not. I don't want to be what I seem to be. I told her that I wasn't going to be a merchant banker but something else, something useful – a doctor, or perhaps a lawyer . . .'

'Your father studied law.'

'Yes. That's what gave me the idea. I'd like to defend poorer people against big companies and the State . . . After all, if God has given one an intellect, one shouldn't use it just to get rich.'

Stefan smiled. 'Especially not when you have plenty of money anyway.'

Teofil blushed. 'That's another thing we agreed. When her parents die we're going to give the money away – form a charitable trust of some sort.'

'Give it all away?'

'Well, most of it. After all, I'll be earning by then and I'd much rather live modestly off what I earn, doing what I think right, than be enslaved by someone else's money.'

'And what did Annabel say to all that?'

'She agrees. She wants to live in London, and I agreed to that. She also wants to have lots of children . . .' He smiled.

'Why not?' said Stefan.

'I'm all for a big family,' said Teofil. 'We were both only children, you see, and not particularly happy . . .'

'You seem to have your life well planned.'

'Yes. If only we can get married.'

'Is there anything that can stop it?'

'Not really, no. But Anna says she'd like to be married from here – not for her parents' sake, but for people like her Nanny and the cook and the gardeners, whom she's known since she was born . . .'

'Don't wait too long,' said Stefan.

'No. It must be decided soon.'

'I should press her . . .'

'I do. I'd really like to go away with her now . . .'

Stefan looked into his nephew's eyes. 'And what about Marryat?' he asked.

'What about him?' asked Teofil.

'Do you like him?'

'Yes I do, rather. In spite of what people say.'

'You don't think he's up to something?'

'What sort of thing?'

'He spends a lot of time with Annabel.'

'I know. He's on our side. He's going to persuade the Felsteds . . .' Teofil took his dinner jacket from the chair and then turned again to face his uncle with such an open smile that Stefan could say nothing more.

Now Stefan began to doubt his own perceptions.

Perhaps Marryat's designs on Annabel are the invention of my imagination? What evidence have I that he intends to seduce her? By repute his mistresses are much worldlier women. It is incontestable that Lady Felsted placed him next to her daughter at table: but her intention might only have been that Teofil should dwindle in Annabel's eyes when compared

332

to Marryat. It is undeniable that Annabel is drawn to him, as she was drawn to me. Marryat's depravity is an expression of his vitality: he is the life with which she struggles – now repelled, now attracted again. Teofil is not the issue. He is gentle and diffident – a brother, a companion. Marryat is the beast, but what evidence is there that she would let herself be seduced by him? Like a child she is fascinated by the beast, but in her mind he is well behind bars. If he escapes she will run in terror and return to her tame cat, curled up by the fire.

On the following afternoon, Stefan went on a walk with Alain and Krystyna. The weather was cloudy and cool, and only the young and hardy had gone to the beach. The de Pinceys had decided to explore the village and Stefan went with them.

'And the charming Sir Jack?' asked Alain. 'Has he gone to swim with the children?'

'I don't think so,' said Krystyna.

'That is because the young lovers are elsewhere,' said Alain.

'Where have they gone?' asked Stefan.

'To visit some neighbours,' said Krystyna.

They walked along the path in silence under the branches of trees.

'Are you worried?' said Stefan.

'About what?' asked Krystyna.

'Marryat.'

'Why should I be?'

'Well . . .'

'He has a reputation,' said Alain.

'Do you mean,' Krystyna asked Stefan, 'that he might be after Annabel?'

'Yes.'

'What nonsense.' She frowned. 'You always had a dirty mind.'

'Don't be so sure,' said Alain, grinning. 'He might gobble them both up . . .'

'Don't be ridiculous,' said Krystyna. 'He's at least twice their age and a friend of her parents.'

Stefan turned to Alain. 'What do you really think?' he asked.

'What I really think is that I don't understand the English. And what I don't understand, I don't like . . .'

333

'He wants to go home,' said Krystyna.

'I've had enough of this grand life,' said Alain.

'But we can't leave them,' said Stefan.

'And what has been decided?' asked Krystyna. 'Are they getting married or not?'

'The English are never explicit,' said Alain. 'You will not know if they are engaged until you read it in *The Times*.'

'I wish we had never got involved with them,' said Krystyna.

'She told me,' said Stefan, 'that she hated the house . . .'

'She may have said so,' said Krystyna, 'but she belongs to them, not to us. Look at the way she slips into this extraordinary life as if it was the most natural thing in the world – swimming in a sea so cold that even the fish must freeze, and then day after day just hanging around . . .'

'So you want to go?'

'I'd go at once if I knew what was decided.'

'What does Teofil say?'

'He says we must be patient; that the Felsteds want to get to know us. So we are trapped. We must wait. For his sake we must wait.'

They came to a wicket gate which led out of the park into the village. They walked down the narrow streets, past shops selling postcards, complaining about the Felsteds, the aunts and the cousins. And when they reached the small port, Stefan turned to his sister and brother-in-law and said: 'So you think there is no danger from Marryat?'

'Danger of what?' asked Krystyna.

'Of his seducing Annabel?'

'Of course not,' said Krystyna.

'It was a joke,' said Alain. 'There is no danger at all, except of Alain de Pincey dying of boredom and bad food.'

They returned to Mulford Park just in time for tea. They sat in a group at the long table in the nursery, separated from the Felsteds by the aunts and cousins. Annabel and Teofil came in together and behaved normally; and when tea was over they left together. Marryat never came to tea.

Between tea and dinner there were empty hours when there was no organized activity. Everyone did what they liked and only met again when they had changed for dinner. Stefan would usually fill this time by reading, or writing in his note-book. On this particular afternoon he went to his bedroom and wrote out a brief conversation with Alain and Krystyna. Beneath it he noted that

those who are neither good nor evil cannot imagine the two extremes. But like knows like, and Marryat knows that I know. His look is evidence; his mockery of me.

At about half-past six he put down his pen and closed his notebook. He looked for something to read but found that he had finished the book by his bedside the night before. He therefore went down to the library to look for a replacement, and there found Teofil, sitting alone.

'Where's Annabel?' he asked.

'Playing tennis with Jack,' said Teofil – his eyes not moving from the newspaper.

'Why didn't you go?'

Teofil looked up. 'I don't know. I didn't feel like it.'

Stefan left the room, slipped out of the house and sauntered towards the tennis court. He had a sudden vivid memory of when he had crossed the lawn at Jezow towards the hayshed; and this memory aroused expectations of the same sights and sounds. But there on the court were Annabel and Sir Jack publicly engaged in a game of tennis.

They were evenly matched. Annabel, though delicate in appearance, was tall and unexpectedly strong. Marryat too was tall and strong, but had some disadvantage in his age. Both had changed for the game and two pairs of taut legs sprung on the hard ground, one pair silken and soft, the other hairy and brown.

Stefan remained quite still, hidden behind the shrubs. He watched them play. Marryat had his back to him, but Annabel faced in his direction – her cheeks pink from her exertion, her eyes gleaming with the struggle, her eyes . . .

There was more, much more, than a game of tennis in her eyes. They were wild and excited. She was hypnotized by Marryat as he hurled himself against the ball. She met each volley with her whole body: each stroke was a response to each stroke of his. Her breasts were abandoned to her movement;

335

her buttocks jumped and twisted; her arms stretched; her legs were open and alert and on her face was a smile – a smile of unmistakable complicity which seemed to confess that the game was not a game but a deadly dance of courtship.

Stefan leapt to the wrong conclusion. 'I'm too late,' he thought to himself. 'They are already lovers.' And then, like an absurd detective, he ran back to the house to look at their sheets to make sure. He did not think that they might have made love elsewhere: in his mind there was only one image – a white sheet with the scarlet marks of her blood.

They were both at the court: he would be safe. He went first to Marryat's room which was near to his own. He went in and looked at the bed which had already been turned down by the servants. He pulled back the sheets. They were creased but unmarked. It was the wrong bed.

He rearranged the beclothes, then glanced around the room – at the ivory handles of Marryat's hairbrush, inlaid in silver with his coat-of-arms; at his silk dressing-gown and embroidered bedroom slippers. Then he slipped out of the room and set out for the other end of the house and Annabel's tower.

When he reached the foot of the spiral stairs, he stopped and listened for footsteps. There was no sound at all. He climbed the stairs, two at a time, and quickly found himself in the bedroom.

The evening sun lit up the white hangings of the bed and the pale blue of the walls. The small china ornaments remained just where they had been before: it was inconceivable that anything gross could have taken place in its confines. All the same, Stefan went to the bed. This too had been turned down for the night, and a white lace nightdress was laid out ready for Annabel to put on.

With a rapid gesture of his right hand, Stefan pulled back the sheets. They had been slept on but there were no marks at all.

He stood there dumbfounded. He had been so certain that one or other of the beds would have had the proof of his suspicions. Then quickly he started to remake the bed. He was struck by the absurdity of what he had done: he did not want to be discovered.

He had put the bedclothes back as he had found them when he saw the nightdress on the floor. He picked it up, and suddenly crushed the soft cloth into his face and breathed in the scent of Annabel. He stood there for a moment, living in the darkness of her aroma: then he realized that someone was standing beside him. He turned and saw Marryat.

The two men stood quite still. For once Marryat did not smile. Then he said: 'Aren't you a little old for that sort of thing?'

Stefan looked at the nightdress in his hand. He dropped it onto the bed. He opened his mouth without any idea of what he was going to say. Annabel came in behind Marryat.

She blushed. 'What are you doing here?' she asked, without meeting his eyes.

'I was looking for you,' said Stefan.

Annabel, like Marryat, was still in her tennis clothes – and still pink and moist from the game. She frowned. 'Well what did you want?'

'It can wait,' said Stefan with a glance at Marryat.

Annabel caught his look and blushed again so strongly that her face, already pink, went red. She looked at Marryat with a brief appeal and he turned away from Stefan and said to her: 'That book. I thought I'd collect it now. I can read it in the bath.'

'Of course,' she said. She went to her bedside table and picked up a book – a small dictionary of wild flowers – without looking at it. Marryat took it and both men left the room.

In the corridor at the foot of the stairs, Marryat turned to Stefan with a mocking smile. 'You're barking up the wrong tree, old chap,' he said. Then he patted Stefan on the shoulder and walked off down the corridor.

Twelve

Stefan returned to his room. He lay on his bed, tired and disgusted. In his mind he cowered from the image of Annabel's glowing face, her breathlessness, her blush. He shuddered at his own decaying body and its kinship to Marryat's. He thought of Bruno – of courage, action, self-sacrifice and death.

He fell asleep. He did not dream, and when he awoke it was five past eight. He leaped off the bed and changed as quickly as he could. He hurried down the corridors and the wide stairs like a child late for school. 'She will see that I have fallen asleep,' he thought to himself, 'like an old man.'

To his relief everyone was still in the drawing-room. He came in, disguising as best he could the vulnerability of his mood. He took a glass of sherry from Lord Felsted and then crossed to Alain and Krystyna. They sat as if nothing had happened. Teofil too, on the other side of the room, chatted to a cousin. Then Annabel came in. Stefan saw her. She did not look at him, nor at Marryat, who stood in his usual position with his back to the fire. Annabel went straight to Teofil and the cousin.

She had recovered her composure. From the look on her lovely, impassive features the scene in the bedroom that afternoon could not have taken place; Stefan might have doubted his own memory had she not so conspicuously avoided his eyes. It was also the first evening for many days that she had not joined the group around Marryat.

At dinner she sat next to Marryat as usual but hardly talked to him; nor did he try to talk to her. This too gave them away. Annabel chattered on about this and that; and when one of her cousins asked what sort of wedding she would have, she blushed, looked prettily at Lady Felsted and said: 'Oh, Mother can decide.'

'The usual sort, I suppose,' said Lady Felsted. She spoke as if the question was of not much interest.

'Some people nowadays,' said the cousin, 'have weddings in the evening with dancing . . .'

'What kind of dancing?' asked Lady Felsted.

'Jiving and rock and roll,' said the mischievous cousin.

Lady Felsted frowned. 'We might have a ball,' she said. 'We have never had one for Annabel. But with waltzes and foxtrots . . .'

'And polkas and mazurkas,' said Alain who sat next to her. 'And of course the polonaise . . .'

'What is the polonaise?' asked Marryat, who sat on the other side of Lady Felsted.

'I thought it was a tune by Chopin,' she said.

'It is also a Polish dance,' said Stefan.

'Then you'll have to teach me how to do it,' said Marryat, with a mocking glance at Stefan. 'That is, if I'm to be asked to the wedding.'

He turned to Annabel. She blushed. 'Of course,' she said, looking down at her plate.

The women withdrew and the men moved up the table towards Lord Felsted. Stefan moved to the other side of the table and sat down next to Teofil. He plucked at his sleeve and drew him away from the general conversation.

'Is anything decided?' he asked him in a low voice.

'About what?'

'Your wedding.'

'I think so, but we're waiting . . .'

'For what?'

'I'm not quite sure.'

Stefan gripped his nephew's arm. 'Do you want to marry her?'

'Of course.'

'More than anything?'

'Yes.'

'Then be more insistent . . .'

'Insistent?'

'Yes. It doesn't flatter a girl to wait around for other people to make up their minds.'

'I suppose you're right.'

'Talk to her,' said Stefan. 'Talk to her tonight. Tell her that you must marry her next month, next week, now. Insist that it is decided: that it is announced in *The Times* . . .'

'Of course you're right,' said Teofil – blanching at the thought of such forcefulness.

'And one other thing . . .'

'What?'

'Don't just hold her hand.'

Teofil looked at his uncle with a creased brow. 'How do you mean?'

'Make love to her. Now. Tonight.'

'But I couldn't,' said Teofil, his face pink with embarrassment.

'You must.'

'I couldn't. Not before we're married.'

'Why not?'

He blushed. 'It would be a sin,' he said, and he turned away from his uncle to talk to the other men.

All Stefan could do was improvise. He sat in the drawing-room, listening to snatches of conversation, watching the faces of the Felsteds, Marryat and an aunt who were playing bridge; and of Annabel and Teofil who faced each other over a back-gammon board. His sister, Krystyna, was talking to him but Stefan hardly listened. His mind was racing for he was now sure, from the way that Annabel never looked at Marryat, that she was expecting him to come to her that night.

At eleven some of the party rose to go to bed. Stefan was among them. He went to his room. He had time because Marryat was still playing bridge: but Annabel had already gone to her room. Even now she was uncovering her body for Marryat, while Teofil slept.

It was half past eleven. Stefan, by now in his pyjamas and dressing-gown, put his hand on the handle of his bedroom door. He had waited long enough. He must act. He turned the handle, opened the door and walked out into the corridor. He started to follow the same path that he had taken that afternoon, from the guests' bedrooms to Annabel's tower. When he came near to it he stopped at a window and looked up. The light still shone in her window. He went further and came to the foot of the spiral stairs. He had no plan of action, and with no plan he sat down on the bottom step.

There he remained like a dog. The stone was hard and the passage draughty. He leaned his head on his hands, propping his elbows on his bony knees. The stable-yard clock struck twelve. He heard voices and footsteps but no one came that way. A dim light shone from the end of the corridor. Then that was switched off. He sat in silence and in darkness.

He waited. He was not tired. In a way he felt elated by the absurdity of his situation. If anyone was to find him there, what would they think? That he was eccentric, even insane? He would not be asked again to Mulford Park. Bagatelle. In any case, it was unlikely that he would be discovered – and if he was, who would know the reason for his presence at the foot of those spiral stairs? Only two, and of those he was only afraid that Annabel would discover him.

The clock struck one. He felt cold. His ribs ached. He was anxious about his heart. He began to waver. Perhaps nothing would happen; perhaps Marryat had come for a book that afternoon – the dictionary of wild flowers; perhaps Annabel had only blushed because she thought he might mistake the situation; perhaps that was why she had not talked to Marryat at dinner. Everything could be invention – a case of a writer trapped within his own story. What a trial it was to be a writer – never to know what was real and what was imagined, like a blind man . . .

In the distance, far away down the corridor, he heard a sound which, as it drew closer, he recognized as the rhythmic shuffle of a pair of slippers. There was no light, but the sound got closer and closer until in the dim light that came from the moon, Stefan could see Marryat standing before him in his embroidered slippers and silk dressing-gown.

Marryat almost stepped on him. He jumped back and cursed. With creaking joints, Stefan got to his feet.

'What the Hell are you doing here?' Marryat hissed at him.

'I couldn't sleep,' said Stefan in a normal tone of voice.

'Then for Christ's sake go and sit somewhere else.'

'No,' said Stefan. 'I am here.'

'You perverse old bugger,' said Marryat.

Stefan said nothing.

'Let me past,' said Marryat.

'I'm afraid that is impossible,' said Stefan.

Marryat moved forward and gripped the lapel of Stefan's dressing-gown. 'Let me past or I'll . . .'

'I shall scream,' said Stefan. 'I shall wake the whole household.'

Marryat let go. 'This is ridiculous,' he said. 'What are you? Some kind of Holy Joe?'

Stefan did not reply.

'You can't stay here for ever,' said Marryat. 'And there's plenty of time before the wedding day.' He turned and walked away with an angrier shuffle from his slippers.

Stefan was there all night. He dozed a little, leaning against the wall. He got colder and colder. He drew his dressing-gown tight around him. His whole body ached. There was a time when he thought he heard Marryat returning, but if he did so he turned away again before Stefan caught sight of him.

Stefan heard every hour and half hour strike on the stable-yard clock, and he remembered the Grand Hotel in Gdynia and the clock striking as he lay by the body of Onufry's whore. He smiled at the contrast between that, and the discomfort of the cold stone step.

The sun rose at five. Slowly the light came through the windows into the gloomy corridor. It grew brighter and brighter. It was going to be a fine day.

At seven there were sounds from below – of servants clearing the ashes from the fireplaces and the cook preparing breakfast in the kitchen; and at eight he heard Annabel come down to her bathroom. Only then did he saunter back to his own room.

He was dazed by his sleepless night and he knew that it could not be repeated. Indeed he knew that he had only hours to find a solution. He could not stand sentinel much longer.

He watched and he listened. He hung around Annabel, who looked grumpy; and when it was clear that she was going to the beach he said that he would go too. Indeed it was such a beautiful day that everyone decided they would go; and the tide was right for a picnic lunch.

Stefan sat in the second Land Rover with the Felsteds, Teofil, Annabel and Marryat. Marryat ignored him. He behaved as if Stefan was not there; but it was clear that he was irritated, and his irritation matched the grumpiness of Annabel. It was as if both had slept badly the night before.

They drove by the village to buy some bread for the picnic, and by the time they reached the top of the cliff the others had already pitched camp on the rocks below. They got out of the Land Rover, distributed the baskets and bathing towels and set off for the beach. Annabel went first down the path, followed by Teofil and then her parents. Marryat came fifteen yards behind them, carrying his bathing trunks and the basket of wine. Last of all came Stefan.

They had got one third of the way down the cliff when they came to a corner where the others were out of sight and the aunts and cousins small points of colour on the rocks below. It was here that Stefan called out to Marryat.

Marryat turned. 'What is it?' he asked.

'You were asking about the polonaise,' said Stefan. 'About how to dance it . . .'

'Oh yes,' said Marryat, turning back to resume his descent.

'It goes like this,' said Stefan. He danced forward along the path, holding a bundle of towels as a partner. His face was twisted into the Kornowski grimace, and when he came level with Marryat he turned so suddenly that the back of his body fell with its full force against Marryat's left shoulder. Marryat, who had not seen him, stumbled to his right: he tottered on the edge of the cliff, seeming for a moment to hold his balance. But the basket of wine slipped from his grasp and in trying to save it he stumbled again and fell over the precipice. Stefan, his face still contorted, went to the edge and saw the body fall unimpeded onto the rocks below. For some seconds he stared at the inanimate blob of colour. Then, his face relaxed into a more placid expression and he continued his descent.

Thirteen

The body of Sir Jack Marryat was sent north to his widow in Yorkshire. It was buried there in a private ceremony attended only by members of his family; but two months later there was a memorial service in London. The church of St Martin's-in-the-Fields was filled with the most distinguished and fashionable members of English society; and at least a dozen women – young and middle-aged – sniffed and sobbed under their veils.

Half the mourners met again a few days later in the parish church at Mulford where Annabel Colte was married to Teofil Kaczmarek. Among them was Stefan Kornowski. He was dressed correctly in a morning coat and was sought out by many of the guests not so much as the bridegroom's Polish uncle but as the witness to the fatal accident which had befallen their beloved Sir Jack. And Stefan rose to the occasion: the story, told so many times already, was polished and refined. 'If only he had dropped the basket,' he would say towards the end: 'We would have been without claret, but at least we should have had him.'

There were other ways in which Stefan Kornowski was the centre of attention. The bride in particular sought him out, took him by the arm and led him among her guests. Time and again she would return to him, perhaps because he was one of the few at the wedding who looked happy. Certainly, her parents never lost their expression of pained duty; all the Colte side looked glum, so that rumours started that the marriage had been forced on them because Annabel was pregnant.

The champagne flowed and in the space of an hour the rumour became an established fact. That Annabel was as thin as she had always been was ignored, but several of the girls among her cousins – seeing Teofil so tall, handsome and benign – said that they did not blame her. 'He's really smashing,' said one, 'and the French make such good lovers.' 'How do you know?' said another – then giggles and more champagne.

The bride and bridegroom left their guests in the huge dining-room of Mulford Park and went to change. Stefan Kornowski stood with his sister, who was slightly drunk.

'Are they married?' she asked him. 'Are they really married?'

'It has only to be consummated,' said Stefan dryly.

'I'm so happy, Stefan,' she said. 'After all we've been through, all our terrible lives, to see Teofil married and safe . . . How happy Bruno would have been.'

Stefan turned down the corners of his mouth.

'When I think of him dead in some ditch, when his son will lie in the mausoleum of the Coltes . . .' Tears began to trickle down her cheeks. 'I always believed in fate. It used to be against me. Now it has made up for everything . . .' The trickle became a flood. 'Just think, Stefan. Think of Jezow and all we lost, and now this . . .' She raised her eyes to the neo-Gothic vault of the ceiling. 'All this will belong to my grandson . . .' She took a scented handkerchief from her bag and wiped her nose.

Stefan said nothing. He watched the doorway and was the first to see Teofil and Annabel reappear in their travelling

344

clothes. They shook hands at random – the guests were now drunk enough to seem happy – and then went to the front door and out onto the gravel where a car waited to take them to Plymouth. Publicly they kissed Lord and Lady Felsted, then Alain and Krystyna de Pincey. Then Annabel looked among the faces crowding around her. 'Stefan?' she asked. 'Where's Stefan?' She saw him watching behind aunts and cousins; she walked towards him; the guests parted like the waves of the Red Sea.

'Goodbye,' she said, embracing him. 'We'll see you in Paris.'

Teofil too came and kissed his uncle. Then they both climbed into the back seat of the car. The chauffeur shut their door, went to the wheel and drove off.

In Paris Stefan returned to his old life of a recluse. He saw Alain and Krystyna on Sundays, but Teofil and Annabel only on their way back to London from the South of France, where they had spent their honeymoon. They had dinner with Stefan in a restaurant, and the young couple held hands throughout. The erotic complicity which Stefan had once looked for in vain, now lurked in their eyes. In the street after dinner they clung together as if they must touch forever: and before they left they confided in Stefan that they thought Annabel was already pregnant.

Stefan had his happy ending and started to write his masterpiece. He knew quite well that marriage is not an end in itself, but for his book it would suffice. His two innocents were impregnable: there was no reason why they should not live happily ever after. So he started the story, staying close to life; but then found that some sort of preamble would be necessary to lift the narrative from a sentimental romance into a novel of ideas.

Every morning he worked on this 'philosophical introduction'. At one he would eat lunch in the same restaurant in the Rue des Saints Pères; then walk for a couple of hours along the banks of the Seine. At four he would return to his flat, make some tea and drink it at his desk. He continued working quite late into the night.

His thoughts were not precise and he knew it. 'I am rambling like an octogenarian,' he thought to himself; and when he looked in the mirror he saw the pale and wrinkled face of a much older man. He also felt tired, but ascribed this to the exertion of his work – the effort of mind required to work out the intractable riddles which obsessed him.

What is the happiness that my characters unknowingly pursue? What is their innocence? Why is the narrator so sure that there is one way, one truth? That the other is evil and wrong? Is it a random preference with no significance beyond the gratuitous choice? Then why does he sit on the stone steps of the spiral stairs? Why does he dance the polonaise on the cliff top?

He is not jealous. He does not want her for himself. Nor does he feel that the marriage of the son is a debt paid to the father who died. The father would have frowned on the marriage: he would rather his son had married a factory girl from St Denis.

The narrator hates the seducer. But why? They are in many ways the same. He is determined to frustrate him. Why? It is not instinct: nature is not on his side. Nature mesmerizes the girl and draws her to the seducer. It is not instinct which finds joy in the triumph of innocence over corruption: it is conscience. But if conscience can be in conflict with nature – then what directs it? What can be beyond nature?

Shortly before Christmas 1958, at ten on a Friday morning, Stefan Kornowski telephoned his sister and asked her to meet him for lunch that day.

'But we'll see you on Sunday, won't we?' asked Krystyna.

'Yes,' he said. 'But there's something I want to tell you . . . something urgent.'

'Tell me now.'

'No. Not on the telephone. But, well . . . do you remember when we were children and Father went bankrupt?'

'Of course.'

'Do you remember what I told you that afternoon . . . in the summerhouse at Jezow?'

Krystyna hesitated. 'Not in particular.'

'I'll remind you at lunch.'

346

'Is it so important?'

'Yes. Yes it is. Because I was wrong.'

Krystyna cancelled the appointment she had made with her hairdresser and at once went to the restaurant to have lunch with her brother. He did not appear. She was irritated, then angry; and at a quarter to two went around to his flat. There was no reply when she knocked on the door. Her anger gave way to anxiety. She called the concierge, who came up and opened the door to the flat. Krystyna went in and almost at once saw her brother lying over the notebook on his desk. She thought at first that he was asleep but when she went to him she saw that he was dead – his eyes closed, his features in repose.